Michael Robotham started his career as a journalist but then became a ghostwriter, writing many bestselling autobiographies in collaboration with politicians, pop stars, psychologists, adventurers and showbusiness personalities. His thrillers have been translated into twenty-two languages and he has twice won Australia's Ned Kelly Award for best crime novel. He was shortlisted for the CWA Steel Dagger in 2007 and 2008 and was also shortlisted for the inaugral ITV3 Thriller Awards.

Also by Michael Robotham

The Suspect
The Drowning Man (aka Lost)
The Night Ferry
Shatter
Bombproof
Bleed for Me
The Wreckage

SAY YOU'RE SORRY

Michael Robotham

sphere

SPHERE

First published in Great Britain in 2012 by Sphere

Copyright © Bookwrite Pty 2012

The moral right of the author has been asserted.

*All characters and events in this publication, other
than those clearly in the public domain, are fictitious
and any resemblance to real persons,
living or dead, is purely coincidental.*

A CIP catalogue record for this book
is available from the British Library.

Hardback ISBN 978-1-84744-524-7
Trade Paperback ISBN 978-1-84744-525-4

Typeset in Bembo by Palimpsest Book Production Limited,
Falkirk, Stirlingshire
Printed and bound in Great Britain by
Clays Ltd, St Ives plc

Papers used by Sphere are from well-managed forests
and other responsible sources.

MIX
Paper from
responsible sources
FSC® C104740

Sphere
An imprint of
Little, Brown Book Group
100 Victoria Embankment
London EC4Y 0DY

An Hachette UK Company
www.hachette.co.uk

www.littlebrown.co.uk

For Alex

Acknowledgements

Say You're Sorry is my eighth novel, which is seven more than I ever dreamed was possible. As always, I wish to thank my agents Mark Lucas, Richard Pine, Nicky Kennedy and Sam Edinburgh, as well as my UK and US editors David Shelley and John Schoenfelder. For their hospitality and friendship I thank Mark and Sara Derry, Ursula Mackenzie, Martyn Forrester, Ian Stevenson and the Honey family recently returned to Harare.

I wish to thank John Leece, who earned the right to name a character in the novel thanks to his generosity in supporting the Dymocks Book Bank project to help 'at risk' children learn to read.

My long-suffering wife Vivien deserves special mention (and a medal) for her love and support. She's my number one fan, my designated reader, my touchstone, my reality check and the person I do this for.

Finally, I wish to thank my readers in the UK, US, Germany, Australia and the many countries in between. I am humbled by the knowledge that my books are bought, borrowed and downloaded. It is a very intimate thing to share a story with another human being. It is a contract. A pact. A promise.

'Do you know how many people have taken me to bed,' I tell my wife.

And she says, 'In your dreams, Pal.'

'*I recognise the moment I'm standing in. This is the moment before. This is the breath you take.*'

Jon Bauer, *Rocks in the Belly*

My name is Piper Hadley and

I went missing on the last Saturday of the summer holidays three years ago. I didn't disappear completely and I didn't run away, which is what a lot of people thought (those who didn't believe I was dead). And despite what you may have heard or read, I didn't get into a stranger's car or run off with some sleazy paedo I met online. I wasn't sold to Egyptian slave traders or forced to become a prostitute by a gang of Albanians or trafficked to Asia on a luxury yacht.

I've been here all along – not in Heaven or in Hell or that place in between whose name I can never remember because I didn't pay attention at Sunday Scripture classes. (I only went for the cake and the cordial.)

I'm not exactly sure of how many days or weeks or months I've been here. I tried to keep count, but I'm not very good with numbers. Completely crap, to be honest. You can ask Mr Monroe, my old maths teacher, who said he lost his hair teaching me algebra. That's bollocks by the way. He was balder than a turtle on chemo before he ever taught me.

Anyone who follows the news will know that I didn't disappear alone. My best friend Tash was with me. I wish she were here now. I wish she'd never squeezed through the window. I wish I had gone in her place.

When you read those stories about kids who go missing, they are always greatly loved and their parents want them back, whether it's true or not. I'm not saying that we weren't loved or missed, but that's not the whole story.

Kids who blitz their exams don't run away. Winners of beauty pageants don't run away. Girls who date hot guys don't run away. They've got a reason to stay. But what about the kids who are bullied or borderline anorexic or self-conscious about their bodies or sick of their parents fighting? There are lots of factors that might push a kid to run away and none of them are about being loved or wanted.

I don't want to think about Tash because I know it's going to make me upset. My handwriting is messy at the best of times, which is weird when you consider I won a handwriting competition when I was nine and they gave me a fountain pen in a fancy box that bit my finger every time I closed it.

We disappeared together, Tash and me. That was a summer of hot winds and fierce storms that came and went like, well, storms do. It was on a clear night at the end of August after the Bingham Summer Festival, when the funfair rides had fallen silent and the coloured lights had been turned off.

They didn't realise we were gone until the next morning. At first it was just our families who searched, then neighbours and friends, calling our names across playgrounds, down streets, over hedges and across the fields. As the hours mounted they phoned the police and a proper search was organised. Hundreds of people gathered on the cricket field, dividing up into teams to search the farms, forests and along the river.

By the second day there were five hundred people, police helicopters, sniffer dogs and soldiers from RAF Brize Norton. Then came the journalists with their satellite dishes and broadcast vans, parking on Bingham Green and paying locals to use their toilets. They did their reports from in front of the town clock, telling people there was nothing to report, but saying it anyway. This went on for days on every channel, every hour, because the public wanted to be kept up to date on the nothingness.

They called us 'the Bingham Girls' and people made shrines of flowers and tied yellow ribbons to lampposts. There were balloons and soft toys and candles just like when Princess Diana died. Complete strangers were praying for us, weeping as though we belonged to them, as though we summed up the tragedies in their own lives.

We were like fairy-tale twins, like Hansel and Gretel or the babes in the wood, or the Soham girls in their matching Man United shirts.

2

I remember the Soham girls because our school sent cards to their families saying our prayers were with them.

I don't like those old fairy tales — the ones about children getting eaten by wolves or kidnapped by witches. At our primary school they took Hansel and Gretel off the shelves because some of the parents complained it was too scary for children. My dad called them PC Nazis and said next time they'd be saying Humpty Dumpty promoted violence against unborn chickens.

My dad isn't famous for his sense of humour, but he does have his moments. He once made me laugh so hard I snorted tea out my nose.

As the days passed, the media storm blew through Bingham. Cameras came into our houses, up the stairs, into our bedrooms. My bra was hanging off the doorknob and there was an empty tampon box on my bedside table. They called it a typical teenager's room because of the posters and my collection of crystals and my photo-booth portraits of my friends.

My mum would normally have gone mental about the house being so messy, but she mustn't have felt much like cleaning up. She didn't feel much like breathing by the look of her. Dad did most of the talking, but still came across as a man of few words, the strong silent type.

Our parents picked apart our last days, putting them together from fragments of information like those scrapbooks people make about their newborn babies. Every detail seemed important. What book I was reading: Curious Incident — for the sixth time. What DVD I last borrowed: Shaun of the Dead. If I had a boyfriend: Yeah, right!

Everyone had a story about us — even the people who never liked us. We were cheeky, fun loving, popular, hard-working; we were straight-A students. I laughed my ass off at that one.

People put a shine on us that wasn't there for real, making us into the angels they wanted us to be. Our mothers were decent. Our fathers were blameless. Perfect parents who didn't deserve to be tormented like this.

Tash was the bright one and the pretty one. She knew it too. Always wearing short skirts and tight tops. Even in her school uniform she *was striking, with breasts like hood ornaments that announced her arrival. They belonged to a grown woman, a lucky woman, a woman who could model bras or be draped over the bonnet of a sports car at a motor show. She lapped up the attention, rolling the waistband of her skirt to make it shorter, undoing the top button of her blouse.*

At fifteen a girl's looks are pretty fickle. Some blossom and others play the clarinet. I was skinny with freckles, a big old head of tangly black hair, a pointy chin and the eyelashes of a llama. My assets hadn't arrived, or they'd been delivered to someone who must have prayed harder, or prayed at all.

I was built for speed rather than low-cut dresses and short skirts. Rake-thin, a runner, I was second in the nationals for my age group. My father said I was part-whippet, until I pointed out that likening me to a dog did nothing for my self-esteem. Homely, was my grandmother's description. Bookish, said my mother. They could have said plain as a pikestaff, but I don't know what a pikestaff looks like. Maybe I make a pikestaff look good.

Tash was an ugly duckling that blossomed into a swan, while I was the duckling who grew into a duck – a less happy ending, I know, but more realistic. Put another way, if I was an actress in a horror movie, you'd take one look at me and say, 'She's toast.' Whereas Tash would be the girl who gets her kit off in the shower and is rescued in the nick of time and lives happily ever after with the hero and his perfect teeth.

Maybe she deserved that happy ending, because real life hadn't been such a picnic. Tash grew up in an old farmhouse half a mile from Bingham, along a narrow lane that is just wide enough for single cars or tractors. Mr McBain rented the farm, hoping to buy it, but he could never raise the money.

I remember my mother saying the McBains were white trash, something I never really understood. A lot of people rent houses and send their kids to public schools, but that doesn't make them any more fucked up than the rich people living in Priory Corner.

That's where I used to live, in a house called The Old Vicarage. It used to house the vicar until the church decided it needed even more

4

money and sold off the house and land. The streets of Priory Corner aren't paved with gold, but our neighbours act as though they should be.

Like everyone else in town, they put up posters in their windows and stickers on their cars after we disappeared. There were candlelight vigils and special masses at St Mark's and prayers at school. So many prayers, I wonder how God missed hearing any of them.

You're probably wondering how I know this stuff about the police search and the vigil. During those first few weeks George let us watch TV and read the newspapers. We were chained up in an attic room with sloping ceilings and a skylight that was stained with birdshit. The room was airless and hot beneath the tiles, but still much nicer than this place. There was a proper bed and an old TV with a coat hanger aerial and a blizzard of static on most channels.

On the third day, I saw Mum and Dad on the screen, looking like rabbits caught in a high beam. Mum wore her black pencil dress by Alexander McQueen and a dark pair of half-pumps. Tash knew the brand. I'm not very good with designer clothes. Mum was clutching a photograph. She'd found her voice and they couldn't stop her talking.

She listed all the clothes I might have been wearing, as though I might have dropped them like breadcrumbs, leaving a trail for people to follow. Then she paused and stared at the TV cameras. A tear hovered halfway down her cheek and everyone waited for it to fall, not listening to what she said.

Mr and Mrs McBain were also at the news conference. Mrs McBain hadn't bothered about make-up . . . or sleeping. She had bags under her eyes and was wearing a T-shirt and an old pair of jeans.

'Like something the cat dragged in,' said Tash.

'She's worried about you.'

'She always looks like that.'

My dad took a shaky breath, but the words came out clearly.

'Somebody out there must have seen Piper and Tash. Maybe you're not sure or you're protecting someone. Please think again and call the police. You can't imagine what Piper means to us. We're a strong family and we don't survive well apart.'

He looked directly into the cameras. 'If you took our babies, please just bring them home. Drop them off at the end of the road or leave them somewhere. They can catch a bus or a train. Let them walk away.'

Then he spoke to Tash and me.

'Piper, if you and Tash are watching. We're coming to find you. Just hold on. We're coming.'

Mum had panda eyes from her mascara running but still looked like a film star. Nobody poses for a photograph like she does.

'Whoever you are – we forgive you. Just send Piper and Tash home.'

My sister Phoebe was put in front of the cameras wearing her prettiest dress, standing pigeon-toed, sucking on her fingers. Mum had to prompt her.

'Come home, Piper,' she said. 'We all miss you.'

Tash's father had his arms crossed through the whole circus. He didn't say a word until the very end when a reporter asked, 'Haven't you got anything to say, Mr McBain?'

He gave the reporter a death stare and unfolded his arms. Then he said, 'If you still have them, let them go. If they're dead, tell somebody where you left them.'

He folded his arms again. That was it. Two sentences.

Something tore inside Tash's mum and she made this small, frightened animal sound, like a kitten squeaking in a box.

There were rumours about Mr McBain after that. People asked, 'Where was his emotion? Why did he suggest they were dead?'

Apparently, you're supposed to quiver and blubber at news conferences. It's like some unwritten law, otherwise people will think you've raped and murdered your daughter and her best friend.

At the end of the questions, my mother held up a photograph of Tash and me. It's the picture that became famous, the one everyone remembers, taken by Mr Quirk, our school photographer (he of the wandering hands and minty breath, notorious for straightening collars, brushing skirts and feeling boobs).

In the photograph Tash and I are sitting together in the front row of our class. Tash's skirt is so short she has to keep her knees together

6

and her hands on her lap to avoid flashing the camera. Flashing the flash, so to speak. I'm next to her with a mop of hair and a fake smile that would make Victoria Beckham proud.

That's the photograph everybody remembers: two girls in school uniform, Piper and Tash, the Bingham Girls.

No matter what channel you switched on, you could see us, or hear our parents pleading for information. Millions of words were written in the newspapers, page after page about new developments, which weren't really new and added up to nothing.

At the candlelight vigil Reverend Trevor led the prayers while his wife Felicity led the gossiping. She's like a human megaphone with a huge arse and reminds me of those dippy birds that rock back and forth, putting their beaks into a glass.

She and the reverend have a son called Damian who should have a cross carved in his forehead because he belongs to the dark side. The little shit likes to creep up behind girls and flick their bra straps. He never did it to me because I'm quicker than he is and I once shoved his asthma inhaler up his nose.

There was standing room only at St Mark's for the vigil. They had to put loud speakers outside so people could hear the prayers and the hymns. The only thing missing were the children. Parents were so terrified of more kidnappings that they kept their little ones at home behind locked doors, safely tucked away.

That was the weekend that the grief tourists began arriving. People drove from Oxford and beyond, circling the streets. They went to the church and stared at our school and at The Old Vicarage.

They watched the reporters talking breathlessly to cameras, making nothing into something, picking the scabs off past tragedies, tossing out names like Holly Wells, Jessica Chapman and Sarah Payne, filling a few more hours with rumour and speculation.

Afterwards the tourists drove away looking slightly disappointed. They wanted Bingham to be more sinister, a place where teenagers disappeared and didn't come home.

1

It's freezing outside – minus twenty-six degrees in places – extraordinary for this time of year. I felt like Scott of Antarctica when I walked to work this morning across Hyde Park – O'Loughlin of the Serpentine, battling the extremes – although I looked more like a bloated contestant on *Dancing on Ice*.

The snow began falling four days ago, big wet flakes that melted, refroze and were covered again, stupefying traffic and silencing roads. There aren't enough snowploughs to clear motorways or council trucks to grit the streets. More grit has been needed, literally and figuratively.

Airports have been shut. Flights grounded. Vehicles abandoned. Tens of thousands of people are stranded at terminals and motorway service stations, which look like refugee camps full of the displaced and dispossessed, huddling beneath thermal blankets in a sea of silver foil.

According to the TV weather reports, a dense block of cold air is sitting over Greenland and Iceland, blocking the jet stream from the Atlantic. At the same time winds from the Arctic and Siberia have 'turbo-charged' the cold because of something called an Arctic Oscillation.

Normally, I don't mind the snow. It can hide a lot of sins. London looks beautiful under laundered sheets, like a city from a fairy tale or a sound studio. But today I need the trains to be running on time. Charlie is coming up to London and we're going to spend four days together in Oxford. This is a father–daughter bonding weekend although she would probably call it something else.

A boy is involved. His name is Jacob.

'Couldn't you find an Edward?' I asked Charlie. She gave me a look – the one she learned from her mother.

I don't know much about Jacob other than his brand of underwear, which he advertises below his arse crack. He could be very nice. He may have a vocabulary. I *do* know that he's five years older than Charlie, and that they were caught together in her bedroom with the door closed. Kissing, they said, although Charlie's blouse was unbuttoned.

'You have to talk to her,' Julianne told me, 'but do it gently. We don't want to give her a complex.'

'What sort of complex could we give her?' I asked.

'We could turn her off sex.'

'That sounds like a bonus.'

Julianne didn't find this funny. She has visions of Charlie succumbing to low self-esteem, which apparently is the first step on the slippery slope to eating disorders, rotten teeth, a bad complexion, tumbling grades, drug addiction and prostitution. I'm exaggerating of course, but at least Julianne turns to me for advice.

We're estranged, not divorced. The subject is raised occasionally (never by me) but we haven't got round to signing the papers. In the meantime, we share the raising of two daughters, one of them a bright, enchanting seven-year-old, the other a teenager with a smart mouth and a dozen different moods.

I moved back to London eight months ago. Sadly, I don't see as much of the girls, which is a shame. I have almost come full circle – establishing a new clinical practice and living in north London. This is how it used to be five years ago when Julianne and I had a house on the border of Camden Town and Primrose Hill. In the summer, when the windows were open, we could hear the sound of lions and hyenas at London Zoo. It was like being on safari without the minivans.

Now I live in a one-bedroom flat that reminds me of something I had when I was at college – cheap, transitory, full of mismatched furniture and a fridge stocked with Indian pickles and chutneys.

I try not to dwell on the past. I touch it only gingerly with the barest tips of my thoughts, as though it were a worrying lump in my testis, probably benign, but lethal until proven otherwise.

I am practising again. There is a bronze plaque on the door saying JOSEPH O'LOUGHLIN, CLINICAL PSYCHOLOGIST, with various letters after my name. Most of my referrals are from the Crown Prosecution Service, although I work two days a week for the NHS.

So far today I have seen a cross-dressing car salesman, an obsessive-compulsive florist and a nightclub bouncer with anger management issues. None of them are particularly dangerous, simply struggling to cope.

My secretary, Bronwyn, knocks on the door. She's an agency temp who chews gum faster than she types.

'Your two-o'clock is here,' she says. 'I was wondering if I could leave early today?'

'You left early yesterday.'

'Yes.'

She departs without further discussion.

Mandy enters, aged twenty-nine, blonde and overweight, with terrible skin and eyes that should belong to an older woman. She has been sent to see me because her two children were found alone in a locked flat in Hackney. Mandy had gone clubbing with her boyfriend and slept over at his place. She told police that she felt her daughter, aged six, was old enough to look after her younger brother, four. Both children are fine, by the way. A neighbour found them fluttering like chickens over the biscuit crumbs and faeces that dotted the carpet.

Mandy looks at me accusingly now, as though I'm personally responsible for her children being taken into care. For the next fifty minutes we discuss her history and I listen to her excuses. We agree to meet next week and I write up my notes.

It's just after three. Charlie's train arrives in half an hour and I'm going to meet her at the station. I don't know what we'll do in Oxford on the weekend. I'm due to talk at a mental health symposium, although I can't imagine anyone showing up, given the weather, but the tickets have been sent (first class) and they've booked me into a nice hotel.

Packing my briefcase, I take my overnight bag from the cupboard and lock up the office. Bronwyn has already gone, leaving a hint of her perfume and a lump of chewing gum stuck to her mug.

At Paddington Station I look for Charlie among crowds of passengers spilling from the carriages of the First Great Western service. She's among the last off the train. She's talking to a boy who is pushing a mountain bike with all the nonchalance of a Ferrari driver. He's wearing a duffel coat and is cultivating sideburns.

The boy rides away. Charlie restores a set of white earbuds to her ears. She's wearing jeans, a baggy sweater and an over-coat left over from the German Luftwaffe.

She offers me each cheek to kiss and then leans into a hug.

'Who was that?'

'Just a guy.'

'Where did you meet him?'

'On the train.'

'What was his name?'

She stops me. 'Is this going to be twenty questions, Dad, because I didn't take notes. Was I supposed to take notes? You

11

should have warned me. I could have written you a full report.'

The sarcasm she inherited from her mother, or maybe they teach it at that private school that costs me so much money.

'I was just making conversation.'

Charlie shrugs. 'His name is Christian, he's eighteen, he comes from Bristol and he's going to be a doctor – a paediatrician to be exact – and he thinks he might work in the Third World for a while, but he's not my type.'

'You have a type?'

'Yep.'

'May I ask what your type is?'

She sighs, weary of explaining things. 'No girl my age should ever date a boy her parents would approve of.'

'Is that a rule?'

'Yep.'

I take her bag and check the departures board. Our train to Oxford leaves in forty minutes.

'So is there any news I should know about? Any latest developments?'

'Nope.'

'How's school?'

'Good.'

'Emma?'

'She's fine.'

I'm interrogating her again. Charlie isn't a talker. Her baseline demeanour is too-cool-to-care.

We buy sandwiches in plastic triangles and soft drinks in plastic bottles. Charlie puts her headphones back in her ears so I can hear the fuzzy *thunga-thunga-twang* as we board the train and sit opposite each other.

She has dyed her hair since I saw her last and has an annoying fringe that falls over her eyes. I worry about her. She frowns too often. For some reason she seems compelled to figure out life too early, long before she has the equipment.

The train leaves on time and we pass out of London, the wheels playing a jazz percussion beneath my feet. Houses give way to fields – a landscape frozen into still life, where the only signs of life are smudges of smoke rising from chimneys or the headlights of cars waiting at crossings.

A couple are kissing in the seats across the aisle, locked together. Her leg is pressed between his thighs.

'That's disgusting,' says Charlie

'They're just kissing.'

'I can hear suction.'

'It's a public place.'

'They should get a room.'

I glance at the couple again and feel a Pavlovian twinge of arousal or nostalgia. The girl is young and pretty. She reminds me of Julianne at the same age. Being in love. Belonging to someone.

Just outside of Oxford, the train slows and stops. The wheels creak forward periodically and then shudder to a standstill. Charlie presses her hand against the carriage window and watches a long line of men move across a snowy field, bent at the waist, as though pulling invisible ploughs.

'Have they lost something?'

'I don't know.'

The train nudges forward again. Through the sleet-streaked window I see a police car bogged axle deep in snow on a farm track. A muddy Land Rover is parked on the nearby embankment. A circle of men, figures in white, are erecting a canvas tent at the edge of a lake. Spreading a domed arch over the spars, they fight against the wind, which makes the canvas flap and snap until pegs are driven into the frozen earth and ropes are pulled tight.

As the train edges past, I see what they're trying to shield. At first it looks like cast-off clothing or a dead animal, but then I recognise the human shape: a body, trapped beneath the ice like an insect locked in clear amber.

Charlie sees it too.

'Was there some sort of accident?'

'Looks like it.'

'Did they fall from a train?'

'I don't know.'

Charlie presses her forehead to the glass.

'Maybe you shouldn't look,' I say. 'You might have nightmares.'

'I'm not six.'

The train shudders and picks up speed again. Snow swirls like confetti from the roof. For a brief moment, the world has tilted out of true and I feel a sense of growing disquiet. There is a void in the world . . . somebody not coming home.

I'm here.

I want to shout it.
Scream it.
I'm here.
I'M HERE
I'M HERE!

Three days. Something has gone wrong. Tash should be back by now. Maybe George caught her. Maybe he hit her over the head with a shovel and buried her in the forest, which he always said he'd do if we escaped.

Maybe she's lost. Tash doesn't have a great sense of direction. Once she managed to get lost at Westgate Shopping Centre in Oxford when we were supposed to meet at Apricot to spend my Christmas money on a beaded belt and a pair of dark wash jeans.

That's the day Tash got into a fight with Bianca Dwyer and threatened to stab her with a pen because she was flirting with Aiden Foster. She would have done it too. Tash once stabbed me with a pen, right through my school tights. I have the world's tiniest tattoo as evidence. She was angry because I lost the friendship ring that she gave me for my twelfth birthday.

Anyway, Tash has a terrible sense of direction – almost as bad as her taste in boyfriends.

I'm so cold it's unbelievable. I'm wearing every piece of clothing – and some of Tash's stuff too. I know she won't mind.

I pull the blanket over my head. Smell my stale breath. Sweat. Every little while I poke my head out and take a few gulps of clean air and then duck under again.

Maybe I will die of the cold before they find me.

It was different those first few weeks. It was summer and the attic room was hot under the tiles. We had a proper bed, decent food and could watch the TV. George told us we'd be going home soon. He didn't seem like a monster. He brought us magazines to read and oversized chocolate bars.

I don't know if George is his real name. Tash came up with it. She said it suited him because he looked like a younger, fatter version of George Clooney, but I think we should have called him Freddy like the guy in Nightmare on Elm Street or that other sicko who wears a hockey mask and carries a chainsaw.

In the beginning George talked a lot about a ransom.

'Your parents are rich,' he told me, 'but they don't want to pay.'

'That's not true.'

'They don't want you back.'

'Yes, they do.'

It was another lie. There was never going to be a ransom demand. How can you pay for something if nobody knows the price?

Chained together on the bed, we watched the TV, waiting for news. Meanwhile, the country watched their TVs and waited for news. Everybody had an opinion. Every rumour was dissected. We were kidnapped by an Internet paedophile, according to one story. He'd met us online in a chatroom and made us take off our clothes. As if!

A clairvoyant from Bristol said we were dead and our bodies had been dumped in water. The police dragged the river at Abingdon and searched dozens of wells and drainage ditches.

Mrs Jarvis, our next-door neighbour, told police she saw a man peering through her bedroom window when she was undressing. Tash laughed at that one. 'Jarvis leaves her bedroom curtains open every night, hoping someone might look.'

A London cabbie claimed he'd seen us outside a cinema in Finchley. And a motorist in High Barnet reported seeing two girls in the back of a white van pressing their hands against the windows.

Why is it always a white van? Nobody ever sees kids being snatched by people in purple vans or yellow vans.

Tash's brother Hayden told reporters that he'd seen a man acting suspiciously in a field not far from Bingham. He took them back to the scene, pointing out the exact place. When he talked about Tash he almost cried, wiping his eyes and threatening to kill anyone who hurt her.

It's amazing how the truth can be stretched so thin that if people turned it sideways it would probably disappear. It's like they invented a fantasy version of our lives and pretended it was real.

The Sun offered £200,000 for information leading to our recovery. Suddenly, there were 'sightings' in Bristol, Manchester, Aberdeen, Lockerbie and Dover – surges of hope and then despair.

The Oxford Mail revealed there were 984 registered sex offenders in Oxfordshire. More than three hundred lived within a fifteen-mile radius of Bingham. Who knew there were so many perverts living so close?

One of them was old Mr Purvis, who has a house opposite the green. He's a creepy old guy who hangs around the train station telling girls they remind him of his daughter.

Police dug up Mr Purvis' garden but they didn't find anything except the skeleton of his dog Buster. By that time, people had marched on the house, calling him a child killer and a paedo.

The police had to rescue Mr Purvis, taking him away with a blanket over his head. You could just see his baggy trousers and his brown shoes with one sock hanging down. Somebody pulled the blanket away and he looked like a frightened old man.

Things just got worse after that. Tash's Uncle Victor drew up a list of people who were new to Bingham – foreigners mainly. Outsiders. He had a mate who was a plumber and they put together a posse of 'concerned locals'. Then they drove from house to house, saying someone had reported a gas leak and they had a legal right to enter.

The police arrested Victor, but not without a scuffle. He told the TV cameras the police weren't doing enough. They should never have closed the local police station, he said. I didn't know Bingham had ever had a police station.

The same people who were quick to weep were quick to hate . . . and to criticise. The police were accused of making mistakes. They reacted too slowly or rushed ahead or searched blind alleys or ignored the obvious or kept families in the dark.

When the chorus grew loud enough, the police pushed back. Rumours begen circulating. We weren't the angels we'd been portrayed as being. We were promiscuous. Feral. Delinquent. Tash was a wild child who had been expelled from school. Her father had spent time in prison. My dad had taken obscene bonuses while taxpayers were bailing out his bank.

Almost overnight Bingham went from being a quaint, sleepy village to being the heart of darkness — full of teenage sex, drugs and binge drinking. The same well-wishers and do-gooders who had searched for us and written sympathy cards and donated money were tut-tutting and shaking their heads. The whole town hummed with disapproval and the country followed.

Flowers rotted in their cellophane, balloons sagged to the ground, soft toys grew damp and the handwritten notes began leaking. The gloss began wearing off Bingham like cheap nail polish and underneath was something ugly and rank.

2

Oxford is blanketed by snow, surprised by its own silence. Mounds of dirty ice have been ploughed to the sides of the roads or shovelled from driveways and footpaths. The dreaming spires look particularly pensive, shrouded by mist and guarded by gargoyles with beards of ice.

I've spent the morning preparing my conference speech, sitting on a sprawling armchair in the lounge of the Randolph Hotel. There is a Morse Bar – named after the fictional detective – with photographs around the walls of the lead characters.

Charlie has been shopping all morning in Cornmarket Street. She's standing in front of the open fire, warming up.

'Hungry?'

'Starving.'

'How about sushi?'

'I don't like Japanese.'

'It's very healthy.'

'Not for whales or for dolphins.'

'We're not going to eat whale or dolphin.'

'What about the blue fin tuna?'

'So you're boycotting all things Japanese?'

'Until they stop their so-called scientific whaling programme.'

My left arm trembles. My medication is wearing off and an unseen force is tugging at my invisible strings like a fish nibbling on a baited hook.

I can give you chapter and verse about my condition, having read every paper, medical journal, celebrity auto-biography and online blog about Parkinson's. I know the theories, the symptoms, the prognosis and the possible treat-ments – all of which will delay the progress but cannot cure my condition. I haven't given up the search. I have given up obsessing over it.

Glancing over Charlie's shoulder, I see two men in the foyer, shrugging off their overcoats. Beads of moisture spray the marble tiles. They have mud on their shoes and a farmyard smell about them.

The older one is in his forties with a disconcertingly low hairline that seems to be creeping down his forehead to meet his eyebrows. His colleague is younger and taller with the body of an ex-fighter who has slightly gone to seed.

A police badge is flashed.

'We're looking for Professor O'Loughlin.'

The young receptionist is ringing my room. Charlie nudges me. 'They're asking for you.'

'I know.'

'Aren't you going to say something?'

'No.'

'Why not?'

'We're going to lunch.'

The suspense is killing her. She announces loudly, 'Are you looking for my father?'

The men turn.

'He's right here,' she says.

'Professor O'Loughlin?' asks the older man.

I look at Charlie, showing my disappointment.

'Yes,' I answer.

'We've come to collect you, sir. I'm DS Casey. This is my colleague Trainee Detective Constable Brindle Hughes.'

'People call me Grievous,' says the younger man, smiling awkwardly.

'We were going out,' I say, pointing to the revolving door.

Casey answers, 'Our guv wants to see you, sir. He says it's important.'

'Who's your guv?'

'Detective Chief Inspector Drury.'

'I don't know him.'

'He knows you.'

There is a pause. My attitude to detectives is similar to my views on priests – they do important jobs but they make me nervous. It's not the confessional nature of their work – I have nothing to feel guilty about – it is more a sense of having done my share. I want to put a sign up saying, 'I've given.'

'Tell your boss that I'm very sorry, but I'm unavailable. I'm looking after my daughter.'

'I don't mind,' says Charlie, getting interested.

Casey lowers his voice. 'A husband and wife are dead.'

'I can give you the names of other profilers—'

'The guv doesn't want anyone else.'

Charlie tugs at my sleeve. 'Come on, Dad, you should help them.'

'I promised you lunch.'

'I'm not hungry.'

'What about the shopping.'

'I don't have any money, which means I'd have to guilt you into buying me something. I'd prefer to save up my guilt points for something I *really* want.'

'Guilt points?'

'You heard me.'

The detectives seem to find this conversation amusing. Charlie grins at them. She's bored. She wants some excitement. But this isn't the sort of adventure anyone wants. Two people

21

are dead. It's tragic. It's pointless. It's the sort of work I try to avoid.

Charlie won't let it go. 'I won't tell Mum,' she says. 'Please can we go?'

'You have to stay here.'

'No, that's not fair. Let me come.'

Casey interrupts. 'We're only going to the station, sir.'

A police car is parked outside. Charlie slides into the back seat alongside me.

We drive in silence through the near-empty streets. Oxford looks like a ghost city trapped in a snow dome. Charlie leans forward, straining at the seat belt.

'Is this about the body in the ice?'

'How do you know about that?' asks Casey.

'We saw it from the train.'

'Different case, miss,' says Grievous. 'Not one for us.'

'What do you mean?'

'A lot of motorists were stranded by the blizzard. Most likely she wandered away from her car and fell into the lake.'

Charlie shivers at the thought. 'Do they know who she was?'

'Not yet.'

'Hasn't anybody reported her missing?'

'They will.'

St Aldates Police Station has an iron and glass canopy over the front entrance, which has collected a foot of snow. A council worker perched on a ladder is using a shovel to break up the frozen white wave, which explodes into fragments on the paving stones below.

Instead of parking at the station, the detectives carry on for another hundred yards and turn right before pulling up outside a Chinese restaurant where denuded ducks are hanging in the window.

'Why are we here?'

'Guv has invited you to lunch.'

Upstairs in a private dining room, a dozen detectives are seated around a large circular banqueting table. The food carousel is laden with steaming plates of pork, seafood, noodles and vegetables.

The man in charge has a napkin tucked into his shirt and is opening a crab claw with a silver pincer. He sucks out the flesh and picks up another claw. Even seated, he gives the impression of being large. Mid-forties. Fast-tracked through the ranks. He has a shock of dark hair and razor burns on his face. I notice his wedding ring and his unironed shirt. He hasn't been home for a couple of days, but has managed to shower and shave.

Beyond the circular table, a series of whiteboards have been set up to display photographs and a timeline of events. The victims' names are written across the top. The restaurant has become an incident room.

DCI Drury tugs his napkin from his collar and tosses it onto the table. It's a signal. Waiters converge and carry away the leftovers. Pushing back from the table, Drury rises with all the grace and coordination of a deck chair.

'Professor O'Loughlin, thanks for joining us.'

'I wasn't given a great deal of choice.'

'Good.'

He belches and pushes his arms through the sleeves of his jacket.

'Can I get you something to eat?'

I look at Charlie. She's starving.

'Excellent,' says Drury. 'Grievous, get her a menu.' He leans closer. 'That's not his real name, Miss. His initials are GBH. Do you know what they stand for?'

Charlie shakes her head.

'Grievous Bodily Harm.' The DCI laughs. 'Don't worry, he's too wet behind the ears to be dangerous.' He turns to me. 'How do you like my incident room, Professor?'

'It's unconventional.'

'I encourage people to feel like part of a team. We drink together. We eat together. Everyone is free to give an opinion. Admit their mistakes. Express their doubts. My department has the best clean-up rate in the county.'

Your mothers must be very proud, I think, rapidly forming a negative opinion of the DCI because of his cockiness and sense of entitlement.

He picks up a toothpick and cleans his teeth. 'You were recommended to me.'

'By whom?'

'A mutual friend. I was told you might not come.'

'You were well informed.'

He smiles. 'My apologies if we got off on the wrong foot. Let's start again. I'm Stephen Drury.'

He shakes my hand, holding it a second longer than necessary.

'I have a double homicide, which looks like a home invasion. The husband had his skull caved in. His wife was tied to a bed, possibly raped, and set on fire.'

The words are whispered. I glance across the room to Charlie, who is spooning fried rice onto a plate.

'When?'

'Three nights ago.'

I glance at the whiteboard, which has a photograph of a whitewashed farmhouse barely touched by fire. Snow was falling when the images were taken, giving them a sepia tone. A smudge of smoke rises from the roofline, etched hard against the white sky.

'What do you want from me?'

'I have a suspect in custody. He worked for the family. We found his prints in the house and he has burns to both his hands. He denies killing the couple and says he was trying to save them.'

'You don't believe him?'

'This particular suspect has a history of mental illness. He's on anti-psychotic medication. Right now he's climbing the walls, talking to himself, scratching at his arms. Maybe he's telling the truth. Maybe he's lying. I can only hold him for twenty-two more hours. That's how long I have to make a case.'

'I still don't understand—'

'How should I treat him? How hard can I push? I don't want some smart-arse defence lawyer claiming I put words in this lad's mouth or browbeat him into confessing.'

'A psychological assessment will take days.'

'I'm not asking for his life story, just your impressions.'

'Where are his clinical files?'

'We can't get access to them.'

'Who is his psychiatrist?'

'Dr Victoria Naparstek.'

The penny drops. I met Dr Naparstek eighteen months ago at a mental health tribunal hearing that involved one of her patients. She called me an arrogant, condescending, misogynistic prick because I bullied her patient into showing his true personality. I got him to admit that he fantasised about following Dr Naparstek home and raping her.

Did I bully him? Yes. Did I overstep the boundaries? Absolutely, but the good doctor should have thanked me. Instead, she threatened to report me to the British Psychological Society and have me disciplined.

Why would she recommend me for this case? Something doesn't make sense.

Drury is waiting for my decision. I glance at Charlie, wishing she were home.

'OK, I'll talk to your suspect, but first I want to see the crime scene.'

'Why?'

'Context.'

3

The Land Rover skids and fishtails through the slush, following a farm track towards a copse of skeletal trees that are guarding the ridge. The ploughed fields are bathed in a strange yellow glow, as though the snow has soaked up the weak sunshine like a fluorescent watch-face before reflecting it back again as an eerie twilight.

The eighteenth-century farmhouse seems to lean against the ridge, protected from the wind. Soot blackens the paint-work above the upstairs windows, like mascara on a teenage Goth.

Released from the claustrophobic heat of the car, I feel the wind tug at my trouser cuffs and collar. Drury leads me across the lawn. He signs a clipboard and hands me a pair of surgical gloves.

'The victims are Patricia Heyman, aged forty-two, and William Heyman, forty-five. Married. One child. Flora. She's studying at one of the colleges in Oxford. Mrs Heyman writes children's books and the husband is a freelance editor. They bought the house three years ago. Both work from home.'

'Any sign of forced entry?'

'The front door was kicked in. Nothing was taken. We found four hundred pounds in a drawer beside the bed and William Heyman had his wallet in his pocket. That's the problem with amateurs.'

'Pardon?'

'They panic and do stupid things. A professional thief wouldn't leave a mess like this.'

The DCI unlocks a padlock and pulls aside a sheet of plywood. Snow tumbles from the eaves. The inner hallway looks largely undisturbed. Glancing through double doors, I notice a sitting room with an inglenook fireplace and exposed oak beams. The dining room has a vaulted ceiling and another fireplace. Cast-iron. Fat-bellied. There is a faint smell in the air, a mixture of smoke, butane and bleach.

Almost without thinking I'm collecting the details: signs of normal, everyday life; cups draining next to the sink; scourers, rubber gloves, scraps of vegetables in a compost bin; a tin of drinking chocolate on the kitchen counter. Open. The Aga stove is cold.

Drury is still talking. 'This is where we found the husband. Face down. Two blows to the back of the head. Something heavy, blunt – a hammer maybe or an axe. He dragged himself across the floor, trying to get away.'

The blood trail has dried into a dark smear.

'What about his wife?'

'She was upstairs tied to the bed. She was still alive when the assailant doused her with an accelerant, possibly lighter fluid.'

'The fire didn't spread?'

'Damaged the room, but didn't get into the ceiling.'

The smell of bleach is stronger here. A side door near the dishwasher leads to the laundry. Wellington boots are lined up – three pairs for mother, father and daughter. A soiled dress is soaking in the tub.

In the living room there are two mugs on a side table. Hot

chocolate. Half-finished. A third mug lies in pieces in the fire-place. A bottle of Scotch rests on the mantelpiece. Opened. Single malt. Twenty years. A drop for special occasions.

Propped against a drying rack, a thin pair of leather shoes. Ballet flats. Charlie wears them.

The DCI continues. 'It happened on Thursday night, during the blizzard. Half the county was blacked out. Roads closed. Phone lines down. Someone made a 999 call from William Heyman's mobile at the height of the storm, but the emergency switchboard was swamped and they were put on hold.'

'How long?'

'Four, maybe five minutes. By the time the operator answered, the caller had gone.'

Drury gives me a baleful stare. 'It was a hell of a night: dozens of accidents, people stranded in their cars; the M40 was like a car park.'

He leads me upstairs. Crossing duckboards on the floor, I reach the main bedroom and recognise the sickly sweet odour of burning flesh, human fat turned to liquid.

Snow swirls through the shattered window before gathering in a corner of the bedroom. Almost every other surface is covered in a fine layer of black soot. The blaze began on the mattress. Layers of bedding are peeled back to reveal the cross-like outline of undamaged fabric. The outline of a body – two arms, two legs, a torso; Patricia Heyman's body had protected the mattress from the flames.

'Her hands were tied above her head,' says Drury.

'Was she clothed?'

'Does it matter?'

'Yes.'

'Pyjamas and a dressing gown.'

There is an en suite bathroom. The frosted glass window is broken, but not from the heat. Someone tried to force it open, cracking the paint that covers the hinges. Cold water fills the bath, coated in soap scum. Matching towels are folded side by side on the heated rail. A third towel – not from the same set – is resting on a wicker laundry basket.

Further along the corridor is Flora Heyman's bedroom. Her wardrobe door is open. Clothes lie discarded on the bed. Someone has searched through them. I check the sizes.

'Does the daughter live at home?'

'She has digs in Oxford,' says Drury. 'Comes home most weekends.'

'Tell me about the suspect.'

'Augie Shaw. Twenty-five. Local lad. Been in trouble before. He does odd jobs around the place – mowing lawns, cutting firewood, fixing fences, that sort of thing. He's worked for the Heymans since they moved into the place, but he was fired two weeks ago.'

'Why?'

'Flora says her old man found Shaw inside the house going through her personal things.'

'Personal things?'

'Her underwear.'

'Who reported the fire?'

'A search and rescue volunteer was driving past the farmhouse and noticed the smoke. He called it in. We found Augie Shaw's car in a snowdrift at the bottom of the hill.

'About an hour later his mother showed up at Abingdon Police Station and said Augie had something to tell us. He had burns on his hands.'

'What was he doing at the house?'

'He says he was collecting his wages. Termination pay.'

'In the middle of a blizzard?'

'Exactly. According to Shaw, the fire was already burning when he arrived. He went inside and tried to save Mrs Heyman.'

'Why didn't he raise the alarm?'

'He went for help but the roads were so icy he put his car into a ditch. He walked the rest of the way to Abingdon and went straight home. Went to bed. Forgot to tell us.'

'He forgot?'

'It gets better. He says his brother told him not to go to the police.'

'Where is the brother?'

'He doesn't have one. Like I said, he's not playing with the full deck. Either that or faking it.'

Retreating downstairs, I follow a side path to a rear terrace garden, where rose bushes, heavily pruned, push through the snow. My gaze sweeps from the gate to the barn and then the orchard, unsure of what I'm looking for.

Several times I walk to the fence and back again. How soon did a person become lost in the trees? How easy is it to watch a house like this and not be seen?

A psychologist views a crime scene differently from a detective. Police search for physical clues and witnesses. I look at the overall picture and the salience of certain landmarks and features. Some roads, for example, act as psychological barriers. People living on one side may almost never cross over to the other. The same applies to railway lines and rivers. Boundaries alter behaviour.

Grievous joins me in the yard, knocking snow off his shoes.

'Some places are just unlucky,' he says.

'What do you mean?'

'This is where Tash McBain lived.'

'Who?'

'You remember her,' he says. 'She was one of the Bingham Girls.'

I feel myself reaching for a memory and coming back with half a story, a headline and a photograph of two teenage girls.

'Her family was renting this place,' explains Grievous. 'But after she went missing, they split up. Divorced. Couldn't handle not knowing.'

'The girls didn't turn up.'

'Never. It's one of those mysteries that locals still talk about. I remember when it happened. This place was crawling with reporters and TV crews.'

'You worked the case?'

'I was still in uniform – a probationary constable.'

'What do you think happened to them?'

He shrugs. 'Five thousand people are reported missing every year in Thames Valley. More than half are kids, twelve to eighteen, runaways most of them. They turn up eventually . . . or they don't.'

Drury emerges from the house and tells Grievous to bring the Land Rover.

'What about the dog?' I ask.

'Pardon?'

'The family had a dog.'

'How do you know?'

'There was a water bowl in the laundry and an empty dog-food tin in the rubbish bin. Something short-haired; black and white, maybe a Jack Russell.'

He shakes his head, but I see a question mark ghost across his eyes. He dismisses it and pulls on his gloves.

'It's time you met Augie Shaw.'

Until we went missing

the worst thing that had ever happened in Bingham was when a German bomber overshot London by eighty miles and dropped its payload on a community hall where people were sheltering. The death toll was never made public – the government wanted to protect morale – but local historians said twenty-one people died.

The next worst thing was the night that Aiden Foster ran down Callum Loach and crushed both his legs, which had to be amputated above his knees. Now he has these stumps, but mostly he wears prosthetic legs made of skin-coloured plastic.

Tash giggled at the term prosthetic. She thought it sounded like prophylactic, which is a fancy name for a condom. That reminded me of when our PE teacher (Miss Trunchbull) put a condom on a banana in sex-ed class. Tash raised her hand and said, 'Why do we need protection from bananas, Miss?'

I laughed so hard I almost wet myself. Tash got sent to see Mrs Jacobson, the headmistress (otherwise known as Lady Adolf). Tash had been to see her so often she should have had a frequent offender's card.

Going missing made Tash and me popular. Sack loads of mail arrived at our houses: letters, cards, poems and pictures from mums, dads, children, churches and schools. The Prime Minister wrote. So did the Prince of Wales.

When school started there were TV cameras outside the gates of St Catherine's. Most of our friends were interviewed: everyone except for Emily, who was kept away from the cameras. She was the other member of our gang. Emily Martinez. She's six months older, slightly overweight and she says 'Wow!' a lot. I didn't like her at first because she had this Little Miss Perfect thing going. Then I felt sorry for her because her parents were getting a divorce and fighting over her.

I never met her father — he was working in America — but her mum was pretty weird, always visiting doctors and therapists. Emily said she was highly strung, but Tash would tip up her hand, making a drinking motion.

On the first day back at school there were trauma counsellors fluttering around the playground like seagulls fighting over chips. They were telling students it was all right to be upset and they should share their feelings. TV cameras were given permission to film the school assembly when Mrs Jacobson said a special prayer for us, getting a little wobble in her voice as she talked fondly about Tash and me.

'Would you listen to her,' laughed Tash. 'A month ago she couldn't wait to get rid of me.'

'Now she wants you back.'

'Sod that.'

A month after we disappeared, George moved us from the attic room to this place. By then the police had stopped looking and everyone assumed that we'd run away. George no longer talked about ransom demands and money. He had rescued us, he said, like some noble knight in a fairy tale. He was going to protect us from all the temptations and evil in the world.

You probably think we were stupid to believe his lies. Naive. Gullible. Moronic. Next time you're drugged and locked in a basement, hungry, thirsty, frightened, then you can judge us. When you have cried as many tears as we did; when you're huddled beneath a blanket with your mind twisted; when you don't have the strength to disobey or disbelieve.

He made us swallow some pills and we woke up in the basement. He cut the ladder so we couldn't reach the trapdoor, not without his help, and we no longer had a TV or a skylight.

When we were good he would leave the lights on. If we misbehaved he would turn them off. You have never known darkness like it; so thick I could have suffocated upon it; so deep it felt like a monster breathing in my ears.

Our lives were managed and manipulated. George decided what we ate and what we wore. He controlled the light and air. There were

33

times when he was kind and we could make fun of him. We could give him shopping lists and tease him into bringing us magazines and extra food.

'I don't want you getting fat,' he said, as he rationed the chocolate.

The magazines were read cover to cover, over and over. There were new faces, new movies, new fashions, but also the familiar. Brad and Angelina. Posh and Becks. Elton and David. The world wasn't changing so much. Prince William married Kate Middleton. Pippa's bottom became famous.

We had no way of knowing if we were close to home. I still don't. It could be miles away. It could be just past the trees. I know there's a railway line nearby because I can hear the trains when the wind is blowing in the right direction.

I miss Tash. I miss being able to reach between our bunks and hold her hand. I miss hearing her voice. I miss watching her sleep.

George hasn't come to see me since she ran away and I know he's going to be angry. That's why Tash has to come back soon with the police . . . before George does.

I'm running out of food and there's hardly any gas left in the bottle.

My handwriting is getting messier, because it's so cold. I can't feel my fingers, which makes it hard to hold the pencil. When the point gets worn down, I scrape the lead gently across the bricks to sharpen it.

Writing keeps me sane, but Tash didn't have anything like that.

She was getting sicker and sicker. Not eating. Chewing her nails until they bled.

That's why she had to get out.

4

Augie Shaw is sitting at a table, propped forward on his elbows, staring at himself in the mirror. He can't see me behind his reflection yet he seems to be gazing directly into my eyes.

Mirrors have an interesting effect in interview rooms. People struggle to lie when they can see themselves doing it. They become more self-conscious as they try to sound more convincing and truthful.

Augie is up now, pacing, talking to himself using gestures and grimaces as though conducting an internal dialogue. Taller than I imagined, he walks with an odd-legged shuffle, his hair falling over one eye.

Pausing at the mirror, he leans towards it, arching his eyebrows and lowering them. He has large eyes and a broad forehead, handsome features on most men. His hands are wrapped in white gauze and he's wearing a blue paper boiler suit.

'Where are his clothes?' I ask.

'We've taken them for analysis,' says Drury.

Augie presses his hands together and closes his eyes as if praying.

'He's religious,' says Drury. 'Goes to a Pentecostal church in town – one of those happy clappy places.'

'I take it you're not a believer.'

'I'm all in favour of redemption. It's the lemming-like leaps of faith that worry me.'

Opening the door, I step inside. Augie's eyes skitter from the walls to the floor, but never to me. There is a smell about him. Sweat. Talcum.

I take a seat and ask Augie to sit down. He looks at the chair suspiciously and then folds himself down into it, with his knees facing sideways towards the door.

'My name is Joe. I'm a clinical psychologist. Have you talked to someone like me before?'

'I see Dr Victoria.'

'Why is that?'

He shrugs. 'I didn't do anything.'

'I'm not suggesting you did.'

'Why are you staring at me? You think I've done something wrong. You're going to blame me. That's why you brought me here.'

'Relax, Augie, I just want to talk.'

'You're going to kill me or electrocute me.'

'Why would I do that?'

'They do that in some countries.'

'We don't have the death penalty in Britain, Augie.'

He nods, running his hands down his hair, flattening his fringe.

'How are you feeling?' I ask.

'My hands hurt.'

'Do you need painkillers?'

'The doctor gave me some pills.'

'How did you burn them?'

'There was a fire.'

I don't ask him about how it started. Instead, I focus on getting a history. He lives with his mother in Bingham. He was born in the area, left school at sixteen and has since done odd jobs as a labourer or farmhand. The Heymans hired him to cut wood and mow their lawns. He repaired some of their fences.

'Why did you stop working for them?'

Augie fidgets, scratching at the gauze on his hands. Minutes pass. I try again.

'You were sacked. What happened?'

'Ask Mrs H.'

'How can I do that, Augie? Mrs Heyman is dead. The police think you killed her.'

'No, no.'

'That's why you're here.'

He blinks at me. 'She's with God. I'm going to pray for her.'

'Do you pray a lot?'

'Every day.'

'What do you ask God for?'

'Forgiveness.'

'Why do you need to be forgiven?'

'Not for me – for the sinners.'

'Why were you at the farmhouse?'

'Mrs H told me to come.'

'Did she call you?'

'Yes.'

'The phone lines were down, Augie. There was a terrible storm. How did she call you?'

'She told me to come.'

'When did she call you?'

'The day before.'

He makes it sound so obvious.

I take him over the details. He borrowed his mother's car and drove to the farmhouse, almost missing the turn because it was snowing so heavily. He couldn't drive all the way to the house because of the snow, so he stopped and walked the rest of the way.

'The house was dark. There was no power. I saw a light in

37

the upstairs window but it was strange, you know, not like a lamp or a candle.' He covers his ears. 'I heard her screaming.'

'Mrs Heyman?'

Augie nods. 'I bashed down the door. Hurt my shoulder. I went up the stairs, but the flames pushed me back.'

He starts to hyperventilate as though breathing in smoke and holds his hands against his forehead, hitting his temple.

'How did you burn your hands?'

'I don't know.'

'Did you hit Mr Heyman?'

He shakes his head.

'Did you start the fire?'

'No, no.'

Without warning, he stands and walks to the far side of the room, whispering to himself, arguing.

'Are you talking to someone, Augie?'

He shakes his head.

'Who is it?'

He crouches and peers past me as though something is creeping up behind me like a pantomime wolf.

'Tell me about your brother.'

He hesitates. 'Can you see him too?'

'No. Tell me about him.'

'Sometimes he steals my memories.'

'Is that all he does?'

'He warns me about people.'

'What does he say?'

'He says they're trying to poison me.'

'What people?'

'It's in the air.'

'Why did you really go to the farmhouse, Augie?'

'To get my wages.'

'I don't believe you.'

Augie puts his bandaged hands together, as though pleading with me. A flush on the back of his neck spreads to his hairline.

'God will judge me if I'm lying.'

'God can't help you now.'

'He can. He must.'

'Why?'

'Who else is going to stop the devil?'

Drury's office is on the second floor. No posters. Minimal furniture. I expect to see commendations and photographs on the walls, but instead he has a whiteboard with timelines, names and photographs – a murder tree as opposed to a family tree.

Condensation beads the window and tiny splinters of ice seem to be trapped within the glass. The DCI leans back in his chair and crosses his legs, brushing lint from his trousers.

'So what do you make of him?'

'He's delusional, possibly schizophrenic.'

'You diagnosed that in an hour?'

'I diagnosed that in five minutes.'

Drury drains a plastic bottle of water, tossing it towards the bin. 'How do I interview him?'

'Right now he's locked into damage control. He's strong physically but not psychologically. Keep the sessions short with plenty of breaks. Don't hammer certain points – let him reveal the story in his own way. If he gets upset, let him retreat. Treat him like a victim not a perpetrator.'

'Will he confess?'

'He's saying he didn't do it.'

'But that's bullshit, right?'

'He's hiding something but I don't know what that is.'

Fierceness fills the detective's eyes and he looks at me with a mixture of impatience and irritation. He gets up, walks round the desk, his body humming with tension.

'It was the worst blizzard in a century yet this kid drives a mile through the storm. I think he went there for revenge. He was obsessed with the daughter. He was angry about being

39

sacked. We can put him at the scene. He had the motive and the opportunity.'

'Whoever did this didn't panic. They tried to destroy any evidence with bleach and fire. This is organised thinking. Higher intellect. That doesn't sound like Augie Shaw.'

'How did his hands get burned?'

'He tried to save her.'

'He fled the scene.'

'He panicked.'

The DCI has heard enough. 'This is bullshit! Augie Shaw murdered the husband and then raped the wife. He wanted revenge. He killed those poor people and I'm going to prove it.' Drury opens the door. 'Thanks for your help, Professor. I'll have a car drop you back to your hotel.'

I pick up my jacket and look at my shoes. A line of mud has dried on the leather uppers above the sole.

'Didn't something about the scene strike you as odd?' I ask.

'What do you mean?'

'The Heymans weren't drinkers. The only alcohol they had in the house was that bottle of Scotch. It was sitting on the mantelpiece, freshly opened.'

'So?'

'You don't open a twenty-year-old single malt for a man you've just sacked.'

'It was cold. The power was out. Maybe the Heymans wanted a tipple.'

'There were three mugs. Only one of them smelled of Scotch.'

'What's your point?'

'There was a blanket on the floor in front of the fire. Somebody was sitting near the hearth, getting warm. Drying her shoes. Ballet flats. Size six. Mother and daughter are both size eight.'

Drury is listening now. We're walking down the corridor towards the lifts.

'A dress in the laundry tub was two sizes too small for Mrs Heyman.'

'Maybe her daughter—'

'Is a size 12. I looked in her wardrobe.'

'I still don't understand what you're suggesting.'

'Somebody ran a bath upstairs. There was an extra towel. The bathroom window was broken.'

'You're ignoring the obvious and fixating on an extra towel and a dress size.'

'What about the missing dog?'

'It ran away from the fire. Died in the blizzard.'

There is a long pause: an uncomfortable silence. Drury presses the lift button impatiently. A small vein on his forehead is beating out a tattoo.

'You don't like me very much, do you?' I ask.

He smiles wryly. 'That's a benefit of reaching my rank. I don't have to *like* people.'

'I'm sorry if I've said something to upset you.'

'Upset me, no. I think you like disagreeing with people, Professor, because it makes you feel superior or smarter than everybody else. But contrary to what you might think, I'm not some dim-witted plod who doesn't read books and thinks Joan of Arc was Noah's wife.'

It's a good line. It reminds me of something a friend of mine might have said: Vincent Ruiz, a former detective inspector with a flair for the telling phrase.

'Do you know how many murders I've investigated?' he asks.

'No.'

'How many bodies I've seen?'

'No.'

'Stabbed, shot, strangled, drowned, poisoned, electrocuted; tossed off cliffs, shoved in barrels, cut up in bathtubs, wrapped in carpets, burned in cars and fed to pigs. You think you understand people, Professor, but I've seen what they can do. I understand more about human behaviour than you ever will.'

The lift has arrived. The doors open.

'What is your wife's name?' I ask.

41

The DCI pauses. 'What's that got to do with anything?'

'I was just thinking that you should change that shirt before you go home. You've been wearing it since yesterday, which means you didn't go home last night. You were with another woman, at her place. Lipstick — left side of the collar, below your ear. You didn't have a spare shirt so you wore this one again and sprayed it with her deodorant.

'I also noticed the box of chocolates in your office — expensive, Belgian — for your wife. You must like this mistress a lot, but you don't want the affair to wreck your marriage. Good luck with that . . .'

Drury hasn't moved a muscle.

'Dead bodies don't interest me, DCI. I deal with the living.'

There is a difference between

a runaway girl and a missing one. Runaways are like spare change
lost down a crack in the sofa. You might find it eventually, but it's not
like winning the lottery.

We slipped through the cracks, disappeared from the headlines. Out
of sight, out of mind. George said that nobody cared except him. He
was our guardian now. He would look after us.

I wanted to believe him. There were times when I looked forward
to hearing him moving boxes and uncovering the trapdoor. Tash always
hated him. She knew him better than I did. She knew more about
men . . . what they wanted, what they did.

We were an odd couple, but that didn't stop Tash and me from
being friends. I walked like a pigeon. She walked like a model. I wore
shorts and trainers. She mini-skirts and platform shoes. I was into
running. She thought sport was a waste of time.

I had blotches on account of my psoriasis. Tash had perfect skin, so
free of blotches and spots it was like looking at one of those manne-
quins you see in shop windows – the normal-looking ones, not the
ones that could be bald aliens. (She once tried to hide my blotches
with foundation, but it made me look like an Oompa Loompa.)

We were born two weeks apart in the same hospital and went to
the same primary school. We thought we were going to be separated
after that, but Tash won a scholarship to St Catherine's, which helped
pay the fees. Her dad works as a scaffolder. Mine works as a banker.
Her mum has a job in a supermarket. Mine doesn't work at all.

We seemed to have nothing in common, but still we were friends.
I spent most afternoons at the training track, doing wind sprints and
pulling a truck tyre across the grass. Tash thought this was hilarious,
but she didn't make me feel stupid. And it's not like she wanted an

43

ugly girlfriend to make her look good. There were way uglier girls than me.

I think Tash liked my family more than she liked her own, particularly my mum who is the Bingham equivalent of a Stepford wife. She calls herself a 'home-maker', which means she does yoga on Monday, tennis on Wednesday and golf on Friday. Before she married she was a model. She said it was on runways, but most of her scrapbook photographs are from motor shows.

She's very elegant and graceful and nothing ever creases or smears around her. She's like a doll that you're not allowed to play with, but instead have to keep it in the original box because one day it's going to be worth a lot of money.

I've never been interested in fashions and make-up and girly things, which disappointed my mother. I sometimes wonder if they got the babies mixed up at the hospital and she was supposed to bring Tash home.

People always talked about me as 'the runner' and 'that tough little thing' or 'the tomboy'. Mum despaired, but Daddy showed off my running trophies and said I was the next best thing to having a son. Being 'next best' was like coming second, but I couldn't be expected to win everything.

The last story I read about us going missing was when my dad doubled the reward. I knew he must love me then. Tash didn't say anything for a long while. Her parents couldn't afford that sort of money.

'Maybe you'll be going home,' she said.

'Don't worry,' I said. 'I won't leave without you.'

For weeks I had begged George to let us write letters. Eventually, he agreed. I wrote one to Mum and Dad and another to Emily. Tash wrote to her folks and to Aiden Foster, her old boyfriend, although I don't know why she bothered.

George told us what we had to say, so we didn't give away any clues. We had to tell them that we ran away and that we were living in London and that people should stop looking for us. I wanted to put in other stuff, but George wouldn't let me.

On a good day he could be kind and generous. On a bad day he was cruel. He enjoyed telling us that our parents didn't want us. My mum was pregnant and having a baby to replace me, he said, and Tash's parents were getting a divorce.

I told Tash not to believe him, but he brought us the newspaper story and said it was proof that they didn't want us back. They were glad we were gone. Good riddance to the bad seeds.

5

Standing alone at the dais, I clutch the lectern in both hands and blink into the brightness. Faces are visible in the light from the stage; pale, winterised, peering from tiered seats that rise into the deeper shadows.

The lecture theatre is half empty. The weather has kept them away, or perhaps I'm not a big enough draw: Professor Joseph O'Loughlin – the trembling psychologist – the man who can supposedly 'walk through minds'.

This is not my usual audience. Normally, I'm lecturing university students with baggy clothes and oily skin. Today I'm facing my peers: psychologists, psychotherapists and psychiatrists, who think I have some wisdom to impart, some remarkable insight into the human condition, which will give them a better understanding of their patients.

I begin.

'Imagine, if you can, feeling absolutely no concern for another human being. No guilt. No remorse. No shame. Never once regretting a single selfish, lazy, cruel, unethical or immoral word or action in your entire life.

'Nobody matters except you. Nobody deserves respect.

Equality. Fairness. They are useless, ignorant, gullible fools, who are taking up space and the air you breathe.

'Now I want you to add to this strange fantasy the ability to conceal from other people exactly what you are, to be able to hide your true nature. Nobody knows what you're really like . . . how little you care for other people . . . what you're capable of . . .

'Imagine what you could achieve. Where others hesitate, you will act. Where others set boundaries, you will cross them, unhampered by any moral restraints or pangs of disquiet, any rules or ethics, with ice water in your veins and a heart of pure stone.

'What will you do with this power? That will depend upon what your desires are. Not all psychopaths are the same. And despite what the tabloid newspapers say, they're not all serial killers or mass murderers.

'Based on the law of averages, at least four people in this theatre match the description I've just given. Maybe you're sitting next to one of them. Maybe you're one yourself.'

There are nervous smiles among the audience, but nobody looks sideways. They are listening.

'We are all different. Some of us are fuelled by ambition or a lust for money or power. Some are lazy. Some are stupid. Some are violent. Some are cowards. Some, as I've explained, are psychopaths. Not monsters. Not madmen. They marry, raise families and create business empires, learning to fake sincerity and hide their secret.

'This concept of the successful psychopath is often forgotten or ignored by the medical profession. We study those on the fringes of society – the dropouts and low achievers, the ones who get caught who have neither the intellect nor the inclination to rule the world. Only in the last few years have we begun to investigate the psychopaths who hide successfully among us.'

Glancing at my audience, I recognise one or two faces. I

worked on a research project with Eric Knox, who is sitting next to Andrew Nelson, a friend from university, who once dated my sister Rebecca and broke her heart. Two rows back, I notice a woman who looks familiar. It takes me a few minutes to put a name to her face: Victoria Naparstek, Augie Shaw's psychiatrist.

'I'm going to end with a story,' I tell them. 'It's about an affable, charismatic man who grew up in a lower-middle-class neighbourhood of New York. Reclusive, stand-offish, slightly aloof, he married his childhood sweetheart and had two sons.

'He started a money management business, handling investments for friends and family. Success followed: a penthouse apartment in Manhattan, shares in two private jets; a yacht moored off the French Riviera. By his seventies he was managing billions of dollars for individuals and foundations, constantly signing up new clients including charities, public institutions and investment firms.

'He shunned one-on-one meetings with most of his investors, but that only increased his allure. He also avoided the Manhattan cocktail circuit, fostering his reputation as a financial mastermind blessed with the Midas touch – the sage of Wall Street. Does anybody know who I'm talking about?'

'Bernie Madoff,' says a voice from the darkness.

'A classic psychopath; a charlatan of epic proportions, a greedy manipulator so hungry to accumulate wealth that he destroyed the lives of thousands of people and didn't lose a moment's sleep.

'He had education, money, opportunity, a magnificent IQ and absolutely no vestige of conscience. Never blinking, never fearing exposure, he engineered the largest Ponzi scheme in history, convinced that he was above the law and that his victims were stupid, unworthy and contemptible.

'Madoff isn't a one-off. There are many like him out there. They choose business, politics, law, science, banking and international relations; pursuing their chosen career with a ruthless, single-minded efficiency, unencumbered by moral uncertainty or guilt, without regard for anyone else.

'They stab colleagues in the back, undermine rivals, ruin enemies, fabricate evidence, shred the truth, lie, cheat, steal and ride roughshod over everyone who stands in their way. Sometimes they marry for money. Divorce for money. Embezzle funds. Bankrupt charities. Start wars. Invade countries. Crush the powerless. Corrupt the innocent. And always with the exquisite freedom of knowing they will sleep peacefully at night.

'These are not the psychopaths who you and I treat in our consulting rooms. Maybe that's a good thing. Maybe it's not an issue of treating them. They're not broken – they just *are*. It's a personality trait, not a personality disorder.'

A hand is raised; a young man, perhaps a postgraduate student. 'Aren't we obliged to treat them?'

'Why?'

'They need our help.'

'What if all we're doing is giving them the skills to fake sincerity and become better psychopaths?'

My inquisitor isn't satisfied. 'Surely you're exaggerating the problem?'

I stop my left arm from trembling. 'I read a newspaper story this morning that anorexia has reached epidemic proportions in this country. There are four times as many psychopaths in this country as people with eating disorders. Does that make it an epidemic or an exaggeration?'

I take a handful of further questions, most of them focused on the empirical data. I warn them not to get too caught up in the statistics. They're important to scientists and students, but less so for clinicians. Human behaviour can't be broken down into bell curves and graphs.

'On July 24, 2000, the Concorde was the safest aircraft in the world. A day later – according to the statistics – it was the least safe airline in the world. Beware the data.'

The lecture is over. Seats slowly empty. Nobody approaches me. Dr Naparstek hasn't renewed our acquaintance, which creates a pang of regret. She's a good-looking woman, attractive without trying. Late-thirties. Slim. Stylish. Out of my league.

Am I even playing in a league?

Julianne put me on a free transfer list three years ago and nobody has made me a serious offer – not even a guest appearance in a friendly.

Outside in the foyer everyone is talking about the weather. A voice makes me stop.

'Augie Shaw didn't kill those people.'

Victoria Naparstek is standing beside the doors. She's wearing a grey woollen sweater dress, black nylons and knee-length leather boots.

'I thought you'd be honest. Fearless. You let Stephen railroad you.'

'Stephen?'

'DCI Drury.'

They're on first name terms.

'You told him what he wanted to hear.'

'I gave him my opinion.'

She steps forward, studying me. Her eyes seem to change colour as she moves. 'They're applying to keep Augie Shaw in custody for another forty-eight hours.'

'Which has nothing to do with me.'

'He didn't kill those people.'

'He was there.'

'He has no history of violence. He doesn't cope well with confined spaces. The last time they locked him up—'

'The last time?'

'It was a mistake. He was exonerated.'

Her hair is cut shorter than I remember. Instead of long rope-thick tresses, she has a chin-skimming bob that sweeps over her cheekbones and ends at the nape of her neck.

'I'm frightened that he'll harm himself.'

'Tell Drury.'

'He won't listen to me.'

She glances at my left hand. My thumb and forefinger are brushing together in a pill-rolling motion.

'Do I make you nervous?' she asks.

'I have Parkinson's.'

Her mouth forms a lipstick circle. She tries to apologise.

'You weren't to know,' I say.

'I'm doing everything wrong today. Can we start again? I could buy you lunch.'

'Or we could go halves.'

A smile this time . . . dimples.

'I know just the place,' she says, marching ahead of me. I check out her figure, forever hopeful. She takes me to the Head of the River, a pub alongside Folly Bridge. Pushing open the heavy door, she takes my coat and hangs it on a hook. Then she chooses a table away from the fire. Orders mineral water. Asks about wine.

'I don't drink.'

'Your medication.'

'Yes.'

'What are you on?'

'Levodopa for the symptoms, carbidopa for the nausea, Prozac to stop me being depressed about having a major degenerative illness.'

'How bad does it get?'

'This is a good day . . .'

We sit a bit, staring at the table as though fascinated by each other's cutlery.

Victoria Naparstek is a little different from what I remember. Her clothes are less feminine, more practical. A string of pearls makes her look older. Maybe she grew tired of being objectified, which would make her unusual among women.

'Are you here alone?' she asks.

'With my eldest daughter Charlie . . . she's out somewhere spending my money.'

51

'You're married?'

'Separated. Three years. Two girls. Fifteen and seven. They live with their mother, but I see them quite a bit; less now that I'm in London.'

'Mmm.'

'What?'

'It's interesting.'

'What is?'

'I asked a simple question and you gave me your entire life story – everything except your favourite colour.'

'Blue.'

'Sorry?'

'My favourite colour is blue.'

I look at the menu. Victoria orders the soup. I do the same. Terrible choice. My left arm trembles.

I change the subject and ask about her practice. She lives in west London, but travels to Oxford two days a week, working mainly for the NHS.

'How did you come to treat Augie Shaw?'

'He turned up at a police station two years ago and confessed to raping a woman, but it was a false complaint.'

'She wouldn't press charges?'

'She'd never seen him before. Augie fantasised about raping her. I think he genuinely believed that he'd done it. He was mortified. Shocked. Angry at himself.'

'You stopped him in time.'

'He stopped himself.' She runs her finger around the edge of her glass. 'Augie started having problems in his late teens. Auditory hallucinations. Blackouts. Disorganised thinking. Chronic headaches. Insomnia. He claimed to get contrary messages whenever he had to make an important decision.'

'Messages?'

'From his twin brother.'

'Drury said he doesn't have a brother.'

'His twin died at birth but Augie believes he's still corded with his brother's soul. He says it's like his twin is trapped inside him and won't leave.'

'Paranoid schizophrenia.'

'Delusional ideas – some grandiose, others paranoid.'

'Medication?'

'Anti-psychotics: olanzapine fifteen milligrams and sleeping tablets. During our sessions, I tried to get Augie to mentally cut the cord, but he's resistant. He thinks half his personality will disappear if he loses contact with his brother.'

'You mentioned claustrophobia?'

'Augie's father used to lock him in a cupboard when he was a boy. He still suffers nightmares. He hates confined spaces. He also believes that inside air is poisonous and that's why his brother died in the womb.'

'You said he had no history of aggression.'

'He doesn't.'

'He *fantasised* about raping a woman.'

'He was delusional.'

'He was sacked by the Heymans for going through their daughter's underwear.'

'Augie said that was a misunderstanding.'

'His fingerprints are all over the murder scene. His hands were burned. He didn't report the fire. Instead, he went home to bed.'

Her eyes have narrowed. 'He panicked.'

'And that's your explanation?'

'He's a schizophrenic. He's convinced he's done bad things, but he hasn't.'

She hears me sigh.

'You should talk to his lawyer,' I say. 'Surrender your clinical notes.'

'He'll have to share them with the prosecution.'

'You're hiding behind protocol.'

'I'm trying to save Augie.'

'The police can get a court order.'

'Fine. When that happens I'll abide by the law. Until then I'll be siding with the angels.'

Our meals have arrived. I choose the bread roll, not willing to tackle the soup.

'You're not hungry.'

'Not really.'

She signals the waitress, whispers something. Moments later another serving of soup arrives, this time in a mug. I should feel embarrassed, but I have gone beyond feeling self-conscious.

'Will you interview him again?'

'Who?'

'Augie. Talk to him.'

'I don't see the point.'

'You'll see I'm right. I've worked with him. He's harmless.'

There's something she's not telling me; some other reason that Augie Shaw went to the Heymans' house that night. He lost his job for inappropriate conduct. He was found in the daughter's bedroom going through her things.

'Is this about the daughter?' I ask.

Victoria Naparstek shakes her head.

'Not the daughter . . . the wife.'

I often wonder what I look like now.

I can see bits of me: my hands, my feet, my stomach and my knees, but not my face. We used to have a mirror but Tash broke it and tried to cut her wrists so George took it away.

She didn't cut very deeply, but that's only because she couldn't find a sharp enough edge. We also lost our only pair of scissors because Tash hacked off my hair. She was trying to make me look ugly. Uglier.

Knives, nail-clippers, all the sharps have been taken away like we're living in some mental asylum. He even took the can-opener because he thought she might use the edge of the baked bean tin, but he gave it back again because we had to eat.

If I lean close to the tap I can see my reflection in the stainless steel, but the curve makes my head look like a squash. It's like one of those funfair mirrors or the weird pictures you can make using Photo Booth on a Mac.

Tash will be back soon. She'll bring the police . . . my mum and dad . . . the army, the navy, the Queen's Guard. Every time I look at the window above the sink, I think about her. Every time I close my eyes.

The reason George hasn't come is because the police must have arrested him. They've locked him up and I hope they beat the shit out of him or he gets raped with a broom handle in prison.

I'm sorry about my swearing. I have a potty mouth. I once overheard my mum telling my Aunt Jean that I might have Tourette's Syndrome so I looked it up on Google and I found out it's when you say fuck at inappropriate times and you do lots of eye-blinking and facial gymnastics. Gordon Ramsay does that all the fucking time, I thought, and I don't swear at the wrong times, I just swear a lot.

I'm curled up on the bunk, wearing all my clothes. When Tash was here we used to lie together to keep warm and tell each other stories. We'd imagine eating make-believe meals like fish and chips, bread and butter pudding and chicken korma, Tash's favourite.

After she cut off my hair, I offered to do hers, but she said it didn't matter because it was falling out anyway. She could pull out chunks like it was some party trick.

When I was a little girl I used to wet my hair and flatten it with a comb, parading in front of the mirror pretending that I had straight hair. I did a lot of embarrassing things, which don't seem so bad any more.

I'm eighteen now – as far as I can tell. I have no idea of the date, but I can count the seasons. Tash woke me one morning last spring and said she was throwing me a party for my birthday. We had biscuits and sweetened tea on a blanket in the middle of the floor.

Right now I know it's winter because of the snow and the naked trees. I can look outside if I stand on the bench and lift myself up on tiptoes. The window is about ten inches high and wider across. If I hold my face close I feel the air coming through the crack at the bottom of the metal frame. At certain times of year, when the sun shines, it angles through the window and makes geometric shapes on the opposite wall that shift and twist. It's my television, my weather channel.

That's the window Tash squeezed through by standing on my shoulders. I've jammed it back in place so that George won't be angry, but he'll know the truth and there's nowhere for me to hide.

I know every inch of this place. I know the crevices and cracks between the bricks, every water stain and smudge and peeling paint flake.

In one corner there are two narrow bunk beds. Tash and I pushed them closer together so we could hold hands in the dark. On the far wall there are shelves with cans of food and boxes of porridge oats. The other wall has a bench with a gas burner, a kettle and a sink. There is a tap with only cold water. A hose snakes through a hole in the wall. If I look along the edge of the hose, I can see a tiny bit of greenery.

The only other furniture is a chest of green-painted drawers and a kitchen cabinet with stencils of geraniums. This is where we keep our clothes. Oh, and I forgot to mention the two straw-bottomed chairs and a table with bamboo legs.

The ladder is attached to the wall opposite the window. It only goes halfway to the ceiling and if I could balance on the very top rung, I might just be able to reach the trapdoor with my fingertips. Behind the ladder there is a poster of Brighton Pier. I think it's Brighton. The words have been torn off at the bottom but you can see the sea and people walking on the pier. They're dressed in old-fashioned clothes with the women carrying umbrellas and the men wearing hats.

There is a camera in the corner of the ceiling, one of those webcams that look like a cue ball, or a beady black eye. I don't know if it's hooked up to anything. Maybe it's another one of George's lies.

There is only one place in the room where the eye can't see us. It is in the corner under the ladder near the sink. That's where I wash myself and where I squat over the bedpan.

When I can't sleep I do OCD stuff like rearranging the cans of food in the cupboard and wiping the benches. There are only four cans. I have plain baked beans, baked beans with sausages, baked beans with barbecue sauce and baked beans with cheese, which is totally gross. I'm out of tuna and sweetcorn and biscuits. After stacking the cans, I count the sticking plasters and headache tablets and little rehydration sachets that you mix with water when you get the runs – the ones that are supposed to be fruit-flavoured, but they taste like medicine.

That's everything in the cupboard. There's nothing for the skin rashes, eye infections, aching teeth, stomach cramps, or period pains; nothing for the boredom or the loneliness.

At least there are no bugs. If this were summer my legs would be dotted with bug bites, which I scratch until they bleed.

I don't mind the darkness any more. It hides my blotchy skin and hairy legs. In the darkness I can be invisible. I can pretend that I don't exist or that George can't see me. He'll think I've escaped and leave me alone.

Some nights I used to think he was watching us. I could feel him behind the beady black eye on the ceiling, which seemed to follow us around the room, but Tash said it was just an optical illusion.

In all those months and years, he only ever looked at Tash. The reason she cut off my hair was to make me less attractive. She was protecting me. Keeping me safe.

6

The snow is thawing but occasional flurries still descend like flakes of dandruff from an old man's scalp. Patches of grass have emerged in the parks and verges, giving dogs somewhere to shit upon.

Poking out my tongue, I taste the falling crystals. Two dozen reporters are waiting in a queue inside Oxford Crown Court, surrendering mobile phones and cameras. Nobody recognises me as I pass through the screening.

I still don't know why I'm here. Maybe I'm a sucker for a pretty face or a kind gesture or a body I'd like to hold myself against.

Victoria Naparstek is close to me now, sitting in the upper gallery, which has been opened to take the overspill of reporters. Beneath us, the courtroom is a mixture of the new and the old: the vaulted ceilings and coat of arms, as well as microphones and digital recording equipment.

I whisper to Victoria, 'So what you're saying is that Augie had a crush on Patricia Heyman?'

'Yes.'

'She's old enough to be his—'

'Yes, I know.'

'Were they sleeping together?'

'Not according to Augie, but I think she was fond of him.'

'Fond?'

'Yes, fond. Are you going to repeat everything I say?'

Augie Shaw appears from below, emerging into a square enclosure of bulletproof glass. People crane their heads to catch a glimpse, wanting to put a face to the crime: see the monster not the man.

He sits, handcuffed, between two court security officers. Turning his head, he gazes into the public gallery, searching for someone. His eyes rest on a small woman in the front row with ragged hair and a sharp nose. His mother, not yet fifty, dressed in a flimsy denim jacket and black jeans.

Augie waves. She smiles anxiously, scared for what's coming.

The prosecutor begins. 'Your worship, this is a particularly gruesome double homicide. A husband had his skull crushed and a wife and mother was set on fire while still alive. A quick resolution is obviously welcome, but not a rushed one, which is why detectives need extra time. They wish to make further enquiries and put more questions to the suspect.'

The defence counsel, a young duty solicitor called Reddrop, stumbles over his own name as he introduces himself.

'Your worship, my client has been co-operating fully with the police and has agreed to make himself available for further questioning. Mr Shaw is a local lad, who lives with his mother and has no criminal record. He does, however, have a history of mental health problems stemming from his childhood. His psychiatrist is here today. She believes his mental state will deteriorate in prison. He is claustrophobic and frightened of authority figures.'

Judge Eccles clears his throat. 'Medication, Mr Reddrop.'

'Yes, your worship, but his psychiatrist Dr Naparstek assures me that he's not a threat and he can abide by reporting restrictions . . .'

The prosecutor hasn't bothered to sit down.

'Until two weeks ago the defendant worked as a farm labourer and odd-jobber for the Heymans. He was sacked for inappropriate conduct concerning items of clothing that went missing from the house – underwear belonging to the Heymans' teenage daughter. She is frightened for her safety and doesn't want Mr Shaw released.'

'Was the theft reported?'

'No.'

Mr Reddrop interrupts. 'These allegations are denied by my client. He informs me that he went to the Heymans' house that night to collect his wages and stumbled upon a crime in progress. He burned his hands trying to save the couple.'

'He fled the scene,' says the prosecutor.

'He went for help but suffered some sort of blackout.'

'How convenient.'

Judge Eccles interrupts both men and tells them to sit down. He scribbles a note to himself and rocks back in his chair, producing a thin whistling noise from his nose like a badly played flute.

'I'm going to grant the police request. Detectives have forty-eight more hours.' He addresses Augie. 'Mr Shaw, you will be held in protective custody for a little longer but I'm going to ask that you be well looked after. In the meantime I want a full psychiatric report.'

Augie glances at his brief, wanting an explanation. Mr Reddrop gives him a sad shrug.

'When can I go home?' he asks in a loud voice.

'You're still under arrest.'

'But I want to go home.'

Augie is being led away between the two police officers. Victoria Naparstek tries to signal him.

'I'm going to be sick,' he says.

'Not here,' says the officer.

★   ★   ★

Outside the court, Victoria weaves between the waiting reporters in the foyer, looking for Reddrop. She intercepts him before the main doors. I don't hear their conversation, but she's clearly a persuasive woman.

'We can see him,' she says, slipping her arm through mine. 'Augie won't be transferred to prison until later in the day. He's downstairs.'

Having emptied our pockets and signed the waivers, we are taken along a bleak corridor by a court security officer, who wears his set of keys like a sidearm. The door is unlocked. Augie is squatting on a bunk with his legs folded beneath him like a complicated pair of springs.

He wipes his cheeks and won't look at Victoria as she takes a seat on the bench opposite.

Some psychologists will tell you that the most important word a patient speaks is the first one. Once events are related, everything that follows becomes a version of the same theme or an attempt to redress a mistake.

I don't agree. I expect people to lie. I expect them to hide things. The truth is a movable feast. It comes out over time or emerges from the static or the facts that people can live with. Augie looks like a bird on a perch, his head cocked towards the lone window.

'If I've done this thing they should just kill me,' he says, scratching at his bandaged hands. 'But I haven't done this thing and I can't stay in here because I'll die anyway.'

Victoria reaches out, but Augie pulls away, shuddering.

'Lots of sperm go into making a baby but only one sperm makes it through to fertilise the egg,' he says. 'The other sperm are trying to get there first, but they die, you know, they all die.'

'You're not making sense,' says Victoria.

'The egg splits. Two sperm. That makes us twins.'

He's talking about his brother.

'. . . cells replicate, atoms fire, the brain forms . . .'

Augie turns to me. 'I'm just trying to keep people from dying.'

'What people?' I ask.

'If I die, how will I save them?'

His eyes are darting from side to side, dancing in his head.

'I raped a woman. You should have listened.'

'You didn't rape anyone,' says Victoria.

'I raped five girls at school.'

'That's not true.'

He stops and stares at me. 'Are you here to kill me?'

'No.'

'You'll kill me eventually.'

'No, I won't.'

Victoria looks at me, hoping I can help. But as soon as I speak Augie reacts with instant hatred, almost snarling at me. Victoria steps back, frightened. 'Are you taking your medication?'

Augie looks at his hands. 'You say I have a chemical imbalance. That I suffer from hallucinations. But you're wrong. What I hear is real.' His shoulders are hunched and a tiny vein throbs at the side of his neck. 'I think I killed her.'

'Who?'

'The woman on the road.'

'What woman?'

He whispers in a little boy voice. 'What was she doing there? She was standing in the middle of the road.' He looks from face to face. 'I think I ran her over. I must have done. I couldn't stop in time.'

My eyes meet Victoria's. She shakes her head.

'What makes you think you hit this person?'

Augie wipes a strand of spit from the corner of his mouth. 'I tried to swerve, but I think I heard a sound. That's why the car went in the ditch. When I got out I looked for her. I called out, but she was gone.'

'Why didn't you go to the police?'

'My brother told me not to. He said I'd be blamed.'

'For the fire?'

'For running that woman over.'

He presses his chin into his knees. 'I looked for her, but then I saw the snowman and I got frightened.'

'The snowman?'

'He came out of the forest covered in snow.'

'You saw him *after* you saw the woman?'

Augie nods.

'This woman, what did she look like?'

'She was beat up, you know, but it was weird. Her shoes.'

'What about them?'

'She wasn't wearing any.'

7

Low grey clouds scud across a dirty sky and the dreaming spires are etched against the southern horizon like vague giants marching out of the mist.

The cab driver manoeuvres deftly on the icy streets, keeping the needle around 20 mph and rarely touching the brakes unless he has no choice. Victoria Naparstek is no longer with me. The moment I mentioned visiting Drury she grew quiet and began making excuses.

'He has a family,' she said, as though that made a difference.

The cab pulls up outside a two-storey house with a gabled roof. A lop-sided snowman is standing inside the front gate dressed in a flowery hat and a Tottenham scarf.

Drury is shovelling snow from his driveway. Working up a sweat, he's peeled down to baggy chinos and a sweatshirt.

A snowball explodes at my feet. A young girl peers from behind a makeshift fort of rubbish bins and a toboggan.

'You missed,' I say.

She holds up another snowball. 'That was a warning shot.'

Drury leans on his shovel. 'Hold your fire, Gracie.'

'I think we should arrest him, Daddy, he looks like a bad'n.'

'Let's see what he has to say first.'

Gracie is wearing a woollen cap with earflaps that make her look like Snoopy in a Peanuts cartoon. Her pale cheeks are dusted with freckles and glasses are perched on the end of her nose. Her younger brother is sitting on the front steps, pushing a toy bulldozer through clumps of ice.

'What are you doing here, Professor?'

'I have a question.'

'It could have waited.'

'I talked to Augie Shaw again.'

'On whose authority?'

'His lawyer and his psychiatrist.'

Drury sets the shovel aside, pulling off his gloves. 'What's your question?'

'Why would a woman go out in the middle of a blizzard without any shoes?'

'You talking about anyone in particular.'

'You have an unidentified female found in a lake.'

'What about her?'

'Augie Shaw said he saw a woman on the road that night. He thinks he might have hit her. That's why he drove his car into the ditch.'

Drury doesn't seem surprised at this. I try again.

'You found a woman's body in a lake. I saw the crime scene from the train. How far is that from the farmhouse?'

Drury doesn't answer. His wife has appeared at the top of the steps, her body framed in the doorway, standing with one hand on her hip. Pregnant. Pretty. Tired around her eyes.

'Is everything all right, Stephen?' she asks.

'Everything's fine. This is the psychologist I was telling you about.'

She smiles. 'You should invite him inside where it's warm.'

'The Professor won't be staying.'

She picks up the young boy and rests him on her hip before turning inside.

I notice the curtains moving at the front window. She's watching.

Drury rubs at his neck. 'Get to the point, Professor?'

'The woman in the lake – was she wearing shoes?'

'I don't know.'

'Did she have any injuries?'

'I haven't seen the post-mortem. Body was frozen solid. They can't cut her open till she thaws.'

The DCI plunges the shovel deep into a pile of snow.

'I think she was at the farmhouse that night,' I say. 'A dress was soaking in the laundry. Shoes were drying by the fire. Someone took a bath . . .'

'You're like a broken bloody record.'

Gracie covers her mouth. 'You said a bad word, Daddy. You know what that means.'

Drury roots in his pocket for spare change. Gracie holds out her gloved hand and her fingers close over the silver coin.

'Go put it in the swear jar,' he says. 'Right this minute.'

She skids across the packed snow and runs up the front steps.

'Take your shoes off before you go inside.'

The door bangs shut. I can hear Gracie's voice – telling her mother that her daddy swore.

'That swear jar earns more than I do.'

He turns to me, stretching his fingers against the cold.

'Dress it up however you like, Professor, but it doesn't change a thing. Augie Shaw murdered those people.'

'What about the clothes on the bed upstairs and the broken window in the bathroom?'

Drury pinches one nostril and blows out.

'OK, let's say you're right and this woman was at the house. Maybe she ran off. Maybe Shaw hunted her down. I'm happy to charge him with a third murder.'

The detective gazes past me at his house where Christmas lights are twinkling behind the net curtains. His wife has gone.

'My father was a detective, Professor. One of the best lessons he ever taught me was to wait until the mud settles so you can see things more clearly.' The DCI glances at his watch. 'We're done here. Have a nice life.'

8

The mortuary supervisor at John Radcliffe Hospital has a face like a chewed pencil and less personality. Rising from his chair, he searches for his reading glasses, which are hanging around his neck.

'Only next of kin can view a body.'

'I don't want to see the body, I want to talk to the pathologist.'

'That'd be Dr Leece. Do you have an appointment?'

'No.'

'Are you a friend?'

'No.'

He blinks at me as though I've asked him to donate a kidney. Perhaps he's unaccustomed to greeting visitors who don't arrive in body bags. I try again, hoping that I'm giving a smile. I can never be sure with my Parkinson's.

Grudgingly, he picks up the handset and punches a number. A brief conversation ensues. The supervisor cups the phone.

'Dr Leece is asking what it's about.'

'It's a police matter. Tell him I've spoken to DCI Drury.'

It's not a complete lie, I tell myself, as I sign the visitor's book and look into the camera. My image is captured, laminated, hung around my neck.

'Through those doors,' he says. 'Straight ahead, turn right at the end of the corridor. It's the fourth door on your right. Not the storeroom, that's too far.'

The wide corridor is empty except for a cleaning trolley and a cart full of test tubes and sample bottles. Glancing through an open door, I notice a stainless steel table in the middle of the room with a central channel leading to a drain. Halogen lights are suspended from the ceiling on retractable arms. Cameras and microphones are positioned above.

I get a flashback of my medical training. I fainted during our first practical lesson working with a cadaver. That's when I realised I wasn't equipped for a career in medicine. I had the memory, the steady hands and the patience, but not the stomach. It took me another two years to tell my father, God's-personal-physician-in-waiting.

Dr John Leece meets me outside his office. Mid-fifties, tall, with greying hair, he has eyes that seem to change size depending upon the angle of his bifocals. It's like watching one of those magic 3D pictures that transform when you tilt them.

He has three pens in the breast pocket of his business shirt. Black. Blue. Red. I imagine the order doesn't change. Every morning he straps on his wristwatch and puts the pens in his pocket, a creature of habit, a lover of order.

'A psychologist,' he says, a pulse of surprise in his eyes. 'I didn't know DCI Drury was so fond of the dark arts.'

'He keeps an open mind,' I say, remembering my last conversation with the detective.

The pathologist laughs and looks over his shoulder at me, assuming I must be joking. He taps a security code into a panel and the door clicks open. Around the walls are filing cabinets and whiteboards. He circles a desk and offers me a seat.

'You have an unidentified body,' I say, hoping to stop Dr Leece from asking any more questions.

'We have four. The oldest has been here two years. We think she's probably foreign but Interpol hasn't managed to come up with a match.'

'What about the most recent one?'

'Yes, of course, the newspapers are calling her the ice maiden. Makes her sound like a character from a fairy tale or a Russian novel. What's your interest?'

'A couple were murdered four nights ago at their farmhouse outside of Bingham.'

'I did their post-mortems.'

'A suspect in the case claims that he saw a woman on the road during the blizzard. He almost ran her down. He says she wasn't wearing shoes.'

'Now there's a coincidence,' says Dr Leece, pushing his glasses further up his nose. 'Our ice maiden was similarly unshod. Do you have a name?'

'No.'

'Pity.' He seems to make a decision. 'Her body has only just thawed out. I'm due to begin the post-mortem. You can watch if you like. Some of my students are coming along.'

'I'm not really—'

'It's an interesting case. I haven't handled a frozen cadaver before.'

'What can you tell me about her?'

'Female. Caucasian. Five-five. There's not much of her – I'd say no more than ninety pounds. Underweight. At the scene I put her at mid-twenties, but the freezing process had altered her appearance. I've since x-rayed her hands and done a comparison using the Greulich and Pyle atlas. Bone development puts her at seventeen or eighteen.'

'What's the margin for error?'

'A year at most.'

He tilts his head. One of the lenses of his glasses catches the light and seems to wink at me.

'What was she wearing?'

'A woollen jumper and leggings.'

'You didn't find any shoes?'

'No, but that's not unusual. People do strange things when they're suffering from hypothermia. Some victims think they're overheating because their skin feels hot and itchy. They take clothes off instead of putting them on. She could have dropped the shoes or kicked them off in the water.'

He picks up a model helicopter from his desk and spins the rotor blade with his forefinger. There are more helicopters on the filing cabinets and shelves.

'I fly them,' he explains, noticing my interest.

'Model helicopters?'

'No, the proper ones,' he laughs. 'I have a Robinson R44. I should take you up some time.'

'I'm only in Oxford for a few days.'

'You sound nervous. I'm a very good pilot. Only crashed once. Mechanical failure. My old heart was racing, I can tell you.' He glances at his watch. 'My students should be here. Come and observe.'

The post-mortem room has a viewing area overlooking the theatre. A dozen chairs rise in tiers. Students have taken up the front seats, leaning forward to get a better view.

Dr Leece tugs on his surgical gloves and waves up to them, checking his microphone. His assistant pulls aside a curtain to reveal a pale thin cadaver, bleached even whiter by the bright-ness of the lights. She is naked, stretched out with her arms against her sides and her legs together.

The dull whiteness of her skin makes her look almost like a marble statue that has been defaced by grazes, scratches, sores and bruises. Her arms and legs are scored with carmine marks and her eyelids are like pools of purple dye. The outline of her rib cage can be traced easily and hip bones stick out sharply where there should be curves.

Dr Leece begins the post-mortem, reading from his notes.

'At approximately 1300 hours on December 19, at the request

of Thames Valley Police, I attended the scene of a death near Abingdon, Oxfordshire. I was logged into the outer cordon of the scene at 1445 hours and approached via a farm track and field. Senior SOCO Marcus Larkin gave me a short background briefing.

'The deceased was a young woman, partially clothed, embedded in ice at the edge of a frozen lake beside a railway line. Heavy snowfall had hidden the body and only her right hand was protruding from the ice.

'Photographs were taken under my direction. She was lying on her side with her head resting on her left shoulder and left upper arm. Her right arm, flexed at the elbow, was wrapped around her chest. Her legs were retracted so that she lay in a foetal position.

'Her clothing consisted of a heavy woollen jumper and dark cotton leggings. She had no underwear. Her feet were bare.

'Ice cutting machinery was necessary to recover the deceased, whose body was transferred to John Radcliffe Hospital, Oxford, on the evening of December 19. The body was received in a white, signature-sealed body bag and wrapped in a black plastic sheet.'

Dr Leece pauses and glances at the students. 'This sort of post-mortem presents a variety of challenges. A frozen body thaws out at different rates – the limbs first, then the head and the torso. Cells can only maintain water if they're unfrozen and undamaged. They are rupturing as they hit room temperature, which is why I have to work quickly.'

He begins describing what he's seeing.

'The deceased is of slim build, approximately a hundred and fifty-five centimetres tall, of malnourished appearance, weighing only forty-two kilos. She has blonde wavy shoulder-length hair, cut roughly. Her pubic hair is denuded. Her ears pierced. Her fingernails bitten.'

Dr Leece pulls open her eyelids.

'At ten degrees Fahrenheit her body would have changed

colour fully to a pale shade of white with maybe a tint of blue. Her corneas became glazed and the pupils have turned a greyish shade.

'She has two inoculation scars on her forearm and an old curving scar around the outer aspect of the right elbow. She has grazes on the outer skin of her thighs at the widest point of her hips.'

His voice washes over me. Raising my head, I glimpse my face reflected in the glass and try to focus on something other than the post-mortem. I feel foolish, almost cowardly. My worst memories of medical school were cutting up corpses, blunting my scalpel on preserved flesh that had the consistency of frozen butter. Surgery 203 – Anatomy – how to dissect a human cadaver.

We were never told the patients' names, only the cause of death, but that didn't stop me imagining their lives, their families, their voices, their laughs, their careers. That was my problem, I was told, I imagined too much.

Dr Leece is still talking. 'The arms and legs are symmetrical and there is no visible evidence of acute injuries. No injection marks. Skin somewhat shiny . . .'

His gloved fingers slide down to her ankles, turning them. 'Both ankles show evidence of bruising and old scarring. The skin has been broken and healed.'

He moves higher, stopping. 'The large bruise on her left thigh indicates an impact injury. Blunt force. Approximately thirty centimetres long.' Glancing up at the window, Dr Leece addresses me. 'This could be evidence of a vehicle impact. It's the right height.'

He carries on, until I hear a sudden intake of breath. Without warning, he steps backwards, raising his arms. He's stumbled against a metal trolley, upending a tray. Instruments clatter to the floor.

From the body, he looks up at the viewing window, like an actor stranded in the middle of a stage, lines forgotten.

Then he finds his voice.

'Get out of here! All of you!'

The students are staring at each other – nobody reacting.

He yells this time. 'I said get out! The lesson is over.'

He turns to his assistant. 'Get me DCI Drury.'

Leece closes his eyes for a second, but opens them, swaying slightly, as though he's trapped on an out-of-control merry-go-round and the world is lurching past him. His hands are resting on the cool edge of the stainless steel bench as he stares at the cadaver. This should have been a routine job. Now it scares him.

When I was a kid

we had this board game called Operation. It's the one where you pretend to be a surgeon and use tweezers to take things out of a patient, stuff like funny bones and broken hearts and butterflies in the stomach.

Right now I feel as though someone has taken something out of me and left a Tash-sized hole behind. I imagine I can feel the outline with my fingers.

I stand on the bench and look through the crack at the bottom of the window. It's daytime. The snow has gone, leaving mud and flattened grass. The trees are like ogres with outstretched arms.

I need a plan. What if George isn't coming back? What if he just leaves me here? What if Tash didn't make it? What if she can't find her way back?

Normally he comes every few days. I'm down to my last can of food: baked beans and cheese. Ugh! When Tash was here we'd have these 'would you rather' discussions. Most people have choices like tongue-kissing your granddad or eating a bucket of snot. But we had to decide between dying of cold or starving to death.

I remember the first time we were in the basement when George came. We heard something heavy being moved above the trapdoor. Then his voice: 'Are you decent?'

He laughed; his little joke.

The trapdoor opened.

'Mind yourselves,' he said. A rope snaked down and slapped against the concrete floor.

Tash tied the end of the rope to the gas bottle and he pulled it up, before lowering down a full one. Then came a basket of food: cans of tuna, baked beans, rice and pasta.

He called for Tash. Told her to climb the ladder. She told him to fuck off. We stared into the blackness of the hole. Waiting. A nozzle appeared. A hose. He released the valve and hosed us down. Water like ice, stinging our backs and legs. We curled up in the corner, hugging each other, trying to escape the spray.

He wet our beds and all our clothes, before he turned off the lights and left us in the dark.

We hung the blankets from the ladder, trying to get them dry. Then we turned on the gas ring and took turns drying our underwear and T-shirts. I thought I was going to die that night.

Two days later he came back. He dropped the rope. Emptied the bedpan. He asked for Tash. This time she went.

Because the ladder doesn't reach all the way to the trapdoor, she had to stand on the top rung and raise her arms. He reached down and grabbed her by her wrists, hoisting her upwards. The trapdoor closed.

It seemed like she was gone for a long time. Longer than a day on Venus, my dad would say, or longer than a month of wet Sundays. I thought of all the things that might happen to her, which only frightened me, so I stopped trying to think.

When the trapdoor opened, I wanted to scream I was so happy.

He lowered Tash down. She wore different clothes − a pretty dress, with clean underwear. She had shampooed her hair. She smelled clean. Fresh.

'What happened?'

She didn't answer.

'Are you all right?'

She crawled onto her bunk and rolled over, facing the wall.

The next morning, she didn't get out of bed. She lay in her pretty dress, not talking.

'Please tell me what happened.'

'Nothing.'

'Did he do something to you?'

'I don't want to talk about it.'

I stroked her hair. We lay there for a long time. She was feverish and then shivering with cold.

'We're not getting out of here, are we?' I said.

She shook her head.

Normally she was the one who cheered me up. She was always coming up with elaborate escape plans that needed things that we didn't have – like shovels, or explosives, or guns.

A week later the same thing happened. George opened the trapdoor. Called her name. Tash climbed the ladder.

Again I worried that she might not come back. I didn't want to be alone.

This time she returned with treats – chocolate and soap and magazines. A part of me was jealous. Her hair was shiny and clean. Her legs were shaved . . . and under her arms. She smelled like a Body Shop and she wasn't hungry. We were always hungry.

I lay on the bunk that night and watched the shadows move across the wall beneath the window. Jealous. She was his favourite. He gave her nice things.

'What happens up there?' I asked her.

'It doesn't matter.'

'Do you know where we are?'

'No.'

'What did you see?'

'Nothing.'

Then she curled up and went to sleep. She didn't have nightmares, not like me. Sometimes she slept so quietly I got frightened that she was dead and would tiptoe over to her bunk and put my face close to her face, listening; or I'd blow gently in her ear until she snuffled and rolled over.

Then I'd be sure.

9

The hospital cafeteria is an echoing space full of scraping chairs and easy-wipe tables. It's mid-afternoon and already dark outside. The lunchtime meals are warmed over in the trays: lasagne and baked vegetables and dried-out roast.

John Leece slumps in a chair, staring at the window as though looking at something that he can't quite bring into focus.

'I've never really understood what people see in alcohol, but sometimes I wish I was a drinker,' he says. 'It seems to bring people comfort. My father wouldn't touch the stuff, but my mother has the occasional sherry or lager shandy.'

'What did you see in there?'

'I can't comment until I talk to the police.'

'OK, we won't talk about the post-mortem. I'll ask you general questions.'

He nods.

'How long would a person survive outside without shelter in a blizzard like the one on Saturday?'

'A matter of hours.'

'The bruises and cuts . . .'

'She was wandering around in a blizzard. She could have bumped into trees and fallen into ditches.'

'Nobody has reported her missing.'

'Maybe she's not a local.'

'They haven't found a vehicle.'

Dr Leece presses his thumbs into his eye sockets. 'I don't know. Sometimes I'm grateful that I don't have to understand human behaviour.'

Augie Shaw saw a woman standing barefoot in the middle of the road. It has to be the same one. She didn't take her shoes off next to the pond. She wasn't wearing any to begin with. Why run off? Why was she outside in a blizzard? Who was she running from?

'Did you notice anything else unusual about the scene?' I ask.

'We found a dog.'

'What?'

'It was frozen with her. Maybe the dog went in after her or she was trying to rescue it. Once she hit the water, the cold overwhelmed her and she didn't have the strength to drag herself out.'

'Was it a black and white Jack Russell?'

The pathologist stares at me. 'How could you possibly know that?'

'One went missing from the farmhouse. Small, black and white, I figured it was probably a Jack Russell.'

'The Heymans' dog?'

'Yes.'

'Why would it be with the girl?'

It's the same question I've been asking myself and I keep coming back to something that Grievous told me at the farmhouse.

'Do you keep the dental records of missing persons?'

'Of course.'

'Can you look up a file for me?'

80

'Certainly. Who?'

'It's a girl who went missing a few years ago. Natasha McBain.'

Dr Leece's eyes bobble behind his glasses. 'She was one of the Bingham Girls.'

'Her family used to live at the farmhouse, but they moved out after Natasha went missing.'

The pathologist's mouth opens; a question half formed on his lips.

'So the dog?'

'What if they left it behind?'

10

Charlie is waiting for me at the hotel suite, sprawled out on one of the twin beds as though bored with life. I kiss her forehead. She looks past me at the TV. Silent. Righteous.

The room is dully corporate, decorated in navy blues, with a high ceiling and an ornate plaster rosette above the hanging light.

'Sorry I'm late. I got held up.'

'All day?'

'I left you a message.'

'Who was that woman you were talking to?'

'Pardon?'

'Outside the college after your lecture: you were talking to her.'

'She's an old acquaintance.'

'Did you go to lunch?'

'Yes.'

'She's very good looking.'

'I hadn't noticed.'

'Dad. Don't.'

'Don't what?'

'Act like you're stupid.'

Even without looking at her reflection in the mirror I know she's scowling at me.

'Her name is Victoria Naparstek. She's a psychiatrist. She wanted to discuss one of her patients.'

'Augie Shaw.'

'How could you know that?'

'He was just on the news. He's being questioned about those murders at the farm. Did he do it?'

'I don't know.'

'He looks like a psycho.'

'We don't call them psychos.'

'They said he burned that woman alive.'

'Allegedly. And you shouldn't think about stuff like that.'

'What am I supposed to think about?'

'Celibacy.'

She's sitting cross-legged on the bed, hands in her lap, treating a grown-up subject like true confessions at a teenage sleepover.

My mobile is vibrating. It's Julianne.

'Hi.'

'Hi.'

'How did your talk go?'

'They didn't fall asleep.'

'That's always a good sign. I haven't heard from Charlie all day. Is she all right?'

'She's here now. I'll put her on.'

Charlie takes the phone and walks to the far side of the room. I can only hear her side of the conversation.

'Yesterday . . . It's OK . . . I went shopping . . . No, I didn't buy anything . . . Didn't like the colours . . . I saw some boots but they didn't have my size . . . Pretty lame . . . He snores . . . I know . . . Yeah . . . I will . . . OK.'

My daughter doesn't mention the murder investigation because she knows that Julianne doesn't like me working for the police. These are old arguments. Lost battles. The war continues.

Charlie hands me the phone and goes to the bathroom, closing the door.

'Have you talked to her about Jacob?'

'Not yet.'

'Don't leave it too long.'

'I'm waiting for the right time.'

She makes a thoughtful sound or maybe it's a doubtful sound.

Our phone conversations are often like this, revolving around domestic issues: the girls, schools, excursions and mutual friends. Julianne is the bright, cheerful one – happier now that she's not with me.

She's working as a translator for the Home Office. I don't know if she's dating anyone. For a while she went out with a lawyer called Marcus Bryant. I had to Google him because Julianne was so guarded and Charlie refused to be my spy. I typed in his name. Started reading. Stopped. His four-year stint with the International War Crimes Tribunal had me worried, along with his pro bono work for Amnesty International. I had visions of him donating a kidney to save his little sister and rescuing kittens from burning buildings.

Charlie is still in the bathroom. I can hear her whispering to someone on her mobile.

Julianne is still on the line. '. . . Emma was going to call you but she's asleep now. She's a snowflake in her ballet recital. She wants you to come. I told her you wouldn't be able to make it.'

'When is it?'

'When school goes back.'

'I'll try.'

'Don't make promises you can't keep.'

'It's not a promise.'

After she hangs up I take Charlie out for dinner. We walk along Magdalen Street past the Martyrs' Memorial, where three bishops were burned at the stake for heresy in 1555: Protestants who offended a Catholic queen. Charlie knows the whole story.

'They hung gunpowder around their necks and when it exploded it took their heads off . . . but this one bishop had wet wood, which only smouldered, and he kept begging for the fire to get hotter . . .'

'How do you know all this?'

'I took the walking tour.'

'Really?'

'Why are you looking at me like that?'

'I'm impressed.'

'I haven't *just* been shopping, Dad.'

We find an Italian place in Broad Street, opposite the Gothic main buildings of Balliol College. Charlie is talking about her day. She doesn't want to go to Oxford University, she says, because it feels like a museum.

'Maybe you want to take a gap year,' I say.

'And do what?'

'Travel. Broaden the mind.'

'People should just call it a holiday,' says Charlie. 'That's what it is.'

When did she become such a cynic?

The waitress leans over to light a candle on our table. I catch a glimpse of her lace-edged bra. Charlie's mobile vibrates on the table. She ignores it. There's no name on the caller display.

'Aren't you going to answer it?'

'No.'

'Maybe it's Jacob.'

She narrows her eyes.

'I know you're still talking to him, Charlie.'

'It's a free country, Dad.'

She wants the subject to end there. I give it a moment and try again.

'Your mum wants me to talk to you.'

Charlie sighs. 'Why don't we save ourselves some time? I'll

tell Mum you gave me a right royal bollocking. You can assure her that I'm straightened out. Everyone is happy.'

'That's not really the point.'

'I'm not going to stop talking to him, Dad. We love each other.'

'He's too old for you, Charlie.'

'He's twenty. You're five years older than Mum.'

'That's different.'

'How?'

'Five years is a lot when you're fifteen.'

'Girls get married at my age.'

'Not any more they don't.'

'They do in some countries.'

'Arranged marriages to men old enough to be their grand-fathers.'

She looks at me defiantly and we both opt for silence. A woman laughs too loudly at a nearby table and two men are arguing about football.

'Maybe we can go back to London tomorrow,' I suggest.

'Haven't you still got work to do?'

'I've done what they asked. We can catch an early train and have lunch at Covent Garden . . . see the Christmas lights on Regent Street.'

She nods and sips her soft drink.

'I could always go back by myself and stay at the flat. You could give me the key.'

'You'd be on your own.'

'I can cook.'

'I don't think your mother would like that.'

Charlie has an agenda. She's testing her boundaries. Separating from me slowly. Growing up. Away. As we walk back to the hotel I notice a dozen teenagers on the street, skinny bow-legged girls in tight jeans and boys with buzz cuts and hooded sweatshirts.

One of the girls whispers to a boy, grinding against him

86

until his neck turns red. He gives her a cigarette for her and her friends.

Charlie notices them, without even appearing to raise her eyes. She walks a few paces ahead, distancing herself from me. Soon they turn the corner and she drops back.

'Friends of yours?'

'Don't be funny, Dad.'

That night I dream of a girl running as fast as she can, bursting through branches and low undergrowth, her feet bare, frozen. She has cuts on her face and hands, the blood mingling with sweat on her skin.

The snow changes the landscape, covering the paths, the rocks, the tree stumps. She wishes she were running on tarmac, familiar streets. She can't find her bearings and moves blindly, the blizzard erasing her footsteps. But the darkness can't conceal her. Something is following, relentlessly.

Stumbling onwards, she climbs fences and thrashes through undergrowth, along farm tracks and through forests. Knee deep in snow, unable to quicken her pace, she can't feel her feet.

Bright lights suddenly blind her and she's caught in the beam like a fly on flypaper. The oncoming car slews sideways and she braces for the impact. Flung backwards into a bank of snow, she feels the powder fold around her like a duvet. Her lungs draw icy feathers into her chest.

She's alive. The wind howls. Trees are lost in white static. A voice calls out. Dragging herself up, she runs again, scrambling over a snow bank, escaping from the thing that hunts her.

In the corner of her eye she sees something moving, a dark shape. An animal. Bounding through the snow, it stops, barks. She shushes the dog. Be quiet. You'll give me away. They run together, company, their fates combined.

In the darkness she cannot see the brittle edges of the lake until she falls, breaking the surface. The shock of the cold catches her breath, drawing water into her lungs. Ice.

In my dream a figure stands at the edge of the lake. He crouches. Waiting for her. He holds out a branch, wanting her to come, but she doesn't take it. She won't surrender. She will not save herself. The cold leaches into her bones. Her limbs cease to work. She cannot hold her head above the water.

In those final seconds of her life, a paralysing certainty descends. There will be no later. Now is where it ends.

After that first time

Tash went up the ladder whenever George asked. He would come every three or four days to bring us food and water. Once or twice he left it a week and the longest was ten days.

We ran out of food and water, but the worst thing was the stink of the chamber pot, which made the cellar smell like a slum toilet in Mumbai. Not that I've been to Mumbai, but I've seen that movie, Slumdog Millionaire, *where the little boy jumps into the pit toilet and is covered in diarrhoea. That was truly gross, but it was a good movie.*

Each time he came, we'd hear things being dragged across the floor. The trapdoor would open and he ordered Tash up the ladder. Each time she returned she would smell of perfume and powder. She brought back more gifts for me. Toothpaste. A hairbrush. Tweezers. She wore clean clothes. Wasn't hungry.

'What did you eat?'

'It doesn't matter.'

'Was it nice?'

'No.'

I grew more and more jealous. I wanted to go upstairs. I wanted to be spoiled . . . to eat nice food and wash my hair properly.

Sometimes we didn't talk for hours I was so angry. I called her a skanky whore. She called me an uptight virgin, which seemed to hurt more.

She shared her new clothes, but that wasn't enough. She wouldn't tell me what happened up there.

'He gave you nice stuff to eat, didn't he? He let you wash. You smell like a Body Shop.'

'It's not what you think.'

'Why? What did he do?'

She shook her head.

'Tell me.'

I didn't give a rat's arse about the gifts she brought back. She was keeping something secret from me. Holding out.

After a day of the silent treatment, we started talking again. Tash told me about the rooms upstairs. She said it was like an old factory full of rubbish and broken furniture. She said there was a yard outside with a shed on brick piers and metal drums against a high fence. She couldn't see any other houses or hear any traffic.

'George said he might give us a radio and some more magazines,' she said. 'And we can get more food, clean sheets and maybe a microwave.'

For everything George promised, only a fraction ever arrived. The clothes we wanted were little girl things – minuscule T-shirts and shorts. Instead of tampons, he gave us sanitary pads.

Slowly we collected more things. Pillows. A clock. Soap. New toothbrushes. Books. But whatever he gave us, he could take away. Tash didn't like asking, because she wasn't sure how he'd react. He could flip from being polite and caring to slamming his fist onto the table and telling her to 'shut the fuck up!'

'Don't you know how lucky you are?' he'd scream. 'I could have killed you. I could have buried you.'

At other times, he'd wheedle and coax her, brushing her hair and fussing with her clothes. She kept him happy. She went upstairs when he asked and did what he asked, but I should have seen what was happening. I should have noticed the changes in Tash.

Whatever she ate upstairs made up for downstairs – where she ate nothing. She started biting her nails until they bled. She began losing weight. She stopped brushing her hair or cleaning her teeth.

When she cut up the magazines she created weird monsters, hybrids with animal heads and human bodies. And she stabbed out the eyes so they were empty.

Each time she climbed back down the ladder, there seemed to be less of her, as though George took a piece or she left it upstairs.

90

One night she wet the bed. I found her shivering in sodden clothes. Peeling them off, I heated water in a saucepan and washed her. She didn't say a word. Didn't cry. Didn't whimper.

'I think it's going to be a beautiful day,' I told her. 'I can hear the birds.'

It was around that time that Tash came up with her plan. We were going to escape, she said, whispering because we couldn't be sure if George was watching or listening.

Tash pulled me beneath the ladder. 'I'm going to do it with this,' she said, reaching behind her back where she'd tucked something into her jeans. She unwrapped it carefully. 'I found it upstairs when he wasn't looking.'

It was an old screwdriver with a broken handle. Tash had bound the damaged end in an old rag so the sharp edges wouldn't cut her hand. She plunged it through the air in a stabbing motion.

'How are you going to do it?' I asked.

'I'm going to creep up behind him and stab him in the neck.'

'What if he doesn't turn his back?'

'I'll pull him towards me and shove it into his guts . . . or in his eye.'

'When?'

'Next time.'

For hours she sat beneath the ladder and practised, stabbing the metal tip into the wood, carving out her initials. At other times she lay on her bunk, listening. When the time comes, she said. When the time comes there will be no more time.

We waited, lying on our bunks, thinking our own thoughts.

'If something happens to me.'

'Nothing is going to happen.'

'If it does.'

'It won't.'

'Don't let him touch you, Piper.'

'I won't.'

'Do you understand?'

'Yes.'

That's when we heard the furniture shifting and we knew George had come back. The trapdoor opened and we went through the routine with the water and food. He lowered a bucket and we emptied the bedpan.

Then it was time for Tash.

I couldn't see George's face in the darkness above. He was just a voice, like Morgan Freeman playing God in all those movies.

'I want Piper this time.'

Tash looked at me. I was rocking from foot to foot, cold all over.

'Take me,' she said.

'It's Piper's turn.'

'No.' Tash thought quickly. 'It's her time of the month.'

George didn't say anything for a while. Tash climbed the rough wooden ladder and raised her arms. Her cardigan rose up above the waistband of her jeans and I saw the screwdriver tucked against the small of her back.

I wanted to tell her not to do it. Don't risk it.

I sat down on the bunk and huddled against the back wall. Every shadow held a withered body.

I prayed. I don't pray very well. We're not a very religious family. My dad says nine out of ten religions fail in their first year.

While I was praying, I was listening, trying to hear what was happening upstairs. I imagined the worst things. Holes being dug and bodies buried. Hideous screams. That's what he always threatened to do: bury us deep where nobody would find us.

I don't know how long I waited. Dozing. Waking. Listening. I shouted at the ceiling.

'Give her back, you bastard! Don't you hurt her!'

I stood on the bench and looked out the crack in the window. There was a moon somewhere and I could just make out the trees and hear the wind moving the leaves.

I woke in the dark again, shivering violently. I sat up. Still alone. I reached across to her bunk. Felt her cold blankets. When I woke again it was almost light enough to see. I threw back the blankets and climbed the ladder, trying to balance, but I couldn't reach the trapdoor.

I stood on the bench. Looked through the crack. I could just make out a wire fence and the edge of another building with a broken window. Rubbish. Weeds. Silence. Nothing moving.

All the next day I waited. Time meant nothing. I was hungry and cold, but I wouldn't eat without Tash. I looked at the black eye on the ceiling. I begged him to give her back. I didn't want to be alone. I needed Tash.

Then I heard the sound of the hatch opening. Gaping darkly. He lowered her down to the ladder. Her legs didn't seem strong enough to support her. I stood beneath in case she fell.

Slowly she descended, flinching, pale. She had blood on the front of her dress. It had dried and darkened. She stumbled. I had to hold her up. Reaching the bunk, she curled into a ball and closed her eyes. Closed to me. Bleeding.

I made her a cup of tea. Heated some baked beans. She didn't eat. She didn't drink. She had stopped living by then. All hope gone.

11

A sound has woken me: a creaking floorboard or a whispered voice outside the door. Maybe it wasn't a sound at all. Dull-headed, I push back the duvet and I tiptoe across the floor, joints popping in my knees.

Turning the latch, I glance along the hotel corridor. Empty. The darkness of the staircase is like an open void. I take a step and feel something wet under my feet. Melting snow, tracked in from outside. Someone has been standing here.

Closing the door, I turn the double lock and go to the window, pulling aside the curtains. It's still dark outside. Charlie is sleeping. She hardly makes a sound. When she was a baby I used to crouch over her cot, fearful that she wasn't breathing at all.

I won't sleep now. I will lie awake and go back over the details of yesterday. I cannot forget the image of the frozen girl. The more I try to push it away, the harder it pushes back. That is the grim inevitability of unwanted thoughts. We cannot empty our heads. We cannot forget.

I wake Charlie just after seven and we eat a quick breakfast before walking to the train station. Supplies for the journey

– a take-away coffee, hot chocolate and the *Daily Telegraph*. Five minutes for the train.

Tyres scorch into the station car park and a police car screeches to a halt. DCI Drury is out the door and sprinting up the steps, leaping the ticket barrier like a gymnast on parallel bars. Grievous struggles to catch up, straddling the barrier and grimacing in pain.

Drury storms along the platform. Breathless. Angry. He almost knocks Charlie over, before jabbing his finger into my chest.

'How in Christ's name did you know?'

I don't retreat, but I'm concerned for Charlie.

'Are you OK?' I ask.

She nods. I look at Drury. 'Please apologise to my daughter.'

He won't be distracted. 'Tell me how you knew. Leece matched the dental records. It's Natasha McBain.'

'I wasn't sure.'

'Did Shaw recognise her?'

'No.'

'How?'

'The dog.'

'You're kidding me! You pulled a name out of your arse based on a dog.'

'It was more than that.' I sound defensive.

'Where has she been? Three years and not a word, then she turns up in the middle of a blizzard.'

'I don't know.'

A train has appeared around a far bend, the carriages straightening, rails humming. For a moment the platform announcer interrupts. Drury waits, loosening his tie.

'You should have told me. I don't like being everybody's prize fuck.'

'I could have been wrong.'

'The chief constable wants to see you.'

'Why?'

'That's his business.'

95

'We're supposed to catch this train.'

'There'll be others.'

Chief Constable Thomas Fryer is a big man squeezed into a uniform that is one size too small for him. Pink-faced with jaundiced eyes, he has an office on the top floor of Thames Valley Police headquarters. It's a blue-sky view and daily affirmation that he's reached the top of his chosen profession.

Removing his rimless glasses, he wipes them with a Kleenex.

'DCI Drury wants to have you arrested.'

'On what grounds?'

'You've made him look foolish.'

'That wasn't my intention.'

Through the vertical blinds, I can see the outer office. Charlie is waiting for me, sitting on a plastic chair, texting on her iPhone. Drury is in the same room, pacing the floor, furious at being excluded from the meeting.

Fryer puts on his glasses.

'He's a good detective. Hot-headed. Noisy. But he gets results.'

The chief constable takes a seat. The silver buttons on his uniform rattle against the metal edge of his desk.

'Are you a gambling man, Professor?'

'No.'

'But you understand odds?'

'Yes.'

'A true punter might wager a few quid on a long shot just to keep an interest in a race, but he doesn't bet his house on an outsider without inside information, you understand what I'm saying?'

The answer is no, but I don't interrupt him.

'A punter doesn't risk his entire stake unless he gets a nod from someone close to the horse, the jockey or the trainer.'

'What does this have to do with me?'

'You're a long shot but I've heard some good things.'

'Good things?'

96

'Detective Superintendent Veronica Cray speaks very highly of you. And I'm led to believe she doesn't say nice things about men as a rule.'

The chief constable has risen from his chair again and walked to the window, admiring his view.

'Hell of a mess, this . . .'

I'm not sure if I'm supposed to answer.

'We need to tread gently. Under normal circumstances, a teenage girl dying in a blizzard wouldn't create too many issues, but this is very different. This is one of the Bingham Girls.'

'Issues?'

'I'll get to that. First I need to ask for your assistance. I want you to hang around for a few more days. Help us understand what happened to Natasha McBain.'

'I have a clinical practice in London.'

'We can pay for your services.'

'It's not about money.'

Fryer places both fists on his desk, propping his body forward.

'The press are going to have a field day. That's why we're not making it public just yet. I've ordered a full media blackout. I don't know how long it's going to hold . . .'

'What about the girl's family?'

'We'll seek their co-operation.'

The silence stretches out. Fryer brings it to a close.

'I have questions, Professor. Do you think Natasha McBain ran away from home and chose the wrong night to come back?'

'No.'

'I thought so. Where has she been?'

'I have no idea.'

Fryer nods and glances at the folder on his desk.

'There are details that I wish to share with you, but first I need your assurance that you'll keep this information confidential and that you'll agree to help.'

'I can't, I'm sorry.'

Fryer doesn't seem to hear me. 'I want you to review the

original investigation. Look for any shortcomings. Assist in the new search . . .'

'I can recommend a good profiler.'

'I'm asking you. You see things that other people miss. In less than a day you uncovered more than two dozen detectives did in a week.'

'I've retired.'

'A man like you doesn't retire. You answer the call.'

He straightens and rocks back on his heels, holding the blunt end of a ballpoint pen against his clean-shaven chin.

'We have a mutual acquaintance, you and I: Vincent Ruiz. I played rugby against Ruiz. It was a long while ago, of course. We both played in the front row. He once landed a punch flush on my jaw and I saw stars for a week. I deserved it. I punched him first.

'If you need help on the review, call in Ruiz. We can employ him as a consultant, put you both on the payroll: a thousand pounds a day. I'm sure he'd appreciate the money . . .'

The chief constable has done his research. He knows that Ruiz has struggled financially since he retired from the Metropolitan Police. He has an elderly mother in full-time care and shrinking savings.

Fryer pauses. There's something else. Resuming his seat, he opens the folder.

'Elements of this case shock me, Professor. I've been a policeman for thirty years and not many things surprise me any more.'

He passes me a photograph of Natasha McBain, naked on a metal bench, her chest sewn together with rough cross-stitches.

'We do some terrible things to people after they die; we cut them open, gut them, stitch them up, but that poor girl suffered more indignities in life than in death.'

He adds a second photograph. 'At a stretch, I can accept why some sadistic prick might rape a teenage girl. Maybe he's anti-social, or impotent, or just plain too ugly to get laid. And I can almost understand why he might keep her locked up as a plaything and beat her around, getting excited by her fear. But this . . . this is beyond me.'

He adds a final photograph – an extreme close-up of Natasha's groin area with her vagina shown in all its anatomical detail. Then I recognise what I'm looking at . . . what I'm *not* seeing. Her prepuce and clitoris are missing.

This is what Dr Leece saw during the post-mortem. This is what left him speechless.

'Dead people have rights too,' says Fryer. 'I don't care what you wish had happened in the past. It's not my concern. I sometimes wish I worked less and was nicer to people and could open a homeless shelter for stray cats, but then I realise that I'm not that sort of person, which is why I don't give a rat's arse about you being tired or retired. It's bogus, a bad excuse.'

The chief constable stabs his index finger at the photographs.

'You're going to help us, Professor, because there's a lot more at stake here than a few bruised reputations and a DCI with his nose out of joint. There were two Bingham girls. The job is only half done.'

12

Drury hasn't said a word since he emerged from the chief constable's office. With his bloodless fists clenched and a manic gleam in his eyes, he strides towards the lift, slapping his palm against the button, trying to bruise the wall.

His arguments are stilling ringing in my ears. Delivered at decibels, they had opened doors along the corridor and raised eyebrows. He demanded a bigger task force. More detectives. Greater resources. What he didn't want was a 'bloody shrink' spouting clichés and telling him the bleeding obvious.

Charlie pretended not to listen. Turning up her iPod, she swung her legs beneath her chair and hummed to herself. Now we're half-running down the corridor, trying to catch up to Drury who is holding open the lift doors like he's Moses parting the Red Sea.

The police car drops us at the hotel where I rebook a room. Charlie has fallen silent, picking at a hangnail, a performance of compressed sullenness. I try to kiss her cheek. She turns her face away.

'I won't be long.'

'What about London?'

'Maybe tomorrow.'

'I can go by myself.'

'Your mother wouldn't like that.'

Drury is waiting downstairs, the engine running.

The lift doors slide closed. I stare at my reflection in the polished steel wondering how I finished up back here – involved in another investigation. Whatever skill I have, whatever ability to understand human behaviour and motives, it has turned into a curse.

People teem with their own information. It leaks from their pores, spouts from their mouths, reveals itself in every mannerism, tic and twitch. Whether they are shy, materialistic, body conscious, vain, fluent in cliché, brimming with aphorisms and tabloid axioms, they reveal themselves in thousands of different ways.

And almost unconsciously I pick up these signals, reading their body language and registering the cues. I used to want to know why things happened. Why would a couple murder young women and bury them in their basement? Why does a teenage boy spray a schoolyard with bullets? Why would a schoolgirl give birth to a baby in a toilet block and dump the newborn in a rubbish bin? Not any more. I don't want to be able to see inside people's heads. It's like knowing too much. It's like living too long or witnessing too many events; experiencing things to the point of fatigue.

People are complicated, cruel, brave, damaged and prone to outrageous acts of brutality and kindness. I know the causes. I know the effects. I have been there and back again and bought the souvenirs. It's not that I don't care any more. I've done my bit. Someone else should shoulder the burden.

DS Casey opens the rear door for me. Drury is riding up front. We're not going to the police station. Instead, we drive to Abingdon, the tyres crunching on gritted tarmac and splashing through puddles of slush. Few cars. Fewer people.

Twenty minutes pass. We pull up outside a red brick and

tile bungalow with pebble dash on the façade. Drury stares through the windscreen and finally speaks.

'Someone removed her clitoral hood and clitoris. That's a religious thing, right? Some Muslim communities do it to young girls. Sew them up . . .'

'It wasn't religious.'

'What sort of sick—'

'It was punishment. Payback.'

'Someone hated this girl?'

'Or what she represented.'

'She was eighteen – what did she represent?'

'Women, youthfulness, beauty, sex . . .'

'It's a sex crime?'

'Yes.'

He blows air from his cheeks and shakes his head.

'I'm not happy about this, Professor, but I don't have a choice. Next time you have a theory or uncover something – you tell me first, understand?'

'Yes.'

'I want a full psychological profile. I want to know where Natasha has been and why she came back. Did she run away or was she abducted? Where was she held? Why was she mutilated?'

'I'm a psychologist, not a psychic.'

'And you're not a detective – remember that.'

The DCI steps out of the car and signals me to follow. He rings the doorbell. We wait. I can hear a TV playing. Footsteps. The door opens. A young man blinks at us. There are tattoos on his forearms and neck. He's wearing a T-shirt that says, POKER – YOU KNOW SHE LIKES IT, and he's holding something out of sight, behind the edge of the door.

Drury flashes his badge. 'Hello, Hayden, is your mother home?'

'She's getting ready for work.'

'This won't take long.'

102

For a moment they stare at each other before Hayden turns his head and yells up the stairs.

'Mum. Coppers.'

A loud noise, something dropped. An exclamation. Then a tentative answer: 'Won't be a minute.'

Hayden slips whatever he's holding into the waistband of his jeans and covers it with his T-shirt. A burst of canned laughter escapes from a TV. He opens the door, inviting us in.

A skinny white girl is sitting on the sofa looking drugged in the watery half-light. She's sitting in an armchair, smoking, her arm bent and her head tilted sideways to let the smoke escape from her lips. Hayden's girlfriend. She looks about twenty-seven but could be seventeen.

Hayden tells her to go home. She blows a fringe from her eyes and ignores him.

'I said piss off!'

This time she grabs her coat and sneers at him, slamming the door on her way out.

Hayden takes her seat in the armchair and picks up a TV magazine, turning the pages, not reading.

The sitting room is cluttered and claustrophobic, smelling of old shoes and cigarettes. There are Christmas cards on the mantelpiece next to a sad-looking Christmas tree. Fake green branches are draped in strips of tinsel and weighed down by cheap ornaments. The crowning angel is too heavy, bending the uppermost branch like a catapult.

Quiet footsteps on the stairs signal Alice McBain's arrival. She's wearing dark trousers, a green-hemmed blouse and a cardigan. A nametag with a supermarket logo is pinned to the pocket. Late-forties, maybe younger, she's a small woman with short straight hair and the slightly dazed, disbelieving air of a refugee or some other figure beaten down by life without ever comprehending why.

'We're here to talk about Natasha,' Drury says.

Alice raises a hand to her mouth. Uncertainty shimmers in

her eyes; not fear or hope, but something that swings wildly between the two extremes. Missing children create a silence around themselves, a vacuum that is filled with every shade of hope and despair.

Drury has taken a seat opposite Alice, their knees almost touching. She tries to speak, but can't summon a sound. This is the moment when all that sadness and dreadful wondering come to a climax.

'Late last night I received a phone call from the senior pathologist at the mortuary at John Radcliffe Hospital. Dental records have confirmed that the body recovered from Radley Lakes four days ago was your daughter.'

Mrs McBain looks at him and then at me. 'But on the radio they said it was a woman.'

'It was definitely Natasha. I am very sorry for your loss.'

Alice shakes her head. Her eyes show no emotion, no focus. She understands the news, but doesn't *feel* it yet.

'Natasha is dead, Mum,' says Hayden.

There is a groan deep in her chest. She puts one fist and then a second over her mouth, pressing them to her lips. She looks at me, wanting confirmation, fearing everything beyond this moment.

Almost as quickly her grief seems to evaporate. She drops her hands and places them in her lap. She's not angry with Drury. She's not hurling insults or making accusations or laying blame. Humble and undemanding, she lowers her gaze to the faded carpet.

'Was she raped?' Hayden asks.

'I can't discuss the nature of her injuries,' says Drury.

'It's been three years – where has she been?'

'We don't know.'

Drury turns to Alice.

'I have to ask you some questions. I know it's difficult. Had you heard anything from Natasha?'

She shakes her head.

'No phone calls? Letters? Emails?'

'No.'

'Did anyone ever call and hang up?'

'No.'

'I need to talk to your husband, Mrs McBain.'

'He's not my husband any more.'

'I still need to talk to him.'

Hayden interrupts. 'I'll give you his address.'

Alice sniffles and twists the sleeve of her cardigan. 'How did my baby die?'

'She drowned in a lake. She was caught out in the blizzard.'

'What was she doing out there?'

'We think she may have been trying to get home. Radley Lakes aren't far from the farmhouse.'

A faint vibration comes off Alice, as though something is spinning inside her at a terrible soundless speed.

'She was coming home?'

'That's just one theory.' Drury acknowledges me and goes back to Alice. 'Did Natasha know a man called Augie Shaw?'

Hayden stiffens. 'Is that the bastard who took her?'

'Please just answer the question.'

Hayden gets to his feet, pulling forward and back like a dog jerking against a leash.

'What did he do to her?'

'I know you're angry, son. That's understandable in the circumstances, but you have to leave this to us.'

Hayden isn't listening. 'I saw him on the news. He killed them people in our old house. Did he take our Tash? What did he do to her?'

Drury looks at Alice, hoping she might intervene, but she seems to be wrestling with the news, fighting her emotions.

The DCI tries again. 'Did Natasha know William and Patricia Heyman?'

Alice shakes her head.

'What about their daughter, Flora?'

'I don't know.'

Hayden picks up a cushion from the floor and holds it against his chest as he paces. Alice stares at the muted TV as though lip-reading.

She whispers. 'You read those stories, don't you, of people who never give up hope. Who never stop believing that their children are coming home . . .' She takes a deep breath. 'I stopped believing. I gave up on Tash. I should have had more faith.'

'There's nothing you could have done,' says Drury.

'Do you know how often I just sat holding the phone, willing it to ring? I did it for weeks, months, nearly a year. Until I finally convinced myself that she was dead. I stopped praying. I stopped thinking she was alive. In the darkest part of the darkest night, I abandoned my little girl . . . and all the time she was alive. She was trying to get home.'

A sob breaks inside her chest. 'I want to see her.'

'I don't think that's—'

'I want to see my Natasha.'

'You have to understand – she's been away a long time – she doesn't look like she once did.'

'I don't care. She's my daughter.'

Drury glances at me, wanting me to dissuade Alice, but I've seen grief in many forms and this mother knows her mind. It's not that Alice doesn't believe Drury or that she's clinging to some irrational hope that Tash might still be alive. She wants to say sorry. She wants to say goodbye.

The DCI relents. 'In the meantime, I'm going to assign a family liaison officer. She'll keep you informed of developments. For the time being we won't be releasing any information to the media. We'd prefer, for the sake of the investigation, that nobody knows it was Natasha in the lake. We have to re-interview witnesses and check alibis. I'm sure you understand.'

'For how long?' Hayden asks, treating it like an imposition.

Drury stands to leave. 'Just a few days.'

'Before we go,' I interrupt. 'I have a few questions for Mrs McBain.'

Alice blinks at me, as though taken by surprise.

'I wanted to ask you about Natasha.'

'What about her?'

'What was she like? I've seen the photographs and read the statements but I want to hear it from you . . . in your own words.'

Hayden looks at me incredulously. 'What difference does it make now? She's dead!'

Ignoring him, I focus on Alice. 'I'm a psychologist. I'm trying to understand what happened. By knowing more about Natasha, I can learn things about the man who took her.'

'You think she's to blame for this?'

'No.'

Hayden wants to protest but Alice touches his forearm with her fingertips. He swallows his anger, chewing on the inside of his cheek. Meanwhile, Alice begins talking softly, describing Natasha. Instead of physical details, she mentions moments, relationships, loves. Natasha had a dog. She got him as a puppy on her twelfth birthday, a Jack Russell. She called him Basher. They used to go everywhere together.

'Tash even smuggled him to school one day.' Alice smiles. 'She could be a terror, but she was a good student, our Tash. Clever. Easily bored. They said she was expelled, but the school would have taken her back. Mrs Jacobson told me so.'

'How did she get on with her father?'

'They had their moments.'

'Moments?'

Alice falters. 'You try to set boundaries, you know. Kids try to cross them. Tash wanted to grow up too quick. Couldn't wait for anything.'

'Did she have boyfriends?'

'She was popular.'

'Did she ever take drugs?'

Her eyes narrow and Hayden answers for her.

'What the fuck does that matter? You can't come in here and say shit like that. She's dead! What sort of moron—'

'Mind your language,' says Alice. 'There's no need for swearing. The man is just trying to do his job.'

Hayden falls silent. Seething.

A car pulls up outside the house. I can hear the *doof doof* bass beat from its sound system, cranked up and shaking the air. Moments later the doorbell rings. There are male voices. Laughter. The letterbox flap opens.

'Hey, Hayden, we know you're in there.'

'Not now, I'm busy.'

'This is business.'

Hayden almost trips over the coffee table trying to reach the door. Cursing, he tells them to leave; mentions the police; more expletives.

Alice stands slowly and looks at Drury. 'I have to go to work now,' she says, almost moving from memory.

She extends her hand. 'I want to thank you. A lot of people made promises to us when my Tash went missing. Not many of those promises were kept. I want to thank you for bringing her home.'

In the entrance hall, Drury pulls on his overcoat and stumbles slightly, bracing himself against the wall. His eyes are shining. Tilting his head back, he stares at the ceiling.

'That woman just thanked me for finding her daughter dead.'

'I know.'

'I hate this job.'

As we leave the house, the car is still parked outside, a Vauxhall Cavalier, music blaring, tinted windows at half-mast. Two white youths are leaning on the open doors, hands deep in their pockets, hoodies like cowls.

Drury wanders across the muddy grass. He knows their names. They laugh too loudly at nothing at all, grinning at each other. The balance of power is evident. The big one is in his mid-twenties, older by five years, with a shaved head. His mate is skinny with fairer skin and a nervous twitch that sends his eyes sideways as though he's constantly looking for reassurance.

Drury returns and slips behind the wheel.

'Who are they?' I ask.

'The local wildlife,' he says. 'The tall one is Toby Kroger. He's a big man on the Blackbird Leys estate, a drug dealer and a pimp. We picked him up two years ago for living off immoral earnings, but the two girls he put on the game refused to give evidence against him.

'The skinny one is Craig Gould. He's a musician with more talent than he deserves. Plays the saxophone. We arrested him a year ago with a vial of Rohypnol in his pocket. He likes his girlfriends to be comatose.'

Drury starts the engine and puts the car into gear. 'I could arrest guys like that every day of the week, but it wouldn't make any difference. They're floaters.'

'Floaters?'

'Turds that don't flush.'

13

Abingdon Police Station never sleeps. Shifts change. Fresh faces replace tired ones. Doors swing open and close behind us. Drury ignores greetings or dismisses them. Reaching the incident room, he throws his coat over a chair and yells to the assembled detectives. A briefing. Fifteen minutes.

I'm to wait in his office. Not touch anything. There is a whiteboard with photographs of the farmhouse and the victims. Natasha McBain's image has been placed off-centre, as though peripheral to the main investigation, yet now she is at the heart of it.

Taking a seat, I glance around the room. A cupboard door is open. There are press clippings stuck on the inside of the door, a bravery citation, photographs of a medal ceremony. Drury is bowing to the Queen. The office door opens before I can read the caption. The DCI is carrying two mugs of tea, presenting one to me like it's a peace offering.

He takes a seat behind his desk.

'OK, let's assume you're right and Natasha was at the farmhouse that night. What happened?'

'She arrived during the blizzard. Wet. Cold. They drew her

a bath. Found her fresh clothes. Dried her shoes in front of the fire. William Heyman tried to phone the police, but the switchboard was overwhelmed.'

'And then Augie Shaw showed up?'

'Someone did.'

A church bell is ringing somewhere. Drury scratches the short hair on the back of his neck.

'Half my team worked on the original investigation.'

'Is that a problem?'

'Decisions were made based on the best available evidence. The girls were classed as runaways. When they didn't turn up after three months the chief constable assigned a smaller task force but the trail had gone cold. Questions are going to be asked. Fingers pointed. This could cost people their careers.'

'Is that your priority?'

The DCI bristles, opening his mouth and closing it again, his lips like thin lines.

'I'm not here to judge anyone,' I say. 'I'm reviewing the evidence not the investigation.'

Drury grunts, unconvinced.

The landscape has changed since the girls went missing. The science has improved. Offenders will have grown complacent. People will have forgotten their motive for lying. Lovers give alibis but ex-lovers take them back. I could make these arguments, but I doubt if Drury will listen. He's protecting his patch and the reputations of his colleagues.

'I'll probably regret this, Professor, but I'm going to give you full access. Don't turn this into a witch hunt. What do you need?'

'I want to visit the farmhouse again.'

'Fine.'

'I'll need the files from the original investigation,' I say. 'Statements. Timelines. Phone wheels.'

'You're talking about more than three thousand statements.'

'I'll get some help.'

Drury swallows something spiky and hard. 'Tell Grievous what you need.'

'I also want to re-interview some of the original witnesses. Talk to the families, filter out some of the biases.'

'You think they lied?'

'People edit out the negatives when they lose someone they love. You heard Alice McBain talk about her daughter. I need to learn everything I can about Natasha and Piper. What sort of girls were they? Were they streetwise, or naive, aggressive or compliant, introverts or extroverts? Did they have boyfriends or ex-boyfriends? Were they sexually promiscuous?'

'You're suggesting these girls were somehow complicit?'

'I'm saying that some women – even young ones – draw attention to themselves. Some are sexually provocative, deliberately or unwittingly. Others are more self-effacing. I need to know Natasha and Piper as though they were sitting opposite me. By knowing them, I can learn why they were chosen—'

'You think they were chosen?'

'Yes.'

Drury breathes deeply, loosening his shoulders, staring at me.

'I've met people like you before, Professor. You study crime scenes and photographs, thinking you can commune with the killer; trying to understand the whys and the wherefores. Me? I don't care about *knowing* the bastard. I just want to catch him.'

Two dozen detectives are gathered in a rough circle, sitting on desks and chairs. They share the same kind of intimacy as soldiers and emergency workers – friendships forged in the heat of battle or during long shifts doing dirty and dangerous work. Not elitist or self-anointed, just tight.

Drury calls for their attention.

'Listen up, lads. Some of you may have heard a rumour about the unidentified white female whose body was found after the blizzard. We now have a positive ID. Her name was Natasha McBain.'

112

The air pressure in the room has suddenly changed, as though someone has opened a distant door letting a cold wind blow through the corridors.

'I am now going to confirm something else,' continues Drury. 'The rumours stop now! Nobody – and I repeat, *nobody* – talks to the media. I'm declaring a total news blackout on this case. Whatever you get asked, the answer is "no comment". I don't care if it's your wife asking the question, you say nothing. Is that understood?'

Nobody interrupts.

'I want to know where Natasha McBain has been for the last three years. Go back over the files. Names. Dates. Places. I want a full list of suspects from the first investigation. Where are they now? What have they been doing?

'We're going to search the crime scenes again – the farmhouse and the lakes. Uniformed officers and civilian volunteers are being bussed in within the hour. The dog squad will try to pick up the scent using Natasha's clothes. Nobody mentions her name. As far as anyone is concerned we're still dealing with an unidentified white female.'

A voice from the back: 'What about Augie Shaw?'

'He's going nowhere. Find out if he knew Natasha McBain or Piper Hadley.'

'And the Heymans?'

'Victims in one crime, suspects in another – it's not the first time.' The DCI looks at Casey. 'What about the prints at the farmhouse?'

'We pulled sixty decent samples from the house and have eliminated all but fourteen of them.'

'Augie Shaw?'

'A palm print in the kitchen.'

'Anything upstairs.'

'There's a partial on the bedroom door.'

'Find out who else has been in the house in the past month. Tradesmen. Friends. Family. What about the semen stains?'

113

'DNA results will take another two days. The daughter says her parents had separate bedrooms and weren't sleeping together.'

'Kids don't know everything. Maybe they were loved up behind her back.'

Another detective speaks. 'There were traces of diluted blood on the broken bathroom window and in the kitchen sink. We'll have to wait for the results.'

Drury looks at another detective. 'What about the family finances?'

'A mortgage. Manageable.'

'Good.' Drury slaps a folder against his thigh. 'At the behest of the chief constable, we are to welcome back Professor O'Loughlin. He is to be afforded every reasonable assistance but don't get carried away with his theories. We're going to solve this case through good, solid detective work, by knocking on doors and interviewing witnesses.'

Point made, Drury doesn't look at me.

'I'm splitting the task force. DS Casey will continue to run the investigation into the double murder at the farmhouse. I'll be in charge of the Natasha McBain investigation, but overseeing both.'

He rattles off names, assigning detectives their new roles.

'Let's do this,' he says, turning and leaving quickly, only letting his mask slip when he reaches the corridor. I see the glaze of uncertainty dulling his eyes like Vaseline smeared on a lens.

Sometimes I wonder why detectives do this work. What pleasure is there in it? Even the satisfaction of solving a case just means another one is waiting. There is never a cessation of hostilities or a negotiated truce, never ultimate victory.

Eventually, the eternal nature of the struggle wears them down — the circle of cause and effect, crime and punishment, guilt and innocence, victims and perpetrators. You don't stop feeling — you just wish you could.

I was born on Mother's Day and

Mum used to say I was the best Mother's Day present in the world. She said things like that when other people could hear her, but never when it was just me listening.

We didn't talk. We competed. We argued. We loved each other. But we hated each other too.

My mother was the world champion at making smiley comments about my hair or my weight or my bra size, slicing and dicing my self-confidence. And she was never happier than when dancing through the tulip fields of the bleeding obvious.

Dad would tell me not to get so bent out of shape, but I was born bent out of shape. I came into the world backwards in a breech birth. Whales breach and so do babies.

Mum is taller than my dad but really skinny. She has these amazing green eyes and eyelashes that look like they're false but they're not.

People say she's beautiful and talk about Dad 'punching above his weight' when he married her, but I think he could have done much better. He could have married someone who didn't care so much about money and what other people thought.

My dad is the nicest person you'll ever meet. Whenever he's disappointed in me he has this way of sagging and letting out a long sigh, as if someone has pulled out his plug and he's crumpling like a bouncy castle at the end of a party. He would die of disappointment rather than raise a finger against me.

Mum used to complain when he spoiled me and Dad always agreed with her before winking at me.

My last birthday at home was cancelled because Mum said I didn't deserve a party or presents because of my ingratitude and my filthy language, particularly the word 'fuck'. Everything was fucking this and fucking that; fucking unfair and fucking unbelievable and you have to be fucking kidding me.

That's one of the reasons I wanted to run away, but it was just talk, you know. I wasn't really serious. Kids always say things they don't mean.

It's morning. I stand on the bench and see if the sun is shining or if it has snowed overnight. No snow. No sunshine. Rain today. It's colder than yesterday.

Standing here, I can almost feel the weight of Tash kneeling on my shoulders and then standing, as she squeezed through that narrow gap. I was afraid that she'd get stuck and I wouldn't be able to pull her back inside. She'd be like Winnie the Pooh in that story where he eats too much honey and gets stuck in Rabbit's front door.

I wet my finger and hold it against the gap, feeling the breeze on my skin. Then I draw a heart in the condensation on the inside of the window. Why do people always draw hearts?

It's been four days since Tash left. That might not seem to be very long after three years, but some days are longer than others. Some days are longer than years.

Only one of us could escape because we couldn't both climb that high. One of us had to lift the other. Tash was smaller. She'd lost so much weight.

Ever since George made her bleed, Tash had been acting differently. I don't know if she tried to stab him with the screwdriver. She wouldn't talk to me. Instead, she scratched at her wrists, biting her nails, sleeping all the time . . . I tried to talk to her . . . to make her eat, but she didn't even have the energy to argue with me.

'You're scaring me,' I said, rocking her in my arms. 'Please come back.'

'We're going to die,' she whispered.

I knew she was right. It was like a message from God. A pretty disappointing message, but I didn't blame him. That's what everything comes down to — dying. Well, not literally everything, but most things.

Tash didn't seem scared any more. Perhaps knowing you want to

116

die makes you less scared. Sometimes there's no rock so heavy or dark or hopeless that people won't crawl under it.

The idea came to me when I was standing like this, looking through the crack. I noticed how the condensation on the inside of the glass had leaked down and frozen along the bottom edge of the window. The ice had expanded in the crack and forced the metal frame to lift. I could see a chink of light where there hadn't been one before. My old science teacher taught me that water expands when it freezes. That's why it can break open granite boulders.

I thought, If it could break a boulder why not a window or a wall?

So I filled a bowl with water and tore up an old T-shirt. I soaked the torn fabric and shoved it into the gap, using a nail file to push it hard into the space. Some of the water squeezed out and leaked down the wall.

It was cold that night. The fabric froze. The next day, I pulled it out and wet it again. Night after night, it froze and refroze. For a long time I didn't think it was working. The gap looked the same. But then one day, I pushed at the window and the whole thing moved.

Some nights weren't cold enough for the fabric to freeze, but then we had a long cold spell. We shivered and huddled together at night, trying to stay warm. And each morning the crack had opened a little more.

I wedged my fingers inside and to my surprise the window moved. I tried again and it gave way. I caught it before it crashed to the ground, falling backwards off the bench. The edge of the window frame cut my forehead, but it wasn't so deep.

Where the window had been, there was now a hole. Tash couldn't fit through it, so she took most of her clothes off. First she knelt on my shoulders and then she stood. Once she put her head and arms through the window, I pushed and she clawed at the ground, trying to pull herself through.

She wouldn't budge. I couldn't pull her back or push her forward. That's when I got really scared. I thought she was going freeze to death stuck in that window, lying half in the snow. I managed to pull off her leggings and then I poured vegetable oil over her hips and thighs.

'I can't do it,' she kept saying.

'Sure you can.'

'I can't.'

'Wiggle your hips.'

'I'm stuck.'

'Keep trying.'

'I am trying.'

She was swearing at me and crying. I had to scream at her and slap her on the thighs. I hit her so hard she slipped right through that hole, her legs and feet slithering out of sight. Snowflakes drifted in. Her head reappeared. I grabbed some more clothes and pushed them through the window.

'I'll be back,' she said, all business. 'Don't go anywhere.'

14

Grievous has been assigned to me. He's drawn the short straw – a fat man's penance or the new boy's forfeit – accepted with grace and good humour. Not fat. Solid. Muscled. Fighting the flab.

I follow him downstairs and through a rear door into the vehicle compound. His grey jacket is slightly too small for him, stretched across his shoulders. He unlocks the car.

'Best ride up front, sir. A drunk threw up on the back seat. Smell doesn't go away.'

As he ducks into his seat, I notice a dull white scar behind his left ear beneath his hairline. Surgery. Rehab. Long past.

Minivans and coaches are parked on the far side of the police compound, waiting for the search parties. Civilian volunteers in white overalls are milling around a brazier, trying to stay warm. One of them waves to Grievous, pulling off a glove to shake hands. The two men exchange pleasantries, commenting on the cold. They talk about the blizzard and the search, wishing each other a Merry Christmas.

'Sorry about that,' says Grievous, as he starts the engine. 'I know a lot of the OxSAR volunteers.'

'OxSAR?'

'Oxfordshire Search and Rescue. I trained most of them. Dentists, mechanics, insurance salesmen . . . they're good lads.'

Cracking the window, he turns up the heating and pulls out of the parking area. In Colwell Drive, he circles the roundabout and heads into central Abingdon where a one-way system funnels traffic around the High Street. Soon cottages and terraces give way to factories and playing fields.

Grievous is a talker. He points out local landmarks and restaurants, showing me where he went to primary school.

'I just want to say that it's an honour to be working with you, sir,' says Grievous. 'I mean, it's a privilege, you being so famous.'

'What makes you think I'm famous?'

'I looked you up, sir. I hope you don't mind. You helped find Mickey Carlisle and catch Ray Hegarty's killer and that guy who kidnapped your wife and daughter. I can't remember his name.'

'Gideon Tyler.'

'That's him. You battled evil and won.'

'I didn't win. Trust me on that.'

'You saved your wife and daughter.'

But not my marriage, I want to add, but instead say nothing. Why spoil a good story? Grievous doesn't have to know that my wife didn't forgive me; that she blamed me for infecting our family with my 'poisonous work' and allowing my daughter to become a target for a sadistic psychopath.

Grievous is still talking. 'I don't know what I'd do if I was confronted by a man like that,' he says, ruminating on the prospect. 'I mean, if somebody took my wife and child, I think I'd want to kill him, you know. Not that I'm married — not yet anyway — but it's a natural reaction. It's comes from in here.' He thumps his chest. 'They cross a line, people like that. They can't expect sympathy or understanding. Yeah, I'd pull the trigger.'

I don't answer.

Grievous glances at me. 'I don't suppose I should say stuff like that — being a detective — but we're human beings, aren't we? You hear all those debates about the death penalty, the pros and cons, but when it's your family it's different, isn't it?'

'Can we talk about something else?'

'Yeah, sure,' he says. 'I shouldn't have said anything. I'm just pleased to be working with you. It's a privilege, you know.'

There are roadworks, a temporary red light. I glance to my right and watch two schoolboy teams playing rugby, muddy armies interlocked, shoving each other off a ball.

'Tell me about the Bingham Girls.'

Grievous nods, gathering his thoughts.

'They went missing on the last Sunday in August. The Bingham Summer Festival had been the day before and they were still packing up the carnival rides and sideshows.'

'What about suspects?'

'Some of those carnie workers were interviewed. That sort of job attracts drifters and perverts. The task force also looked at a band of travellers who were camping in a farmer's field on the edge of the village. They raided the camp three days after the girls went missing, but found nothing. A week later, two caravans were gutted by fire and a little girl got burned.'

'Why did people think the girls ran away?'

'They were planning to, according to one of their friends. Emily Martinez was supposed to go with them.'

'What happened?'

'The girls didn't show up. Police checked the buses and trains that left that Sunday morning. They interviewed drivers and passengers, but nobody saw Piper or Natasha.'

'What do you think happened?'

'They got in the wrong car. Natasha was known to hitch-hike. She wasn't exactly the shy retiring type.'

'Meaning?'

He hesitates, tugging at the collar of his shirt. 'There were rumours, you know. Drinking. Drugs. Lipstick parties. You know about those?'

'Sadly, yes.'

121

'According to some people, Natasha was charging money for blowjobs.'

'What about Piper?'

'She was quieter, a good athlete.'

'You know the families?'

'Not really, just the rumours.' He indicates left and turns. 'Hayden McBain is a small time dealer, selling dope and amphetamines – makes more in a week than I do in a month. Every time we arrest him he gives the judge a sob story about his sister going missing. Blah, blah, blah. He walks.'

'You don't believe him.'

'He was dealing before she went missing.'

A burst of static from the two-way interrupts his train of thought. He turns it down. For a big man, he has a boyish face and soft eyes. He cocks his head each time I ask a question.

'What about Piper's family?'

'They've never stopped talking about her – giving interviews, going on radio, putting up posters, writing to politicians. Every year they hold a candlelight vigil. It's like the McCanns – you know, Madeleine's folks – they're never going to stop looking. They've got websites and newsletters and posters. You'll see. It's just up ahead.'

Moments later we pass a WELCOME TO BINGHAM sign and arrive in a pretty little village that clings to the banks of the Thames. Painted houses shine brightly in the angled light and smoke swirls from chimneys. A mixture of old and new architecture, the village has three pubs, a pharmacy, café, clothing store, butcher, bakery and two hair salons.

Grievous pulls up at the pedestrian crossing. Signposts on either side are decorated with yellow ribbons along with something else – a photocopied poster covered in plastic. MISSING is printed in bold letters across the top, above a photograph. More writing below: *Have you seen Piper?*

'The street cleaners take them down, but they go up again just as quickly,' says Grievous. 'Wait here, sir.'

He pulls over and gets out of the car. Collecting a poster, he hands it to me. The plastic cover is beaded with rain.

Piper Hadley
Age: 18
Missing since August 31, 2008
Last seen wearing blue jeans and black and red striped T-shirt.
Call Crimestoppers: 0800 555 111
Reward Offered: £400,000

I study the image of a brown-eyed girl with a lop-sided grin and a shock of dark hair. She's almost defying the camera, challenging the result even as the shutter captures the moment.

Grievous steers us through the village and out again, along a narrow tarmac road flanked by hedgerows and puddles of melting snow. Occasional clumps of hawthorn and gorse emerge along the ditches where the fences have collapsed or rotted with age.

The road turns sharply. Straight ahead a padlocked gate prevents access. The sign advertises a concrete and gravel haulage business. Mounds of broken rock and shingle are visible beyond the vertical bars of the gate.

Steering onto a sidetrack where the potholes grow deeper, we pass clumps of snow that have survived in the shady hollows. The trees suddenly thin and I notice a grey expanse of water, whiter at the edges. Not water, ice. The frozen lake is beginning to break up in places, creating darker patches, black as onyx, dotted with a few brave waterbirds.

'They used to be gravel pits,' explains Grievous. 'Over time they flooded to form lakes. There were more of them, but in the eighties the Electricity Board began filling them in with waste ash from Didcot Power Station. The locals complained and organised a campaign to save the rest of the lakes.'

'How far away is the power station?'

'Four miles south of here.'

I remember seeing the six huge concrete chimneys from the train.

'What about the Heymans' farmhouse?'

'As the crow flies, about a mile.'

He pulls over. 'You got any other shoes?'

'No.'

He shrugs and pulls on an oilskin jacket. I have the woollen hat that Charlie bought me for my last birthday.

The cold nips at my cheeks, the chill of wind over water. The trainee detective constable leads. I follow. The track is part rubble, mud and grass, skirting the edge of the lake only a few feet from the water.

'This is where they found her,' he says.

The white tent has gone, but the crime scene is still marked by yellow police tape. On a nearby fence someone has pinned a bouquet of flowers, the petals withered by frost.

The lake glitters like a field of broken glass. A railway line flanks the eastern side.

Ducking under the police tape, I stand at the spot where Natasha's body was cut from the ice with machines and icepicks. A misshapen hole marks the spot, now full of black water and dead leaves.

Squatting on the ground, I pick up a blade of flattened grass, holding it between my thumb and forefinger. Closing my eyes, I listen to the winter silence, which is almost absolute. An image forms in my mind, a replay of last night's dream – a girl running as fast as she can, bursting through the branches and undergrowth, her feet bare, the blizzard erasing her footsteps.

She crossed the railway line and tumbled down the slope, feeling the ice crack beneath her and give way. She must have fought for the surface, the cold sapping her energy, unable to drag herself out. Someone chased her here. Watched her die.

She lay for two days beneath the ice until the sun came out and created a halo of splintered light around her body. A couple walking their dog raised the alarm.

'Which way to the farmhouse?' I ask.

Grievous raises his arm and points across the tracks.

'Can I walk it?'

'I can drive you.'

'Give me the directions and I'll meet you there.'

The farmhouse looks different from this angle, framed by a hard blue sky and ploughed fields, streaked with snow, that look like marbled meat. The buses and minivans have arrived. Searchers stamp their feet to stay warm and police dogs pull at leashes, sniffing the air. Some of these men and animals have scoured these fields already, but Drury wants it done again – every inch between the farmhouse and Radley Lakes.

Grievous is waiting for me at the house. He lifts the make-shift door aside and I walk through the rooms, reacquainting myself with the layout.

Pausing at the laundry, I remember the floral dress that was soaking in the tub. Summer not winter wear. Bagged. Labelled. Taken for tests.

'What are you looking for?' asks Grievous.

'I'm trying not to *look* for anything.'

'Huh?'

'The trick is to keep an open mind. When you search for something specific, you can fail to see a more important detail. Beware desire.'

'But how will you know if you find it?'

'I just will.'

'I see,' he says, when obviously he doesn't.

'Did you bring the photographs?' I ask.

He opens a satchel and hands me a ring-bound folder of crime-scene pictures. The first images are location shots of the farmhouse taken from every angle. For a hundred yards in every direction the pristine snow is untrammelled. No footsteps. No tyre tracks. No signs of life.

The images move closer, skirting the fire engines and showing the shattered front door. The interior shots reveal a clean, comfortable house with no immediate signs of a disturbance apart from the evidence markers on the floor.

Taking a photograph from the folder, I prop it on a chair in the sitting room. I choose a second image, this one of William Heyman, and place it on the kitchen table. He's lying on his stomach, head to one side, blood pooling beneath his cheek.

Closing my eyes, I try to picture that night. A blizzard raged outside, groaning through the roof beams and rattling the windows. The power lines were down. The Heymans lit candles on the stairs and in the kitchen. They were sitting in front of the open fire.

A teenage girl knocked on the front door. Wet. Cold. Covered with scratches. She wasn't barefoot, but she was wearing a floral dress and perhaps other clothes that aren't here any more.

William and Patricia Heyman weren't living in the area when the Bingham Girls went missing. They moved into the farmhouse a year later. The girl who came to their door was a stranger. They took her in, drew a bath, found her fresh clothes and dried her shoes by the fire.

She told them the story and William Heyman called 999, but the switchboard was overloaded and he was put on hold. Someone else was outside in the blizzard, following Natasha.

The attack was sudden . . . fierce. Mr Heyman turned and tried to run. He was struck from behind before he reached the kitchen. He crawled a dozen feet before dying, smearing the tiles with his blood.

The weapon? Something blunt and heavy: an axe perhaps. I noticed a woodpile with a chopping block at the side of the farmhouse.

Natasha was upstairs in the bath. She must have heard the commotion. Pulling on her clothes, she smashed the bathroom window and crawled through, cutting herself on the broken glass.

Patricia Heyman fled upstairs but the killer followed. She tried to barricade herself in the bedroom but the lock didn't hold.

Looking at the photographs, I notice little evidence of fire in the hallway but once inside the main bedroom the visual impact of the blaze is instantly clear. It burned intensely over a few square feet, yet covered every surface of the room in oily black soot, creating a strange 'shadowland'.

The only 'un-sooted' item on the bed is a blanket covering the body. It was placed on Mrs Heyman *after* the fire. Augie Shaw wanted to shield her, to protect her privacy. He's a schizophrenic. Interpreting his actions is perilous. It still doesn't make sense. Why would he kill her, burn her body and then tenderly protect her modesty with a blanket?

Whoever killed the Heymans worked calmly and quickly, wiping benches and pouring bleach, removing traces of his presence. He didn't come prepared. He made do. He didn't plan ahead, but neither did he panic. He stayed afterwards to clean up or came back later.

Meanwhile, Natasha fled from the farmhouse, barefoot and bleeding, across a silent landscape. She knew he was coming . . . following . . .

Some girls are cutters

or slicers or jabbers. Some are bulimic or anorexic. I'm a runner and a writer. I jot things down. Messages. Shopping lists. Quotes. Names. Ever since I learned how to write I've been filling exercise books, notepads, journals and diaries.

I like words. Sometimes they pop into my head randomly or I see them out of the corner of my eye, like shadows or flashes of light or stray eyelashes. I have favourites. Incandescent is a good word. So is serendipity. Epic. Perpendicular. (Tash said I only like it because it has a 'dick' in it.) Audacious. Rapscallion. Oxymoron. Hullabaloo.

I have three exercise books, which I keep hidden beneath my mattress. I write in the corner beneath the ladder, just in case the camera is watching.

When I write things down, I own them. They're no longer hanging in mid-air like cartoon bubbles or wisps of smoke. They're made real. Solid. Conversation doesn't last. Spoken words fade. We stop listening. Forget.

This is what I wrote down this morning.

- I dreamt last night that I had a mono-brow.
- Cramps. My period is coming.
- Spaghetti and meatballs . . . again.
- The gas bottle is running out.
- Must wash socks, but I'm wearing every pair.

Before I was taken, my lists were very different. I used to write down why I was unhappy.

- Because Mum and Dad row all the time.
- Because I'm ugly.

128

- *Because I'm not a vampire.*
- *Because my room's a mess.*

My handwriting is getting smaller and smaller, as though I'm shrinking. The real reason is that I'm running out of pages so I try not to waste the margins or the white spaces, filling them with words to pass the time. I have one page left after this one. Every word has to count.

Filling hours. Wasting days. Tash cut up our magazines and made a collage on the wall, sticking photographs and words together to form these weird worlds where people have dog heads and bikini bodies. It's really clever because if you stand at the far side of the room you can see that all the random images and letters form a bigger picture — a portrait of a girl. Tash said it was of me, but I'm not that pretty and nobody will ever paint a picture of me.

You're probably thinking I have low self-esteem. My mother taught me to lower my expectations. She was a debutante and a model at motor shows, but she talks as though she was the muse to Yves Saint Laurent and Versace.

And she makes out that her family was wealthy and upper class, but I know she came from Brighton where Gran and Granddad had a bed and breakfast on the seafront and they sent her to the local grammar school.

I don't know what my dad sees in Mum — apart from her looks, of course — but beauty is only skin deep and short-lived and in the eye of the beholder. I know my clichés. In their wedding photographs, my mother looks like Natalie Portman and Daddy looks like Natalie Portman's father, walking her down the aisle.

I don't have his patience or his sense of duty when it comes to loving Mum. 'Anything for a quiet life,' he used to say. I can give you more clichés: don't rock the boat or make waves or upset the apple cart.

Mum was always going off to health spas because she needed to recharge. Daddy didn't seem to mind because he could relax for a week. When she came home she'd throw these lavish parties, filling the house with freeloaders and hangers-on, who would eat our food and drink our booze, while she played lady of the manor.

I used to dream about leaving home. I wanted to go somewhere where I could lose myself. Bingham isn't big enough to get lost in. It's boring. Dullsville. It's like going to a relative's house when you know in advance where you're going to eat and refuel and what songs you're going to sing and what colour cordial makes you throw up. And when you arrive, someone is going to pinch your cheek and tell you how much you've grown.

I don't know why I'm writing stuff like this down. I don't imagine anyone will ever find my notebooks or read them. And if they do, I don't know if they'll be young and sad. That's the sort of reader who will understand me: young and sad and lonely.

15

The main doors of the church are shut, but I find a smaller door at the side of the south transept. Dr Leece's wife told me that I'd find him here. Stepping inside, I let my eyes adjust before searching along the high-backed pews, looking for movement or a silhouetted head.

From somewhere above me, an organ strikes up in a blast of music that vibrates the air and shakes dust from the beams. Following the sound, I climb the stairs to the choir loft. John Leece is sitting with his back to me at an organ keyboard, facing a wall of pipes and plugs. Working his feet and hands, he produces deep resonant chords that fill every corner of the church.

As the final notes fade, he folds the sheet music. I clear my throat and he turns, blinking, his eyes floating behind thick lenses.

'I'm sorry, I didn't hear you,' he says.

'I was enjoying the music.'

'I play here every Sunday,' he says, packing away his things.

'That piece didn't sound very religious.'

He glances at me guiltily.

'I'm sure God won't mind me rocking it up occasionally. How did you find me?'

'Your wife.'

Dr Leece looks at his hands, closing his eyes for a second.

'You've come to ask me about the post-mortem?'

'Yes.'

'Are you a Christian, Professor?'

'I'm not really anything.'

'I was an altar boy. I even thought about becoming a priest, but I became a doctor instead.'

The pathologist is staring at his hands, turning them over as though studying them for the first time.

'I have done more than four hundred post-mortems, but nothing like the one yesterday. Every body presents a new challenge. It's like reading a road map of broken bones, scars and diseases, but you expect there to be certainties; things you know are true.'

There is a chair in the corner. I pull it closer. With barely any inflection in his voice, he relates the details of the post-mortem, describing the various tests and measurements, screening for drugs and analysis of stomach contents.

'She was chronically underweight, physically stunted, with anaemia, Vitamin D and iron deficiencies, skin lesions and sores.'

'Best guess?'

'She was imprisoned away from the natural light.'

'For how long?'

'Months rather than weeks.'

'Years?'

'Quite possibly. There were twin lateral scratches on both her hips, suggesting she may have squeezed out of somewhere narrow.'

'The bathroom window at the farmhouse?'

'No, somewhere else.' Dr Leece opens his hands. 'She cut her forearm on the bathroom window. The lateral scratches were made earlier.'

'How much earlier?'

'A few hours.'

He unrolls his sleeves and buttons the cuffs.

'Ever heard of Locard's Exchange Principle?'

'No.'

'It's a theory developed by Edmond Locard in the nineteenth century. It states that whenever someone comes into contact with another object or person, there is a minute exchange of particles. I found several fibres in Natasha McBain's hair and beneath her fingernails – synthetic material, a dark colour, totally different to her clothing.'

'When you examined Augie Shaw's clothes – did you find similar traces?'

Dr Leece shakes his head. 'Her dress was heavily soiled. I've done an early analysis. The dirt is a conglomerate of things – plants, animal matter, microscopic particles of glass, paint, cement and machine oil . . .'

'An industrial site?'

'There were also traces of creosote and chlorinated hydro-carbons. Creosote has been used to treat railway sleepers and chlorinated hydrocarbons can create all sorts of things: pesticides, plastic, synthetic rubber, you name it. I've sent the samples to a lab in Switzerland that specialises in identifying contaminants. It may give us an idea of the industrial process.'

'What about her stomach contents?'

'She hadn't eaten in her last twelve hours. There were traces of vegetable matter and meat, but I won't have a definitive answer until tomorrow.'

He pauses for a moment, gazing past me at a stained glass window showing the apostles at the last supper.

'She was circumcised,' he whispers.

'I know.'

'The procedure was poorly executed but required some medical knowledge. She could have died of infection.' The pathologist lowers his forehead, faltering. 'Why was it done at all?'

I don't answer him.

'How far could she have walked in a blizzard in those clothes and shoes?'

'Not more than an hour or two.'

I make the calculation: four to seven miles, depending upon the terrain.

'Natasha was wearing an ankle bracelet,' says Leece. 'A silver chain, not expensive. I went back over the old case files – there was a list of the clothes they might have taken with them. Jewellery was mentioned.'

'Did Natasha have an ankle bracelet?'

'No . . . Piper Hadley had one.'

The church grows even quieter, as though someone has turned the volume down, muffling our voices. Piper Hadley has rarely been mentioned in the investigation, yet she's like a jagged hole at the centre of every scenario. A silent victim.

Outside, I breathe in the cold air, smelling woodsmoke and chestnuts roasting over charcoal. I buy a bag from a man on the corner, peeling off the blackened skins and tasting Christmas. People pass me on the wet pavements, hunched and hurrying, carrying bags full of Christmas presents and groceries. They have no idea how the world has changed since yesterday.

A ridge of lead-coloured cloud is burning like magnesium along the edge of the horizon, silhouetting the rooftops, making the dark seem darker. Stillness gathering.

I once thought of studying meteorology to learn how it works, the flow of things, air currents, wind, clouds, circling the earth. I thought the planet might be easier to understand than the mind.

Shifting my weight from one foot to the other, I wait for Mr Parkinson to fall into step inside me. Together we walk back to the hotel, going over the details again. One girl escaped. One remains elusive.

These are urgent times and I'm a weary man.

16

There's a note from Charlie written on hotel stationery.

Gone to a party. Won't be late. Cxx

A party? No mention of where, when, who she's with. What constitutes 'late'? It's only six o'clock. She's allowed to have a social life. She's sensible and mature for her age, but looking seventeen doesn't change the fact that she's only fifteen. Two years is a lot when you're that age. Fifteen is more Britney than Barbie. Fifteen scares the hell out of me.

I try her mobile. She's not answering. Maybe she's ignoring me on purpose because I wouldn't let her go to London on her own.

Four sealed boxes have been delivered in my absence – statements from the original investigation, along with time-lines and phone wheels. Drury has written a note: 'Knock yourself out.'

I pick up the first of the transcripts.

It's dated Monday, September 1, 2008. Sarah Hadley, Piper's mother, told police that she'd woken just after seven on Sunday morning and thought Piper had already gone to her riding lesson because she wasn't in her room.

At nine o'clock she phoned the riding school and one of the instructors, Mrs Clayton, told her that Piper hadn't shown up. Piper's mobile had been confiscated when she was grounded for an earlier indiscretion so there was no way for Mrs Hadley to call her.

'I was angry at first,' she told police. 'It was obvious Piper had snuck out of her room and stayed all night with that McBain girl, who is nothing but trouble. We told Piper she couldn't go to the funfair, but she disobeyed us and went out anyway.

'Piper has a blind spot when it comes to Natasha McBain. I don't like pointing the finger at particular people, but that girl is bad news. We tried to tell Piper, but what can you tell a teenager, eh? They never listen.'

I carry on reading statements, periodically glancing at the digital clock between the beds. At midnight Charlie still isn't back. If I call Julianne she'll panic. Blame me. I try Charlie's number again, leaving another message, trying to take the strident tone out of my voice.

Where is this party? Charlie doesn't know anyone in Oxford. She could have met them today, which isn't reassuring. Then it dawns on me. How stupid! She's not in Oxford; she's in London.

I dial Julianne's number, fortifying myself. She's awake instantly.

'What's wrong?'

'Do you have a number for Jacob?'

'Why?'

'I think Charlie is with him.'

'When did you last see her?'

'This morning.'

'Christ, Joe!'

There are so many things I know Julianne wants to say, but

136

thankfully she holds back. I can picture her in her flannelette pyjamas, fire-engine red, padding down the hall to Charlie's bedroom, looking through Charlie's desk, her corkboard, her address book.

'Why do you think she's with Jacob?'

'She said she was going to be at a party and wouldn't be late.'

'What party?'

'That's just it – I think she went to London instead.'

'Where were you?'

'I've been busy today.'

It sounds like a lame excuse.

'I can't find a number,' she says. 'Her friends might know.'

'No. Wait. Look at the last mobile phone bill. Charlie's calls will be listed.'

Julianne goes downstairs to the kitchen where we keep the household bills in a drawer with the chequebooks and our passports. I listen to her breathing, which sounds judgemental. Accusatory. I was supposed to settle this issue of the inappropriate boyfriend.

Julianne is looking down the list of numbers. She tells me one comes up more than any other. It must be Jacob.

'Do you want me to call him?' she asks.

'No, I'll do it,' I say, jotting it down.

'Ring me back.'

'As soon as I know something.'

She won't sleep now. She'll lie awake worrying.

I try the number. The first attempt goes to Jacob's voicemail. I try again. This time he answers, shouting to be heard above thumping music He's at a party or a nightclub.

'Yeah.'

'I need to speak to Charlie.'

'What?'

'This is Charlie's father. Where is she?'

He hesitates. 'Charlie who?'

'I know she's there, Jacob. Put her on.'

Another pause. I can picture him, lean and sharp-faced, with drooping trousers and a leather biker jacket. Blood surges into the top of my skull and I can feel my fingers working on the phone.

'I don't know what you're talking about,' he says. Wasted. Drunk. High.

'Listen, Jacob, up until now I haven't had reason to hate you or want to hurt you. Charlie is fifteen. You're an adult. There are laws.'

'I've done nothing wrong.'

'Is that a licensed venue, Jacob? Is Charlie drinking? You're corrupting a minor. There are laws about grooming underage girls.'

'Fuck off!'

'Did Charlie tell you about me? Did she mention that I work with the police? They're tracking this mobile. They can pinpoint your location to within fifty yards. I'm giving you the opportunity to help yourself, Jacob. Let me speak to Charlie.'

He pauses. Tells me to hold on. I'm listening to whining synthesisers and thumping bass beats. Is it a dance track or a techno song? I've never known the difference.

Charlie picks up the phone.

'Hello.'

'Are you OK?'

'I'm fine.'

I swallow the lump in my throat. 'Where are you?'

'London.'

'Where in London?'

'Camden.'

She starts to explain, growing tearful.

'I meant to be back by now. I thought I could catch a train and you'd never know. Jacob wanted to go to this party and now he's wasted . . . and my phone is dead . . . and it's too late to get a train.'

I can picture her standing slightly pigeon-toed, pushing her fringe from her eyes. My mouth is clogged up and I can barely speak.

'It's OK, Charlie.'

'You're angry.'

'No.'

'Please don't be angry.'

'We'll talk about it later.'

'That means you're *really* angry.'

'How much money do you have?'

'Eleven quid.'

'What's the address of the party?'

'Are you going to call the police?'

'Someone else.'

Vincent Ruiz answers on the second ring. Insomnia replaced his third wife or maybe he just retired from sleeping when he quit the Met and handed back his badge.

Ruiz is a friend of mine, although we started off disliking each other when we first met eight years ago. That's one of the intuitive things about life: meeting people that we seem destined to know. Ruiz is like that. Our initial mistrust grew into respect then admiration then genuine affection. Sacrifice comes last. Ruiz would give up a lot for me, perhaps even his own life, but he'd take a dozen people down with him because he doesn't surrender without a fight.

'This better be important,' he barks down the phone.

'It's Joe. I need your help. Charlie's in trouble.'

I can hear him sitting up, swinging his legs out of bed. Cursing. Fully alert now.

'What's wrong?'

'I stubbed my toe.'

He's looking for a pen. I give him the address.

'What do you want me to do?'

'Pick her up. Put her to bed. I appreciate this. I'll take an early train.'

139

'I'm on it.'

That's what I like about Ruiz. He doesn't need to rationalise or debate the pros and cons of a given situation. He goes with his gut and it rarely lets him down. Other people need to feel good about themselves, usually at the expense of others, or they keep a ledger of favours owed. Not Ruiz. When Julianne and I separated, he didn't take sides or pass judgement. He stayed friends with both of us.

Before he hangs up: 'Hey, Professor, did you hear they just brought out a new "Divorce Barbie"? She comes with all of Ken's stuff.'

'Fetch my daughter.'

'Done.'

Julianne picks up on the half-ring.

'Charlie's fine. Ruiz has gone to pick her up.'

'Where was she?'

'With Jacob.'

'Where?'

'He took her to a party and then got wasted instead of bringing her home. She's pretty upset.'

'She should be.'

'I'm sorry – I should have been watching her.'

Julianne doesn't respond. I know she's angry. I had one job to do – look after Charlie – and I proved myself incapable. Useless. Feckless. Pointless. Aimless.

I wish she'd shout at me. Instead, she says goodnight.

I lie awake until Ruiz calls to say that Charlie is asleep in his guest room. It's after three. I won't sleep now. So I pack Charlie's things and check out the train timetables. I'll take the first available service to London and then drive Charlie home. We'll work out a story in the car, polishing the script until we have something that Julianne accepts.

I miss this. I know that sounds bizarre, given what's happened tonight, but I miss the daily dramas of being married, the ins and outs of everyday domestic life. We've been separated for three years, but whenever something goes wrong Julianne still calls me. In the event of an emergency, I'm still her go-to man, the number one person in her life.

There's a downside, of course. She wants me to handle the bad stuff, not the good stuff.

I don't hear him coming.

I don't hear him move the furniture or open the trapdoor. It's strange because normally I'm such a light sleeper.

When I do wake, I think it must be the police. Tash has brought help. They've found me. But then I hear his voice and my heart freezes and the cold reaches all the way to the ends of my fingers.

He's already down the ladder. Standing over me. He grabs my hair and pulls me out of bed and throws me against the wall, bouncing my head off the bricks. He does it again, holding my hair, making syllables into words as my head hits the wall.

'YOU . . . THINK . . . YOU . . . ARE . . . SO . . . FUCK . . . ING . . . CLEV . . . ER!'

I crumple on the floor, trying to crawl away, but he grabs my leg and pulls me across the concrete. I can feel the skin being torn from my knees and elbows.

A forearm snakes around my neck. He pulls me back into his chest and wraps his fist in my hair.

'I'm sorry, I'm sorry.'

'What are you sorry for?'

'Please don't hurt me.'

'Tell me – what are you sorry for?'

'I don't know.'

The blade of the knife is pressed under my left eye, digging into the skin.

'Do you remember how I cut her? Do you want that to happen to you?'

I shake my head.

'When are you going to learn?'

'I will.'

'I'm trying to save you,' he says, almost pleading with me now, still tightening his arm across my neck. 'I'm trying to save you from yourself.'

I try to nod, but I can't move my head.

'You smell!' he says, pushing me away. 'Don't you ever wash?'

'I'm sorry.'

'You keep saying that. You think I'm stupid?'

'No.'

'You think you're clever helping her escape. She's not coming back. She's dead. You killed her. It's your fault.'

I don't believe him. He's lying.

I'm lying on the floor. He kicks me before I can curl into a ball. I do it anyway, trying to protect myself, covering my head.

I hear him moving, but I don't look up. I can hear water echoing against the metal sides of a bucket. He stands over me, pouring the water slowly over my head and my arms and legs. The cold takes my breath away. He fills the bucket again. I don't move.

Here it comes again. He kicks me.

'On your back! Open your legs!'

I turn over. He pours the water on my groin and tosses me a scrubbing brush with hard bristles.

'Wash yourself.'

I don't understand.

He kicks me again. 'I said, wash yourself.'

I use the brush, rubbing it along my arms.

'Not there! There!'

He points. I put the brush between my thighs.

'Scrub!'

I hesitate.

'You do it, or I'll do it for you. That's it. Harder! Harder!'

I can't see through the tears. I can barely hear him.

When he's satisfied, he takes the brush away from me. Then he collects the remaining food in a plastic bag, my last can of beans. He carries it up the ladder and turns off the light.

'When you're really sorry, we'll talk again. Maybe then I'll turn the lights on.'

The trapdoor shuts. The darkness comes to life, breathing into my ears, whispering, sighing.

On my hands and knees I crawl across the room to the sink. The vomit that comes out of me is bitter water. My clothes are soaked. The bunks. The bedding. I still have gas in the cooker.

I make myself a cup of tea, feeling my way around the basement. Then I sit with my head over the bedpan, wanting to be sick again. I'm not scared of the dark any more. I'm used to it now. The darkness used to be like death, now it's like the womb.

He told me nobody wanted me. He told me they stopped looking because nobody cared. He said Tash was dead. I'm not going to believe his lies.

I shake the ladder. I shout at the trapdoor. 'I need a dry blanket.'
Nobody comes.
'I need a dry blanket.'
Still nothing.
'I'm sorry.'

17

It's still early when I arrive at Ruiz's house in Fulham. Mist hangs over the Thames, blurring naked trees on the distant bank. Rowers appear from the shroud, pulling into view with choreographed strokes like a ballet on water.

Ruiz answers the door in a short bathrobe, bare legs and Ugg boots.

I look at his feet. 'You're wearing dead sheep.'

'How observant of you. No wonder you're a psychologist. They were a gift from Miranda. They're so ugly I've grown fond of them.' He wiggles his toes. 'I'm thinking of giving them names: Lambchop and Shaun.'

His arms fold around me in a proper hug. Not many British men can hug, but Ruiz makes it feel as easy as a handshake. I follow him down the hallway to the kitchen.

'Do you want to put some trousers on?'

'No.'

'Charlie?'

'Still asleep.'

'Did she say anything?'

'She puked her little heart out about 3 a.m. I gave her an aspirin and put her back to bed.'

Ruiz fills a teapot and covers it with a knitted cosy. Sits opposite. Pours. Milk. Sugar. Even dressed in a bathrobe he can look intimidating, yet there is a gentle stillness about him that I've always admired, a quiet dignity. He doesn't offer unsolicited advice. His two children are grown up. One of them is married. Guidance might be reassuring, but it's rarely helpful.

'So how are you doing?'

'Good.'

'Seeing anyone?'

'No.'

'How's Julianne?'

'She's being reasonable and polite. I wish she'd get angry.'

'Not everyone is like you.'

'You think *I'm* angry?'

'I think you're furious. I think you wake up in the morning and if you're not angry you hold a mirror over your mouth to see if you're still breathing.'

Not rising to the bait, I try to change the subject. I don't want to talk about Julianne. Instead, I start telling him about Oxford and the Bingham Girls.

He remembers the case. That's one of the remarkable things about Ruiz – his memory. For him there has never been such a thing as forgetting. Nothing grows hazy or vague over time, fraying at the edges. Some people think photographically or chronologically, but Ruiz connects details like a spider weaving a web, threading one strand to the next. That's why he can reach back and pluck details out of the air from criminal cases that are five, ten, fifteen years old.

'Natasha McBain's body was found four days ago in a frozen lake.'

'How long had it been there?'

'Thirty-six hours.'

Ruiz whistles through his teeth. 'So she's been alive all this time. Any idea where?'

'No.'

'How did you get involved?'

'They want me to review the original investigation.'

'And you said no.'

'Correct.'

'But you're doing it anyway?'

'Yes.'

'Why you?'

'I'm an outsider.'

'Which would normally count against you.'

'The chief constable is concerned about the fall-out. He wants to avoid allegations of a cover-up. It's not a witch hunt.'

'Not yet,' says Ruiz, swallowing half a mug of tea and pouring himself another. 'I remember they suspected a school caretaker and they also looked at Natasha's old man. Isaac McBain served five years for armed robbery. He got mixed up with a couple of gangster-wannabes called the Connolly brothers who knocked over a payroll in London. When it all went pear-shaped, McBain copped a plea and grassed up the Connolly brothers for a lesser sentence. After the girls went missing, the police thought the brothers might have orchestrated the kidnapping as payback.'

'What happened?'

'They were interviewed; denied everything. Then the abduction theory ran out of steam.'

'What changed?'

'There was a third girl,' he says. 'Emily Martinez.'

'The best friend.'

'She told police that Natasha and Piper were planning to run away. I guess everyone expected the girls to turn up once they'd run out of money or had a falling out, but it never happened.'

'And the investigation?'

'The Hadley family kept up the pressure. You must have seen the mother on TV. She can't pass a camera without making a speech. She's a good-looking woman, if you're into hard-bodied, gymrat chic.'

'Not your sort of thing?'

'I like a woman with something to hold on to.'

'Handles?'

'Curves.'

Ruiz clamps his hands on the edge of the table and presses down hard, rising to his feet. He puts two slices of bread in the toaster.

'The chief constable says he knows you,' I tell him. 'Thomas Fryer.'

'Ah, yes, Fryer. I once punched him on a rugby field. He got up again, to his credit.'

'He says if I need help he'll put you on the payroll as a consultant; a thousand pounds a day.'

'He thinks I can be bought.'

'I'd appreciate your help.'

'The trail has been cold for three years.'

'Look upon it as a challenge.'

His lips separate. It might be a grimace. He could be smiling. I cannot tell the difference. Retirement has never sat easily with Ruiz. He's like an old racehorse put out to pasture: when other horses run, he wants to run too.

Behind him I glimpse Charlie clinging to the door jamb, ghostly pale. Heavy lidded. She's wearing one of Ruiz's old shirts.

'If you're going to puke, Princess, please don't do it on my floor,' he says.

She scowls at him and slumps at the table, putting her head in her hands.

'How are you feeling?' I ask.

'Like crap.'

Ruiz begins opening cupboard doors, looking for a jar of

148

jam. His bathrobe is too short. Charlie gets a glimpse of buttocks.

'Now I *am* going to be sick.'

'Don't be cheeky,' says Ruiz, tugging it lower.

Charlie blinks at me and sighs. 'OK, get it over with: the lecture. Tell me, "I told you so", and "What were you thinking, Charlie?" and "We raised you better than this, Charlie" and "You're grounded until you're eighteen".'

'Twenty-eight,' says Ruiz, who's enjoying this.

Charlie shoots him a look.

'Just don't give me the silent treatment. Mum does that. She looks at me with her big sad eyes like I've just drowned a sack of kittens.'

'What do you want me to say?'

'Nothing. I screwed up, OK? I lied. I broke the rules. I didn't listen . . .'

'And?'

'I'm never drinking again.'

Ruiz pours her a glass of orange juice. Charlie takes a sip and hiccups. 'And anyway – it's not all my fault. If you hadn't been so unreasonable – never letting me do stuff.'

'You're fifteen.'

'Almost sixteen.'

'Too young to be in London on your own.'

'You want to keep me locked up like some princess in a tower.'

'When have I locked you up?'

'I'm speaking figuratively.'

Ruiz laughs. 'Figuratively speaking, you don't look much like a princess. Unless you mean Princess Fiona – you're the same shade of green.'

'Fuck off.'

'Spoken like a true princess.'

I tell her to mind her tongue. Charlie sulks for a moment and then stands, putting her arms around Ruiz's waist.

'Thank you.'

'What for?' he asks.

'Coming to get me.' She turns to me. 'I'm sorry about what happened.'

'I know.'

'How long before you think I've learned my lesson?'

'Some time shy of the next decade.'

Mid-morning I drive her back to Wellow. She sleeps most of the way with the nape of her neck against the back of the seat. I glance at her occasionally, studying her face. Her nose has a bump on the bridge and a smattering of freckles.

Watching her brow furrow and her lips part slightly, I wonder how much her behaviour now is due to what she's suffered in the past – the kidnapping and imprisonment. Gideon Tyler stole a part of her childhood – I can't say how much – when he knocked her off her pushbike and bundled her into his car.

Psyches are harder to bandage than flesh. For all my training and experience, I don't repair damaged minds. The best I can hope for is to help people cope.

Just outside of Bath, we stop for lunch. The pub has an open fire, fake rafters and smoked yellow walls, decorated with horse brasses and fox-hunting prints. The publican is a big slow man, polishing a pint glass, who frowns vacantly as though trying to remember something important.

Our meals arrive – cottage pie and a Ploughman's. Charlie sips a soft drink.

'Are you ever going to get married again?' she asks, out of the blue.

'I'm already married.'

'She's not going to take you back, Dad.'

'I don't have a girlfriend.'

'But you could . . . if you wanted. That woman likes you.'

'What woman?'

'The one you had lunch with. She was flirting.'

'No, she wasn't.'

'Of course she was. Women can tell.'

'You mean *you*?'

'Yes, Dad, I'm a woman and I could tell.' She pops a chip into her mouth. 'If you do get remarried, I won't be a bridesmaid.'

'Why not?'

'I'm not wearing some lame burnt-orange dress that makes me look like a lampshade.'

'Understood.'

The cottage is near the end of a narrow lane that leads to a bridge over Wellow River. It's barely a bridge and barely a river. Julianne is waiting at the door. Her hair is pinned up and she's wearing old jeans and a sweater, but still looks like she could be starring in a TV commercial for multi-vitamins or shampoo.

Charlie accepts her hug and glances back at me, blinking through a veil of hair that has fallen over her eyes. There's something knowing in her look – a shared secret.

Separating, she disappears inside, climbing the stairs to her bedroom. Julianne watches her go. Relieved. Anxious.

I'm expecting her to be angry, to slam the door on me, but instead Julianne opens her arms and hugs me.

'She messed up.'

'Yes.'

'What should we do?'

'Nothing. She made a mistake. We've all done that. The important thing is that she doesn't give up. We want her to wake up tomorrow and shoot for another perfect day.'

'You make it sound so easy.'

'Not easy.'

Julianne asks if I want a cup of tea. Normally, I'd jump at the chance to spend twenty minutes in her company, surrounded by the familiar.

'I have to get back.'

'To London?'

'Oxford.'

I can't tell her about Natasha McBain. She'll know soon enough. Then she'll put two and two together and realise that I'm helping the police again and look at me the way she always does, like my personal star is shining a little less brightly than before.

She kisses my left cheek and her lips brush against mine as she moves to my right cheek.

'Thank you for bringing her home.'

Charlie unlatches the window upstairs and pushes it outwards, leaning half her body through the opening.

'There's a story on the TV about that guy.'

'What guy?'

'The one you talked to in Oxford – Augie Shaw.'

'What about him?'

'He tried to hang himself.'

I have this counting game.

I start counting backwards from a hundred and tell myself that Tash will come back before I get to zero. When I get to the end, I start again. I always slow down when I get to single figures, listening between each number in case I hear footsteps or voices.

It's just the wind.

She's not coming back.

Early morning, it's dark inside and outside. Dark enough for the trees to look like a monstrous wave moving towards me.

When the sun rises pale and cold, I stand on the bench and look at the brightening sky. A train passes. Without it, I might be on another planet. I might be dead. I might be the only person left in the world.

I have no more paper to write upon. I have used up the last page. When George hosed me down, the book was under my pillow. The pages were wet and now they are buckling and curling as they dry. My pencil is just a stub, so I guess it doesn't matter about the paper. From now on I'll have to write in my head. Compose my lists. Gather my thoughts. File and forget.

People say that my generation lacks imagination and that we have a short attention span. We're also super-sized and lazy and have no decent music. This is criticism from a Boomer generation that loves telling stories about the 1960s – the sex, drugs and rock 'n' roll – but who swapped their protest placards for property portfolios and pension funds. My parents are like that: small people with small lives.

When I reached the England Indoor Age Championships and had to go to Birmingham to run, my mother didn't come to watch me. She said running wasn't very ladylike and suggested that I had a mutant gene that didn't come from her side of the family. She also joked about checking my adoption papers or said that she must have shagged Seb Coe instead of my father.

She was always talking Dad down like that. 'I didn't marry you for your looks' she'd say, 'but where are the brains you were supposed to bring to the family?'

After I came second at the nationals for my age group my parents gave me a brand-new Raleigh bike. I was sick of running by then, but I liked my new bike. I rode everywhere, for mile after mile.

My grandmother died that month. When I got the news I rode my bike to Abingdon Station and waited for one of the express trains to come roaring through so I could swear and scream at how wrong the world was to take my gran. That's what I want to do now. I want to scream at the top of my lungs, but this time I want the world to hear me.

18

Homeopaths say that water can retain a memory; why not walls? They can be scrubbed, graffitied, painted and plastered yet somewhere beneath the layers, the memories remain.

The guard ahead of me has pale blond hair that is combed across his forehead like he's going to primary school. Occasionally, he glances over his shoulder, making sure I'm still following.

'One of my colleagues found him,' he says, as we stop outside a cell. 'He opened the viewing hatch and saw him hanging there. Raised the alarm.'

The cell door opens. I'm expected to look. The guard is still talking. 'My colleague wrapped his arms around the prisoner's waist, supporting him until someone could cut him down.'

The guard points to the far wall. 'The belt was looped around that heating pipe. He must have stood on the bench.'

The room has no windows, bare walls and a concrete floor.

'They took him to the Radcliffe, unconscious but breathing. Could be brain damaged. Oxygen deprivation. I heard one of them paramedics talking.'

The guard is gazing at something beyond the walls. 'There'll be a full investigation. No belts. No laces. That's the rule. Somebody fucked up.'

I need to get outside. Fresh air. It's not until I reach the car park that I realise I've been holding my breath. Ruiz is waiting for me. He's wearing a heavy woollen overcoat that looks like it survived both world wars. A boiled sweet rattles between his teeth.

'You found the place,' I say.

'Trained investigator.'

He has a different car. He once drove an early-model Mercedes – his pride and joy – but it didn't survive a collision with a motel room wall. Now he has a box-like Range Rover with a dark-green paint job.

'It looks like a tank.'

'Exactly.'

We drive together to the hospital. Sinatra is in full voice on the stereo: 'That Old Black Magic'. Ruiz's musical tastes haven't escaped from the fifties. I once asked him about the sixties and he told me that he was too busy arresting hippies to ride the peace train.

'So you missed out on the free love.'

'Oh, it's never free, Professor. Never free.'

There are police cars outside the main doors and a uniformed constable is stationed at the ICU. Tall. Good looking. Nurses keep smiling at him as they pass.

Augie Shaw is lying half naked on a bed, handcuffed to the side-rail. The capillaries have burst in the whites of his eyes. There is a woman sitting beside him, canted forward with her head resting on the bedding, eyes closed. His mother, even more diminished than before, fading away.

DCI Drury is talking to one of the doctors. We wait.

'I hate hospitals,' says Ruiz, expecting me to ask why.

I humour him. 'Why?'

'Healthy people die in them.'

'You've lost me.'

'Sick people get better in hospitals. Healthy people die. Think about it. That's what you read about in the papers: people going into hospital for minor operations and dying because of stupid mistakes and overworked nurses and exhausted interns. You don't hear about really sick people dying.'

'That's because they're really sick.'

'Exactly.'

I don't bother pointing out the flaw in Ruiz's logic.

'I should be made Minister for Health,' he adds. 'I could sort out the problem with waiting lists straight away.'

'How so?'

'I'd stop people at the door of Accident and Emergency and quiz them on how they got injured. Food poisoning or a dog bite or a broken arm, they'll have to wait fifteen minutes. But if they arrive with self-inflicted slashes or a Hoover nozzle stuck up their arse, it'll be six hours.'

'Are you sure you don't read the *Daily Mail*?'

'I'm being harsh but fair. There are too many idiots using up our health budget.'

Drury has finished his conversation. He opens his palms, looking like a Mafia godfather. 'Where have you been?'

'I had to take my daughter home.'

'Tell Grievous next time. He's been running around like a lost puppy.'

I introduce him to Ruiz and the two of them size each other up with a handshake. Drury seems less aggressive today. Perhaps he hasn't met his normal quota of fools.

'If it weren't for Piper Hadley I'd be wishing that boy dead,' says Drury, talking about Augie Shaw. 'Sign of a guilty man, a suicide attempt.'

'Or a desperate one,' I say.

The DCI pushes spare change into a machine and makes his choice. A bottle of water drops into the tray. He cracks the top and drinks noisily, wiping his mouth with the back of his hand.

He looks at me. 'You still think Augie Shaw couldn't have kidnapped Natasha McBain and Piper Hadley?'

157

'He hasn't the intellect or the experience.'

'Maybe you're right, Professor, but while you've been playing happy families, we were checking the registered sex offenders living in the area and running a full background check on suicide boy in there. A very interesting name came up – his old man Wesley Shaw once faced eight counts of child rape but managed to plea-bargain it down to one count of attempted unlawful penetration of a minor. And you know where he was on the night the Bingham Girls disappeared? He was working on the rides at the fairground.'

'Where is he now?'

'He died eighteen months ago. Ran a red light and got pancaked by a bus in Stoughton Street.'

Drury tosses the empty plastic bottle into a metal bin.

'Wesley George Shaw. He also had a few aliases: WG Buford, David William Burford, George Westman. Born in 1960, the son of an aircraft mechanic stationed at RAF Abingdon working on fighter planes. First arrest at age twenty-four: attempted rape. Charges dropped. Second arrest: kerb-crawling and engaging the services of an underage prostitute. You see where I'm going, Professor? Wesley Shaw's name came up in the first investigation, but his old lady gave him an alibi. She lied for him.'

'Is that what she told you?'

'She just confirmed it.'

'But Wesley Shaw is dead.'

'He was alive when the girls went missing. He could have kidnapped them; set the whole thing up. Augie just inherited them. Like father like son.'

At the far end of the corridor, a door opens and Victoria Naparstek appears. Tall, pale, purposeful, her face enamelled with anger. She confronts Drury, stopping inches from his face.

'I warned you.'

He raises his hands, but Victoria knocks them away.

'I told you what would happen.'

'Let's take this somewhere else. Take a deep breath. Calm down.'

'Don't tell me to calm down.'

He's gentler with her than I expect. 'Somebody messed up. I'm sorry.'

'Have you told his mother that? No. That might mean a lawsuit. Compensation. Instead, you're going to close ranks. Collude. Get your stories straight.'

'This isn't the time or the place.'

He's whispering to her, trying to lead her away; holding her arm, talking like they're old friends. She shudders at his touch. Disappoints him.

'Don't patronise me,' she says. 'Never, ever patronise me.'

Then she leaves, storming down the corridor. The police officer on guard follows her progress, his eyes glued to her posterior.

'What are you looking at, Constable?' barks Drury. 'Keep your eyes to the front.'

19

St Catherine's School is set amid trees and boot-churned sporting fields on the northern outskirts of Abingdon, a mile from an old RAF base, which was decommissioned in the nineties.

A lone student is sitting in the administration office. Sulking. She swings her legs beneath a vinyl chair, awaiting judgement for some indiscretion. Dressed in a grey skirt, white blouse and v-neck burgundy jumper, she looks up as we enter in a flurry of cold air. The door closes. She looks down again.

A school secretary is seated behind sliding glass. Grievous flashes his warrant card and asks for the headmistress. The secretary misdials the number twice. All thumbs. Perhaps an unpaid parking ticket is preying on her mind.

The headmistress, Mrs Jacobson, is a big woman in a beige dress. Her dyed hair is brushed back and fastened with a comb. 'Come, come,' she says, herding us like pre-schoolers into her office, her shoes echoing on the parquet floor.

'This is about Piper and Natasha, isn't it? Is there news?'

'There have been some developments in the case,' says the young detective. 'The details are confidential for operational reasons.'

'Of course, I understand. Sit down. Coffee? Tea? Help your-self to biscuits. Such a terrible business – it took our girls a long time to recover. Some of them needed counselling, but we're a very stoic bunch here at St Catherine's.'

A spare seat is found for Ruiz, who hasn't said a word since we arrived. Grievous picks up a chocolate biscuit, which crumbles when he takes a bite. He makes a little sound and tries to catch the falling crumbs. Mrs Jacobson walks to the side table and comes back with a plate and a paper napkin, silently admonishing him. She settles again behind her desk.

'Darling Piper, I can't imagine why she'd run away. Her father is such a generous man. And her mother is so beautiful and charming.'

'Not like the McBains?' asks Ruiz.

The headmistress flinches. 'Excuse me?'

'Natasha's father served a five-year stretch for armed robbery. Surely you know that.'

'We don't discriminate at St Catherine's.'

'Neither do we,' says Ruiz.

There is a look between them. Nothing warm.

'We were hoping to talk to some of the teachers who taught Piper and Natasha,' I say. 'And to look at their student files.'

'I'm afraid the files are confidential, but most of their teachers are still with us. We don't have a big turnover of staff.'

'What about caretakers?' asks Ruiz.

The headmistress hesitates. 'If you're referring to Mr Stokes, he's no longer working at St Catherine's.'

'He was sacked.'

'Yes.'

'Why?'

'I don't see how that's relevant.'

'He took inappropriate photographs of the girls.'

'An unfortunate incident. We did all the proper checks.'

'Where is Mr Stokes now?'

She stares at Ruiz icily. 'We haven't kept in touch.'

They hold each other's gaze for a moment and then Mrs Jacobson looks at her small gold wristwatch. 'It's lunchtime. You'll find most of the teachers in the staff common room.'

The schoolgirl in the waiting room is instructed to escort us. Her name is Monica and she walks with a pigeon-toed gait and sloping shoulders. We climb the stairs and follow a corridor past classrooms and science labs.

I fall into step beside Ruiz. He's limping more today; the legacy of an old bullet wound. He's too proud to use a walking stick. Vain.

'Why did you give her such a hard time?'

'She reminded me of my old physics teacher.'

'Is that all?'

'You didn't meet my physics teacher.'

Monica knocks on the door of the common room and asks for Miss McCrudden. The English teacher is in her mid-thirties, wearing dark trousers and a blouse with a coffee stain. Her fingers are spotted with blue marker pen.

Most of the tables are taken by groups of teachers eating sandwiches or reheated soup. We take a seat in the corner.

Miss McCrudden looks at me nervously.

'This isn't an official interview. Nobody is taking notes. I'm a psychologist working with the police. I'm trying to learn whatever I can about Piper and Natasha.'

She makes a clucking sound deep in her throat. 'Such lovely girls.'

'What do you mean?'

'Pardon?'

'You answered automatically and said they were lovely girls.'

'They were.'

'How were they lovely?'

'They were very friendly.'

'Did they have a lot of friends?'

She hesitates. 'Some.'

162

'Not a lot then?'

'Are you *trying* to disagree with me?'

'I'm *trying* to get to the truth.'

The teacher eyes me accusingly. 'Are you calling me a liar?'

'Yes. You see, Miss McCrudden—'

'Call me Kirsty.'

'Kirsty. By most accounts Natasha McBain was a bit of a tearaway. Always getting into trouble.'

'She was high-spirited.'

'There you go again – making excuses for her. Apologising. Trying to soften the edges; airbrushing the truth.'

She gives me a hard stare and starts again. 'Natasha could be difficult. Hard to control.'

'In what way?'

'She didn't respect authority. I don't think St Catherine's was the place for her.'

I wait for something more. She sighs. 'I shouldn't really talk – I was a complete nightmare at school. Not as bad as Natasha, mind you, but my parents were always being summoned to explain or apologise.

'Some girls are suffocated by a place like this – the discipline and routine. We talk a lot about pastoral care and not leaving a girl behind, but let's face it, we want students who make us look good, who aren't management problems, who do well in their exams . . .'

'Natasha didn't fit.'

'She was a brilliant student. A complete natural, the sort who wins awards and gets scholarships without even trying.' The teacher lowers her voice. 'But she was also restless, preoccupied, often crude. When she wasn't terrorising teachers, she was flirting with them – male and female.'

'Did she flirt with you?'

Kirsty smiles knowingly. 'Natasha enjoyed being provocative, but there's a difference between physical maturity and emotional maturity. She made a lot of bad decisions.'

'What about Piper?'

'Completely different. A born storyteller. One of the best creative writers I've ever taught. She daydreamed. Often I'd catch her staring into space, or studying the ground as though it were a river she couldn't cross. And she had a way of touching things, tapping them lightly with her fingertips, as though playing a secret game.'

'Academically?'

'She struggled.'

'Is she the sort of girl to run away?'

Kirsty doesn't answer immediately. She turns to the window, watching girls outside in the playground.

'Natasha was one of those rare creatures who truly didn't seem to care what people thought. Compliment her or criticise her and her reaction didn't change. Piper was more self-conscious. I think there was some hero worship involved.'

'How did Natasha react?'

'She loved being adored. Piper was like her faithful retainer.'

'Why didn't they have many friends?'

'They had issues.'

'Such as?'

The teacher falters slightly. 'I think a lot changed after the accident.'

'What accident?'

'There was a fight between two local lads. One of them drove a car into the other. Left him disabled. The driver was arrested and charged with attempted murder.'

'What does that have to do with Natasha?'

'It was her boyfriend. They were fighting over her.'

'When was this?'

'About four months before the girls disappeared. You should really talk to Emily Martinez.'

'Is she here today?'

'I don't know. She misses a lot of school.'

Ruiz has pulled an old notebook from his pocket and is

jotting down details. It's not that he needs reminding – he won't forget – but old habits are hard to break.

Kirsty turns to Grievous. 'Has there been some news?'

He doesn't answer, but the knowledge still reaches her. Fear thickens her vowels.

'Are they dead?'

'I can't comment,' he says.

She looks at me. 'Oh dear, you've made me do a terrible thing.'

'You've told me the truth.'

A bell rings. Bodies fill the corridors outside; girls in motion, laughter, musical voices and sentences that end with upward inflections. The English teacher has to go. She stands and brushes the front of her trousers. She touches the corner of one eye, then her hair.

'We all have reasons to run away,' she says, before turning. 'Most of us find the strength to stay.'

20

Ruiz turns off the ignition and we sit in silence, watching the empty street. A Network Rail sign indicates the entrance to Radley Station and beneath it is an information board with a poster for a visiting circus.

Beyond a bus stop is the Bowyer Arms, a chain pub with pale washed walls. Ruiz fumbles in his pocket, pulling out a tin of boiled sweets. He chooses one and sucks on it thought-fully.

'Explain to me why we're here?'

'This is where they were supposed to meet,' I say. 'According to Emily's statement, they were going to rendezvous here at ten o'clock on Sunday morning, but they didn't show up.'

I take out a copy of the original missing persons report. Alice McBain told police she last saw the girls at just before 8 a.m. on Sunday August 31. Piper had slept over at Natasha's house after the Bingham Summer Festival. Alice knocked on Natasha's door and told them to get out of bed. Natasha had a waitressing shift at a café in Abingdon at ten that morning, but failed to show.

'Why did they want to run away?'

'In the last week of the school year Natasha was expelled from school for pulling a prank on a couple of teachers. The details were never released and the expulsion was rescinded when the girls went missing.

'According to Emily, they planned to run away to London. They packed bags and saved money, but the idea seemed to lose potency as the summer wore on. It came up again on the last night of the Bingham festival. The girls went to a funfair. Piper was supposed to be grounded, but she climbed out of her bedroom window after her parents had gone to bed.

'Dozens of people saw the girls during the course of the evening. The fairground rides closed down at eleven. Emily had gone home an hour earlier after a phone call. Her mother had suffered some sort of turn and been taken to hospital.'

'What sort of turn?'

'It's not clear. Piper and Natasha were seen near the entrance to the village green just before ten.'

'Who saw them?'

'A police patrol.'

The boiled sweet rattles against Ruiz's teeth. I continue.

'Some time shortly after midnight, Piper Hadley knocked on Emily's bedroom window. She was upset, but wouldn't say why. She said they were leaving, running away. If Emily wanted to come, she had to meet them here at 10 a.m.'

'Did Emily see Natasha?'

'No. Emily showed up at Radley Station at 9.50 a.m. but the girls didn't show. She waited for nearly two hours then went home.'

'She didn't raise the alarm?'

'No. A search wasn't launched until late Sunday afternoon. Police interviewed passengers on the trains and the City35 bus service, but nobody remembered seeing the girls.'

'What about their mobile phones?'

'Natasha's phone was turned off just after eleven on Saturday night. Piper didn't have one with her.'

'How far is the farmhouse from here?' he asks.

'Just over half a mile.'

Ruiz is still contemplating the pub in the distance. 'Maybe Drury is right about Augie Shaw.'

'Augie doesn't have the intellect to have done this.'

'What about his old man?'

'Wesley has been dead for a year and a half. Even if he abducted the girls, I don't think Augie could have carried on without him. It takes food, water, heating, security . . .'

'Why keep the girls?'

'Could be a number of reasons. It's sexual, but there's definitely a revenge element. It's also about possession; owning something special, being completely in control.'

Ahead of us a bus lurches to a halt and schoolchildren of various ages get off. I notice a pair of teenaged girls, one model tall, the other short, stout and brunette, walking along the footpath.

Ruiz steps out of the car.

'How's it going, ladies?'

They both smile and say hello, but keep their distance.

'Can I ask you a question?'

'Sure,' says the taller girl. She has a blue school bag with neon stickers.

'The bus that comes through here – does it run on Sunday mornings?'

'Every hour.'

Ruiz takes out his notebook and jots something down. 'I'm just doing a little detective work,' he explains. 'Two girls went missing from this spot a few years ago. Do you remember the Bingham Girls?'

'Everybody knows about them,' says the brunette, taking a few steps and looking into the car. 'Are you really detectives?'

'Working a case.'

'Piper Hadley was a really good runner,' says the tall girl.

'Did you go to the same school?'

168

'No.'

'What about Natasha McBain?'

'She was just, like, you know . . .'

'I don't.'

Eye-rolling. 'She had, like, this reputation of being a slag.'

'A wannabe-dot-com,' adds the brunette.

Ruiz glances at me, already tired of talking to the girls.

'My dad thinks they're, like, dead,' says the tall one.

'Is like dead the same as being *really* dead?' asks Ruiz.

They look at him blankly.

Further along the road I notice a familiar-looking Vauxhall Cavalier slow and pull over. Tinted windows. Fat tyres. Two-up. Toby Kroger and Craig Gould emerge. Gould is wearing stylised baggy pants, a leather jacket and an oversized T-shirt like he's an LA gang-banger an ocean away from home. Kroger has on the same cotton hoodie and battered jeans that I saw him in two days ago.

'Afternoon, ladies,' he says, grabbing the crotch of his jeans. 'Are these old pervs hassling you?'

The taller girl giggles. The brunette stands with one foot behind the other, pushing her breasts forward.

Opening the car door, I join Ruiz on the footpath.

'You know these clowns?' he asks.

'The local yoof.'

Kroger tugs at his hood, pulling it over the brim of his baseball cap.

'I like your hoodie,' says Ruiz. 'Justin Bieber wears one just like that.'

The girls are giggling.

Kroger takes a moment to formulate a response, peeling back his lips to show splinters of gold in his teeth.

'Two girls were kidnapped around here, so when we see two old guys putting the hard word on local girls, we get concerned.' He winks at Gould and then at the brunette. 'We're like guardian angels.'

'Oh, that's so sweet,' says Ruiz. 'They're angels. I don't see any wings. You know what they say about angels with small wings?'

Kroger's eyes seem to click open and his feet are set before he swings. His fist bounces off the side of Ruiz's head. That was his one half-chance. Before he can set himself again, he's doubled over with a fist deep in his stomach and no air in his lungs.

With the minimum of fuss, Ruiz twists Kroger's arm behind his back. A shirt button pops loose and rolls into the gutter where it spins like a bottle top.

I don't see Gould's arm move. He punches me hard in the side of the face and I fall against the car, bouncing onto my backside. My jaw is simultaneously numb and on fire.

Ruiz pulls me up. He's still holding Kroger and nearby Gould has curled up on the pavement, shielding his head.

'A hundred thousand sperm and you guys were the fittest. It makes you start to question Darwin's theories, doesn't it? Survival of the fittest. Natural selection.' Then he addresses the girls. 'Maybe you should run along now. Careful how you go.'

They leave quickly, short skirts swinging against their thighs.

'This is assault,' whines Kroger.

'I didn't throw the first punch.'

Gould is still lying on the ground, moaning slightly, his teeth like a row of dirty pebbles.

Ruiz speaks next. 'We can play this one of two ways, lads. We can call the police, take statements, lay charges, meet up again in court . . . or you can run off home.'

Kroger and Gould look at each other. Ruiz makes a buzzer sound. 'Time's up.'

He walks away and opens the car door.

'Try not to let your minds wander, lads. They're too small to be out on their own.'

If a broken mirror can bring

seven years of bad luck, what's the penance for breaking someone's body? On the scale of sins, how do you measure something like that? How many Hail Marys and Our Fathers?

Callum Loach got crippled and Aiden Foster went to jail. That's when Tash's life turned to shit. They say a person's life can spin on one event – one chance meeting or a mistake or a piece of good luck. It's true. I don't believe in fate or destiny, but sheer blind-arsed bad luck . . . that's another story.

Tash had been sort of dating Aiden Foster for three months when it happened. I say 'sort of' because nobody ever formalises these things. It's not like those American teen movies where people badge each other or swap college rings.

Aiden was four years older and one of Hayden's friends. They would have been in the same year at school if Aiden hadn't left after GCSEs to become an apprentice at his father's garage. He always had dirty fingernails, which turned me off, but Tash didn't seem to mind.

She liked making him jealous. She could do it without even trying. Aiden was jealous of her clothes because they got to touch her skin all day. That's what he said. And he even carried a pair of her panties around in his pocket, used ones, which is just plain creepy.

He was also a complete tosser most of the time. He had his hair gelled back like he was standing in a howling wind or skydiving. And he thought he was hot shit because he played guitar in a band, which used to get hired to play at parties, mostly by friends. Eighteenths. Twenty-firsts.

That's why we went to the party in Abingdon. It was somebody's birthday. I lied to Mum and Dad and said I was spending the night with Tash. Aiden picked us up in his car. He drove the whole way with his hand sliding up and down Tash's thigh.

The party was at a big old house near the centre of Abingdon with arches over the doors and windows. The place was full of college-age kids; boys with crew cuts and leather jackets and girls in postage-stamp dresses smelling of Pantene and cigarettes.

Tash was in a good mood. She was younger than any girl at the party (and prettier) but nobody was going to kick her out. Hayden had given her some stuff to sell and she road-tested the merchandise in advance. Her eyes were like black marbles and she was swaying and giggling.

A guy called Simon tried to chat me up by telling me dirty jokes. I stopped him halfway through and said I'd heard the joke before.

'What's the punchline then?'

'I can't remember,' I said. 'But I know I've heard it before.'

'When was the last time you laughed?'

'Yesterday. Eleven thirty-four a.m. And I'm gonna laugh tomorrow when I think about you.'

He left me alone then, muttering something under his breath.

People were smoking and drinking and popping pills. I recognised some of them from school, but they were way ahead of me.

Tash was dancing with Aiden, grinding against him until he was drooling in her ear. Aiden's friends were watching her, particularly Toby Kroger and Craig Gould. Craig was always looking at Tash in a funny way, like he was hungry and she was a Big Mac and fries.

Aiden and Tash disappeared for a while. They went upstairs. Tash came back fifteen minutes later, carrying her shoes. She kissed me, wrapping her arms around me and pushing her tongue hard against mine, before pulling back and giggling at the applause.

The boys were egging her on. The music was too loud.

Outside, there was a patio and a swing seat. I was getting some fresh air, drinking a Bacardi Breezer, watching three girls and two boys smoking a joint. They offered me some. Told me their names. I told them mine. I coughed when I tried to hold the smoke in my lungs, but I kept trying because I wanted them to like me.

172

That's when I saw Tash in the garden. She was puking. Callum Loach was with her, holding back her hair and making her lean over so she didn't mess up her dress.

Callum was tall and strong and played football. Tash had been teasing him all summer. I remember her wearing a bikini and parading past him at the leisure centre. Later, when she rubbed suntan oil on her shoulders, she pulled one triangle of her bikini top aside so that he got a glimpse of her breast. Callum looked embarrassed. Tash laughed.

Now he was looking after her. He went and got her a bottle of water, wiped her face and unhooked her belt because it was too tight around her waist.

Then Aiden turned up, eyes jittering and his skin all waxy. He told Callum to get his 'faggot hands' off Tash.

Even though Tash was completely wasted, she told Aiden to piss off, but he didn't listen.

'Is he a good fuck for a faggot?' he screamed.

'Better than you,' she said. 'Maybe you should ask for some pointers.'

'Wha? From the dickless wonder?'

'At least I could find his dick.'

Toby Kroger and Craig Gould laughed. Aiden tried to slap Tash, but Callum pushed him away. Next came a punch, which missed by a mile. Everybody laughed. Aiden sulked.

Callum offered to drive us home. He had his mum's car. Tash had the window open and her head resting on the door so the fresh air could sober her up. I was in the back seat, feeling woozy, but glad to be away from the party.

When we got to the farmhouse, Tash still felt sick and wanted Callum to drive her around a bit longer. She rested her head on his shoulder. 'I want to kiss you but my mouth tastes like puke.'

'That's OK.'

'I could do something else.'

'You don't have to do anything.'

That's when Tash remembered her handbag. It was back at the house. It had her mobile phone and some of Hayden's stuff so she couldn't leave it behind. So we drove back to Abingdon and Callum went inside.

He came back out and I saw him looking around. Craig Gould and Toby Kroger were yelling something at him. I noticed that Aiden's car was gone. Callum opened the driver's door and I saw Aiden's Subaru coming towards us. I yelled out, but there wasn't time.

Aiden didn't brake. Nothing locked or screeched. There was a sickening crunch of metal on bone. The impact threw Callum up and over the bonnet of Aiden's car, spinning him backwards through the air. It was like watching an acrobat tumbling, head thrown back, almost graceful until he landed with a dhoof! *sound and crumpled.*

Aiden kept going. Gravel spraying.

Callum lay on the tarmac with his arms flung wide, blood in his hair, and an innocent trickle coming from the corner of his mouth.

Tash screamed. She kept screaming, even when she didn't make a sound. It was like that painting of the melting face screaming. Munch. We studied it in art. That's what she looked like.

I grabbed Tash and pulled her away. I pulled her along the road. I left her sitting on the grass and then ran between houses, hammering on doors, screaming at people to call an ambulance.

Emily was there. I'd almost forgotten about her. She kept wailing that her mum was going to kill her and that her dad would use it as another excuse to get custody.

Doors opened and people came out onto the street. I don't remember their faces. I wanted to run. I know it sounds stupid, but I thought if I could run fast enough, I could stay ahead of what had happened. That Callum wouldn't be dead and I wouldn't have to see him tumbling through the air and hear the sound of his body hitting the tarmac.

He wasn't dead, but I didn't know that then. An ambulance took him to hospital and the doctors induced a coma, keeping him alive with machines that kept his heart pumping. But they couldn't save his legs. The bones had been crushed and one was already partially amputated, so they kept going and finished the job.

These memories are flooding back to me, filling my lungs, making it hard to breathe. I take a big gulp of air and look at my hands, which are bunched so tightly that my fingernails have left red marks on my skin.

Muddy light has broken through the gloom outside the window. Another day begins.

21

Isaac McBain lives in a shack on the edge of a building yard that smells of mildew and wet wood. Ruiz knocks on the door, but there's no answer.

I peer through the dirty front window. In the gloom I see a living room full of indistinct lumps of furniture, a bar fridge and a fifty-inch flat screen. The man has his priorities. Along one wall is a record collection: hundreds of vinyl albums stacked upright on shelves; a lifetime of music, catalogued into genres and filed alphabetically.

'Can I help you, lads?'

The voice belongs to a big man with tight curls, who is standing behind a wire fence. Dressed in a Nike sweatshirt, baggy trousers and expensive trainers, he's holding a bull terrier on a shortened leash. The dog lunges at the fence, all fangs and fury but no bark. The animal's voice box has been removed or damaged in a fight. The man jerks at the chain, hauling the terrier off its feet.

'We're looking for Isaac McBain,' I say.

'Who told you he was here?'

'His son.'

Most of the man's attention is focused on Ruiz.

'Are you debt collectors?'

'No.'

'You work for the Connolly brothers?'

'No.'

This must by Vic McBain. Natasha's uncle.

'It's about Natasha,' I say. 'Did Isaac tell you?'

'Yeah, he told me. What was Natasha doing at Radley Lakes?'

'We don't know.'

There is another long pause. The bull terrier has calmed down.

'Nice dog,' says Ruiz.

'He could rip your throat out.'

'Must be good around the kids.'

Vic rubs his mouth. 'You look like a copper.'

'Used to be,' says Ruiz. 'Now I'm doing a bit of freelance work. Better hours. Fewer rules.'

'Isaac didn't turn up for work today. Can't say I blame him.'

'Any idea where he'd be?' I ask.

'Drunk by now. Self-medication. Dulls the pain.'

'Where does he normally drink?'

'The White Swan in Abingdon.'

Vic McBain turns away and walks back through the muddy building yard, between the racks of scaffolding pipes and lumber. The dog limps after him, nosing at a metal drum and casually cocking a back leg.

The White Swan is one of those pubs you won't find unless you're a local or a lost traveller. We had to ask twice for directions. The only interior lighting consists of the neon tubes above the bar and the ambient glow from two open doors that are marked oxymoronically as LADIES and GENTS.

The barmaid has punked blue hair, shaved on one side, and black fingernail polish.

Ruiz leans fully over the bar, studying the taps. 'The sign outside says you have a fine collection of real ales.'

177

'So?'

'You have one hand-pump of Morland's Original. That's hardly what I call a selection.'

She looks at me. 'What's his problem?'

'He thinks he's a connoisseur.'

Isaac McBain is sitting at the far end of the bar beneath a Union Jack flag. Between his forearms he has a pint glass and a whisky chaser centred on matching cardboard coasters. Making his choice, he lifts the shot glass and downs it in a swallow.

We pull out bar stools on either side. Isaac turns slowly, his eyes swimming in an alcoholic haze.

'I'm not in a talking mood,' he slurs.

'Your brother told us you'd be here,' says Ruiz.

'He called me. Said you were coming.'

'We're sorry for your loss,' I say, making the introductions. My outstretched hand is ignored. Withdrawn.

Isaac blinks slowly and I get a whiff of the ashy stink coming from his hair. I see a man who is torturing himself with alternative scenarios. What if he hadn't gone to jail? What if he'd been a better father? Would his daughter still be alive? Could he have protected her?

These thoughts have haunted him for three years, sweating through his dreams, hooking his heart whenever he turned a corner and caught a glimpse of someone who looked like Natasha.

'They let me see her,' he whispers. 'That body didn't look like Tash, you know. I mean, it did, but it didn't. She was beautiful, you know.'

He drinks half his beer, his throat moving noiselessly.

'They're saying she was held prisoner.'

'Yes.'

'Someone kept her alive.'

'Yes.'

'And . . . and did things to her?'

'Yes.'

His face creases in pain and I can tell that he's screaming internally.

'I need a cigarette.' He stands and takes his beer through a rear door into a courtyard with a handful of wooden tables and benches. He lights up. White smoke curls around his wrist.

'A lot of folks blamed me,' he says. 'Even the police. That's why they wanted us to do the media conference when the girls went missing. They were studying me, analysing my words and my body language.'

'That's pretty standard practice,' says Ruiz. 'Look at the families first.'

'Yeah, well, I had everyone looking at me sideways. They leaked the story about me having done time, you know. Lads I used to drink with suddenly didn't fancy standing at the same bar with me. My local publican told me I should find some-where else to drink. I finished up at this shithole.'

The barmaid has come out for cigarette. 'I heard that.'

'Fuck off.'

I can see the glint in Isaac's eyes and know I'm witnessing the other side of him – the wildness that saw him go to prison; the wildness that Tash inherited.

'I pissed them off early – the cops. When Natasha and Piper went missing we organised our own search. We had hundreds of volunteers. Friends. Neighbours. Strangers. Vic did most of the work. We were chomping at the bit, but the police kept telling us to wait. Then I overheard this inspector saying that he didn't want to compromise the evidence – like he thought the girls were already dead.

'I argued with him. "For fuck's sake – it's my daughter. We have to find her. It's not rocket science." This guy told me to step away and lower my voice. I didn't. Then he threatened to have me arrested. It was bullshit.'

We let Isaac talk, venting his anger.

'They still think it's me, you know. They came and asked me where I was during the blizzard. They were sweating on me,

179

trying to get me rattled, thinking I might confess. As if I'd be scared. I've been bounced off prison walls by cons who'd shank you quicker than look at you. The police don't scare me.'

'Why were you in prison?' says Ruiz.

'Here we go.'

'I'm just asking.'

'Armed robbery. Sentenced to five, I served three. I don't shy away from it. No point. Small town like this, everyone knows. But tell me something, Mr Ruiz. How is that piece of information going to help you catch my daughter's killer? I'm just asking.'

'I don't mean to offend you. I'm just wondering whether you could have made any enemies; someone who might hold a grudge?'

Isaac blows air out of his mouth. 'You're talking about the Connolly brothers. You don't have to dance around the subject.'

'You gave evidence against them.'

'I told the truth.'

'Maybe what happened to Natasha was payback.'

'The Connolly brothers don't take revenge on children.' He crushes the cigarette beneath his heel. 'If they wanted to punish someone – they'd punish me.'

'Perhaps they are,' I say.

He shakes his head.

'The Connolly brothers didn't take Tash and Piper. Payback wasn't necessary.'

He closes his eyes as though picturing a scene from his past.

'My ex-wife blames me too. She thinks I let Tash down, that I could have done more. But not many people could stop Natasha doing stuff, not when her mind was made up.

'She were only ten when I went inside. When I came out she weren't a little girl any more. We were strangers, you know. I know she hated school and wanted to get out of this place, but she wouldn't have gone without saying goodbye, you know. That's why I knew she hadn't run away.

'Or if she did, she'd have left a letter or sent us a card. She loved her mum. She would have called her to reassure her. All those birthdays, Mother's Days, Christmases, they came and went . . . not a word. Nothing. Tash wouldn't do that.'

He sighs ruefully, turning towards the pub. 'Now we know, eh?'

'Can I buy you a drink?' asks Ruiz.

'No, thanks anyway. Only want one thing from you – find out who did this to my Tash.'

22

The door opens hard against a security chain. I see one eye and a fringe of teenage hair.

'Are you Emily Martinez?'

No answer.

'Is your mum home?'

'No.'

'What about your dad?'

She glances past me. 'He'll be here soon.'

'It's you I came to see, Emily.'

She blinks at me. 'I'm not allowed to let strangers inside the house.'

'That's very wise. Maybe we could just talk here. You could stay in there and I'll stay out here.'

She pushes back her fringe and I can see both her eyes and the braces on her teeth.

'You weren't at school today.'

'I wasn't feeling very well.'

'I talked to Miss McCrudden. She said you miss quite a lot of school.'

Emily shrugs. She has a small neat nose, but carries weight beneath her chin.

At that moment a Black Lexus pulls into the driveway and a middle-aged man gets out, flipping the keys back and forth over his knuckles. Early-forties, tall and fine-featured, he looks like he's just stepped off a movie set, dressed in sharply pressed khakis and a business shirt. His curly hair is tipped with blond.

He mounts the stairs two at a time. Smiles. Open as a sunny day.

'This looks like good timing. We weren't expecting visitors.'

He shakes my hand. Emily unhooks the chain and opens the door. Mr Martinez hands her his briefcase and coat.

'I'm sorry, I should have called ahead,' I explain. 'I'm assisting the police in an investigation.'

'Is this about Natasha and Piper?'

'What makes you assume that?'

He looks at Emily. 'What else would it be?'

'I was hoping to talk to Emily.'

'Oh, I see, well, Em's been off school today. She had one of her dizzy spells this morning.' He puts an arm around her shoulders. 'Are you feeling better, honey?'

She nods.

He continues, 'She's already given the police three statements.'

'Yes, but I'm looking at these things differently. It won't take long.'

Mr Martinez glances at Emily. 'What do you think?'

She nods.

'Right, let's get inside. It's cold out here. Put the kettle on, Em?'

The lounge is a long narrow room with high ceilings and expensive furniture and paintings. The armchairs have the carved wooden legs of animals, as if they lead secret lives when everyone else is asleep.

Emily has gone to the kitchen. Phillip Martinez lights the

gas fire and fluffs up cushions on the sofa. He has a smooth, almost feminine face with pale, barely existent eyebrows.

'This whole thing has been a terrible business – young girls running away. Not knowing what happened. It makes you wonder . . .'

'About what?' I ask.

'Excuse me?'

'What does it make you wonder about?'

'Their families.' He makes it sound so obvious. 'If things at home had been fine, they wouldn't have run away.'

'What if they were kidnapped?'

'Well, that changes everything.' He studies me for a moment. My left arm trembles.

'What stage?'

'I beg your pardon?'

'Your Parkinson's – what stage?'

'One.'

'How long?'

'Eight years.'

'It's slow – you're lucky.'

'That's how I try to look at it.'

'It's not really my field.'

'Your field?'

'I'm a research scientist. I work at the Biomedical Sciences Department at the university. We do a lot of gene therapy research into things like diabetes, Alzheimer's and muscular dystrophy. Parkinson's is one area. Some of my colleagues are doing some important research. You should come and have a look. I could organise a tour.'

'Thank you.'

'That's one of the reasons Emily is quite wary of strangers.'

'I don't understand.'

'We use animals in our testing. Chimps mainly. There were problems during construction of the lab. Protests. Fire-bombings. Threats.'

'Were you threatened?'

'My last car had acid poured over it and you should see some of the letters I received. I've taught Emily to be vigilant.'

'I hope I didn't frighten her.'

'Oh, she's fine. Highly strung. A bit like her mother.'

Emily reappears. She's carrying a tray with a teapot and cups. Mr Martinez takes it from her.

'I'm going to leave you two alone. I have emails to answer. I'll just be upstairs.' He turns to Emily. 'Honey, if you know something that could help, you tell him.'

Emily nods and listens to her father climbing the stairs, following his progress, picturing him moving steadily through the house. Higher. Further away. Satisfied, she smooths her dress over her thighs and sits on the edge of the sofa, toying with one sleeve of her jumper. Cautious and tense, she has a defeated expectancy about her, as though at any moment she expects to be admonished.

I've read her statements. Emily's story hasn't changed. But I know from experience how perceptions alter over time. I start gently, asking her about Piper and Natasha; how they met, what they did together.

She chews the skin around her thumbnail and occasionally nods and shakes her head. She doesn't want to talk to me and I don't have the codes to unlock her defences – the mysterious combination of trust and shared experience that causes a teenage girl to prattle non-stop to her friends, but stop immediately when an adult walks into the room. If I knew the numbers, I could talk to my own teenage daughter.

'Do you have secrets, Emily?'

'What do you mean?'

'You understand what secrets are?'

She nods nervously.

'We all have them. Secret hiding places, secret crushes, secret regrets. We have faces that we don't show other people, only our friends.'

Emily is staring at me with the dull frowning air of an amnesiac.

I try again. 'Why did you want to run away?'

She shrugs.

'You must have had a reason. I know Natasha had some problems at school – what about you?'

'No.'

'At home then?'

She hesitates and glances at the stairs, worried that her father might be listening.

'My mum had been sick. She had a breakdown.'

'Where is your mum now?'

'She lives in a hostel in London. She's getting better.'

'That's good.'

Emily tugs at the hem of her tartan skirt. She hasn't touched her tea.

'Whose idea was it to run away?'

'Tash's.'

'Where were you going to go?'

Her shoulders rise and fall.

'You must have imagined a new life.'

'Yes.'

'You didn't like this one?'

Again she looks at the stairs. 'It was just talk at first. I didn't think we'd actually do it – not for real. It was exciting . . . something different . . . but then . . .'

'Then what?'

'Tash got serious.'

'Why?'

'It was after the night Aiden Foster ran down Callum Loach. We made a sort of pact because things were so shitty at school and at home.'

'Why were things bad at home?'

Emily raises her eyes to the ceiling.

'Your parents were divorcing.'

186

She nods.

'Tash sort of lost interest in the idea but then she got into trouble at school and Miss Jacobson said she couldn't come back after the holidays. Tash didn't tell her folks. She was going to run away before they found out.'

'What happened on the night of the Bingham festival?'

'What do you mean?'

'You were with Piper and Natasha.'

'Only until ten o'clock.'

'What happened then?'

'I got a call saying that Mum was in hospital. I came straight home.'

'But you saw Piper later?'

'She woke me. I heard her knocking on the bedroom window. Straight away I knew something was wrong, but she wouldn't tell me. She said they were running away in the morning. I said I couldn't come – Mum was in hospital.'

'But you changed your mind?'

'Yes.'

'Why?'

She shrugs.

'How were you going to live in London?'

'Tash had money. She said her uncle owed her. She used to work for him.'

'What did she do?'

'Filing in his office.'

'I thought she was a waitress.'

'That too.'

'Did she get on with her uncle?'

Emily reacts as though slapped, holding her cheek.

'What was that?'

'What?'

'That thing you just did?'

'What thing?'

'You reacted when I mentioned Tash and her uncle.'

Emily lets out an avian squawk, shaking her head. 'I didn't say anything! I didn't! You're putting words in my mouth.'

'I'm sorry. I didn't mean to upset you.'

She calms down, sinking back into the sofa.

'Tell me about the accident.'

'We went to a party at this house in Abingdon. It was thrown by one of Aiden's friends. He was Tash's boyfriend: Aiden Foster. The party was full of university students and stuck-up girls who treated us like we were in pre-school.'

'Tell me about Aiden.'

'He was all right, I guess. Older. He had a car. Tash didn't like taking the bus so she sort of used him. Aiden got wasted at the party and Tash started flirting with Callum Loach. He was a couple of years ahead of us, but went to a different school.

'Aiden got pissed off. He grabbed Callum and acted like a complete psycho and then laughed.'

'You saw this?'

'Piper told me later. I was inside.'

'What happened then?'

'Tash was sick. Callum offered to drive her home, but he came back for her phone, which was upstairs. Callum was getting back in the car when Aiden came around the corner in his Subaru and he just ran him down.' Emily bites down hard on her lip. 'We thought he was dead. He flew into the air and over the car and landed on the road.'

'What happened to him?'

'He lost both his legs. He's in a wheelchair.'

'And Aiden?'

'He went to jail.'

'Is he still in prison?'

Emily shrugs.

'Would your dad know?' I ask.

She stares at the ceiling. 'I don't want to ask him.'

On the morning after the party,

two police officers came to Tash's house and took her to hospital where they tested her blood for alcohol and drugs. Then she went to Abingdon Police Station and made a statement.

Aiden Foster arrived at the station late that afternoon, along with his father and a big-shot barrister. He was charged with attempted murder and was granted bail the next day. They confiscated his car and told him not to approach any of the witnesses.

The police came to my house on the Sunday and asked me a lot of questions. I was a minor so I had a social worker with me during the interview. The only bits I left out were about the drugs. I was scared they might charge me for having puffed on a joint.

That night I heard Mum and Dad arguing downstairs, saying that I had 'run off the rails' and 'gone feral' and was going to finish up in prison or worse. The next morning I didn't get woken for school. Mum didn't knock on my door. I dressed in my school uniform and came downstairs, but she told me to go back and get changed. That's when I noticed the suitcase in the corner of the kitchen.

Two men came to get me. Their van was so clean and shiny that clouds rolled across the sides and the roof. I thought I was going to the police station, but instead they took me to some sort of boarding house with gardens and high walls. Not in Oxford or in London. It was surrounded by fields and had the sea on one side.

Mum came with me that first day, but she didn't stay.

'Please be a good girl and you'll be home in no time,' she said.

I grabbed her arm and begged her not to leave.

'This is only because we love you,' she said.

Parents always say things like that – like 'this is going to hurt me more than it hurts you', but how can that be true?

That night I heard them lock my door. And every couple of hours someone came along the corridor and looked through a hatch. I couldn't turn the lights off even if I wanted to. The next day I kicked off at one of the nurses and she threatened to handcuff me to the bed. I didn't believe her, until she waved the cuffs in front of my face.

That day they gave me all these different tests, showing me pictures and shapes. Some of them were just images flashed onto a computer screen and I had to press either a red or green button depending on how the picture made me feel. I assumed the red was supposed to symbolise anger and green was calm. I tried to throw the results out by pressing red on the pictures of puppies and green on the pictures of riots.

My therapist was called Vernon and he asked me if I ever touched myself. I tried to think of what Tash would say. 'Constantly. I use cucumbers, candlesticks, anything I can get my hands on.'

There were group sessions with other girls. Never boys. Some of them were anorexics or bulimics or were suicidal or into cutting themselves. The therapists were never specific in the group sessions. It was all about 'feelings'.

'You want my feelings – I feel pissed off about being in here,' I told them. That lost me TV privileges for the evening. I told them I didn't give a fuck about the TV, which lost me dessert privileges for a week. I lost a lot of privileges. I can't even tell you what they were because I lost them before I had the privilege.

They gave us each a work roster. We had to set the tables or clear away dishes, or help in the kitchens. Our beds had to be made and rooms tidied. It was like being at boarding school because even our socks had to be folded in a certain way.

'Don't knot them together – fold them with a smile,' the matron said.

'Mine are smiling like the crack of your arse,' I told her.

That lost me games room privileges.

At least they let me write. It was encouraged. I had to write lists of things I liked about myself and the things I disliked. The way I looked, for instance; my swearing; my temper; the fact that I'm crap at maths . . .

I was allowed to make one phone call every week to Mum and Dad. I begged them. I cried. I tried to guilt them into letting me come home. My father's voice would start to shake, but Mum would grab the phone from him before he broke down.

I didn't have a mobile. I couldn't talk to Tash or find out what had happened to Callum or Aiden. Days stretched into weeks. A month. Two. There were more therapy sessions and lectures on drugs and alcohol.

My parents thought I was a drug addict — or well on the way. I was 'heading down the slippery slope', they said.

After eight weeks they let me go home. They didn't tell me until half an hour before my parents arrived. Even then, the matron just said, 'Pack your suitcase.'

Mum came to the reception room. Dad stayed outside, standing by the car. That was it. We drove home in silence and I went to my room. I looked at my computer and at my mobile. I didn't call Tash. I didn't email anyone. I pulled out all my old toys and played with them. My Barbie dolls. I combed their hair and changed their clothes. I hadn't done that in years.

Miss McCrudden, my English teacher — the one who loves my stories — always told me not to have passive characters when I wrote. They have to make things happen, she said, not just have things happen to them.

That's when I realised what she meant. I was a passive character in my own life, letting things happen instead of forging my own way, finding my own path.

Not any more, I decided, never again.

23

The caretaker is easy enough to track down. He hasn't covered his tracks or crawled into a deep hole. Nobody is far from the surface these days – not with emails and Facebook pages and Twitter accounts. They leave an electronic trail behind like mouse droppings in cyberspace.

Nelson Stokes works as a street cleaner for Oxford City Council, pushing a barrow in the pedestrianised precincts and laneways too narrow for the machines.

Thirty-eight, with long hair and an angular face, he's wearing a plaid wool shirt and a reflective jacket. His barrow is propped outside a shoe shop while he rolls himself a cigarette. Inside the shop, a young salesgirl is standing on tiptoes, putting boxes on a high shelf. Stokes is watching her thighs and rump flexing beneath her short skirt.

'Mr Stokes?'

He turns his head slowly. 'Do I know you?'

I hand him a business card. He reads it carefully, taking a moment to decide if I'm an inconvenience or an opportunity. I've seen his police file, which is depressing reading. Arrested twice in his early twenties for accepting stolen goods, he pleaded

192

guilty and was given the benefit. Before that he was studying engineering at university but lost his place for cheating in his first year exams. Odd jobs since then; married; divorced; one failed business. He worked at St Catherine's as a caretaker/ groundsman for two years before being fired.

According to the police file, a handful of senior students at St Catherine's complained about Stokes taking photographs of them. It emerged that some of the girls had opted to do a quick change at the back of the sports hall after gym instead of going to the locker room upstairs. Stokes had used a digital camera to record them. Pictures of Natasha were found among the images.

The caretaker spent two days in custody and was interviewed for eight hours, but he had an alibi for the Sunday morning that the girls disappeared.

Propping his broom in the barrow, Stokes takes a seat at a bus stop and lights his cigarette.

'I was hoping we could talk about the Bingham Girls.'

'What's that got to do with you?'

'I've been asked to review the case.'

'Nothing to do with me.'

'You knew the girls.'

'Found them, have they? The bodies.'

'What makes you think that?'

'Stands to reason.' He blows smoke from the corner of his mouth. 'Missing all this time – they must be dead.'

He raises his eyes and glances across the street where a group of girls are chatting outside a Starbucks. I notice the heat in his eyes and his unwashed smell.

'I know about the photographs.'

'I never touched those girls. Not a hair.'

'You took pictures.'

He flicks ash. 'That's all. Why you bringing this up again? Did one of those little bitches make a complaint? Wants to sue. She can go ahead. Got no money. Can sue me for the barrow.' He laughs and nods to his brooms.

Stokes isn't a practised deceiver. If you're going to lie, you show your hands, let people see you're unarmed. And you lean forward a little to reinforce your convictions, without breaking eye contact.

'Where were you on the night of the blizzard?' I ask.

'Saturday? I would have been washing my hair.'

'Is that your alibi?'

'Why would I need one?' He smiles at me sadly, a bitter taste in his mouth. 'It's the uncle they should be looking at. I told the police. I told them what I saw.'

'What did you tell them?'

'I told them about that girl and her uncle, Vic McBain.'

'What about them?'

'I saw them together. He was dropping Natasha at school one day and the two of them were in the front seat of his car. She was sitting on his lap and they were kissing. Not just any kiss. Not a peck on the cheek. Open-mouthed. You know what I'm saying? At first I thought it was one of the senior girls and her boyfriend, but then Natasha got out and I saw the bloke she'd been kissing. She went skipping off to class like it was right as rain.'

'You're sure it was Vic McBain?'

'Yeah. I talked to Natasha. She said she knew about my taking pictures and that if I told anyone she'd tell the police that I touched her. That's a lie. I never laid a finger on any of them girls.'

'And you told the police this?'

'Yeah, I told them.'

'Who did you tell?'

'A detective; I don't know his name.'

I've read the files. There were no allegations of an improper relationship between Vic McBain and his niece.

Stokes squeezes his cigarette until the paper and ash disintegrate. He sweeps them into a dustpan on a stick.

'She could be a real bitch that McBain girl, so full of herself, strutting around like she was on a catwalk. A prick-tease at fourteen, a runaway at fifteen, that girl was nothing but trouble. Maybe she got what she deserved.'

'What did she deserve?'

He doesn't answer. Instead, he turns away and lifts a hard-bristled broom from the barrow.

'I got work to do.'

24

A pint of Guinness is resting between Ruiz's elbows and he's studying the bubbles as they settle into a creamy head. We're not drinking in the Morse Bar. He chose a pub around the corner, where the prices are cheaper and happy hour twice as long.

'I've got nothing against TV detectives,' he explains. 'They're all equally full of shit. You take Columbo.'

'Peter Falk?'

'The guy wears the same raincoat for twenty years and pretends to be bumbling and stupid so people underestimate him. I know detectives who've been doing that for twice that long and haven't solved more than a crossword puzzle. You know what happens to them?'

'I have a feeling you're going to tell me.'

'They get promoted.'

His pint glass is empty.

'It's your shout,' he says.

'I'm not drinking.'

'That's not my fault. It's called a tradition.'

I go to the bar. When I get back to the table Ruiz has taken out his notebook and is licking his thumb as he turns the pages. While I've been interviewing Emily Martinez and Nelson Stokes, he's been tracking down details of the accident.

He rattles off the facts: Aiden Foster, twenty, and Callum Loach, eighteen, had an altercation at a party in Abingdon. Later in the evening Foster drove a car into Loach and fled the scene.

'Foster was arrested the next day. He copped a plea and the charge was downgraded from attempted murder to GBH. He's been inside for the past four years.'

'What happened to Loach?'

'He had both legs amputated above the knee. Lives at home.'

'And the fight was over Natasha?'

'Apparently so.' Ruiz takes a sip of Guinness and wipes his top lip. 'It didn't make her very popular.'

'How so?'

'When she gave evidence at the trial people abused her outside the court, saying it was her fault. Foster's barrister made her sound like Slutty McSlut from Slutsville. Witnesses said she was dealing drugs at the party.'

'So the families blamed Natasha?'

'Looks like it.'

Ruiz raises an eyebrow. He knows I'm trawling for motives, looking for anomalies or angles the police might have overlooked.

'What was Aiden Foster doing with a fifteen-year-old girlfriend?' I ask.

'What was Vic McBain doing with his niece?' he counters.

'I don't know if I believe Stokes.'

'Why would he lie?'

'To deflect attention. What do we know about Vic McBain?'

'He and Isaac used to be business partners. They started a scaffolding business together ten years ago. It's a niche market, very lucrative and competitive. Vic doesn't so much win clients as lose competitors.'

'What do you mean?'

'Other companies have trucks clamped or jobs cancelled or scaffolding collapse, but Vic's business is bulletproof. When it comes to winning contracts, Vic seems to always be the low bidder or the last man standing.'

'Why aren't the brothers still partners?'

'They had a falling out. Vic bought Isaac's share of the company. Now Isaac works for him.'

'What did Isaac do with the money?'

'Lost it on the wheel of fortune – the one with the red and black numbers and the bouncing white ball. That's probably why he fell in with the Connolly brothers. He owed fifteen grand to a loanshark called Cyril Honey.'

'So he opted for the last resort – he robbed an armoured van.'

'And now he's living in a shack while Vic owns five hundred square yards of a property on the Thames and a chateau in France.'

Ruiz closes his notebook and slips a rubber band around the pages. 'You think Stokes is good for this?'

'Maybe. I'd really like to know why his statement didn't mention Vic McBain.'

'You should ask DCI Drury. Make his day.'

My mobile is ringing. I don't recognise the number, but the voice is familiar.

Victoria Naparstek apologises for her behaviour at the hospital and asks me what I'm wearing.

'Why?'

'I want you to take me to dinner and I'm just making sure you're not wearing that tweed jacket.'

'Is tweed a problem?'

'It makes you look like a supply teacher.'

'That's good to know.'

'I've booked us a table at Branca. It's an Italian restaurant in Walton Street. I'll see you at eight.'

I end the call. Ruiz has an arched eyebrow. 'You have a date?'

'Just a meal.'

'With that very fetching psychiatrist.'

'She wants my opinion on something.'

'Not your body then?'

Ruiz is the only one of my friends who doesn't try to convince me that Julianne and I are going to get back together. I think he hopes it, but would never say as much. Although he talks a lot about sex, the only woman in his life is his ex-wife Miranda, who seems to have decided that Ruiz was a lousy husband but perfectly adequate as an occasional shag.

'I have to get changed,' I tell him. 'She doesn't like tweed.'

'Obviously a woman of taste.'

'Out of my league.'

'Chin up. Even the shittiest player can fluke a goal.'

Victoria Naparstek is waiting for me in the hotel foyer. She's wearing contact lenses and sexier clothes – a mid-thigh black dress, leggings and boots that make her taller than I am. It's one more thing to be self-conscious about.

The Italian restaurant has tea candles in red globes on every table. It's perfect lighting to hide a myriad of flaws and blemishes – mine not hers.

'How is Augie?' I ask.

'That's what I wanted to tell you. He was granted bail this afternoon. He's out.'

'Where?'

'At his mother's house.'

'What happened?'

'The judge was so angry about the suicide attempt that he wouldn't listen to any more excuses. The police failed in their duty of care, he said. He granted bail with conditions. Augie has to wear an electronic ankle tag.'

She raises her glass in a mini-celebration, pushing her hair behind her ears.

'Did the prosecution mention Augie's father?'

'Inadmissible. You can't blame a son for something his father did or didn't do.'

One of my shirt cuffs has come undone. I don't have the dexterity to do it up again. Victoria notices and reaches across the table.

'There,' she says.

'Thanks. I don't know what I'd do without you.'

A smile. She has the kind of dimples that leave a mark on a man's mind.

We make small talk and eye contact. Naparstek is a Jewish name. Her great-grandparents escaped from Poland in 1935. She's an only child, which meant she was rather spoiled and bookish. She grew up in Glasgow, went to boarding school and was head girl. Her father makes corporate videos. Her mother is a speech therapist.

I listen and tell myself to remember this – how it feels to talk to an attractive woman and flirt a little. What I don't mention is that I woke up this morning with an erection, imagining Dr Naparstek with her very smart business skirt hiked up over her hips and the base of my penis grinding against her pubic bone.

'I'm sorry I seem to be doing all the talking,' Victoria says. 'You don't mind, do you?'

'Not at all.'

'Liar!'

'It's true.'

She carries on, telling me about performing the lead in her school drama and flirting with the idea of becoming an actress. The conversation blossoms and we grow comfortable together, discussing the edited highlights of our lives. Then, out of the blue, she asks, 'Do you remember when we first met?'

'Yes.'

'You told the mental health review tribunal that my patient was fantasising about raping women . . . about raping me.'

'How is Liam?'

'Let me finish,' she says, steeling herself. 'After the hearing he was denied release and went back to the secure unit. Six months later he applied again and was given approval for escorted day trips, weekend leave, that sort of thing. Two months after that he abducted and tried to rape a childcare worker walking her dog on Putney Common.' She lowers her head, whispering. 'He cut her neck, but she fought him off. You were right. I should have listened.'

I think about saying something, but there are no words I can offer her. Silence is kinder.

We walk back to the hotel. This is the bit that terrifies me. There have been two women since Julianne and I split up, both one-night stands – a teacher at Charlie's school, and a divorcee I met at dance classes. You could call it pity sex or lonely sex, hungry and sad: two people trying to forget rather than to forge something new.

Why am I thinking about that now? I rationalise things too much. I should just act.

Victoria Naparstek takes the decision for me, pulling me into a shop doorway, kissing me like a teenager. Then she takes me by the hand and we continue walking.

'Before you invite me upstairs,' she says, 'let me warn you that I'm going to say no.'

'Oh.'

'I'm just warning you – but you should still ask.'

'The point being?'

'I'll be flattered.'

'You like me then.'

'I do. You're a nice guy . . .'

'There's a "but" in there somewhere.'

'I get the feeling that you're hung up on a nice girl . . . and it's not me.'

'I could get hung up on you.'

'I'm not very patient and don't like waiting in line.'

'That's no reason we shouldn't sleep together.'

'Is that an invitation?'

'Yes.'

She laughs and kisses me again. As she steps away, I grab her and pull her close, hearing her exhale softly. Her mouth opens. There is nothing left to say.

Later that night or early the next morning, she is lying next to me, her head resting on my shoulder and her right arm across my chest.

'I thought you were going to say no,' I say, tracing my fingers over her breasts.

'I have no self-control.'

'Maybe I should apologise.'

'It's a bit late now.' She kisses the tips of my fingers. 'It was certainly different.'

'In a good way?'

'Definitely worth repeating.' She rolls out of bed. 'Not tonight, sadly, I have an early start.'

'So you're loving me and leaving?'

She's in the bathroom, getting dressed. 'It's not like that.'

'What is it like?'

'Complicated.'

'You're seeing someone else?'

'This was probably a mistake.'

'Don't turn it into a tragedy. Nobody got hurt.'

She's studying herself in the mirror, adjusting her hair. There is something very sensual about a woman preparing herself.

'Are you married?' I ask.

'No.'

'What is it then?'

'Nothing.'

She pulls on her overcoat and kisses my cheek. There is a

note on the floor, pushed under the door. She picks it up and reads the name, her forehead buckling.

It's a handwritten message from DCI Drury.

Blackout over: the storm breaks.

I haven't heard him coming.

*He is sitting in the shadows with just his hands and knees in the
light. My heart stops and I take a juddering breath, scrambling to the
end of the bunk.*

He leans forward, his face now visible.

'Good morning, Princess.'

The skin wrinkles around his eyes.

*When there were two of us he would never come down the ladder.
He's more confident now that I'm alone. I haven't had a chance to
study him up close for a long time – not for years. He's a forgettable
man; one you wouldn't notice twice. Once even.*

'You must be hungry. Are you ready to come upstairs?'

I shake my head.

'I have a warm bath waiting. Hot food.'

He's smiling with a mixture of compassion and dry humour.

'Where's Tash?'

'Don't worry about her.'

'Is she all right?'

*George glances at the window. 'You were very foolish helping her
escape like that. I know what you did. I know how you did it.'*

My bladder is full. I have to use the toilet.

*He walks around the basement, stopping at the sink and examining
the empty cans as though frightened he might catch something.*

*He points to the ladder. 'I'm going up now. You know what's going
to happen if you don't come to me? Remember the hose?'*

*He grips the ladder and climbs easily, balancing on the uppermost
rung before swinging through the open hatch like a gymnast. He peers
back through the hole.*

'Come on now, Piper. You know you want to.'

'Are you going to hurt me?'

'Why would I do that?'

'You hurt Tash.'

'She didn't do as she was told.'

I scan the room, looking for something – a weapon or a way out.

'Don't make me wait, Piper.'

I don't want to go up the ladder, but it's been three years living in a hole. I want to see different walls.

'I have hot food,' he says again. 'A warm bath.'

I climb. One hand follows the other. Higher. I hold my arms above my head. He reaches down and grabs me by the wrists, lifting me easily. Hoisting me to the edge of the trapdoor and then higher onto my feet.

He lets me go. The room is dark. I'm standing under a set of iron stairs. George walks through a door into a second room, motioning me to follow. He's wearing a jacket and corduroy trousers – the sort of clothes my father would wear.

We're in some sort of workshop or factory, with high ceilings and narrow windows running along the top of the walls. The plaster is crumbling, the roof panels are broken. I notice a chest freezer with a blinking red light; a table, two plastic chairs, boxes, metal drums. Then I smell the food. Barbecued chicken. Still warm.

He tears open the bag. I think I might faint from hunger. The bag is from the Chicken Cottage in Abingdon. I know that shop because the man who runs it has one of those mail-order brides from the Philippines who looks like she's about seventeen.

'Maybe you should wash first,' says George.

I shake my head.

He offers me a chair. My hands are shaking. Stomach cramping. I can see the greasy warm flesh, the golden brown skin, the fat drumsticks . . .

He sits down opposite and watches me eat. I keep cramming chicken into my mouth because I'm scared he might take it away.

'Something to drink?'

He opens a can of lemonade.

'You'll make yourself sick. Maybe you should slow down.'

But I keep eating. I can't chew quickly enough. I swallow and almost choke.

He takes the corner of the greaseproof bag and pulls it away from me. My eyes and hands follow the food, but he smacks at my wrists, telling me to slow down.

I can't answer. A wodge of food is caught in my throat. I can't breathe. He stands and puts his arms around me, tightening his grip, forcing air out of my lungs. I cough up a ball of masticated chicken.

He sets me down on the chair.

'Do as you're told next time.'

That's when I puke. He steps back but not in time to save his shoes. He calls me something. I don't catch the words. My whole insides are coming out. I feel as though they're going to finish up on the floor with the regurgitated chicken and lemonade.

I wipe my mouth and nose with my sleeve.

'Where is Tash?'

'I caught her.'

'Where is she?'

'I killed her.'

'I don't believe you.'

He laughs. 'She's in another room – just like this one.'

'Can I see her?'

'No, I'm punishing her.'

'Punish me instead.'

He doesn't answer.

'Please, let me see her.'

'No.'

'Why are you doing this?'

Again, he doesn't answer.

'I want to go home. Please let us go. We won't tell anyone.'

'I thought you had outgrown all this,' he says, sounding disappointed.

'Let me see Tash.'

His hand shoots out and grabs my face so hard that my jaw feels like it might collapse. He lifts me up. My toes are barely touching the ground.

'Shut up! Understand? Stop whining.'

He says it in a tiny whisper that echoes in my skull.

'Do you hear me?'

He forces my face up and down. Then he lets me go. I don't know how I stay upright. He sniffs at his fingers and wrinkles his nose.

'Time to get you cleaned up.'

He leads me away from the table to a bed and a big old-fashioned bath on clawed feet. A wood-fired boiler is warming the room and heating the water. The bath is already half full. He turns on the tap. Steam billows. Bubbles froth. A large trunk at the bottom of the bed is open. There are shampoos, soaps, body washes, lotions, conditioners, moisturisers, perfume, bubble bath – it's like he's raided every hotel in the country, taking all those little complimentary bottles.

Adding more bubble bath into the running water, he watches it froth and foam. Then he opens a second trunk and takes out a big fluffy towel.

'You haven't undressed.'

'I don't want to.'

'Why not?'

'Not in front of you.'

'I'm not going anywhere.'

'Please,' I ask, in a squeaky voice.

I look at the bath and then the open trunk. It has a mirror fixed to the inside of the lid. I catch a glimpse of my reflection. My hair is matted into rat's tails. My eyes are red.

The bath is ready. He dips his fingers into the water.

'You have nothing I haven't seen before.'

But that isn't true. He hasn't seen me naked before. Not up close. Not like this.

He takes hold of my face again, forcing me to look into his eyes, which peer deep inside my head. His fingers tighten. Tears fall on the back of his hand.

'Don't disobey me, Piper. You know what I can do.'

I take off my clothes. He holds them between his finger and thumb, dropping them into a plastic rubbish bag. I cover my breasts with my forearm.

He motions to my knickers. Soiled. Yellow.

'Those next.'

'I want to leave them on.'

He shakes his head.

I push them down, turning my back, stepping quickly into the bath and sliding beneath the surface, curling up into a ball. He pulls his chair close so his knees touch the edge of the bath.

He hands me a pink disposable razor.

'Do your legs.'

I hesitate. He reaches into the water and grabs me by the left ankle, lifting the leg upwards. I don't have time to grip the sides of the bath. I slide completely underwater. He's holds my leg higher, keeping my head under. I can't breathe. I may never breathe again.

When he drops the leg, I come up spluttering and coughing, leaking snot, eyes stinging.

'Either you shave or I do it for you.'

I shave, one leg at a time, propping each on the edge of the bath. He watches. My hand is shaking as the blade carves a track through the foam.

Then he tells me to stand up. I cover my groin and breasts. He points to my pubic hair.

'We have to do something about that.'

I don't understand.

'Shave it off.'

My hand is shaking. I can't do it.

Nobody has ever touched me there. Nobody. The only guy who ever tried was Gerard Bryant who pushed his hand up my skirt at the Odeon in Oxford, but got a punch in the stomach for his troubles.

I don't punch George. I stand very still and taste the tears that are running into the corners of my mouth. He talks to me as he works, but the words don't register. When he's finished he holds up the towel, putting it around my shoulders, drying me gently, my arms and legs, between my toes . . .

He lets me keep the towel around my shoulders as he opens the

208

trunk and removes the top shelf. Beneath there are bras, knickers and lingerie. He chooses a nightgown.

'Put this on.'

'Why?'

'Because I want you to.'

I raise my arms. The fabric slides over me. I stand self-consciously, still feeling naked. He puts his hands on my shoulders and makes me sit while he brushes my hair and pulls my face towards his, using a tube of lipstick to paint my lips.

He puts his hand under my chin and lifts my head so that I'll look at his face. His thumb and forefinger are digging into my cheeks, pulling my mouth out of shape. I don't want to look into his eyes. Instead, I try to concentrate on a spot just above them, a patch of dry skin on his forehead.

'Don't you look pretty?' he says, pointing me towards the mirror. He makes me stand.

'Do a twirl.'

I shuffle in circles. Then he leads me to the bed and forces me forwards, his hands urgent, lifting the nightdress over my hips, bunching it around my waist. His breath quickens with the march of his fingers.

I should fight. I should bite and scratch. I should jam my fingers into his soft bits. Instead, I squeak like a kitten as his fingers invade me.

I don't know what happens next. My mind goes blank. He's talking to me but the sound is washed away. I'm writing in my head, putting words together randomly.

I become a different person. I can be somewhere else . . . in a safe place. Why can't I be an angry person, who can fight and punch and kick? Why can't I set loose the dogs of war? I don't know what the 'dogs of war' are or if they're real dogs but they sound pretty scary.

He's unbuckling his belt. Sliding down his trousers. My face is pressing into something soft − a blanket made of fur, so soft and warm.

'Do you know what you're lying upon, Piper?' he whispers. 'Lots and lots of animals; pretty little dead things all sewn together. Once they were alive and now they're not.'

The words echo inside my head.

'Rabbits. Baby seals. Foxes. Beavers. Shall I tell you how they died? They were bludgeoned or electrocuted. They were skinned, their pelts pulled over their bleeding heads. Their little hairless bodies were thrown onto a pile, some still breathing, blinking, dying . . .'

His lips are pressed to my ear.

'If you ever disobey me, Piper . . . if you ever try to escape . . . I will strip off your skin and toss your body on a pile just like all those pretty little dead animals.'

His hand snakes around my head and covers my mouth and nose. My head snaps back. I claw at his hands and a rushing sound fills my head, drowning out my silent screams. I don't feel pain. My mind has gone blank. He cannot touch me now. He cannot reach inside my head.

I have found my hiding place.

25

On an icy morning the news runs hot and normality lifts from the streets of Bingham like a flock of startled birds. Residents read the headlines over breakfast or watch the reports on morning TV.

Natasha McBain. Three years missing. Five days dead.

By ten o'clock there are broadcast vans parked on Bingham's village green and reporters are going door to door to get reactions from neighbours and friends. Memories are revisited and raked over like the embers of last night's fire, while the girl in question is being reinvented and rebranded. Natasha McBain is no longer the troublemaker and delinquent who ran away from home. She is a victim. Abducted. Imprisoned. Sexually violated. A predator is living in their very midst – one of their own, perhaps – a neighbour, a work colleague or that strange man over the road whose basement lights burn all night.

The police car navigates through a crowd of reporters who are milling outside the gates of The Old Vicarage. Two constables force them back onto the road and the gates close again.

Grievous steers the car along a crushed marble driveway, pulling up outside a double garage. Ahead of us, the gardens spread across two acres, dotted with huge old trees, garden beds and patches of manicured lawns. There is also a pond, a tennis court, a croquet lawn and greenhouses full of spring seed trays.

'This is some place,' he says. 'Must be worth a pretty penny.'

'Dale Hadley is a banker,' I say, which says enough.

I glance at the detective constable. He has toothpaste in the shell of his ear. I point it out and he tilts the rear-view mirror, examining himself. Annoyed.

'The lads put toothpaste on my desk phone,' he explains. 'Old dogs, old tricks.'

DCI Drury is already inside the house, trying to explain to Piper Hadley's family why they weren't informed that Natasha McBain had been found.

Dale Hadley is a short, stocky man with greying hair and deep lines around his eyes. His shoulders are as wide as his waist and his clothes look ill-fitting on his odd-shaped frame. He's pacing the kitchen, fists clenched.

'What else haven't you told us? What else are you hiding?'

'I understand you're upset, Mr Hadley, but the news blackout was necessary. We had to check the whereabouts of suspects. Establish alibis.'

'Which includes me! That's why I had one of your detectives come here asking me where I was during the blizzard.'

'You have to understand—'

'No, *you* have to understand. I will not be treated like a fucking criminal. My daughter has been missing for three years. We've heard nothing. Not a whisper. Now we learn that you've been keeping information secret.'

'I will never lie to you,' says Drury, 'but there will be certain things the police must keep to ourselves.'

Through an open door, I see a sunken living room where a girl of about eleven is holding her hands over her brother's ears.

'Daddy!' she says.

'Sorry, Phoebes.'

The children go back to watching TV.

Dale Hadley turns again to Drury. 'You must have some idea where she is.'

'We're looking, I promise you. I have officers going door to door and dozens of volunteers searching the fields around the farmhouse. They're going to keep looking, I promise you.'

'What farmhouse?'

'We think Natasha was trying to get home. It's likely she didn't know her parents had divorced and moved house.'

Mr Hadley's face bends like a white rubber mask. 'Oh, Christ. So Piper might have been with her. They both could have escaped.'

'It's too early to say.'

'You must have some leads.'

'We are questioning someone.'

'Who?'

'A man who was in the area when Natasha was found.'

'What's his name?'

'I'm afraid I can't tell you.'

'Does he know where Piper is? Have you asked him? Did he leave her somewhere safe?'

Drury opens his palms. 'I can't answer those questions.'

A woman enters the room, her hair freshly brushed and make-up applied. She's carrying a toddler in colourful leggings and a bright-red smock.

She admonishes her husband. 'You shouldn't be talking in here, Dale. Not in front of the children.'

Sarah Hadley is a tall, attractive woman in her early forties, dressed in a dark silk shirt, cashmere cardigan and designer jeans that might never have been worn.

'Phoebe, can you please feed Jessica?' she asks. 'She wants Rice Krispies. Make sure she wears a bib.'

Phoebe takes her sister, lifting her onto a booster chair.

Sarah insists on talking in the drawing room. The precisely

furnished room has sofas and armchairs arranged around a walnut coffee table. A Christmas tree, decorated in white, fills the bay window.

Sarah perches on the edge of an armchair, hands on her lap, knees together. The whites of her eyes are threaded with tiny red veins and her breath smells of something sweet: a drink to steel herself.

'They've arrested someone,' says Mr Hadley. 'They think he might know where Piper is.'

'I didn't say that,' says Drury. 'At this stage it's not wise to speculate.'

Sarah turns her head and stares past the Christmas tree into the garden. The sun has come out and turned the frosty lawn into a carpet of diamonds.

'Natasha was the strong one,' she whispers. 'If she couldn't survive, what hope is there for Piper?'

Her husband hushes her and reaches for her hand, but she withdraws it almost instinctively. They're an odd-looking couple. Sarah looks like a former beauty queen with flawless skin, seemingly devoid of pores and such artfully applied make-up that it appears almost non-existent. Dale is short and stocky with a moon face and acne scars.

Each seems to have reacted differently to the news. Dale has allowed himself to hope for the first time in a long while. Now he wants to be outside, kicking down doors, shaking the trees and yelling Piper's name from the rooftops.

Meanwhile, Sarah, who has spent three years publicising Piper's disappearance, keeping her in the public eye, giving interviews, putting up posters and running a website, has been hollowed out by the news of Natasha's death.

I have seen hundreds of couples overwhelmed by loss. Some can look straight into each other's eyes without needing words. Others are like strangers sitting on a long-distance train. Some fall to the ground shrieking while others remain unmoved, seemingly devoid of emotion. Some blame themselves, and others search for someone to blame, while a few drink themselves into oblivion or pretend nothing has changed.

I can picture this couple lying side by side in bed at night, hollow in heart and soul, wondering if Piper is still alive, one abandoning hope, the other clinging to it − until today when the roles have been reversed.

I have been there. I have lain awake staring at the ceiling, my bones aching with exhaustion, knowing Gideon Tyler had taken Charlie,wondering if she was still alive. I have been visited by every shade of grief and know that it doesn't come in black or white.

Dale Hadley takes me upstairs to Piper's bedroom. He pauses outside the door, as though unwilling to cross the threshold.

'I haven't set foot in this room,' he explains. 'Not since she went missing. Piper had this thing about her privacy. She didn't like anyone invading her space.' He uses his fingers to make inverted commas around the last statement.

'She was secretive?'

'Aren't they all? Teenagers, I mean.' He scratches his unshaven jaw. 'We let her put a lock on her door, but we took it off after she and Natasha got into trouble. They went to a college-age party . . . there was an incident.'

'I heard.'

'We knew Piper had been drinking and we caught her with pills in her bag. That's why we grounded her. She wanted to go to the festival, but we told her no. She snuck out anyway. That's the last time . . . you know . . .' He sighs. 'The last words she said were that she hated me.'

'She didn't mean it.'

'I know.' He glances at the single bed. 'We blamed Natasha. She was always a wild child. You know how girls like pretending to be grown-up, dressing in their mothers' clothes, tottering in high heels? Natasha acted like she was *always* grown-up. Precocious isn't the right word. She was trouble. We tried to separate them by sending Piper to one of those camps for troubled teens, but that didn't do any good.'

'You tried to stop her seeing Natasha.'

'Did we do the wrong thing?'

'You shouldn't punish yourself.'

'Why not? Maybe it was our fault.'

His eyes close in a delta of wrinkles. Dale Hadley, like Isaac McBain, has spent three years debating the 'what if's and 'if only's. What could he have done? How could he have changed things?

Piper's room is exactly as she left it. Her desk has textbooks stacked smallest to largest and there are pictures pinned to a noticeboard, mostly of Natasha. It is a typical teenage girl's room, full of lip gloss, bracelets and acne creams. Nothing strikes me as being odd or out of the ordinary, except for the fact that none of the posters or photographs feature boy bands or sex symbols.

Everywhere there is evidence of girlhood adventures: a jumble of novelty pens, knick-knacks, key rings and cheap jewellery. I run my fingers over the bookcase. One shelf contains cloth-coloured notebooks.

'She liked writing,' explains Dale, still standing in the doorway. 'We found them all over the place after she'd gone – behind the radiator, under the mattress, in the cavity behind her drawers. Some were wrapped in masking tape so that her sister couldn't read them.'

'You gave them to the police?'

'Of course.' He sighs. 'She wrote some hurtful things about the family. You know what teenagers are like. They love and hate in the same breath.'

I pick up one of the journals. 'Can I borrow these?'

'Go ahead.'

He looks absentmindedly at his watch. 'I have to make some calls. They'll have heard the news at work, but I should say something . . .'

He turns and leaves, walking like a man submerged in water.

Taking the journals, I cross the corridor to a small home office, which is the 'mission control' centre for the 'Finding Piper' campaign. There are posters on the walls, along with newspaper clippings, emails and photographs of Piper in every stage of her young life.

One image shows her digging earthworms from a muddy bank, concentrating so hard that her brow is furrowed. It's an inconsequential moment frozen in time, but something about the way it is framed and displayed makes Piper seem almost deified, like a child chosen for a higher purpose.

I'm aware of someone else in the room. Phoebe is sitting on the office chair with her legs crossed, watching me intently.

'Hello.'

'Hello.'

'You must be Phoebe.'

'How do you know my name?'

I tap the end of my nose.

'Are you a detective?' she asks.

'No.'

'Are you looking for Piper?'

'I am.'

'If you find her, will I still be invisible?'

'Pardon?'

'Do you think Mum will see me then?'

'You think you're invisible?'

'I'm not like Piper. She's the one people talk about. She's the one they want to see – not me or Ben or Jessica. We're invisible.'

'I'm sure that's not true. Your mother loves you.'

Phoebe rocks forward and puts her feet on the floor. From downstairs, I can hear her brother Ben calling her.

'Goodbye,' she says. 'I'm glad you can see me.'

Sarah Hadley is not in the house. I find her outside in the

garden hitting golf balls into a practice net. Pieces of ice fly off the mesh every time a ball smacks into the hanging curtain. I can imagine her in the summer at her country club, her long tanned legs in tailored shorts.

She drives a ball, wrapping the club around her back and holding the pose. Her shirt rides up over her flat stomach.

'Nice swing.'

'I used to play on the county team.'

At first glance her complexion had looked golden and almost unblemished but now I notice the skin around her eyes has been tightened. Repairs have been done. She takes a swig of something from a glass. Alcohol has glazed her eyes but hasn't numbed anything else.

'Maybe you should ease up on that,' I tell her.

'Bit late now. I was two years sober until this morning.'

'I could give you someone to call?'

'Therapy? Tried that too. None of it lasts.'

'Where is your husband with this?'

'He makes excuses for me. He's not one to complain.'

She swings at another ball and this one shanks to the right. 'You know the saddest thing about all this?'

'What's that?'

'Phoebe doesn't know how to ride a pushbike because we haven't taught her. She's never taken the school bus or walked to the shops by herself. I'm scared that if I let her out of my sight she might not come back.'

'That's understandable,' I say, remembering my conversation with Phoebe.

'It's affecting her, you know. Little by little, I see her regressing. She was always a strong-willed little madam, but now I've made her helpless. She has nightmares, wakes up crying and shouting. Dale has to calm her down.'

'Not you?'

'She doesn't settle so easily for me. You should see her bedroom. She kept every single one of the soft toys that people sent. The attic is bursting with them. Dale wanted to donate them to charity, but Phoebe wouldn't let him.'

Sarah glances over her shoulder at the house, proud of her family but unable to explain the mix of feelings that marriage has brought her. The Christmas tree is visible through the drawing room window.

'We still hang Piper's stocking every year. And we have a cake on her birthday, with just the right number of candles. We've been going through the motions, but now it seems more real . . . more real than yesterday.'

She tees up another ball, checks her grip, makes a practice swing.

'I've grown used to being stared at. People whisper behind my back – they think I'm a publicity-seeker. Phoebe came home from school one day and said a boy had told her that Piper was dead and that I should shut up and stop talking about her.

'That's what people think. They think our little girl was murdered or ran away because we were awful parents. They think I waste my time, banging on pointlessly . . . putting up posters, not letting them forget. Do you know why I've never given up?'

'No.'

'I talked to a medium . . . a psychic. She told me that Piper and Natasha were still alive. She said they were together and were trying to get home. She said, "They are beneath the earth, but not a part of it. Breathing in the darkness."'

'How did you meet this medium?'

'Vic McBain was going out with her.'

'Natasha's uncle?'

Sarah nods and something feverish passes across her face. She doesn't strike me as being the sort to hang her hopes on the cold reading capabilities of a psychic, but three years is a long time without news and desperation is a cold cup of coffee.

'What else did this medium say?'

'She said she could see flashing lights and a tall building like a smokestack or a windmill without any sails. The girls were under the ground, but not *in* the ground. Alive, that's what she said, definitely alive.'

There is a sound from the bushes behind the practice net. A face appears. Young. Brazen. The reporter has mud stains on his knees.

'Mrs Hadley, I spoke to Hayden McBain. He said that Natasha was raped and mutilated by a paedophile. Is that what you fear for Piper?'

Sarah's fists tighten around the driver. She marches towards the reporter swinging the club through the air like a two-handed machete.

'You are a grubby little man,' she screams. 'You're a vulture . . . a ghoul . . . get off my property!'

He turns and runs, leaping onto the wall, his shoes scrabbling for purchase on the wet bricks.

Sarah drops a golf ball onto the lawn and takes her stance. The club swings through a graceful arc and she drills the ball towards the reporter, who has just reached the top of the wall and raised his arms to celebrate his escape. The ball hits him between the shoulder blades and he drops like a felled tree, making an *oof* sound as he lands in the neighbouring garden.

26

'We've had five hundred phone calls since six this morning,' says Drury, staring out the car window. 'Each one of them has to be logged, categorised and followed up . . . I'm all in favour of public support, but we're getting calls from every nutter, do-gooder and pissed-off ratepayer with a grudge against his neighbour.'

'Who broke the news blackout?'

'Hayden McBain took thirty pieces of silver from the *Sun*.'

'The news would have leaked eventually.'

Drury shakes his head in disgust, silent for a long moment. His job has become a lot harder. People are scared. Parents want reassurance and a quick resolution. The media will be demanding answers. Progress. Daily briefings. Failure will bring blame.

The road out of Bingham is choked with traffic, belching fumes into the frigid air. Drury tells Grievous to use the siren. Motorists pull over and the unmarked police car squeezes past.

Sarah Hadley's words are still grinding through my mind. Grief has kept her busy for three years, held her upright. The news of Natasha hasn't restored her belief, it has caused her to doubt.

'I want to ask you about Victor McBain,' I say.

The DCI glances over the seat. 'What about him?'

'Nelson Stokes claims that he saw Natasha kissing her uncle in the front seat of his car. It wasn't a peck on the cheek. He says he told police, but I can't find any mention of it in his statement.'

Drury seems to be chewing on my question, deciding how much to say.

'We looked at Vic McBain,' he says, speaking to the windscreen. 'You know how it works. When a child goes missing or is murdered we look at the family first, then friends. Ninety per cent of the time it's a fair assumption.'

'Why wasn't the allegation included in Stokes' statement?'

'McBain threatened to sue the police if anyone repeated the claim.'

'Were the allegations investigated?'

'Of course.'

'So there's no truth—'

Drury interrupts. 'He gave Natasha some inappropriate gifts.'

'What gifts?'

'Bikinis, booze, condoms.'

'Not the sort of things an uncle gives a niece.'

'I saw Vic McBain three years ago. He would have torn this town apart to find Natasha. He also had an alibi for the morning the girls disappeared.'

'What about the night of the blizzard?'

Drury loses patience. 'If you have new information, Professor, let's hear it, but don't play twenty questions with me. I don't have the time.'

'Sarah Hadley said she talked to a medium – some woman who was introduced to her by Vic McBain. This medium claimed that Natasha and Piper were being held somewhere against their will. She used the phrase "Beneath the earth but not a part of it".'

'Don't tell me you believe this psychic shit? Do you know

how many mediums and mystics we've heard from so far? Dozens of them.'

'This could be different. This medium saw a smokestack or a windmill. The pathologist found traces of heavy metals on Natasha's clothing. What if Vic McBain fed her some of the details.'

'Why would he do that?'

'I don't know, but there's something else that bothers me. When the girls were planning to run away, Natasha told Emily that her uncle owed her money. When I asked Emily why, she clammed up and got upset.'

'You think Natasha was blackmailing her uncle?'

'It's possible.'

'OK, OK, we'll take another look.' Drury squeezes his nose and blows out his cheeks as though adjusting the pressure in his head. 'I'm getting a head cold. My daughter gave it to me. If you ask me, rats got a bum rap for the plague. I blame kids.'

Phillip Martinez is causing a commotion downstairs at the police station, arguing with the desk sergeant, whose blood pressure is glowing in his cheeks. A dozen people are waiting to be seen. Emily hangs back, hands buried in the pockets of a donkey jacket.

Martinez looks relieved to see me. 'Professor O'Loughlin, you'll understand.'

'What will I understand?'

'We have important information. Emily does. There's something she didn't tell the police. She received a letter.'

'A letter?'

'From Piper.'

Drury is shaking out his coat and spins around as though struck. He yells at the desk sergeant to let Mr Martinez and Emily through. A button is pushed. The door unlocks. Father and daughter are ushered quickly upstairs to the DCI's office.

Emily hasn't raised her eyes. She doesn't dress like most girls her age. No clunky shoes, acid-coloured skirts or livid lipsticks. Instead, she's wearing a long skirt and baggy jumper.

I notice a music folder sticking out of her bag.

'What do you play?' I ask.

'The piano.'

'What grade?'

'Six.'

'She's taking extra lessons during the holidays,' says Mr Martinez. 'Her teacher says she has perfect pitch.'

Emily looks embarrassed, wanting him to be quiet.

Drury enters, apologising for the delay. I watch Emily side-long, looking for more signs of inner turmoil.

Mr Martinez does the talking. 'She only told me about the letter this morning. I tried not to touch it. That's why I put it in a plastic bag. I thought it might have fingerprints, you know, or DNA.'

Drury takes the letter and places it on his desk. The paper is poor quality and almost perished at the creases, but the sentences are still legible, written in fading pencil.

Dear Em,

Please, please don't tell anybody about this letter - not my parents or the police. You have to promise. This has to be our secret.

Everybody knows we ran away now and hopefully they'll stop looking soon. We're living in London, by the way, just like we said. It's a big house, but I'm not supposed to tell you the address.

Tash is OK. We both miss you. We're sorry we left you waiting for so long at the railway station, but it's probably best you stayed. One day when we're all eighteen we can get a place together.

I guess my mum is happier now. She can

concentrate on Phoebe and Ben without me getting in the way. They deserve better than me.
I wish I'd been nicer to them.
  Until we meet again.
  Lots of love,
  Piper xxxooo

I recognise the handwriting as Piper's. The loopy letters and square capitals are pencilled hard into the cheap paper, leaving specks of graphite glinting in the furrows.

'When did you get this?' I ask.

Emily brushes her fringe from her eyes. Her father answers for her. 'I've told her she did the wrong thing. She's very contrite. It won't happen again.'

'When exactly did it arrive?'

Once more Mr Martinez answers. 'The envelope has a London postmark. The date is blurred, but it might be October 2008.'

I look at Emily for confirmation. She nods.

'Why didn't you show it to anyone?'

'Piper told me not to. She made me promise.'

'That's no excuse, Emily,' says her father. 'You should have told me.'

Drury has picked up the phone, asking forensics to collect the letter and envelope. Tests will be done on the paper and the stamp.

'Does anything about the letter strike you as odd?' I ask Emily. She looks at me blankly.

'How did Piper know that you waited at the railway station? You didn't see her there. It was never made public that you were there.'

Confusion fills her eyes.

'Who else knew that you were waiting for them at Radley Station?'

'Nobody.'

I look at Phillip Martinez. 'Did you know?'

He shakes his head.

'Did you tell anyone, Emily?'

'I don't think so.'

'Did you see anyone?'

'No.'

'Where did you go afterwards?'

'I tried to call Tash, but she wasn't answering her phone. I sent her text messages and went to the café where she worked on Sundays. I thought she might turn up.'

'Who did you see there?'

'I can't remember.'

'Think really hard. It's important.'

'I talked to the manager and the other waitress.'

'Anyone else?'

'Natasha's uncle was having breakfast at one of the tables. He saw my bag and said it looked heavy. He made a joke about me leaving home.'

'Do you think he knew?'

Emily shrugs. I glance at Drury, gauging his reaction. Something about this bothers me. Teenage girls don't usually write letters. They send emails or texts or they phone.

Drury is asking Emily if Natasha ever talked about her uncle. She shakes her head more adamantly than necessary.

'How did she get on with him?'

'OK, I guess.' Emily looks at her father. 'Can we go? They have the letter.'

The DCI hasn't finished. 'When you planned to run away, what money did you have?'

'Tash had money.'

'Where did she get it from?'

'She had a job.'

'Was she selling drugs for her brother?'

Emily seems to hold her breath, as though the answer can be avoided as long as she doesn't exhale. She nods. Breathes. 'It was just some pills and stuff.'

'Where?'

'Parties. It's not like she was selling to pre-schoolers.'

Phillip Martinez doesn't hide his disgust. 'Don't try to defend her. It's wrong!'

Emily averts her gaze.

Her father stands. 'I think she's said enough.'

Drury pushes back. 'She withheld important evidence from a police investigation.'

'She made a mistake.'

'She owed it to their families.'

Emily blinks back tears, looking utterly miserable. 'I'm sorry, I'm sorry. I thought they were in London.'

Mr Martinez gets to his feet. 'We're leaving. Come on.' He puts his arm around Emily's shoulders and she shrinks under his touch. Drury doesn't try to stop them.

Pausing at the door, Martinez turns to me. 'That research study I mentioned. I checked with my colleague. There are still places. I could recommend you.'

'Thank you,' I say, embarrassed that the offer is so public. 'I'll look into it.'

Drury leans forward in his chair, thumbs massaging his temples, a swarm of thoughts crowding together.

'Is it genuine?'

'Yes.'

'So they were in London?'

'Not necessarily.'

I study the letter again, looking at the syntax and sentence structure. I have no doubts about the handwriting, but the language lacks Piper's customary flourishes, her self-deprecating sense of humour, her fatalism or her swearing.

'I think the letter was dictated. Piper was told exactly what to write, giving away as little as possible.'

'Why send a letter at all?'

'Let's assume it was sent in October, two months after the

girls went missing. That's about the time the police were discounting the runaway theory. Maybe the kidnapper wanted to create more confusion.'

'He expected the letter to surface.'

'Wouldn't you?'

Drury stands and walks to the window, staring in dull bewilderment at the street below.

I still have questions. 'How did Piper know that Emily was waiting at the station?'

'Emily could have been lying about having no other contact,' he says.

'She seemed contrite. Frightened.'

'So what's your theory?'

'There are three possibilities. Either someone saw her at the station or Emily told someone, or the kidnapper gained access to information that wasn't in the public domain.'

'Vic McBain was at the café,' says Drury. 'I'm going to put him under surveillance.'

'It could still be a coincidence.'

'Yeah, well, you know what they say about coincidences . . . some of them take a lot of planning.'

He didn't rape me.

I threw up again . . . all over his little dead animals. The roast chicken came out quicker than it went in.

George hit me across the face and I felt something warm dripping from my nose. Then he threw me back into my hole and took away the blankets.

He left behind a walkie-talkie, a green plastic thing with a small aerial and a button on the side. It looks like something a child might play with.

'When you're nice to me you'll get your blankets back,' he said, before closing the trapdoor and sliding something heavy on top of it.

I'm curled up on the bunk. Aching. My bones are sore and cold against the thin foam mattress. I finally drift off to sleep but wake in the middle of the night, feeling strange and sort of shivery. Straight away I think of Tash. George said he was punishing her. Does that mean she's in another room? Is she lying awake like me? Wondering.

I pick up the walkie-talkie and press the button.

'Hello? Can anyone hear me?'

Nothing.

'Hello? Is anyone there?'

I jump when he answers. 'Are you ready to be nice to me?'

I drop the walkie-talkie and it bounces off the cement floor. A small piece of plastic breaks off, but it's still working. George is talking, but I don't answer. Instead, I curl up on the bunk and put a pillow over my head. Eventually, he goes away.

I understand why Tash went up the ladder to be with George. She did it to protect me. She knew I was a virgin. Inexperienced. Naive. But each time she came back to the basement, a little less of her climbed down the ladder. It's as though George took a piece of her as a souvenir or she left it upstairs.

Tash loved me. Not in the same way I loved her, but I don't care. I know what it's like to love someone and not be able to tell her because it will screw up the friendship; and having that person as a friend is better than losing her completely.

That's what it was like with Tash. At first I thought it was just a schoolgirl crush, a girl thing, you know, but then I realised it was something more. Tash was always trying to line me up with boys, but none of them interested me. I wanted to spend time with her.

Everybody fancied Tash: men and boys and grandfathers. The ones who asked Tash to babysit and offered to drive her home afterwards; the shopkeepers who hired her and the teachers who let her flirt with them. I caught my father sneaking glances at her. I used to stare at her too.

It was just a game for Tash. She flirted, preened and teased, raising expectations and crushing them, inadvertently and on purpose. Expecting Tash to change was like telling the Pope to stop praying. She was full of contradictions – old before her time, young at heart, living on the edge.

She used to tell me that she'd stop when she reached the point of no return, which didn't make any sense to me. There's no stopping at the point of no return. You're over the edge. You're falling through the air. Gravity can't change its mind. Although I did once hear a story about a woman who jumped off the Clifton Suspension Bridge and her long skirt blew up and acted like a parachute. I remember thinking, Lucky cow, but she probably didn't see it the same way.

I've thought about suicide. Not so much killing myself but picturing everyone at my funeral – all the people who made my life so terrible. That seems childish now. My life wasn't so bad back then. Things are pretty relative when you're locked in a basement.

There are worse things than dying. I saw Callum Loach come home from the hospital in his wheelchair. I have lived in this dark hole. I have watched my best friend wither and give up hope.

When Callum came home the ambulance had a little ramp at the back and his folks built more little ramps all over his house and changed the dining room into a bedroom so he didn't have to climb the stairs.

230

A whole lot of people were there to welcome him, but he looked embarrassed rather than happy. He wanted to be left alone.

He was home in time to give evidence against Aiden Foster at the trial. Photographers took pictures of him arriving at the courthouse, dressed in a suit, being pushed by his father. He didn't have his prosthetic legs by then and his trouser legs flapped pointlessly where his legs used to be.

His father sat stony-faced in the public gallery. They could have invented that description for Mr Loach: 'stony-faced' – he could have been chiselled out of rock. He could have been on Mount Rushmore.

Aiden arrived wearing a suit and a haircut that made him look like a choirboy. He even had a side-parting. Instead of swaggering, he kept his head down and walked between his mum and dad.

Emily had to give evidence first. She was used to going to court because her parents were fighting for custody. I waited outside in the foyer, sitting next to my dad, who kept squeezing my hand, saying, 'Just tell the truth. That's all they want.'

They called me. The big door creaked open. I walked between the benches and the tables. Aiden was sitting in a box. I had to raise my right hand and swear on a Bible. Then one of the lawyers began asking me about that night and what I saw. I told them what happened.

Then Aiden Foster's lawyer asked me more questions. He wanted to know how much Tash had been drinking and what drugs she took. He made her sound like some drug kingpin; and whenever I tried to say something nice about her, his eyebrows were riding high like he didn't believe a word of it.

'Do you have a problem with telling the truth?' he asked.

'No.'

'Well, just answer my question – yes or no.'

'Not every answer is that simple,' I said. 'What about multiple choices?'

People laughed, but the barrister had forgotten how. He just showed his sharper teeth.

After the judge dismissed me, I got to sit in the courtroom and listen. Tash walked in like a movie star. When she got to the witness box she removed her sunglasses and tugged down her dress as she crossed her legs.

Aiden Foster's barrister couldn't wait to get to his feet. Right through Tash's statement, he pulled faces and fidgeted, showing his frustration. When it was time for the cross-examination, he smirked and smarmed and slimed his way across the courtroom.

Every question seemed to have a double meaning. Whenever Tash tried to answer both possibilities, he would tell her, 'Just yes or no, Miss McBain.'

After a while she got confused, saying yes when she meant to say no. Once he found the slightest flaw, he wouldn't let it go. He would twist this big invisible knife inside her, occasionally glancing at the jury to make sure they were listening.

Aiden Foster wasn't on trial. It was Tash. Every word she spoke was skewed and stretched, giving it a different meaning. She grew angry. She swore. The judge told her to mind her language. The barrister smiled at the jury.

Before the misery ended, Tash was like a poor defenceless animal and the cross-examination was like a blood sport. Nobody felt sorry for her except me.

People shouted as she left the old stone courthouse. They hurled abuse and spat at her, Aiden's friends and Callum's friends, united against a common enemy. They blamed Tash for everything that had happened.

Izzy Cruikshank tried to slap her, but a security guard pushed her away. Tash didn't react. Instead, she kept walking as though nothing was wrong.

Later that night, she knocked on my window.

'I'm leaving,' she said.

'When?'

'Soon as.'

'Where?'

'Anywhere.'

They say when you're young you cry tears of pain and when you're older you cry tears of joy. That's why I want to grow up.

27

Ruiz is waiting for me in the hotel lounge, having comman-deered a table and armchair big enough to make him look small. He's spent the morning reading up on the original investigation, looking for patterns or disparate details.

'Eight thousand interviews, three thousand statements, more than a million hours of police work,' he says. 'I could spend the next ten years reading this stuff and miss the bloody obvious.'

'Does anything jump out at you?' I ask, picking up a folder.

'The silence,' he says. 'The girls disappeared on Sunday morning some time after 7.40 when Alice McBain left for work. Nobody saw them on the footpath into Bingham or crossing the fields or waiting at the train station. That strikes me as odd.'

'Someone could have picked them up before they walked very far.'

'Which means it had to be someone they knew. Girls that age don't get into a stranger's car.'

'Maybe they were overpowered.'

'It would take more than one kidnapper.'

'You don't often see that.'

Ruiz is hungry. We go looking for a café that does an all-day breakfast.

The sun is out and pigeons are fighting over crumbs on the pavement, beating their wings in a desperate dance. The waitress has a dreamy stare, loose hair escaping from a clip. Ruiz orders a full English with mushrooms, cooked tomato and baked beans.

'Wholegrain toast,' he tells her. 'My doctor wants me to eat healthier.'

She doesn't smile. Ruiz polishes his knife and fork with a paper napkin.

'I did come across one detail – Augie Shaw must have known Natasha McBain.'

'Why?'

'When the Heymans moved into the farmhouse, Augie was already mowing the lawns. He worked for the McBains.'

'What about his old man?'

'I can't find a link, but Drury has a dozen officers looking for one.'

'I still don't think Augie Shaw kidnapped those girls.'

'Maybe you're right. Maybe you're thinking nice thoughts because your new girlfriend is his therapist.' A small smile tugs at Ruiz's lips. 'How was your date last night?'

'None of your business.'

'That sounds promising.'

He grins and jiggles a tea bag in boiling water.

'You'll be pleased to know that I too can flirt. I chatted up a very nice middle-aged divorcee in the front office of the County Court.'

'The reason being?'

'I got a peek at the court transcripts for Aiden Foster's trial. The jury found him guilty of GBH with intent and the judge gave him seven years with a non-parole of four.'

'Where is he now?'

'Her Majesty's Prison, Bullingdon.'

'What about Callum Loach?'

'He still lives locally.'

Ruiz reaches into his jacket pocket.

'I took the opportunity to peruse copies of the local rag at the library. Came up with this.'

He hands me a pile of photocopied stories from the *Oxford Mail*, most of them concerning the trial. One clipping has a photograph of Natasha at the courthouse, being escorted through an angry crowd. The shutter has captured the moment when she flinches under the abuse and a faceless security guard pushes someone aside.

'They blamed her for what happened,' says Ruiz, whose afternoon breakfast has arrived. He eats like a condemned man, with his elbows either side of his plate.

In the meantime, I read the articles. The last of them reports that Callum Loach has been selected in the British Paralympic Team. A photo shows him sitting in his wheelchair nursing a basketball.

Ruiz pushes his plate away. Belching quietly. 'Being crippled is a powerful sort of motive . . . so is being sent to prison. I doubt if Aiden Foster shed many tears when Natasha McBain went missing.'

'Maybe we should ask him,' I reply.

'I'm way ahead of you.' Ruiz pulls a ten quid note from his wallet and slides it under the teapot. 'I booked us a visit. Visiting hours end at 4.30.'

HMP Bullingdon is eighteen miles north-east of Oxford on the southern outskirts of Bicester. A category C training prison, it houses inmates who fall somewhere between serial killers (high security) and disgraced Cabinet ministers (open prison).

Wives and girlfriends have already started to gather at the visitors' centre. Some of them have children, who fidget and fight, wanting to be somewhere else. Once inside we are searched, ID'd and have our belongings confiscated and put into lockers. Gifts are vetted in advance. Anyone wearing clothes too similar to prison garb is asked to change.

The formalities over, we are escorted to a large annexe, which has fixed tables and chairs. Visitors must stay outside until the prisoners are brought from their cells. Dockets are presented and the doors opened. Visitors and prisoners are kept apart. Knees cannot touch or lips meet. Hands can be held and children lifted over the divide. Some kids are fine. Others are howling. Some don't leave the safety of their mothers' skirts, peeking out at the stranger sitting opposite.

Aiden Foster is twenty-three now, but looks younger. His pale blond hair is gelled into peaks like a seismic chart and he sits with his legs splayed as though he has weights hanging from his testicles. He's a boy playing a man, trying to survive in a place where men who look like boys get turned into women.

He gazes around the room, expecting to see someone else. Then his forehead creases. Mentally, the floor seems to tilt up and away from him.

He slouches loosely, rocking slightly. I notice the bruises on his neck and the shadows beneath his eyes. He has done it hard. Parole is coming.

Ruiz pulls a paper bag from his pocket. Inside are two packets of cigarettes and chewing gum. Aiden peers into the bag as though examining his school lunch. He stacks the cigarettes on the table with the gum on top.

I introduce myself and Ruiz does the same. Aiden doesn't react. He's trying to give the impression of being completely at ease. A small silver crucifix swings on a chain around his neck.

'We want to talk to you about Natasha McBain,' I say.

'Has she turned up dead?'

'What makes you say that?'

'Why else would you be here?' He smiles.

'You don't seem very upset, Aiden.'

'Oh, don't worry, I'm crying on the inside.'

Again he smiles. Ruiz folds his arms, unimpressed. He's met a lot of smart-mouthed punk kids and has never lost his desire to punch them.

Certain people don't seem to match their voices and Aiden Foster is one of them. His tone is pitched too high, but he tries to roughen it up by adopting a growl. I've read his police file and the trial transcripts of his evidence. I know his type. He's a bully when he can be and a victim when it suits him. I knew somebody like him once, a lad called Martin Payne who made my life a misery at boarding school. Martin joined the army when he graduated. He fought in Bosnia and Kuwait, winning the Queen's Gallantry Medal. Despite these heroics, I always considered Martin to be most at risk of being struck by a random thought. As it happened, I was right. After drinking fourteen pints he bet a friend that he could jump between two platforms on the London Underground – a leap that would have made Bob Beamon proud. Martin landed six feet short and perished on the live rail. Undone by idiocy.

Aiden leans back in his chair, scratching his groin. I point to his crucifix.

'Does God help you sleep at night or does he play well with the parole board?'

'The priest here has been good to me.'

'Let's talk about Natasha.'

'What happened to her?'

'She fell through the ice on a frozen lake.'

'In London?'

There is a pause, before Ruiz asks the obvious question. 'What makes you think she was in London?'

Aiden hesitates, preparing to lie.

'Had you heard from her?' I ask.

'No.'

'Why then?'

There is another long silence. Ruiz speaks first. 'Let me give you some free advice, Aiden, since you've still got six months to go. Most of the cons in here are uneducated, violent, washed-up drug addicts and habitual criminals. They know how to work the system . . . to survive. But you, Aiden, you're a fish. You're too young and pretty for a place like this. I bet the wolves have been sniffing around, waiting to introduce you to a little prison romance.'

'No fucking way, man.'

Something drops with a loud bang on the far side of the room and Aiden spins around as though shot. After a beat of silence, conversations begin again. Aiden tries to shrug it off but he's less sure of himself.

'Shower-time must be a nightmare,' says Ruiz. 'What do you do? If you fight them they punish you. You get shanked in the breakfast queue or lighter fuel thrown on your bed while you're sleeping. Are you getting much sleep, Aiden? I wouldn't be. I'd keep my back to every wall.'

Aiden's eyes are wide.

'Or maybe you've found yourself a benefactor, someone who looks after you. What do you give him in return? Are you bending over for someone, Aiden? Or maybe you're muling drugs or lining up other fish?'

'You got it all wrong.'

'I wonder what your mates are going to think when they hear you're somebody's prison bitch.'

'No way, man! I'm nobody's bitch.'

'That sort of rumour is hard to shake. Girls won't treat you the same way. They'll want you to take an Aids test just to look at them.'

Aiden's eyes are filming over. 'This is bullshit!'

'I'm not telling you anything you don't know,' says Ruiz. 'Maybe it doesn't matter what your mates think. So what if they tell stories about you behind your back – about how some hare-lipped, flat-nosed con found you alone in the shower and uttered sweet nothings in your ear.'

'That didn't fucking happen.'

'I believe you, truly I do.' Ruiz looks at me. 'I don't know how these rumours start.'

The silence lasts a dozen heartbeats.

'She sent me a letter,' says Aiden.

'Who?' I ask.

'Tash.'

'When?'

'A few months after she went missing.' He squints at something on the ceiling. 'She said she and Piper were in London. They were living in a squat and she was working for some guy who ran a place in Soho.'

I look at Ruiz.

'Why did she write to you?'

'She said she was sorry.'

'Sorry for what?'

'What do *you* fucking think?'

'Do you still have the letter?'

'Oh, yeah, I put it in my scrapbook with my pressed flowers and needlework.'

Aiden thinks that's funny. He wants an audience.

'Did you write back?'

'Why would I write to her? She put me in here. She put Callum Loach in a wheelchair. If it weren't for that little prick-tease, none of this would have happened.'

I can see Ruiz's shoulders flexing beneath his shirt. It isn't so much Aiden's whining that he dislikes, but his cocky self-importance and how he wants to blame his own immeasurable stupidity on a schoolgirl because the alternative requires too much self-analysis and accountability.

'Why didn't you tell anyone about the letter?' I ask

'Why should I? Nobody did me any favours.'

Taking a photograph from my jacket pocket, I place it on the table between his elbows. The image is from the post-mortem. Natasha's thin body laid out on the stainless steel bench, swollen and exposed, her eyes blank. Aiden is staring at me, unwilling to look. Slowly he lowers his gaze. Hesitates. Recovers.

'She's not so pretty now,' he says, turning his face away from the photograph.

'You still think she got what was coming to her?' asks Ruiz.

Aiden smiles ruefully, showing all the compassion of a shark loose in a colony of seals.

'Been going to church while I been in here. Learned a few things. It's like the Bible says: "Whatsoever a man soweth, that shall he also reap". Man, woman, same difference. She got what she deserved.'

As we leave the prison, Ruiz takes a boiled sweet from his tin and sucks it hard as though wanting to get a bad taste from his mouth.

'You know how most people in prison deserve to be there.'

'Yeah.'

'Some deserve it more than others.'

28

Late afternoon I drive across Oxford in mist that can't decide if it wants to be rain, or perhaps it's the other way around. The streets are crowded with cars and tourist coaches. The schools are closing, holidays starting, last-minute Christmas shoppers buying last-minute gifts. At the colleges, parents are arriving to fetch their offspring home from university. Trunks are hefted down narrow stairways and loaded into car boots.

It makes me remember my own university days. I had expected a four-year slumber party full of sex, alcohol and soft drugs. Instead, I fell in love with a string of unattainable girls, who thought I was great fun to have around, but not very shaggable. They seemed to prefer rugby players or boys called Rupert whose parents had country estates. Normally all I could offer was my undying love and a bottle of warm Lambrusco Bianco.

Victoria Naparstek comes to mind, her shy eyes and over-wide mouth. I remember seeing the same gratitude in her eyes that I felt was in mine; an appreciation that she was there and that I hadn't completely embarrassed myself.

Parking outside the sports centre, I push through the double doors and hear the echo of basketballs rattling backboards. At the front counter, a woman is wearing a tracksuit on her thin frame and twenty years of sun damage around her eyes. I ask for Callum Loach.

She points through another set of doors. 'He'll be inside with the Ayatollah.'

'Sorry?'

'Theo. That's his old man.'

There are three basketball courts side by side, but only one is being used. Theo Loach is pacing the edge of the court. Yelling instructions, he ducks and weaves as though he's shadowboxing or playing the game from the bleachers. A Para tattoo on his right forearm has faded into a blue stain.

'Hey, Cal, watch for the quick break. That's it . . . cover him.'

I've never seen a wheelchair game of basketball. The speed surprises me. With a flick of forearms, competitors are hurtling up and down the court.

I recognise Callum from his photograph. He's sitting in a lightweight chair with wheels that are canted inwards and give the impression they're collapsing into his lap.

Theo yells, 'Good block! See who's open. That's it. Go . . . go!'

Nursing the ball on his lap, Callum pushes twice on the wheels and dribbles, leading a charge of pumping arms and blurring wheels.

'All the way!' shouts Theo.

Callum shoots and lands the basket, colliding with an opposing player and toppling sideways. The chair seems to roll 360 degrees and he flips it up again, laughing and high-fiving his teammates.

Theo rubs his hands together as if keeping them warm. Then he looks up.

'Can I help you?'

'I was hoping to speak to Callum.'

'Game's almost over.'

I take a seat on a bench and rest my jacket over one thigh. Theo is no longer paying as much attention to the action. Periodically, he glances my way until curiosity gets the better of him.

'I'm Cal's father. What's this about?'

'You've heard the news about Natasha McBain?'

'Sure.'

'I'm assisting the police in the investigation.'

'What's that got to do with Cal?'

I delay answering. The silence fills with a referee's whistle, a foul and a free throw. Theo's face is as round as a pie tin under a baseball cap. He takes a seat next to me, his knees creaking.

'We have a policy in our house that nobody mentions that girl's name.'

'Why's that?'

'Isn't it obvious?'

'Natasha didn't cripple Callum.'

Theo doesn't say anything. His gaze shifts and he studies cobwebs hanging from the lights. I notice his tattoo again.

'You were in the army.'

'Yeah.'

'See any action?'

'The Falklands.'

He licks his lips and drapes his hands over his thighs. 'You got children, Professor?'

'Two girls.'

'How old?'

'Fifteen and seven.'

He nods. 'We were only blessed the once. You read those stories about women popping out babies like they're Pez dispensers even though they can't afford to feed them. I'm not just talking about in Africa and poor countries. Look at the single mums in this place – never working, living off welfare, having three kids with as many different men. It's fucking criminal, you know.'

I don't answer.

Theo scratches his cheek with three fingers.

'Cal doesn't normally play in this league. He's part of the Olympic squad.'

'Congratulations.'

'It's going to be a big year for him.'

His eyes mist over. 'He used to play football. When he was twelve he was taken down to Arsenal to look around the Emirates Stadium and meet some of the players. There was talk of a contract.'

'What happened?'

'Becky didn't want him leaving home. Only child. You understand?'

'I do.'

'We had a few arguments but she was right. She let him go at sixteen. He was in their youth training squad. You should have seen him. So much speed and poise. He could ghost into positions like he was invisible, you know, and then pounce.' Theo takes a deep breath and then stares at his shoes. 'He was going to fly so high, that boy. But then some whackjob, rattling with pills, drives a car into him and takes off his legs. I can remember the day. I can tell you the time and place. You don't forget details like that. You don't forget how someone puts your boy in a wheelchair. Destroys his dreams.'

'I talked to Aiden Foster earlier.'

Theo nods and glances at the game.

'He's due out next year.'

'Yeah, well, he's done his time,' says Theo. 'They'll let him go and he'll have two good legs for the rest of his life. Won't matter. He's always going to be a deadbeat scumbag, a poster-child for losers.'

'Did you blame Natasha too?'

'She wasn't behind the wheel.'

'That's not an answer.'

He looks at me, holding a pocket of air in his cheeks. 'She

provided the drugs. She started the fight. What do you think? If that bitch hadn't . . . if she . . . my boy would . . .' He can't finish. 'Ah fuck it, I don't want to talk about this.'

For a long while he remains silent, watching the game, not concentrating.

'Aiden Foster never called. He didn't write a letter. He didn't say he was sorry. Wait, no, that's not true. His legal team came to us and wanted to organise a meeting between Cal and Aiden, a reconciliation, they said. They turned up with a TV crew. They wanted to film the whole thing, so they could show the judge and get Aiden a lesser sentence. Maybe if Aiden had showed up without the cameras. Maybe then I'd have believed him.'

The referee has blown time. Handshakes. High-fives. Callum rolls away from the circle, crossing the polished boards. A good-looking boy with shoulders like a butterfly swimmer, he has a flop of blond hair that he flicks back, showering the sprung floorboards with beads of sweat. He looks like he should be advertising Gatorade or appearing on a BBC sports quiz show or dating a hot-looking girl. Theo tosses him a towel. Callum chugs the contents of a water bottle, wiping his mouth, tossing the empty bottle into his kitbag. He misses.

'First one I've missed today,' he says, grinning.

'This is Joe O'Loughlin,' says Theo. 'He's working with the police. He wants to ask you about "you know who".'

'You can say her name, Dad.'

Callum shakes my hand. Apologises for the sweat.

'I told him you don't know squat,' says Theo.

'Why would anyone think I did?' asks Callum.

'That's what I told him. I said you didn't. I said you've got more important stuff to think about. That girl was nothing but trouble.'

'Don't talk about her like that, Dad. She's dead. What happened is in the past.'

Callum spins the chair to face me. 'What happened to her? I mean . . . where has she been all this time?'

245

'We don't know.'

'They must have some idea.'

'Do you have one?'

The pause extends a beat past comfortable. Callum shakes his head.

Theo tells him to put on a sweatshirt so he doesn't get cold.

'The Olympics – that's a big deal,' I say, noticing the British team logo on his kitbag.

'Yeah, it is.' He rocks backwards, balancing the chair on two wheels. 'It was my dad who suggested wheelchair basketball. He took me to see a game. I told him if I can't play on my feet, I don't want to play.'

'What changed your mind?'

He shrugs. 'Before this happened to me, playing sport came naturally. Football. Training. I didn't have to think. After my injury I became more self-conscious about my body and staying healthy. I started this to keep fit. Now it makes me happy. Earns me respect.'

'You must have regrets.'

'About what?'

'Being disabled.'

'I lost my legs. Now I have these.' He opens his kitbag and shows me two prosthetic limbs, skin-coloured and sculpted to look real. Trainers are laced to the feet.

'Who do you blame?' I ask.

'Do I have to blame someone?'

'Most people do.'

'Why?'

'It helps them come to terms with things.'

'You mean it gives them an excuse?'

'Maybe.'

He shakes his head. 'When I woke up in hospital and looked down at where my legs used to be, I went through that whole hard-nosed, why-me response. I denied it, grieved over it, screamed at the unfairness and wanted to crawl into a dark

246

hole. I did for a while. I hated Aiden Foster. I hated Natasha McBain. I hated everybody who was able-bodied and walking around on two legs.'

'What changed?'

He shrugs. 'Time passed. I stopped making excuses. Winners don't make excuses. When I'm on a basketball court, or staring at a flight of stairs – I don't make excuses. I find a way.'

Strapping on his legs, he tugs down his tracksuit pants then rubs a towel over his hair, drying the sweat. Theo has gone to get the car.

'If you see Mr and Mrs McBain – tell them I'm sorry for their loss. Tell them I didn't blame Natasha.'

'What about your father?'

He glances at the double doors and smiles sadly. 'Don't judge him too harshly. He shattered his knees in a skydiving accident and the army pensioned him off. The pain doesn't go away.'

'And your mum?'

'She left us years ago.'

'Did she leave *him* or you?'

'Does it make a difference?'

A car horn sounds from outside. Theo is waiting.

Balancing on his wheels, Callum spins his chair and rolls away, his shoulders flexing like a boxer throwing punches at a bag. He has to turn to move backwards through the swinging doors.

The woman at the front desk yells goodbye and a chorus of other voices wish him good luck. Callum grins and waves back, sitting up straight in his wheelchair – a man with useless legs trying to stand as tall as his dreams.

Once Tash got an idea in her head

she didn't let it go. Running away was her new project. Her eyes would light up from the inside when she made plans, talking about how we'd live in London and hang out with celebs.

Getting more and more excited, she'd spin sentences together each beginning with 'and then'.

'And then we'll find somewhere to live, not a squat, but somewhere nice in Fulham maybe, or Notting Hill. And then we'll get jobs. I could be an actress or a model. I don't mind getting my kit off. Just the top half like Katie Price, you know. Glamour shots. Lots of girls do that. They make loads.'

'I think you've got to be eighteen to be a glamour model,' I said.

'I look like I'm eighteen. I've got my fake ID.'

'Some of those photographers can be real sleazebags.'

'You'll come with me. We'll look after each other.'

'Won't they come looking for us if they see you on page three of the Sun?'

'They'll have stopped looking for us by then. You can divorce your parents, you know. It's, like, legal and everything. You just get a lawyer and he goes to court and asks a judge.

'We'll get invited to all the cool clubs, no queuing, straight to the front of the line. And then we'll buy our own place. I'm gonna have a circular bed and automatic blinds that go up and down and I'm going to be friends with David Beckham and David Tennant and that guy from the Arctic Monkeys whose name I can't remember.'

Tash had only been to London a few times, but she always sounded like an expert. She knew exactly where she wanted to live and how much it would cost and where all the celebrities lived. She was an expert on Katie Price, having read all her books and the magazine articles.

Our English teacher Miss McCrudden said that if Tash had studied her schoolbooks the way she read magazines she could be a genius. She was getting straight As anyway, so she couldn't really complain. I was the one who was dumber than a box of hair.

The only reason Lady Adolf was so nice to me is because Daddy organised for the school to get a cheap loan from his bank so they could build a new assembly hall. We had names for everyone at the school. The physics teacher Mr Fielding we called Mr Bean because he had this weird overbite and he drove a Mini. Miss Kane, the PE mistress, was called Miss Trunchbull because she used to be a javelin thrower. (If you haven't read Matilda, you won't know what that means.)

Everybody at school knew that Miss Trunchbull was having a fling with Mr Bean. We used to see them flirting with each other in the playground and Tash saw them kissing in the alcove near the assembly hall. That's when she came up with a cunning plan. She put a digital recorder on the windowsill of the PE staffroom. It was mid-July and the window was open.

Listening to the recording afterwards, you could easily hear what they were doing. Mr Bean, who has this lisp, was going, 'Oh, oh, yeth, yeth, yeth', while Miss Trunchbull was so loud we couldn't tell if she was getting shagged or tortured.

That should have been the end of it – a good laugh and no harm done – but then Miss Trunchbull made fun of Tash in PE class because she wouldn't do a cartwheel, saying she was a prima donna. Tash's period had started unexpectedly and her knickers were stained, which is why she wouldn't do the cartwheel.

After that Tash uploaded the audio onto a YouTube post which included photographs of Mr Bean and Miss Trunchbull taken from the school website.

I warned her. She wouldn't listen.

The school hired these computer geeks to track down the person who uploaded the files. Even though Tash took it down straight away, they still kept looking. It took them three days to find her and she was hauled into the headmistress's office where she took the blame.

Mr Bean was there, his face bunched in fury. 'Look at her eyes,' he said. 'She's high as a kite.'

Lady Adolf tut-tutted. 'Have you been taking drugs, Tash?'

'No.'

'You're lying.'

'I'm not.'

Denying a lie made it no less a lie, according to Lady Adolf. I remember wondering if admitting a truth would make it more of a truth.

She had made up her mind. Tash wasn't welcome at the school any more, she said.

Welcome? When was she ever welcome!

29

For the past three hours I've been reading Piper's stories and poems. Her handwriting is full of loops and swirls, punctuated by drawings, doodles and emoticons. At times I feel like I'm eavesdropping on my own daughter's life, yet I don't feel guilty. Maybe I'll learn something. Understand more.

Most of the entries are undated, but I can see how they grew messier and more secretive in the months before she disappeared. There are code words that I don't understand and nicknames for people. One of her teachers is 'Mr Bean' and another 'Miss Trunchbull'.

She writes letters to herself and to her parents, a lot of them full of angst and anger.

Dear beautiful Daddy and the ice maiden,
By the time you find this letter I will be gone.
Maybe I'll have killed myself. Maybe I'm too
hopeless to do that properly. I mess everything
else up. Either way, I'll no longer be your
problem. You should be happy now, Mum. You'll
have a perfect daughter in Phoebe and a

beautiful little boy and the ugly one will no longer mess up the family photographs or get in the way.

I used to think I was adopted. I still do. Then you had a proper baby and realised that I didn't fit in with your perfect family. Maybe you should have given me back to the agency when you had the chance.

I think it's best you forget me. Please look after Phoebe and Ben. Tell them I love them.

I am sorry but goodbye.

As always,

Piper.

Another journal entry begins on Piper's fourteenth birthday, after what she describes as 'the worst year of my life'.

Sometimes I feel that there is no point my living if I'm not going to be anyone. I'd hate so much to be just an ordinary nobody. I can't imagine having a quiet life and then fading away, not to be remembered. The other day I read this: 'You're not a child any more when you have discovered that childhood is the best time of your life.'

If that's true then pass me the razor blades.

Reading more of the pages, I discover Piper's likes and dislikes. Favourite films. Worst fashion crimes (gypsy skirts and black mesh vests). Coolest bands. Possible careers. 'Reasons to hate my mother'. 'Why little sisters should be boiled in oil'. Occasionally I laugh out loud at some of her observations – a bad haircut makes her look like 'a startled hamster', while some boy she met at junior athletics has 'an IQ two points lower than a rock'.

Wedged in the pages of one journal I find a strip of

passport-sized photographs. Piper and Tash are sitting on each other's laps in a photo booth, pulling faces at the camera, laughing behind smears of crimson lipstick.

It's the only photograph that I've seen of Piper in which she doesn't look self-conscious. Instead, she's relaxed and revelling in the moment, completely happy.

Glancing at the pile of journals, I'm still no closer to uncovering her secret life. Condoms were found in Tash's room, along with two cannabis cigarettes. She had older boyfriends and was sexually active. She went to parties and dabbled in drugs. Piper knew these things, but didn't write about them.

Villages like Bingham are often deceptive. Viewed as rural idylls and perfect places to raise families. People get nostalgic about them, harking back to bygone days, imagining a world of picket fences, corner pubs and village bobbies.

The reality is sometimes very different. Bigger towns expand, swallowing up villages, turning them into satellite suburbs or commuter belts. Areas become run down. Pockets of poverty emerge. Unemployment. Domestic violence. Boredom.

Teenagers feel it most. Too young to drink or to drive, without cinemas, shops or youth centres, they find other amusements, crashing parties and experimenting with sex, soft drugs and alcohol. Young girls like Natasha are drawn to older men. Boys their own age are slower, shyer, less worldly, whereas older men have cars and money to splash around on restaurants and nice clothes. The girls are excited by the fact that a grown man might be interested in them, but are too young to understand the danger of stoking a man's desire.

At some point I fall asleep fully clothed, a journal open on my chest. A phone enters my dreams. My mobile. Buzzing. A name on the screen: Victoria Naparstek.

She speaks before I can utter a word, yelling down the line. 'Please, please help me! They're outside!'

I can hear shouting in the background.

'Where are you?'

'At Augie's house . . . there are people outside . . . they want to kill him. They're saying they're going to burn him out.'

'Where are the police?'

'I called them.'

'What about Augie?'

'He's here . . . with his mother. They're scared. *I'm* scared.'

'Are the doors and windows locked?'

'Yes.'

'OK, stay away from them. I'm coming.'

Ruiz isn't answering his phone. I leave a voicemail and juggle my shoes and socks as I run for the lift, taking it downstairs. The streets are deserted. Christmas lights twinkle and blink from shop windows and behind net curtains.

Jumping red lights at empty intersections and swerving around trucks gritting the roads, I reach the house in less than fifteen minutes. There must be fifty people outside, spilling across the footpath and grass verge onto the normally quiet street. More cars are arriving.

A dozen police officers are lined up in front of the two-storey house. Outnumbered. Nervous. They're yelling at people to go home but the protest has already gained too much momentum. Hayden McBain is at the centre of the crowd. His uncle is at his shoulder.

'He's a child-killer,' yells Vic McBain. 'And we don't want him here! There are kiddies in this street. We don't want that evil pervert touching them. This is our town. These are our kids.'

The crowd punctuate each statement with a cheer and then begin to chant.

'Scum! Scum! Scum! SCUM!'

Fighting my way to the front, I recognise one of the constables. Yelling above the noise.

'Where are the rest of the police?'

'They're coming.'

'Can I go inside?'

He nods and opens the gate. Victoria answers the door and closes it quickly. Relief in her hug. Fear. I glance along the hallway and see Augie, peering from the kitchen, half hidden behind the door frame. His mother is next to him, wearing her dressing gown, her hair unbrushed and skin looking almost jaundiced.

'Is everyone OK?'

They nod.

Augie has his mother's dark solemn eyes but his gaze, even at its steadiest, keeps pulling distractedly to one side. His hands are no longer bandaged, but the skin looks pink and painful, smothered in cream.

From outside the chants are growing louder. Going to the front room, I open the curtain a crack. More police have arrived, linking arms to form a human chain, but they're easily outnumbered. A bottle explodes on the tarmac, scattering diamonds of green glass.

Joining the others in the kitchen, I try to calm their nerves. 'How about a cup of tea.'

Victoria fills the kettle.

'Why can't they just leave us alone?' asks Mrs Shaw.

'They're angry at me,' says Augie.

Victoria shakes her head. 'It's not your fault.'

'Whose fault is it?'

'You should never have gone to that farmhouse,' says his mother. 'You should have stayed away from those people.'

Tightening her robe, she looks through the pantry, trying to find a packet of biscuits. 'I know I had some,' she says. And then to Augie, 'Did you eat the biscuits?'

He lowers his head.

More police have arrived, but so have more protesters. Bottles and bricks are being thrown. Bodies forced back. Regrouping. Coming again. Each chant of 'scum' makes Augie flinch. He presses his hands to his ears, trying to block the sound. He whispers in a little boy voice, 'It's my fault. I couldn't save them.'

'Who couldn't you save?' I ask.

'All of them.' He puts his finger to his forehead, corkscrewing it as if drilling into his skull. 'I couldn't save Mrs Heyman from the fire. I couldn't save my brother. I couldn't save the girl.'

'Natasha?'

'The snowman took her.'

'Why do you call him the snowman?'

'He was made of snow.'

A window smashes in the front room. Mrs Shaw screams. Almost simultaneously, glass shatters upstairs. Bricks and bottles are landing against the house.

'Everyone stay here,' I say.

Crouching, I run along the hallway to the front room. The curtains are billowing. Broken glass glitters on the carpet. I move to the window and glance outside. The police have surrendered ground under a hail of missiles.

Bottles and bricks are bouncing off parked cars, occasionally finding windows. A police van made it halfway down the street before being abandoned. Rioters are rocking it from side to side, creating momentum. It topples. Metal on tarmac. The mob cheers.

A rock cannons against the window frame above my head. Another shatters a picture in a frame on the mantelpiece.

Crawling to the entrance hall, I press my ear against the front door. I can hear a policeman outside, radioing for help, sounding desperate. I open the door a crack. Blood streams from a split on the bridge of his nose, running across his lips.

'Stay in the house, sir,' he orders.

I see his head snap back as a half-brick hits him flush in the face. He goes down, his helmet rolling across the steps. At that same moment, I see a flash of yellow and hear it smash as it lands. A *whump* sound fills the front room. Petrol igniting. Flames. Light.

'There's a fire!' screams Mrs Shaw.

'Stay in the kitchen,' I yell back.

Retreating down the hallway, closing the doors, I reach the kitchen. I look out the window and notice a gate at the rear of the yard.

'Where does it lead?'

Mrs Shaw looks confused for a moment. 'There's a lane. It runs behind the houses to Lovett Road.'

'Where's Augie?'

'I thought he was with you.'

'No.'

'He must be upstairs.'

'I'll get him. You go. Take your coats. Call the fire brigade when you get to the lane.'

'I'm not leaving without Augie,' says his mother.

'I'll get him.'

Covering my mouth and nose, I climb the stairs two at a time. There are three rooms upstairs, two of them bedrooms, crammed with too much furniture. I call Augie's name. No answer. I can't see him.

Walking around the beds, stepping over clothes, I glance out a broken window at the street. A phalanx of police wearing helmets and black body armour are marching from the northern end. Reinforcements. They're pushing the crowd back, clearing the street like a human bulldozer. Behind them the road is littered with shattered bricks and broken glass. The police van is burning.

I can't find Augie. I search the wardrobes and peer under the beds. He's not here. The smoke is getting thicker and my eyes are streaming. I crawl across the landing, bumping my head against the wall. My fingers find the skirting board and I feel my way towards the bathroom.

By touch, I find the sink and turn on a tap, washing out my eyes. I manage to open the window a few inches and press my face to the gap, sucking in fresh air. Turning back, I notice a dark shape to my right. Augie is sitting in the bath, his arms wrapped around his knees.

I grab his arm. Shouting. 'We have to get out.'

He looks at me. Tears stain his cheeks.

'Come with me.'

He pushes my hand away.

'You can't stay here. We have to go.'

'I can't,' he says, pointing to his ankle bracelet. 'The judge said I couldn't leave the house.'

'This is different. You're allowed.'

'But they'll kill me outside.'

There is a whooshing sound from below. Flames sweep across the ceiling of the entry hall. Wood crackles and burns. The window won't open far enough for us to get out. I can't carry Augie and he won't come with me. He's too frightened.

I can't leave him here and I can't stay.

Turning on a tap, I wet a towel and drape it over his head. 'Stay here, I'll get help.'

He doesn't answer.

I wet a second towel and cover my head. On my hands and knees, I reach the top of the stairs. Face first, I slide down the steps, losing control, landing on my shoulder and rolling. The burning ceiling twirls and dips.

I'm breathing more smoke than oxygen. Blindly, I try to reach the kitchen, but everything has slowed down. I keep hitting my head on the wall. I can't find the door. It's dark. Poisonous. Hot.

Curling up on the floor, I place my lips against the carpet, trying to find clean air. If I could just get one lungful, I could keep going. I can feel the heat on the back of my legs.

Wood splinters and the air pressure changes. The fire feeds on the oxygen and bursts through the door of the front room. Strong hands grab me, lifting me, carrying me along the hallway. I try to help, but can't support my own weight.

My legs are bumping down the steps. I feel soft earth beneath me. Fresh air. I'm dragged across the garden and rolled onto my back. Coughing. Sucking in air. I can't open my eyes, but I recognise Ruiz's voice.

'Is there anyone else inside?'

I nod, but can't speak. Another question, a different voice. Grievous is with him. I point upstairs. Every window at the rear of the house is lit up by fire. Firemen appear from the laneway, dragging hoses through the gate. The detective constable yells at them. 'There's someone still inside. Upstairs.'

The fireman nods and uses his radio, calling for breathing apparatus. Flames are spilling from windows, licking at the eaves. Ruiz helps me to stand. I don't want to leave. I reach out towards Grievous, wanting to thank him, but he's already gone, issuing commands, growing in stature.

Ruiz walks me along the lane past the fire engines and police cars. In the darkness I can't see the smoke, but an orange glow is silhouetting the rooftops and the sparks look like bloated fireflies rising on the heated air.

The crowd has gone silent. No longer hurling missiles, they watch the blaze like children around a bonfire, cheeks glowing, light dancing in their eyes, energy draining away.

One group of young men is loitering on the far side of the street, swigging from cans of lager. Two of them I recognise: Toby Kroger and Craig Gould. Kroger sees me and raises his drink in a grinning toast. Nelson Stokes is another spectator, gazing at the fire as though he expected something more impressive and shouldn't have bothered coming out.

Ruiz is still with me.

'How did you know?' I ask.

'I got your message. I came as soon as I could. Your girlfriend told me you were still inside the house.'

'Thank you.'

'I guess we're even.'

How does it make us even?'

'You'll save my life one day.'

Victoria Naparstek is sitting in a police car with the door open and a grey blanket wrapped around her shoulders.

She looks relieved and then searches the road behind me. 'Where's Augie?'

'He wouldn't come out. I tried. I'm sorry.'

Her first reaction is anger, then hurt, then sadness. She walks into my arms, resting her head against my chest, wiping her nose with the corner of the blanket.

'They killed him,' she whispers, barely making a sound.

This is how I wake,

sliding warily out of sleep, listening for every sound, watching the shadows. He crept up on me last time, caught me by surprise. I won't let it happen again.

Squatting, pants around my knees, I listen to the tinkling in the bedpan beneath me, gazing at the dull white square of the window. Quiet. No birdsong.

Afterwards, I climb on the bench and look at the pale nude sky.

I wonder if George will come today. Until Tash left, I didn't consider the idea that I was lonely. Now it's driving me crazy. I can handle the hunger and the cold, but not this. I need George. Next time I'll be nicer to him and he'll bring me food and more gas and warmer blankets. If I'm nice to him, he'll let me wash and give me clean clothes.

I know what he wants and I don't care any more. He can stab me with his filthy penis. He can kiss me with his slimy tongue. I just want to know he's coming back. I want to talk to someone. I don't want to die down here alone.

I've tried to use the walkie-talkie but I think it's broken or the batteries are dead. I took them out and put them back in again, but it didn't make any difference. The eye is still peering from the ceiling but I don't know if it's turned on or if George is watching. I've begged him to come back, but nothing happened.

It's cold. I pull on three layers of clothes and go to the gas burner. It's empty. The tap is frozen. I'll have to wait. The pipes will thaw when it warms up outside.

When I'm hungry like this I think about home. I think about cottage pie and baked pears. Phoebe. Ben. I used to be able to describe The Old Vicarage down to the last detail, every crack and creak and wobbly window, but over time I've started to forget things.

If I concentrate really hard, I can imagine throwing rocks into the pond and hear them land with a satisfying plonk before muddy bubbles break the surface. Then I can hear my mother calling me inside for breakfast but I keep standing in the garden, not wanting to leave, watching the first rays of sunshine reach across the lawn towards the greenhouse.

Phoebe will be up early. She's a morning person, always buzzing and chatting, treating each day like the start of a new adventure. If it's Saturday morning she'll watch TV, curled up on the sofa, creating a fort of pillows around her. She'll get Ben breakfast because he gets hungry before Mum and Dad get up.

I have a new baby sister. I don't know her name. George didn't tell me what they called her. I can't remember much about Phoebe being a baby, but Ben came along when I was twelve. I saw him at the hospital, lying in a cot in the maternity ward. I thought he looked like Gollum from Lord of the Rings.

There's a sound above me. Boxes are being moved. For a fleeting second, I'm hoping that Tash has come back, but then I hear his voice.

'Honey, I'm home,' he sings from the far side of the trapdoor.

My bowels seem to liquefy. Stupid, stupid, stupid me! I wanted him to come. I prayed for it. Now I would take it back. I would take it back a million times.

The trapdoor opens. His face appears.

'Are you ready?'

I draw back, shaking my head, waiting.

'I heard you asking for me.'

'Where's Tash?'

'I have food.'

'I want to see her.'

'Forget about her. She's being punished. If you're good to me, I'll let you talk to her. Come on. Climb up. That's it. Raise your arms. One, two, three, upsy daisy.'

30

The paramedics have flushed out my eyes and checked my lungs. Victoria Naparstek has waited for me, sitting in silence in a police car, lost in her own thoughts.

DCI Drury steps over the hoses and shakes water from the shoulders of his coat, pausing to study the house. The front two or three rooms have been completely gutted but the main structure is intact.

Avoiding a fountain of spray, he finds the senior fire officer, who is uncoupling the harness and lifting his tank onto the back of a truck. The fire chief has thick sideburns that make him look like the circus ringmaster. He takes off his helmet and wipes soot from his forehead, smudging it into a dark stain beneath his fringe.

'There's a body in the upstairs bathroom. Young. Male. Tag on his ankle.'

Drury grimaces as though acid reflux is scalding his oeso-phagus. He swallows and turns away, striding back towards the police lines. Ignoring the spray, oblivious to it, he yells instruc-tions to DS Casey.

'Get these people away from here. Call SOCO. Secure the scene.'

'We don't have the personnel,' says Casey.

'Wake them up.'

Drury notices me. One eyebrow arches. 'What happened to you?'

'I was inside. Grievous and Ruiz pulled me out.'

'What were you doing here?'

'She called me.'

He turns his head and recognises Victoria Naparstek. Something softens in his eyes and he draws forward, crouching beside the open car door, talking to her softly. Ash smudges her right cheek. He reaches to wipe it away. She pushes his hand away. Trembling.

'I'm sorry,' he says. 'We should have had more officers . . . nobody expected this.'

Victoria looks hard into his eyes, testing his honesty.

'Who started the fire?' asks Drury.

'I don't know.'

'Did it start inside or outside?'

'Something was thrown through the window. They wanted to kill him.'

Shakily, Drury stands, stiff-kneed, joints creaking like armour. He stares at the house for a moment and then turns to Casey.

'Get a warrant.'

'Who are we arresting?'

'Hayden and Victor McBain.'

Victoria Naparstek lets me drive her home. We stop halfway because she wants to be sick. The fresh air makes her feel better. We walk in silence along the river, the mist shrouding the far bank where canal boats are groaning against their lines.

Her shoulder brushes mine. I can still see the smudge of ash on her right cheek. Drury had tried to wipe it away. It was a gesture of intimacy, accompanied by something vague and bright in his eyes, a painful rapture.

I should have seen it earlier. The clues. Drury had looked

like a married man in the midst of an affair. Victoria acted like a woman trying to escape from one. I understand now why she wouldn't go to the DCI's house. She didn't want to see his wife and children. That's why she reacted so angrily towards him at the police station and again at the hospital. She expected more from the DCI because she had given so much of herself.

I am not surprised. I don't disapprove. Who am I to judge? Had I asked for honesty? No. The truth is an overrated quality. Lies make a dull world more interesting. They take things in unexpected directions. They add complications and layers of texture.

Victoria tugs the collar of her coat more tightly around her.

'How did you and Drury meet?' I ask.

She is silent for a long time. 'I did a psychiatric report for a defendant and gave evidence at the trial. It was Stephen's case. He won. He took me for a drink afterwards. One thing led to another.'

Another silence, longer this time.

'Are you in love with him?'

'No.'

'Is he in love with you?'

'He says he is.'

'And now you feel trapped.'

She looks up at me and back at the river. 'Pretty much.'

The wind is buffeting her, pushing her coat against her body and shaking her hair. We've reached a turn in the path. There is a pub ahead with closed shutters and Christmas lights blinking around the door. I push against her and kiss her clumsily, my hand slipping inside her coat to find her breast.

Her mouth tastes of smoke and something yeasty and exciting. It's the sort of kiss I would have taken for granted a few years ago – deep and unhurried – but now it feels like a rare gift. Pushing me away gently, Victoria looks past my shoulder and I have a sensation that she can see someone behind me, watching us from the shadows. It's that same impression that I often get with her; that she's dreamily preoccupied or looking for something other than me.

'We had sex,' she says. 'It wasn't a good idea.'

'Why not?'

'There was always a conflict of interest. You are evaluating one of my patients. It could be misconstrued . . .'

'The sex?'

'Yes.'

'I know it wasn't earth-moving. Nobody is going to write poetry about it or paint a mural, but I'd be happy to do it again.'

She laughs. 'You're a wonderful man, Joe. Far better than you give yourself credit for.'

'And?'

'You have no idea what you're getting yourself into.'

I feel like saying, I'm the one with the disease.

We each exhale, our breath condensing and combining in a single cloud.

Behind her, I notice a deserted bus stop and I remember Natasha and Piper. They were supposed to meet Emily that Sunday morning, but disappeared somewhere between Natasha's house and Radley Station, a distance of half a mile, mostly along the edge of fields and on footpaths.

I try to picture the scene again, but I can't get a fix on the girls. I have been to their houses, I have learned about their personalities, but I cannot picture them making that journey.

Almost in the same breath, I taste something different in my mouth.

'They were never there,' I say out loud.

'What?'

'The girls were never there.'

'Are you all right?'

'No. There's someone I need to see.'

'It's three in the morning.'

266

'I know.'

We walk quickly back to the car. Reversing and doing a U-turn, I head towards Abingdon, following the white lines, floating over humps. The hedgerows turn to tarnished silver in the headlights and the countryside rushes to meet us. Twenty minutes later we pull up outside the familiar pebble-creted house. There are three police cars parked on the street. The doors are open. Lights flashing. Two detectives escort Hayden McBain from the house. He is handcuffed and smiling, his teeth bleached white by the spotlights.

Alice McBain is yelling at them. 'Get your hands off my boy! He's done nothing wrong!' Her eyes are smeared and splintery with tears.

Drury steps in front of her. 'Bag his clothes. Search the house.'

Elsewhere in the street, porch lights have blinked on and curtains are twitching.

DS Casey is standing at the open car door. He pushes at the top of Hayden's head. The door closes. Locks.

Crossing the lawn, emerging through a gap in the hedge, I feel as though I'm stepping onto a brightly lit stage. Mrs McBain doesn't recognise me at first. She tries to step around me.

'Did you see the girls that morning?' I ask her. It sounds like an accusation.

Alice flashes me a look and goes back to worrying about Hayden, who is being driven away.

I try again. 'You said you talked to Piper and Natasha on that Sunday morning. You knocked on Natasha's door and told them to get out of bed.'

'So what?'

'Did you see them?'

'Of course I did,' she says, less sure this time.

'Did you open the bedroom door?'

Alice frowns, trying to remember.

'How do you know they were in the bedroom?'

'I knocked. They answered.'

267

'Who answered?'

'I don't remember,' she says, annoyed wth herself..

I can almost see her mind working, the nerves fizzing and popping under her skin.

'What did you hear?' I ask.

'They were playing music.'

'Did Natasha have a radio alarm?'

'Yes.'

'What time did she set the alarm for?'

'Seven-thirty.'

'You knocked on the door at seven-forty, but you didn't open it. What if you heard the radio and not the girls?'

Alice squints at me, unsure if I'm trying to trap her. She wants to argue. She tries to think. She comes back empty.

Drury is next to her. 'What's this about?'

'It changes everything,' I say. 'What if the girls weren't at the house on Sunday morning? Alice didn't see them. She heard the radio alarm.'

'You're saying they didn't go home.'

'They went missing the night before.'

He pulls me close to him,

his unshaven cheek brushing against my forehead.

'You're like an ice block. Let's warm you up.'

One hand takes hold of my hair like it's a piece of rope and his other hand slides down to the bottom of my spine.

'Mmmm,' he says. 'You're a lovely one for hugging.'

He wraps a blanket around me and points me towards the open door. My bare feet make little slapping sounds on the floor as I walk. I know he's a step behind me. I still haven't looked at his face, his eyes.

A bath has been drawn. Water steaming. Clothes set out.

I taste copper in my mouth and wonder if I've bitten my tongue.

'I'm hungry.'

'This time you eat afterwards.'

He's humming to himself, fussing over the towels. I undress and slip beneath the water, leaning my head against the bath. I can feel his gaze drifting over me, dismantling my body as though dissecting it with a knife. Cutting me into little pieces.

I am going to be nice to him. I am going to moan and tell him how good he makes me feel. If I'm nice to him, he'll let me see Tash. We'll be together again and I'll look after her. If I'm nice to him, he'll let his guard slip and I'll find a way of getting out of here.

He calls me his 'poor defective monkey' as he washes me. I don't feel his hands.

After the bath I let him rape me. Is it even rape if I let him do it?

He breaks my hymen. I bleed. I look at his face when he ejaculates and he doesn't look human. It twists and grimaces and looks like a rubber mask.

269

Afterwards, he lets me eat. Satay sticks of chicken and beef. This time I eat more slowly, sore between my legs. My cup of tea is on the table with a swollen brown bag submerged in it, growing cold.

How calm he seems. How little difference it makes. He sits there, staring at me, sipping his tea as though nothing has happened.

'Can I see Tash now?'

'No.'

'You told me I could see her.'

'Not yet.'

I feel like crying. 'You lied to me.'

'She needs a few more days.'

'I did what you asked.'

He laughs sarcastically and I stare at him with narrowed eyes. This is a mistake. I am aware of his temper, how easily he could injure me. The sensation creeps along my spine like a spider crawling on bare skin.

Afterwards, he falls asleep next to me, chained to my ankle. I look at his white cheesy body asleep on its back and listen to the wet gurgling in his throat. His right arm hangs down over the side of the mattress and his left hand is touching my thigh.

I do not sleep. I want to be awake. I want to put my hand over his mouth and nose until he stops breathing. I want to drive a knife into his heart. For the moment, I lie still next to him, listening to him gurgle, thinking how fear is different when it's real. I used to love those fairground rides that take you higher and drop you faster, but that was a fear that came wrapped in pleasure. This sort of fear has no upside or happy ending.

He's awake now. Stretching. I force myself to snuggle up against him. His breath smells like sour milk.

He strokes my cheek. 'You missed me?'

'You were away so long . . . I got frightened.'

This pleases him.

'Can't I come with you? I won't try to run away.'

'That's not possible, my little monkey.'

I ask about Tash. Is she close? When can I see her?

His mood suddenly changes. It's like flicking a switch. He slaps my face, knocking my head against the wall. He raises his hand again, showing me his palm, challenging me, daring me.

'Forget about her.'

'I'm lonely.'

'I'll find you another friend.'

'What?'

'Someone to keep you company, eh?'

My mind suddenly stops. Is he suggesting what I think?

'No . . . who?'

'I can find someone.'

'No! No! Please don't!'

He takes a photograph from his wallet. 'How about if I bring her?'

My throat closes. It's a picture of Emily. I have seen it before. We were mucking around in a photo booth at Oxford Station, pulling funny faces.

'She's your friend?'

'No!'

'You wrote a letter to her.'

'I don't want a friend.'

Even as the words come out of my mouth, I know a part of me isn't convinced. I want someone to talk to. I don't want to be alone. I push the thoughts away. Horrified. Hating myself.

'I just want to see Tash. Nobody else,' *I say.*

'That's not possible. She's still being punished.'

He takes me back to the trapdoor and kisses me. Then he lowers me down until my feet touch the ladder.

'If you want a friend, I promise I will get you one.'

'No. Please let Tash come back.'

The trapdoor is closing.

'That I can't promise.'

31

It's been sixteen hours since the fire. I slept through most of them, waking to more snow, which has bleached the pavements and parks, dipping the world in white. The newspapers are full of headlines about mob justice and public lynching.

Ironically, for perhaps the first time in his life, Augie Shaw has become a sympathetic figure, a victim not a villain. The police are to blame according to the *Guardian*. They took too long to react. The *Daily Mail* says Augie Shaw should never have been granted bail; the judge was clearly out of touch or deranged.

Putting aside the newspapers, I arrange a dozen photographs around the hotel room, propping them on chairs and the TV cabinet. I take a seat in the middle of the room, directly in front of an image of Natasha and Piper sitting side by side in a class photograph, light and dark, blonde and brunette, salt and pepper.

Radiating an odd mixture of vulnerability and sensuality, Natasha has a classical beauty. Piper, by comparison, looks almost boyish and angular.

I am beginning to understand this crime. The details have

been floating just out of reach, but are now falling into place. The person responsible is no longer a figment. No longer a mystery. No longer a part of my imagining. I can see the world through his eyes; hear what he hears.

He's a collector. He enjoys owning things, rare objects, valuable artefacts, things he's been denied in the past. Some collectors fall in love with great works of art. A few arrange to have them stolen to order, knowing they can never hope to resell such a famous artwork or put it on public display. That doesn't matter. It is about possession not largesse; owning something unattainable and bathing in the brightness of its perfection.

He's an aesthete, who craves control and order in a disordered world. A man of strong discipline, trained to reason and compute, yet he has no moral base. He doesn't believe he is bound by the same rules as other people but is willing to abide by the law because it helps him conceal his desires. Others wouldn't understand what it feels like to 'own' something, to have complete control over another human being – life, death, light, darkness, warmth, cold and sustenance.

What causes this yearning? Where does it begin? A powerless childhood, a chaotic past, impossible expectations; it could be any number of things, but along the way he developed a sense of entitlement or an anger at being denied his right.

Closing my eyes, I try to picture him, not his face, but his mind. There you are! I see you now! You're a clever thief, bold as brass; you snatched two teenage girls who had known each other since infanthood – same hospital, same primary school, same classes. You planned this in advance, first in your fantasies, then adding elements from the real world.

But why choose these girls? Surely a prostitute would have suited your purposes. Easier to acquire, more anonymous than most, prostitutes are always disappearing but they rarely earn headlines or have a nation on alert. Missing schoolgirls aren't forgotten. They're cherished and prayed for and expected home.

You chose Piper and Natasha because they meant something to you, or represented someone. Possession and ownership, that's how it began, but later the motive changed. Perhaps the lustre wore off. You grew bored, or the girls weren't as compliant as you wished. The reality was never going to match up to your fantasies.

That's when you discovered another form of control. Punishment. Inflicting pain. Look what you did to Tash. What more intimate example is there of punishing a woman than to deny her something that makes her a woman? You removed her clitoris. You denied her sexual gratification. She might still be a sex object, but would never enjoy sex in the same way.

You expected to be horrified . . . to feel guilt or remorse, but it didn't happen. Instead, it was the purest of joys because you had never known anything so intimate or invasive or final. It was the most inspiring and fulfilling moment of your life.

Now you've lost one of your possessions. Tash managed to escape and almost get home. She would have unmasked you and destroyed your elaborate secret life.

You'll be chastened. You'll go to ground for a while. If Piper is still alive she is alone, more vulnerable than ever. The closer we get to you, the greater danger she'll face. You'll protect yourself by removing all trace of her.

Taking a notebook, I begin jotting down bullet points.

- *Mid-thirties to late fifties.*
- *Above average intelligence.*
- *He will live alone or with an ageing relative or a subservient wife – some form of domestic arrangement where nobody will question his movements or unexplained absences.*
- *Tertiary qualifications or training that requires discipline and accuracy.*
- *Knowledge of the area. (The girls disappeared quickly.)*
- *Knowledge of the victims. (He chose them for a reason.)*

- *He doesn't see himself as a monster. He deserves this. This is his reward.*
- *In the beginning he focused on interaction with the girls, but he has become a sadist.*
- *He craves order in a disordered world, but is constantly being disappointed because nothing and nobody matches up to his high expectations.*
- *He is forensically aware. Careful. Practised.*

The cab drops me at Abingdon Police Station. DCI Drury is in the CCTV control room. He hasn't been home. Rings of perspiration stain his armpits and his body odour follows him like a noxious cloud. Hayden McBain and his uncle are being held in separate cells. Left to sweat or to cool off.

The control room has six TV screens and a console that looks like something from an episode of *Star Trek*. Attention is focused on one screen: forty-four seconds of grainy black and white footage showing a man siphoning petrol from a parked car. He's wearing a hooded sweatshirt and a baseball cap.

The spiky-haired operator adjusts the controls. 'The camera is only four blocks away from the house.'

'I can't see his face,' says Drury.

'There aren't enough pixels. Pull it up any further, you lose quality.'

'Can you try?'

The operator adjusts the brightness and contrast.

Drury turns to me. 'Is that Hayden McBain?'

'Could be anyone.'

'Christ, what a mess!'

Drury's team has gathered upstairs for a briefing. Sleep-stung, nursing cups of takeaway coffee, many of them I now recognise, although I don't know their names. A female DS introduces herself. Karen Middleton. She has wide-apart eyes and too much make-up.

Grievous is cleaning the whiteboard and making sure the marker pens have matching lids. He has taken a shine to Ruiz and the two of them have matching extra-large cups of coffee.

Ruiz raises his cup to Drury. 'Morning, Columbo.'

'You're not as funny as you look.'

Ruiz grins. 'Day's still early. Wait till the caffeine kicks in. I'm a certified barrel of laughs.'

Drury enters the circle of detectives, shrugging off his jacket and rolling up his sleeves. The symbolism isn't missed or necessary. Around him, detectives are perched on the edge of desks and sitting backwards on chairs.

'You all know what happened last night,' says Drury. 'We now have another death to investigate.'

'You must be joking,' mutters one of the sergeants.

The DCI turns his head slowly. 'You see me laughing, DS?'

'No, boss.'

'A man was killed last night. A crime was committed.'

'Yes, boss.'

'That crime has to be investigated. If you don't want to do your job, you can fuck off now.'

'Yes, boss.'

The briefing continues with Drury breaking the task force into teams. A dozen detectives will investigate the riot and the fire. The rest are to review the original investigation into the Bingham Girls, based on a new timeline.

'We now believe the girls may have disappeared on Saturday night instead of Sunday morning. That means rechecking alibis, interviewing suspects and studying photographs for the Bingham Summer Festival.

'I want the new time frame run through the computer database. Let's see what HOLMES2 comes up with. Where did they go on Saturday night? Who did they talk to? Who saw them?'

Chief Constable Fryer appears in the incident room, wearing

his full dress uniform, peeling off leather gloves, a big man, full of confidence, on a mission.

Detectives find their feet. Fryer only has eyes for Drury.

'Your office. Now!'

The chief constable notices Ruiz and pauses. 'Vincent?'

'Thomas.'

'You've grown fat.'

'No fatter than you.'

The two men stare at each other.

'We should have a beer,' says Fryer, turning and striding towards Drury's office. He slams the door with such force it bounces open again, allowing everyone to hear his contained fury.

'What in fuck's name were you thinking arresting Hayden McBain? Have you heard the radio? They're crucifying us. They're saying we arrested the grieving brother of a murder victim – a teenage girl we took three years to find. Do you see how it looks?'

The DCI tries to hold his ground. 'With all due respect, sir, we can't let a mob rule the streets. Augie Shaw is dead. Someone threw a petrol bomb through his front window.'

'Someone? You don't know who?'

'McBain and his uncle incited the riot. We have witnesses. He doesn't have the right to take the law into his own hands.'

'Don't tell me about his rights, Detective.' Fryer drops his voice. 'Did Augie Shaw have an opportunity to escape from the house?'

'Yes, sir.'

'So he was complicit in his own death.'

'He didn't start the fire.'

'I accept that, DCI, but answer me this: do you believe Augie Shaw killed the Heymans?'

'Yes, sir.'

'Did he kidnap Natasha McBain?'

'Quite possibly, sir.'

'Augie Shaw could be the answer to your prayers, Stephen.

Wrap this up. Close the file on the Heymans and let the coroner decide what happened to Natasha McBain.'

I knock on the open door. 'You're making a mistake. Augie Shaw didn't kidnap the Bingham Girls.'

Fryer's face reddens. 'And you know that for certain?'

'It was someone older, more experienced. Someone with knowledge of the case.'

'What knowledge?'

'Police didn't publicise the fact that Emily Martinez waited for the girls on Sunday morning. Whoever took the girls knew this, which means it had to be someone close to the families or close to the investigation.'

Fryer waves his gloves dismissively. 'That's a big call from someone who's only been here for a few days. This case has been the subject of two police investigations and a judicial inquiry.'

'If you close the file you're giving up on Piper Hadley.'

'I've kept an open mind on this, Professor, but there isn't one piece of credible evidence to suggest that Piper is still alive. If she escaped with Natasha McBain, we'd have found her by now. If she didn't, the question is why? My guess is that she's dead. She died three years ago or some time between now and then.'

'You don't know that.'

'In all fairness, Professor, neither do you.' His voice softens. 'You're the sort of poker player who doubles down because you're losing badly and you think that's the way to catch up. It's not. You double down when you're winning, not losing. Trust me. Walk away.'

The chief constable turns to Drury. 'What's your plan of action?'

'I've organised a media conference with the Hadleys. In the meantime we're doing another search of the area, checking alibis and re-interviewing witnesses. If nothing comes up, I'll scale the investigation down for Christmas and prepare a file for the coroner.'

Fryer nods approvingly. 'Covering the spread. Wise move.'

32

Ruiz joins me in the lift and we ride down together in silence. My medication is wearing off. I can feel the other 'man' waking inside me, ready to dance like a drunk.

'They don't believe Piper is alive,' I say.

'Maybe they're right.'

'She deserves more.'

The doors slide open. My right leg stops swinging and I pitch forward. Ruiz catches me. I straighten and pull back my shoulders, trying to pretend that nothing has happened. I can see our reflections in the large pane of glass beside the door – a man with a limp and another with a twitching arm. Both proud. Both damaged.

'You don't have to stay,' I tell him. 'You should go back to London. Where are you spending Christmas?'

'Claire has invited me to her place. I'm worried Miranda might be there.'

Claire is Ruiz's daughter. Miranda is his most recent ex-wife, the one he's still sleeping with.

'I thought you two were tearing up the sheets.' I say.

'I'm not complaining about the sex but she wants me to have feelings.'

'Feelings?'

'I told her that I have three of them.'

'Three?'

'I'm hungry, horny and tired – in that order.'

'How did that go down?'

'Not so well.'

We've reached the main doors. I remember to ask him something. 'That mate of yours – the computer geek.'

'Capable Jones.'

'Are you still in touch?'

'I own his soul. What do you need?'

'Can you ask him to access aerial maps and photographs of Oxfordshire. I'm interested in factories, past and present, that manufactured pesticides, plastics or synthetic rubber, that sort of thing. The forensic report showed traces of heavy metals and chlorinated hydrocarbons beneath Natasha's fingernails.'

'What's the search area?'

'Four or five miles from the farmhouse.' He gives me a look. 'You think I'm clutching at straws.'

'Atheists aren't supposed to ask for miracles.'

Downstairs in the charge room Victor McBain is being released after ten hours in custody. Dressed in a blue paper boiler suit, he signs the release form and is handed his clothes and personal possessions, sealed in plastic.

'I hope you washed and pressed them,' he says.

'No, but we checked for traces of accelerant,' says DS Casey, unmoved by the sarcasm.

Opening one of the plastic bags, McBain pats his trouser pockets and pulls out his cigarettes and a Zippo lighter. In one motion, he flicks the lighter open and strikes the wheel with his thumb. Holding up the flame, he smiles at the detective before flipping it shut again.

'Where can I get changed?'

Casey points him down the corridor. McBain recognises me as he passes, blinking with gin-pale eyes.

'What are you looking at?'

'You.'

I hold his gaze. He pushes past me.

'Can I ask you a question?'

'Been there, done that.'

'I'm not the police. We're not being taped. I'm just trying to understand a few things. Why did you give your niece condoms?'

McBain looks at me for a long time, his nostrils flaring and his lips curled back as though he's talking to someone who is completely deaf or stupid.

'She asked me for them.'

'Why?'

'Her parents wouldn't buy them.'

'You don't think it's slightly odd — a man your age buying condoms for a teenage girl?'

'She was having sex. I wanted her to be safe.'

'Who was she having sex with?'

'Her boyfriend, I assume.'

'You assume?'

'What's that supposed to mean?'

'Nelson Stokes saw you kissing your niece in the front seat of your car when you dropped her at school.'

'Who the fuck is Nelson Stokes?'

'The school caretaker.'

'She gave me a peck on the cheek.'

'And you slipped her the tongue.'

McBain screws up his face. 'You're a sick bastard! You repeat that in public and I'll sue you for slander.'

'Were you having sex with your niece?'

'Get out of here! You have no right to come in here saying stuff like that.'

McBain is pulling on his trousers, cinching the belt. He

pushes his arms into a T-shirt before looping it over his head.

'On the night before she disappeared, Natasha came to see you. She asked you for money. Was she blackmailing you?'

'No.'

'So she didn't come and see you?'

'No.'

'Why would Emily lie about something like that?'

'Sometimes Tash did some work for me, filing and stuff.'

'Did you see Tash on the night of the Bingham festival?'

'Yeah, I saw her.' He crouches to lace his boots. 'I don't know what the big deal is. Tash didn't go missing until Sunday morning.'

'That's where you're wrong. Alice McBain made a mistake. She didn't see the girls that morning, she heard Natasha's radio.'

The realisation dawns on him. His mouth opens and closes.

'What time on Saturday night did you talk to Natasha? Maybe you were the last person to see her.'

He doesn't speak now. His mind is weighing up the possibilities.

'You don't have an alibi for that night, do you? Just like you don't have an alibi for the night of the blizzard.'

'I was with my brother.'

'No, you weren't.'

He opens the door and strides along the corridor. I try to block his path.

'Listen, Vic, the police are looking at you now. They're going to pick apart your life. They're not going to stop until they find something. Where were you during the blizzard?'

He steps around me and crosses the foyer, reaching the main doors, which slide open automatically. Reporters and photographers have surrounded a car outside. Sarah and Dale Hadley appear from the open doors, quickly flanked by detectives, who shepherd them into the station.

Vic McBain stops and steps back as the couple approach the door. Sarah Hadley looks up and their eyes meet. She looks away. In that moment something passes between them – a knowledge that goes beyond the familiar. Pain. Hurt.

Sarah passes through the revolving door and takes hold of her husband's hand. There are hairline cracks in the make-up around her lips. McBain watches her, studying her body as she enters the lift and the doors close. Turning, he pushes past the media scrum, head down, his shoulders hunched.

I have seen that look. I have seen it in the mirror. I saw it last night in Drury's eyes when he couldn't comfort Victoria. It diminishes a man when he can't make a woman happy . . . when he makes her unhappy. The world is no longer rich and colourful. All he can see is the poverty of things.

How did it happen? I wonder. I picture Sarah Hadley standing beside Piper's bed, holding an article of her clothing, as if discovering something new about her daughter. Recalling the best moments. Trying to keep her alive. She clutched at every piece of misinformation and rumour, consulting psychics and fortune-tellers. Vic McBain introduced her to one of his girlfriends who claimed to have the gift. She told Sarah the girls were alive. She gave her comfort. Hope.

Mourning can be lonely. Grief can be shared. Sarah couldn't look at her husband because he reminded her too much of Piper. Vic McBain understood. And then one night they came together, most probably in some out-of-the-way hotel room or a clumsy adolescent-style coupling in the back seat of a car. I don't know who seduced whom. It doesn't matter. Vic McBain had made it possible for Sarah to be herself again – not the campaigning mother or the media spokesperson or the woman locals took pity upon when they saw her pushing a trolley in the supermarket . . .

She could escape the whispers and stares, becoming anonymous for a few hours, suspended between fantasy and reality, feeling pleasure instead of loss, or perhaps feeling nothing at all.

For all her campaigning and sacrifice, Sarah Hadley has a streak of self-loathing that is wider than the M25. She married an unattractive man with money, a man who loved her, but she didn't feel the same way about him. She fucked her way to the middle rather than the top. She could have accepted that and slept in the bed she made, but then her daughter went missing and she blamed herself, thinking she deserved to be unhappy. She deserved a marriage on life support and sordid sex in a cheap hotel room overlooking a cut-rate carpet ware-house.

Vic McBain has reached the corner and is waiting for the lights to change. I catch up with him.

'I know what you're hiding,' I say.

He doesn't answer.

'Just tell me one thing. After that I promise I'll leave you alone. On the night of the blizzard, were you with Sarah Hadley?'

He blinks at me, a strong, silent man, lost for answers.

'I'm not going to tell her husband,' I say. 'Nobody else has to know.'

He wipes a finger across the corner of each eye.

'She deserves better than me,' he says. 'She deserves to find her daughter.'

33

Behind the glass door of the conference room a volley of flashguns are blasting light through the frosted panels. From outside it looks like a gunfight without the noise. Reporters and photographers are crammed into the overheated room, taking up every vantage point.

Dale and Sarah Hadley enter through a side door. The light seems to imprison them. Phoebe is clutching her mother's hand, eyes downcast. The younger children have been left at home, cared for by friends or relatives.

The family are seated at a long table. Camera shutters continue clicking. Once again Piper Hadley has captured the nation's attention. For a second time her fate is being debated across garden fences, in pubs and office canteens. Comparisons are being drawn with other high-profile kidnappings, names like Sabine Dardenne, Elizabeth Smart and Natascha Kampusch; the miraculously returned.

DCI Drury takes a seat beside the Hadleys. He waits for the camera shutters to fall silent.

'The body recovered from Radley Lakes six days ago has been identified using dental records and next of kin of the deceased have been notified. I am now in a position to formally release the name. We are investigating the death of Natasha McBain, aged eighteen, who went missing from the village of Bingham on the weekend of August 30, 2008. The official cause of death is drowning.'

There is another volley of flashguns.

'We have reason to believe that Natasha was kept imprisoned somewhere prior to her death. Her former home, a farmhouse outside Bingham, was the scene of a double homicide on Saturday evening. We are now certain that Natasha was at the farmhouse at some point that evening. We don't know if she played a role in the deaths of William Heyman and his wife Patricia, but it appears that she fled from the farmhouse before the fire started and fell through a frozen lake, succumbing to the cold.

'As I'm sure everyone is aware – Natasha McBain didn't disappear on her own. Another teenage girl also went missing that day: Piper Hadley, then aged fifteen. On behalf of the families I want to appeal for public help in both these cases.

'Someone knows what happened to Piper. Somebody knows where she and Natasha were held. Perhaps you've seen the girls or you've seen someone acting suspiciously. It could be a friend or a neighbour or a loved one who has a secret life, a basement or a lock-up that you're not allowed to visit. Someone who keeps strange hours.'

Drury pauses.

'I have more than eighty officers and volunteers searching the surrounding farmland. We're using helicopters, tracker dogs and ground-penetrating radar. The search will continue until we have ruled out every possibility.'

A reporter yells from the floor, 'Has there been any contact?'

'No.'

'Do you have any proof that Piper is alive?'

'No.'

'So she could be dead?'

Sarah Hadley confronts the questioner with steel in her voice. 'Our daughter is alive.'

Drury puts a hand on her shoulder. Sarah falls silent.

'The chief constable has ordered a review of the original investigation in light of the new information. In particular, we are seeking witnesses who may have seen Piper Hadley and Natasha McBain on the evening of Saturday, August 30, 2008. That was the last night of the Bingham Summer Festival.' Drury looks directly at the TV cameras. 'Did *you* see the girls? Did you talk to them? Did you see them getting into a car? Please ignore past information that has been made public. Whatever you may have heard or read, don't assume the police know everything about the last movements of Piper and Natasha.'

Drury takes a sheet of paper from his pocket and unfolds it on the table.

'I'm going to take the unusual step today of releasing details of a psychological profile drawn up by Professor Joseph O'Loughlin – a clinical psychologist who has been assisting our investigation. I'm not going to release the full profile for operational reasons, but I will give certain details, which I hope will trigger memories or encourage witnesses to come forward.

'According to Professor O'Loughlin, the suspect we are looking for is likely to be aged between thirty-five and fifty-five, of above average intelligence, with a detailed knowledge of the area. This wasn't a random kidnapping – he chose Piper and Natasha for a reason. He may well know them.

'He is likely to live alone or in a domestic arrangement where nobody questions his movements or unexplained absences. He has an isolated house or a secret room or basement where he was holding Natasha McBain. He brought her food, water, clothing . . . someone must have seen him come and go.

'He was out in the blizzard last Saturday night. Perhaps you saw him. He may have smelled of smoke or had stained clothing. Please come forward if you have any information.'

Again the questions start and Drury raises his hand, calling for quiet.

'Please, I will leave time for questions. For the moment, can we let Mr and Mrs Hadley speak?'

He pushes the microphone along the table. Dale Hadley leans forward.

'First of all, I want . . . I mean, we want . . . we want to thank the public for its support and kindness. We also want to offer our condolences to Natasha's family and say how sorry we are that she didn't make it home. I know they never gave up hope.' He takes Sarah's hand. 'Neither have we. That's why we're appealing for your help. Whoever did this has torn my family apart. So if you do know something, if you suspect someone, if you have seen or heard something suspicious, please pick up the phone.'

The flashguns are firing, revealing every tic and tremor, pain measured in micro-expressions. Sarah takes the microphone. There is something cold and brittle about her, like ice forming into crystals. The search is what sustains her. It is the sinew that holds her together. Everything else might crumble, but not her desire to find Piper. She will not rest. She will not sleep. She has to know the truth.

I have experienced that sense of certainty. When Gideon Tyler kidnapped Charlie. When he knocked her from her push-bike and chained her to a sink with masking tape wrapped around her head and a breathing tube in her mouth. When these things happened, I remember how my throat tightened and my bowels liquefied and panic carved through my soft organs. But I knew one thing for certain. I would never stop looking until I found her.

Sarah stares directly into the cameras. 'If you're the person holding Piper, if you're listening to this or watching this, the time has come to let her go. Let her come home.'

Questions come again, shouted from the floor.

'Do you blame the police?'

288

'Will you consider taking legal action?'

'Have you talked to Natasha McBain's parents?'

'What makes you so sure Piper is alive?'

Answers become shorter. Yes. No. I don't know. The media conference is curtailed. Police officers flank the family as they leave through a side door. Phoebe has almost been forgotten. She lowers her head and follows her parents, running to catch up.

The family pauses inside the rear doors of the station, waiting for their car. Phoebe looks up and notices me.

She smiles. 'Are you going to find Piper?'

'I'm going to try.'

'Do you think she'll still like me?'

'Why wouldn't she?'

'Mum says that she's still with us. That's why we hang up Christmas stockings and set a place at the table and have a cake on her birthday, but that scares me a little because she's like a ghost. There's an empty chair and an empty bed, but she's still here.'

'People cope with loss in different ways.'

Phoebe nods and looks at her parents.

'Is anything the matter?' I ask.

She shrugs. 'They just seem different.'

'In what way?'

'They become different when they talk about Piper.'

'They're just concerned about her.'

Phoebe puts her hands over her face and rubs her forehead with her fingers.

'So I should stop worrying.'

'Yes, stop worrying.'

She notices a stain on the sleeve of her dress and tries to rub it away with her thumb.

'I hear them coming up the stairs at night,' she says. 'They brush their teeth and turn off the light, but they don't talk.'

'What is it you want, Phoebe?'

Her voice drops to a whisper. 'I want them back.'

My gums are bleeding.

Mum always said I'd get scurvy if I didn't eat my fruit. Now I'm not eating anything – not since yesterday. I've decided to go on a hunger strike until he lets me see Tash.

I'm not going to wash. I'm not going up the ladder. I'm not going to let him touch me.

He can beat me. He can hose me down. He can turn off the lights. He can take away my blankets. I'd rather starve or freeze to death than go on without Tash.

The only thing I've ever been good at is running. I used to imagine that if I could run fast enough, I could catch a glimpse of my future. I might round a corner or crest a hill and see myself disappearing into the distance. I can't do that when I'm stuck down here. I can't glimpse the future. I can't imagine one.

Lying on my bunk, I remember happy times like the day we went to Tash's uncle's place and he let us drive his old station wagon around the paddocks, bouncing over the potholes and squashing the cowpats. We drove with the windows down and the music cranked up, pretending we were cruising along that famous road in the South of France with the clifftops and tunnels – the one where Grace Kelly died. Another tragic princess. I grew up listening to fairy tales where everyone lived happily ever after, but in real life princesses die in car crashes or get divorced or flog diet products.

Tash once told me that most people settle for second best, but maybe there's a reason for that. Second isn't so bad. I came second in the nationals. When you come second you don't have to keep looking over your shoulder or worry about inflated expectations.

I had a nightmare that George came back with Emily. He must be watching her. How else would he have her photograph? He said he was watching Tash before he kidnapped us, but I don't remember seeing him until that night.

Reaching beneath my pillow, I feel for the bamboo satay skewer. I took it from the table the other day when George wasn't looking. I slipped it under my dirty clothes. Now my fingers slide along the wooden shaft and touch the sharpened point. I have a weapon.

It probably won't kill him, not unless I stab him through the eye or through the ear. Maybe I could wait until he is sleeping and then do it.

I remember the broken screwdriver. Tash had the same idea. She was going to stab him in the neck. That's when she came back with bloody thighs and curled up on her bunk. That's when she gave up hope.

Lying on my back, I stare at the ceiling and try to steady my breathing. Slow it down. Not a hunger strike. I need my strength if I'm going to escape. I'll eat, but that's all.

Slipping out of bed, I go to the cupboard and find a can of baked beans. The can opener is blunt and it takes me twenty minutes to peel back the lid. While it's heating up, I take a spool of masking tape and use my fingernail to lift the sticky end. I carefully wrap a length of tape around the skewer, leaving the sharpened end protruding.

The tape is a handle. I hold it in my fist and make a stabbing motion. I don't feel very confident. I try again. Then I picture Tash lying on a bunk, curled up in pain. This time I stab easily at the air. I think of Mum and Dad and Phoebe and Ben and the baby sister they had to replace me – all the time stabbing at the air.

I play the scene over and over in my head, imagining how I plant the skewer in his back. How I push him down through the hatch and call him a sadistic prick and he looks up at me, surprised, hurt, scared.

I've never done any serious violence to anyone, but I'm going to make an exception for George. I'm going to hurt him. I'm going to pay him back for what he's done.

34

'Explain something to me,' says Grievous, beating out a rhythm on the steering wheel. 'Why do people always talk about how fast a car can get from nought to sixty? I mean, what's the big deal about sixty miles an hour? It's like people think aliens are going to land and only be able to do fifty-nine. They'll suck out our brains unless we can do nought to sixty in less than ten seconds.'

He pauses, expecting a response.

'I've never thought of it that way,' I say.

'Revheads don't have brains,' he adds. 'The aliens wouldn't be interested.'

The holiday traffic has slowed to a crawl, edging between lights and roundabouts.

'Did you always want to be a detective?' I ask.

'Oh, no, sir, I came to it late,' he says, pleased with the question. He pulls a creased photograph from his inner pocket.

'That's me there,' he says. 'Second from the left.'

Still warm from his body, the image shows a group of teenagers in combat gear, resting on their haunches, weapons propped between their knees.

'You were an army cadet?'

'Yes, sir.'

'Why didn't you join the army?'

'Failed the medical.' He points to the scar above his left ear. 'I had a tumour. Benign. But it was pressing on part of my inner ear. I was deaf in that ear until I was twenty-one. People thought I was slow. Stupid, you know.'

'That's why you turn your head to one side.'

'Pardon?'

'I noticed it when I first met you. You cock your head a little when you're listening to people.'

'Force of habit.' He laughs, putting the photograph away. 'When I couldn't join the army, I worked as a nurse and then became a court security officer. That's where I saw police officers giving evidence at criminal trials and I thought, Yeah, I could do that. I guess I wanted a challenge . . . to make a difference. Does that sound like a cliché?'

I shake my head.

Phillip Martinez's car is parked out front of the house, but nobody is answering the doorbell. The curtains are drawn. Lights off. I'm about to give up when I hear a tooting sound coming from the garage. I knock on the large double doors. A latch lifts and the right door opens a few inches.

Mr Martinez takes a moment to recognise me.

He apologises. 'Were you knocking? I'm very sorry. I get so caught up.' A bell jangles behind him. He opens the door wider. 'My hobby,' he explains. 'It's rather embarrassing . . . a grown man playing with trains.'

A model railway fills the entire floor space of the garage, twisting back and forth on different levels. There are mountains, rivers, roads, underpasses, tunnels, stations, hoardings, signposts, rolling stock, engines and carriages. The attention to detail is astonishing, right down to the tiny figures of people and animals; animate yet immobile, inhabiting a recreated world.

He has fashioned entire towns with factories, warehouses,

railway yards, shops, post offices, restaurants and cinemas. Pedestrians are caught in mid-stride on crossings. Cars wait for the lights to change. Town hall clocks are poised, ready to strike the hour.

Along one wall I see his workbench. It is lined with off-cuts and panels of balsa wood, along with electric fittings, wires and racks of steel train tracks. Tiny pots of paint are arranged according to colours. A magnifying glass on a retractable arm bends above the bench, with a bright light behind it.

The detective constable has followed me inside and is studying the workmanship.

Even the cast-offs in the dustbin look perfect, yet some small defect or flaw must have consigned them to the scrapheap.

Mr Martinez adjusts a figure that has fallen over on a platform – a stationmaster wearing a uniform and holding a flag.

'Only three tracks are running today,' he explains. 'There are normally five. Would you like a tour?'

'Please.'

He takes me to the control panel and flicks several switches, setting more engines in motion. Boom gates open and close. Trains pause at level crossings. Whistles sound. Bells peal. The movement and sound seem to bring the models to life and I can almost imagine the little manikins moving.

'How long has this taken you?'

'A couple of years.'

'Is it finished?'

'I keep changing my mind and rebuilding things.'

'A work in progress?'

'A Sisyphean task.'

Grievous has picked up a dining carriage. 'Hey, there are little people in here. You can see the food on their plates.'

'Please don't touch,' says Mr Martinez. 'Some of the pieces are very delicate.'

The detective constable sets down the carriage, wiping a smudge of oil from his fingertips.

On the wall of the garage I notice a photograph of Emily. The image has been folded in the frame, concealing the other person in the shot.

'I was hoping to speak to Emily.'

'She's at work today. She has a part-time job in Abingdon.'

'Can I ask you a question? Why did Emily want to run away?'

Mr Martinez doesn't react. He flicks more switches. Another train is set in motion. 'It was during the divorce. They were difficult days.'

'Emily's mother lives in London.'

'Yes.'

'You don't share custody?'

Mr Martinez pauses, squeezing his temple between this thumb and forefinger. 'My wife attempted suicide a few years ago. It had been on the cards. Amanda had problems with alcohol and drug dependency, painkillers in the main. She stopped acting like a responsible adult, which is why I sued for custody.'

'She fought the case?'

'Yes, but common sense prevailed.'

'When did she attempt suicide, before or afterwards?'

His smile is long forgotten. 'I don't feel comfortable with a question like that.'

'I'm sorry. It came out the wrong way.'

'I doubt that, Professor. You don't strike me as someone who speaks without thinking.'

'You have a slight American accent,' I say, changing the subject.

'I worked there for seven years. Amanda never really settled and her drinking got worse. I came home one day and she and Emily had packed up and come back to England.'

'You followed them.'

'Not immediately. My work was too important.'

'That must have been hard, being away from Emily.'

'I tried to get back and see her when I could. Amanda

wouldn't let Emily fly on her own to the States. In the end I sacrificed everything to come back – my research project, my funding.'

The trains are still circling, their lights flashing and whistles sounding.

'I did that for Emily because I could see what was happening. Amanda's drinking had got worse. She went to AA for a while, but kept falling off the wagon. She had always been flighty and highly strung, but she'd become positively destructive. Popping pills. Blacking out. Twice Emily couldn't wake her up and had to call an ambulance. That's why I fought for Emily and I didn't give up until I'd won her back.'

'You make her sound like a prize.'

He gives me the flattest of looks. 'All children are gifts.'

'Your daughter wanted to run away.'

'We took a while to get to know each other. There were bumps along the way.'

'Bumps?'

'Amanda suffered a relapse and was committed to a psych ward. Emily blamed me.'

'Why?'

'I don't know. You should ask her. Amanda going to hospital was probably why Emily stayed. She visited her mum every day and in the meantime we got to know each other. Things became easier . . . she understood the rules.'

'Rules?'

'The normal stuff – no drinking, no smoking, no drugs, no junk food, no staying out late . . . Her weight was all over the place and her school grades were terrible. All that changed when I took charge.'

'She was going through puberty.'

'Exactly. Teenagers shouldn't be treated like adults. They don't have the emotional and intellectual skills. That's half the problem in this country – lack of supervision, children being allowed to roam the streets. Look at the London riots. Young kids were breaking windows, trashing cars and stealing flat-screen TVs just because they were bored and they had no role models at home.'

'What's the other half of the problem?'

'Pardon?'

'You said children were half the problem in this country.'

He stops and apologises. 'You've got me on my hobby horse.'

'Trains are probably a nicer hobby,' I say, wanting to be outside, breathing different air.

He gazes at me with a formless smile. 'I sense that you disapprove of my methods, Professor, but my daughter loves me. I'm just glad she didn't go with those girls. She might have been kidnapped too. Do you have children?'

'Two girls.'

'It's difficult . . . raising kids. The world gets more complicated every day. They're getting information from magazines, TV shows, the Internet, social networking sites and instant messaging. We have to worry about net porn, cyber bullying and online grooming. They all want to be famous. They think they're entitled. It's scary out there.'

Out where, I want to ask him, but I'm tired of listening to his complaints and his paranoia. My left arm is trembling. There are too many fragile things around me; if I stumble I could crush entire buildings, ruin streets, derail trains . . .

'Do you mind if I talk to Emily?' I ask, moving towards the door. He gives me the name of the pharmacy where she works.

'Tell her I'm cooking linguini tonight. It's her favourite.'

35

The sun seems to be resting on the rooftops, angling through the windscreen. Grievous drives cautiously in the glare, bullied by cab drivers and dark-coloured BMWs and Audis.

Ruiz answers his mobile on the first ring. He's out of doors, wheezing like an ex-smoker.

'Do you know how many abandoned industrial sites border railway lines in Oxfordshire?'

'Is that a trick question?'

'I've visited nine so far and every one should be bulldozed.'

'I thought Capable was going to get aerial photographs and maps.'

'You can't see shit from an aerial map. A ten-storey building can look like a tennis court.'

'So you're climbing over fences.'

'I've been chased by two dogs and some old biddy threatened to have me arrested.'

'Charmer. I need another favour from Capable Jones.'

'And you've caught me in such a good mood.'

'I need a background check on Phillip Martinez. He's a

research scientist in the Biomedical Sciences Department at Oxford University.'

'Why the sudden interest?'

'He annoys me.'

'Is that all?'

'He's a self-righteous spiteful social conservative, who treats his daughter like she's a bank account he kept secret from his ex-wife in the divorce settlement.'

'Did you tell him that?'

'I was more polite.'

'You shined his shoes with your tongue.'

'It's called being professional.'

Ruiz laughs and ends the call. My mobile rings almost immediately. It's Julianne. She's in the car and I can hear Emma, my youngest, singing along to a nursery rhyme CD. Whenever I hear Julianne's voice I get a sort of aching bliss and I wish I could think of something to say to her, something that would fill her with excitement or wonder.

'Hi,' she says.

'Hi.'

'How are you?'

'I'm good.'

'I wanted to know what time you'll be here tomorrow?'

'Tomorrow?'

'Christmas Eve, silly. You're coming to spend it with us.'

'Yeah, of course.'

'The girls want to hang their stockings when you get here – well, Emma does. Charlie still isn't talking to me. I'm going to cook something nice. We'll let them open one present before they go to bed.'

'Just like old times.'

'Are you being sarcastic?'

'No.'

'So what time?'

'I'm not sure.'

'Well, try to miss the holiday traffic and don't buy me a present.'

'OK.'

She hangs up and I suddenly wonder what present I can get her. She'll have bought something for me. She'll have thought about it, planned ahead and whatever I do won't match her efforts.

We near the pharmacy. Grievous pulls over and parks, pointing across the road.

'That's the place. I'm going to get something to eat.' He pats his stomach. 'I have the caveman gene – always hungry. My girlfriend has me on this diet until the wedding. She's filled my fridge with healthy crap – celery, lettuce, cottage cheese . . . No beer. No pizzas. Right now I'd kill for a burger and a bowl of chips.'

'Killing is a bit extreme.'

'You're right. I'd beat someone up very badly so they couldn't move.'

He pulls down the sun visor, displaying a THAMES VALLEY POLICE notice. 'I'll wait for you here,' he says, locking the car.

Emily is unpacking boxes of shampoo and conditioner and lining them up on the shelves, labels facing outwards. A price gun rests on top of the stepladder. Something shivers in her eyes at the sight of me.

'I'm working – I can't talk,' she says.

'It's important.'

She glances over her shoulder. Chews her bottom lip. 'Maybe I can take my break.'

We go to a café across the road. She orders a skinny hot chocolate and ponders the muffins, making her choice seem like an act of rebellion. I doubt if her father would approve of an oversized blueberry muffin.

She's wearing a black skirt and white blouse with a nametag on the breast pocket. Taking a seat, she hunches over her drink, as though she's embarrassed to be seen with me.

'I need to talk to you about that night again.'

'What night?'

'You were with Piper and Natasha at the Summer Festival. When was the last time you saw them?'

'They were opposite the dodgems. There was a shoot-the-basket type game and Tash was trying to win a panda. I remember her arguing with the guy, saying the game was rigged because the balls were extra bouncy and they wouldn't go through the hoop or kept bouncing off the rim.'

'What time was that?'

'Just after nine.'

'Who were the girls with?'

'Nobody really.'

'Was anyone hanging around?'

'They were talking to some boys.'

'Who?'

'I don't know their names. They were Hayden's friends.'

'Was Hayden there?'

'No.'

'Who else?'

'Everyone from town – kids and grown-ups – it was a big deal in Bingham.'

I try to get names and to plot where the girls drifted to during the course of the evening. Emily talks, large-eyed, nodding faintly now and then.

'Was there anyone who made you feel uncomfortable,' I ask. 'Someone who looked odd or stood out in some way?'

'I don't know.'

'What about Tash's uncle?'

'He was running the tombola. He was quite funny – some of the things he was saying. Getting people to buy more tickets.'

'Who else did you see?'

'Some girls from school . . . the vicar and his wife . . . Callum Loach was there with his family. People felt sorry for him. It's not as though he could go on the rides.'

301

'Did he talk to Tash or Piper?'

'I don't think so. I heard his father say something about Tash.'

'What did he say?'

She picks at her muffin, pulling out the blueberries. 'It was pretty awful. He called her a prick-tease and a slag. Everybody knows he hates her.'

'When Piper came to your house that night, where was Tash?'

'I don't know.'

'Did Piper say anything?'

'I knew something was wrong. Her clothes were dirty. She had mud on the knees of her jeans and on her elbows. I thought she must have fallen over. She sat on my bed and left dirt on the bedspread.'

'Was she hurt?'

'No.'

'Had she been crying?'

'Piper never cries.' Emily runs her fingers through her hair, hooking it over her ears.

'You left the funfair at nine o'clock. Why was that?'

'Mum had gone to hospital.'

'Who called you?'

'My dad.'

'You said your mum lives in London now.'

'Yeah.'

'How often do you see her?'

'When Dad lets me.'

'How often would you *like* to see her?'

A hurt helplessness ghosts over her face. Only crumbs remain on her plate. 'I have to go. I only get fifteen minutes.'

'Just one last thing,' I say. 'Was there a special place where you girls used to hang out?'

'You mean like a clubhouse?'

'A favourite place.'

'You make us sound like we're eight and still using secret passwords.'

I laugh. 'It's just that Piper and Tash took so little with them. No clothes were missing. I thought maybe they could have hidden bags. You said you were planning this.'

'We were.' She peers out into the street. 'That summer we hung out a lot at the leisure centre. The pool. We used the lockers. Tash used to hide stuff there.'

Emily pushes her empty cup away. She's said too much. 'I have to go.'

Without waiting, she grabs her coat and I watch her skip across the road, looking both ways. A sense of disquiet has been growing within me like the beating of a war drum, repetitive, dull, getting stronger every day.

She stops on the far side of the road and looks over her shoulder, holding my gaze for a fraction of a second as though worried about what she's left behind, but determined to go on without it.

My dad once told me that people

can sometimes do amazing things when they're in life-and-death situations. Mothers can lift cars off their trapped babies and people have survived falls from aeroplanes.

When the time comes, maybe I can do something amazing. Every time I contemplate stabbing George, my throat starts closing. It feels like a heart attack, although I don't know how a heart attack is supposed to feel. I imagine like heartburn only a million times worse because you don't die of heartburn.

I know it's a panic attack. I've had them before. Tash used to help me get through them. She would hold a bag over my mouth and get me to breathe slowly or she'd rub my back, telling me to picture something that made me happy, a place or a person.

That's what I do now. I imagine I'm lying on the grass on a beautiful sunny day in our garden beside the pond. Phoebe is next to me and I've made her a clover crown and a matching bracelet and necklace. Mum is in the kitchen cooking chicken Kiev, which is my favourite.

I know it sounds corny, like a scene from a washing powder advert, but it takes my mind off my panic attack. After a few minutes I start to breathe normally again. I go to the sink and wash my face. Boiling water in a saucepan, I cook pasta and mix it with a teaspoon of oil. I can only swallow a few mouthfuls. My nerves are too bad for eating.

I look at the trapdoor and listen. If not today, maybe he'll be here tomorrow.

I've washed out an empty can of baked beans, which I'm using as a hearing device. I hold it against the wall and put my ear to the base, hoping to hear Tash on the other side. I even imagine that she's doing the same thing, listening for me. Our heads might almost be touching.

On the night we finally decided to run away our heads were touching

304

and we made promises to each other. I thought Tash was unbreakable but that night she shattered into a million little pieces and I tried so hard to pick them up again.

Ever since Aiden Foster's trial she had talked about running away. Getting expelled from school simply created a timetable. We had one more summer in Bingham, she said. When school went back, we'd have to leave.

The Summer Festival was on the last weekend of the holidays. There were funfair rides, stalls and sideshows on Bingham Green. The local pony club put on a display and Reverend Trevor judged the dressage competition.

The entire day was supposed to be a celebration. It began with morning tea in the gardens of The Old Vicarage – one of the traditions that Mum and Dad had to agree to when they bought the house. Apparently, according to local historians (by which I mean busybodies), the vicarage had hosted a morning tea for estate workers and townsfolk for the past a hundred and sixty-two years.

I don't know what an estate worker is, but most of the visitors were old biddies from the church, sitting at long tables on the lawn. There were scones, sponge cakes, trifles and summer puddings under muslin to keep the flies and sticky fingers away. Jasmine Dodds brought her new baby, whose scalp was all scaly like it was moulting, but that didn't stop everyone ooh-ing and ah-ing every time it burped. Jasmine used to babysit me when I was a kid.

At lunchtime Mr Swanson, the town butcher, set up a spit and roasted a pig that looked so much like a naked person it made me feel like a cannibal when my mouth watered.

Mum and Dad made me work all day, serving tea and cakes, then clearing away dishes and washing up. I stacked chairs and replaced divots in the lawn. Meanwhile, I listened to squeals from the Disco Rider and saw people climbing the giant slide and heard the PA system telling parents where to pick up their missing kids.

Finally my temper got the better of me. I said it was fucking unfair and told Mum she was being a vindictive bitch. Dad's shoulders slumped like he was deflating. I'd disappointed him again.

I was sent to my room. Grounded. I could hear Mum and Dad arguing about sending me away again. She was saying I was out of control and he was telling her not to overreact.

Tash sent me an email from her phone with a photo attached. She and Emily were sitting in the pirate ship, their hair flying as it swung back and forth. I couldn't even text them. My phone had been confiscated. What would they take away next?

At eight-thirty I made a show of brushing my teeth and getting ready for bed. Phoebe and Ben were already asleep. As soon as I heard Mum and Dad start watching a movie in the lounge, I opened my bedroom window. From the roof I could climb onto the old stables and slide down the tree onto the woodpile. Crossing the garden, I silenced the frogs and crickets. Slipping through the side gate, I was only two minutes from the green.

Tash and Emily were near the bungee trampoline. They'd been riding the roller and were laughing how their dresses would flip up every time the cars went upside down.

It was only nine o'clock and the fair didn't stop until midnight. We walked arm in arm between the sideshows. Tash was in her element, batting her eyelids and tossing her hair. Boys and grown men were looking at her, some like puppies, others like predators.

Soon after nine Emily got a phone call about her mum being taken to hospital. It wasn't the first time. We were getting used to Mrs Martinez being sick. I remember wishing my mum would get carted off to hospital, which makes me feel guilty now.

Tash slipped her hand down her pants and pulled out a small pillbox, pulling my hand until we were behind one of the tents.

'I only have one. We'll have to share.'

She popped it in her mouth, slipped her arm through mine and kissed me, pressing her tongue hard against mine until the pill crumbled and dissolved like aspirin. She pulled away giggling. My cheeks were burning.

'I think you liked that,' she said, teasing me. Already I could feel the E filling me up with chemical joy. I could taste the music, which was fizzing in my brain like lemon sherbet.

She took my hand again.

'Let's go swimming.'

'But the pool's closed.'

'I know how we can get in.'

She was talking about the leisure centre. Tash was pulling at my arm, dragging me with her. The idea of going swimming with her brought a flutter of happiness inside me. There were some drunken teenagers talking to the police near the park entrance. Tash steered me around them and we ran all the way to the leisure centre.

It was a hot night, full of insect sounds and the smell of honeysuckle and jasmine. Every one of my senses seemed to be heightened. I could have run faster than ever before. I could have run all the night and into next week.

The only thing that seemed strange was my voice. I didn't sound like me.

'We have to get out of this place,' said Tash, with the exhausted affectation of a bored housewife. 'It's so small and mean and . . .'

'Boring?'

'If we don't escape, we'll go mad with boredom. We'll be trapped. We'll get married and pregnant and buy a house and be stuck here for fifty years like our parents.'

She twirled onto the street with her arms outstretched, shouting, 'We're going to be free!' and spinning round and round before collapsing drunkenly onto the grass, dizzy and laughing uncontrollably.

The leisure centre has two small outdoor pools and a larger one indoors beneath a domed roof where pool lights shone blue and painted patterns on the interior walls.

We walked around the outside, following the wire security fence. Someone had parked a builder's skip behind the administration block, next to one of the brick pylons.

Tash climbed onto the skip.

'You'll have to give me a leg-up.' She flipped the hem of her dress, showing me her thong. 'No peeking.'

I cupped my hands together and she stepped into my palms. Then she shimmied upwards onto the brick pillar where she posed like a sea captain, staring into the distance.

'I see water.'

'What about me?'

'Follow the fence. I'll let you through the gate.'

It was dark and I cracked my shin against a bike rack, cursing and hopping on one foot, rubbing the other. I called out to Tash. She didn't answer.

I peered through the fence, wondering where she'd gone. Then I spied her near the gate, her short dress hanging loosely from her shoulders, her hair askew. Through the drugs and dark, she looked like a mermaid who had shed her tail and learned to walk.

She was looking over her shoulder and then she began to run, kicking up her feet like a newborn foal. At first I thought she was running away from me, but then I realised that she was running in my direction. She didn't slow down. She smacked into the wire fence headlong and fell backwards. Up again, she tried to climb, but couldn't get traction. Not strong enough.

'Run, Piper,' she said. 'Run!'

36

Drury gazes from his office window at the grey winter day, the eve of Christmas Eve. A wind has sprung up but the clouds seem too solid to move. Concrete. Summer might never come again.

'It's not Victor McBain,' I say.

The DCI doesn't seem to be listening. After a long pause, he turns to me and gives himself a heave as though shifting a heavy load from one shoulder to the other.

'What changed your mind?'

'On the night of the blizzard he was with a woman at a hotel. He doesn't want to implicate her.'

'We need a name.'

'Will it be made public?'

'Not unless it's relevant.'

'Sarah Hadley.'

'He told you that?'

'Yes.'

'And you believe him?'

'I do.'

Drury's eyes move around the office, focusing on his desk,

the back of his chair, the windowsill, but his mind is elsewhere. Perhaps he's contemplating his own infidelity or trying to remember a time when people didn't disappoint him.

'I don't know how many people I'll have left by tomorrow,' he says. 'People want to get home for Christmas. My budget is blown and I can't pay them overtime.'

'What about the search?'

'We're going over old ground. I'm scaling it down.'

Voices interrupt him, the sound of a commotion. He turns back to the window. A crowd has gathered on the footpath outside. TV cameras, reporters and photographers: encircling Hayden McBain. He's wearing a blue blazer and has combed his hair.

'My sister is dead and they have the nerve to arrest me,' he yells, pointing at the station. 'They locked *me* up. They threatened *me*. They told me to shut up. Well, I won't stay quiet. I'm going to sue these bastards for wrongful arrest, personal injury and emotional suffering. I'm going to sue them for destroying my good name.'

Drury rests his forehead against the glass, leaving an oily mark.

'Look at that toe-rag,' he mutters. 'He's got himself an agent, some Max Clifford type who's flogging his story to the highest bidder. He should have been charged.'

'It would have made things worse.'

'He's profiteering. There should be laws.'

Another interruption. Dave Casey this time.

'You're going to want to see this, boss. Sky News just posted new pictures of Natasha McBain on their website. They're saying they were taken on the night before she disappeared.'

Casey types the webpage address on the desktop computer. The page loads with photographs beneath a headline: 'Natasha's Last Dance'.

The images are poor quality, taken on a mobile phone, but

the subject is instantly recognisable. Natasha McBain is wearing a short summer frock and appears to be dancing. Spinning. The movement causes the dress to lift from her hips.

She has an audience of men, although I can't see their faces. They're sitting on benches or standing around her, watching her dance.

> **These are the last images ever taken of tragic teenager Natasha McBain, who disappeared three years ago with her best friend Piper Hadley. The photographs were taken only hours before Natasha went missing from a summer festival in Bingham, Oxfordshire, on August 30, 2008.**
>
> **Natasha's body was discovered last week in a frozen lake half a mile away from her home.**

'I want the originals,' orders Drury. 'I want to know who took them.'

Fifteen minutes later a call is patched through to the deputy director of news at the cable channel. Nathan Porter has a Brummie accent full of chummy bonhomie. He's on speakerphone.

'How can I help, Detective Chief Inspector?'

'You have photographs of Natasha McBain. Where did they come from?'

'A member of the public provided them.'

'I need a name and contact address.'

'Our source wished to remain anonymous.'

Drury tries hard to control his temper. 'This is not WikiLeaks, Mr Porter. This is a murder investigation.'

'Sky News has an obligation to protect our journalistic sources. In a free society . . .'

Drury picks up the phone unit and pretends to bash it against the desk. Porter is still talking.

'. . . media independence is an important pillar of democracy . . .'

Any goodwill that existed between the two men has gone.

'Let's be serious, Mr Porter, you're not protecting democracy,
you're protecting the killer of a teenage girl.'

'Steady on,' says the news editor. 'I think you're exaggerating
the situation. All we've done is find a good story.'

'That's all this is to you, a *good story*. A girl is dead. Another
is missing. You have fifteen minutes to provide police with the
identity of your source. If you fail to do so, I will call another
media conference. I'm sure Mr and Mrs Hadley would appreciate
the opportunity to comment on a news organisation that with-
holds important evidence that could help find their daughter.'

There is a long pause. Some silences have their own grammar
and syntax.

The news editor speaks first. 'Please hold the line. I'm seeking
advice from our lawyers.'

'The clock is ticking,' says Drury.

We wait, listening to a promotion for Christmas programmes
on Sky Premier.

Five minutes later, Porter returns.

'There seems to have been a misunderstanding,' he says,
apologising for the delay. 'Crossed wires.'

'How so?'

'We always intended to hand over the photographs. We
certainly didn't want to impede or hinder your investigations.
Perhaps, in return for our help, you might consider making the
Hadleys available for an exclusive interview.'

'That's not possible,' says Drury.

'Perhaps *you* would agree to be interviewed.'

'You don't want that, Mr Porter.'

'Why not?'

'I might say something you'd regret.'

'I see.'

'Who gave you the photographs?'

'A man called the newsroom and offered us the images. He called himself John Smith – clearly a fake name. He wanted cash. We paid him five hundred pounds.'

'Just like that?'

'Our security cameras took footage of him when he came to collect the money. Give me an email address, I'll send you the grab.'

'What about the photographs of Natasha?'

'They were taken on a mobile. He gave us four stills, which seem to run in a sequence, possibly taken from a video. I'm sending the email now.'

Moments later the computer chimes. Drury has mail.

'Thank you for your co-operation, Mr Porter.'

'Always a pleasure to assist, DCI.'

Drury hangs up and clicks on the inbox. The attachment opens in a new window; a video file. Loading. The security footage shows a man entering a revolving door and crossing a foyer. He's wearing a hoodie pulled up over a baseball cap. Baggy jeans. Hands in his pockets. He talks to a receptionist and refuses to be photographed for a visitor's pass. Instead, he waits in the foyer until a female journalist appears in a mid-length skirt. He studies her, checking out her calves. The exchange takes place. He turns for the door.

'There!' says Drury.

The footage pauses. The man who called himself John Smith has glanced up at the CCTV camera, revealing his face for just a fraction of a second.

'Shit!' says Drury, grabbing his coat from the back of his chair. He opens his door and yells across the incident room. 'Blake, Casey, Middleton . . . with me.'

37

Blackbird Leys is one of the largest council estates in Europe, dating back to the fifties when urban planners thought the way to solve inner-city deprivation was to move the inner poor from the tenements and rundown neighbourhoods to greenfield sites on the fringes of town. Out of sight, out of mind.

Instead, this utopian idea produced a cement and breeze-block badlands, as bleak as anything Dickens described, full of drug dens, illegal factories, brothels, squats, second-hand car yards, chop-shops and convenience stores with metal grates over the windows.

This isn't tourist Oxford or mortarboard-and-gown Oxford. It's where the 'townies' live – the cleaners, maids, factory workers, delivery drivers and tradesmen who keep the city running; as well as the employed and the unemployable, the working class and the underclass.

The local landmarks are twin towers: Windrush and Evenlode; fifteen-storey monuments to function that would be improved immeasurably by a wrecking ball or twenty pounds of Semtex.

The service entrance of Windrush smells of disembowelled bin bags, disinfectant and cat piss. I watch as a dozen officers in body armour climb the stairs. Another four of them use the lift and look like astronauts on their way to the command module.

Toby Kroger lives on the seventh floor with his younger brother. Their neighbours have been quietly evacuated. The SWAT team is in position. The lead officer has a helmet camera providing a live feed. Drury stares at the screen, an earpiece in his right ear.

'Door's opening. Someone's on the move.'

'It's the brother.'

A kid, barely seventeen, comes out of the flat carrying a black bin bag. He leaves the door open and walks to the rubbish chute. Three seconds and he'll reach the stairwell where the officers are waiting.

'He's going to clock them,' mutters Drury. And then into the radio, 'Get ready to move.'

The brother dumps the bag and reaches behind his back. He could be scratching himself. He could be reaching for a gun.

'Go now!' says Drury, screaming into the radio. 'Go! Go! Go!'

The camera bounces and shakes as the wearer runs along the corridor to the open door. There are flashes of helmets and weapons.

'POLICE! GET DOWN! ON THE GROUND! NOW!'

Officers pile into the flat one by one until I can't imagine there's any room inside. Kroger is shirtless, lying flat on the floor. Spread-eagled. The TV is on. Joysticks. Pizza boxes. Beer cans.

Moments later, Kroger emerges, half-carried, handcuffed, looking like he's just stepped on the third rail. From elsewhere in the building a dog barks, a baby cries, someone yells for quiet.

The entire operation has taken two minutes, yet it feels like I've watched it in slow motion. Blackbird Leys is unchanged. I glance along the empty street and notice a man walking along the footpath carrying a plastic bag. He stops suddenly, taking in the scene before ducking sideways into an alley. Moments later I see him crossing open ground, moving quickly, whippet-like. It's Craig Gould.

Drury has gone upstairs to search the flat. Karen Middleton has stayed behind, manning the radio. I signal to her silently. Pointing. Gould is cutting between two buildings, heading away from us. Putting both hands on the top of a wall, he heaves himself up, right leg over. Gone.

Middleton to Drury on the radio: 'Boss, someone clocked the police cars and started running. He just jumped the south wall. I'm in pursuit.'

Holstering her radio, the sergeant is already moving across the parking area. A short solid woman, convex rather than concave, she runs with surprising speed. Climbing on the bonnet of a parked VW, she goes over the wall head first, swinging out of view.

I go after her, skirting the wall and taking a walkway between two rows of terraces. Ahead I can see businesses, shuttered shops and a garage forecourt. Where has she gone?

There is waste ground to my right, protected by a wire fence. I see a shape, a mound of rags, moving. I climb the fence, swinging one leg over, cold metal on my testicles, the other leg, dropping hard on the far side. DS Middleton is lying there, winded, moaning, a cut on her bottom lip.

I take her radio.

'Officer down, repeat, officer down.'

She takes it from me. 'I can do this.'

There's a building ahead. The windows shattered. Derelict. My eyes follow the fence to a break in the wire. Gould can't be too far ahead of me. Ducking through the hole, I follow the lane past lock-ups and garages. There's a footpath. Bollards. Pedestrians only.

Forty paces and I reach a cross-street. Cars are parked on either side, already white with frost, fluorescent. I look both ways, trying to find him. A car engine fires up and rumbles through an illegal muffler. Designer noise. Moments later a Ford Escort roars towards me, Gould at the wheel, a manic gleam in his eyes. I'm standing in the middle of the road. He swerves and touches the brakes too hard. The rear end of the Escort slides out and clips a parked four-wheel-drive. Gould tries to correct. The car fishtails, losing traction.

He hammers the brakes, locking the wheels in a cloud of burning rubber. Sliding sideways, the Escort crumples into a van, metal embracing metal.

SWAT officers appear with guns drawn. Crouching. Aiming. Gould struggles to get his hands in the air. He can't hear their instructions over the double-bleat of half a dozen car alarms.

Drury arrives, his eyes like black gravel.

'Get him out. Secure the area.'

Karen Middleton is with the DCI, bruised but unhurt.

Gould is dragged free. Handcuffed. Bundled into a police car. An open palm raps against the metal roof sending the car on its way.

'Are you OK?' asks Drury.

'I'm fine.'

'What were you thinking?'

'She went on her own.'

'Which is her problem. Not yours.'

Heavy boots are moving through Toby Kroger's flat. A search is underway. Officers are opening drawers, cabinets and wardrobes, sliding hands beneath a mattress and a poster of a topless girl making love to a motorbike.

The flat reeks of bacon fat and old water. I watch from the hallway as covers are pulled off the unmade beds. DVD cases are opened and discarded.

The laptop is found in a drawer. Blinking. Asleep. Drury flips it open. The screensaver is a photograph of a heavy metal band. He double clicks the Apple icon in the top left corner of the screen and works his way to the main control panel. No password required.

Kroger has an inbox with 4,327 messages. His sent file contains 2,512.

Drury opens 'Finder' and looks for a media file. A list appears, numbers instead of names. The thumbnails take longer to load. There are hundreds of video files, mostly porn clips and trailers.

'This computer is less than a year old,' says Drury. 'The footage of Natasha was taken before then. Maybe he didn't transfer the old files to the new machine.'

'He wouldn't have deleted the Natasha footage,' I say.

'Why?'

'Look at the other clips he's downloaded. Most of them are rape fantasies or women submitting to force. The Natasha footage will have special significance because he'll feel a sense of ownership. Try searching for the earliest dates.'

Drury clicks on 'View options' and ticks the box for 'Date created'.

'He registered the computer in May. Look at how many files share that date?'

'He must have imported them from his previous computer,' says Drury, opening files. He watches several seconds of each clip. Pretty women with painted mouths, taken by force, penetrated, pretending. There is nothing erotic or titillating about the footage; instead, a mind-numbing banality, pain for the heartsick.

A new clip opens on screen. The poor-quality camerawork shows the floor and then a wall, before it focuses on a girl in a floral dress and messy hair being made to dance as wet towels flick at her legs and thighs. The music is coming from a mobile phone: Beyoncé's 'Single Ladies'.

The men are sitting on wooden benches or standing. Balaclavas or handkerchiefs cover their faces. Natasha is begging them to let her go. One of them flicks a lit cigarette at her legs. She dances away. Exhausted. Slowing down.

318

'*Give us a spin.*'

She obeys.

'*You can do better than that.*'

'*Faster!*'

She turns faster. Her dress flies up, showing her underwear.

One of the men gropes Natasha's breasts. She pushes him away. Another set of hands close around her waist, lifting her off the floor. Someone is reaching between her legs.

'*No,*' she pleads. '*Please, let me go.*'

'*I thought you liked dancing.*'

'*I'll dance, but don't touch me.*'

'*Come on, shake that little tail.*'

The footage stops and starts again. The angle is different. The towels are still whipping at Natasha's thighs and stomach but now she's naked.

There are six men visible on the video. A seventh is holding the camera.

'*Yeah, give it to her!*' says a voice.

'*Show us how you move.*'

A fist grabs her hair and jerks her head up.

'*Don't cry, missy. When this is over you'll walk funny for a while, but you'll still have two legs.*'

A dream.

What I heard.
  What I saw.
  What I wish I could forget.
  They must have followed us from the funfair, but I don't know how they got inside the leisure centre. Tash was trapped behind the wire, unable to get away.
  I ran. I made it almost back to the main road where there were streetlights and houses, but I tripped over the bike rack, the same one as before. I thought my leg was broken. I hobbled towards the road.
  A shadow moved on my right. His hands closed around my waist and his fingers covered my mouth, pressing against my nose. I couldn't breathe and I couldn't tell him. I kicked and squirmed, but he held me tighter.
  He carried me back to the leisure centre. I thought I was going to suffocate. Instead, he put me down and tied my hands behind my back. I was sitting on the concrete outside the changing room.
  I could hear music inside. They were laughing. Tash was begging them to let her go.
  The man pulled my head up. He put a smooth stone in my mouth. 'Don't you swallow this or you'll choke,' he said, as he pulled a piece of fabric between my teeth, tying it behind my head. Then he pulled up my shirt until it covered my face. I was embarrassed because he could see my bra.
  'We're not going to hurt you,' he said. 'Your friend is being taught a lesson.'
  I couldn't see his face, but I smelled his sweat and the alcohol on his breath.
  I heard voices inside. Music playing. Laughter.

'Swing those hips,' someone said.
'Show us how you move.'
'Lift your chin. I want to see your face.'

38

Toby Kroger sits with his legs splayed, fingers locked behind his head, endeavouring to look like a man who has never known a moment of doubt or hesitation. Internally, there is a dynamic at work. He's scared. Bewildered by the speed of his arrest. Wondering what moment of catastrophic inattention had led to this abrupt change in his fortunes.

I have read his file. Unemployed, uneducated, he's one of three children whose parents divorced when he was seven. His grandfather and father worked on the production line at the Morris Motor Company in Cowley until the downsizing of the eighties saw the workforce cut by 90 per cent.

Kroger was kicked out of school at fifteen and arrested twice before his seventeenth birthday. There were no factory jobs. The mines had closed and the manufacturers had moved offshore. The state paid him welfare and wondered why a kid like this would turn to crime, when the only 'paid work' on offer was coming from the drug dealers and crime gangs on the estates. So they hired more police and built more prisons and hoped the underclass would shrink and die.

Drury is behind me in the observation room. 'What's your take on this guy?'

'He'll stonewall you,' I say. 'He isn't fazed by police interviews because he's been here before.'

'I'm a patient man.'

'That won't be enough. You have to shake him up. Keep him off balance. I can help with that. Let me sit in.'

The DCI doesn't dismiss the idea. 'Make your case.'

'Right now Kroger doesn't know why he's been arrested, but he must suspect this has something to do with the photographs. People get nervous around psychologists. They think I'm going to mess with their heads or read their thoughts. It might be enough to unsettle him.'

Drury ponders this for a moment. Makes a decision. 'Let's do this.'

Kroger doesn't look up as we enter. I take my chair and move it around to his side of the table. He looks at me sideways and then to Drury.

'What's he doing here?'

'Professor O'Loughlin is a psychologist. He's here to observe you.'

'Can he do that?'

'Relax, Toby.'

'But why is he here?'

'It doesn't matter.'

Kroger looks at me again. The clock ticks through half a minute.

'I want him to stop doing that,' he moans.

'Doing what?'

'Make him stop staring at me.'

Ignoring him, Drury opens a folder and shuffles pages. Kroger picks up his chair and moves it further away from mine, crossing his arms. Enclosed. Defensive.

Another minute passes.

'What are you waiting for?' he asks.

'I'm giving you time to compose yourself,' says Drury.

'Huh?'

'I'm giving you time to come up with a story. It helps to have a good story when you're going to be charged with sexual assault.'

'I didn't touch anyone. If she said I did, she's lying.'

Drury pauses. 'Who do you think we're talking about, Toby?'

Kroger hesitates. 'I don't know. Some bitch.'

'Natasha McBain. We found footage of her on your computer.'

Kroger falters and takes a moment to recover. 'That's not my laptop.'

'We found it in your flat. It's linked to your email account.'

'A guy sold it to me.'

'When?'

'A few weeks back.'

'Where?'

'In a pub.'

'Which pub?'

'The Ox.'

'The Ox has been closed since March.'

'Must have been another pub. I can't remember.'

Drury shakes his head. 'I gave you extra time, Toby.'

'It's true! A guy sold it to me. He was blond, fat, about forty. I think he was one of them problem gamblers you hear about, because he only wanted sixty quid.'

'And all the porn on the computer?'

Kroger grins, his gold tooth gleaming. 'That's not illegal.'

'The photographs you sold of Natasha McBain, who took them?'

'Don't know what you're talking about.'

'We have CCTV footage of you collecting the money from a journalist, who has just identified you as being the source.'

His grin fades. He glances nervously at me. 'I found them on the computer. The guy didn't wipe his hard drive.'

'You recognised Natasha McBain?'

'Yeah.'

'Why didn't you call the police?'

'I saw an opportunity to make a few quid.'

'She was being sexually assaulted.'

'I didn't watch the whole thing.'

'Maybe you think she deserved it.'

'None of my business.'

'Who took the footage?'

'I told you.'

'Some fat guy you met in the pub?'

'Yeah.'

'Last chance, Toby. I want the truth.'

Drury signals to the mirror. Moments later there is a knock. Dave Casey enters holding a mobile phone.

'Is this your phone, Toby?'

Kroger hesitates.

'It's a pretty straightforward question,' says Drury. 'It's registered in your name. You took out the plan. What's the security code?'

'I don't have to tell you that.'

'Don't worry – we've unlocked it already.'

Kroger is staring at the phone like it might detonate. 'That's my private property. You need a warrant or something for that.'

'That's where you're wrong.'

The DCI slides his finger across the screen.

'We've searched the memory. We found the footage.'

He turns the screen longways. Footage begins playing. Natasha is dancing on the small screen. Kroger won't look.

'There was no fat man in the pub, Toby. You took the footage. You filmed what happened. She was fifteen years old. I counted six grown men. Seven counting you.'

'I just filmed, I didn't touch her.'

'You raped her.'

'No, no, no.' He shakes his head from side to side, pleading with Drury to understand. 'We just frightened her. We flicked her with towels. We made her dance. Nobody raped her.'

'Bollocks!'

'It's true. Nobody raped her. I swear.'

'Where was it taken?'

Again Kroger hesitates. Drury slaps his hand on the table.

'How long do you think it's going to take us to triangulate the signals and find out exactly where you were? And how long will it take before we trace the signals from other mobile phones at the same place at the same time? We're going to get the names of everyone on this video and we're going to charge them with sexual assault and kidnapping and maybe even murder.'

'What? No, no, we didn't murder anyone. We didn't kidnap her. It was just a bit of fun. Payback for what she done.'

'What did she do?'

Kroger stops himself. He's said too much.

'Payback for what?' Drury asks again.

'Nothing. I mean, she was a prick-tease, you know. She was asking for trouble.'

'So you raped her?'

'Will you stop saying that?' Kroger looks at me for under-standing and reacts angrily. 'And you can stop staring at me.' He folds his arms. 'I want a lawyer.'

'That's your prerogative, Toby.'

'I'm not answering any more questions.'

'Fine. Have it your way. I am charging you with the impris-onment and sexual assault of Natasha McBain. You don't have to say anything, but anything you do say will be taken down and can be used as evidence against you . . .'

Kroger tries to speak, but Drury drowns him out.

'You had your chance, Toby. Go back to the cells and come up with a better story. Be more creative. Amnesia maybe. Insanity. You're going down for this. The Professor here has a daughter that age. That's why he's looking at you like that. He can see inside that festering little brain of yours. He knows you get off watching rape pornography.

'Imagine what it's going to be like in prison – hundreds of blokes staring at you, wanting to cut your balls off for raping a minor. That makes you a kiddy fiddler, a paedo, a molester. They'll be waiting for you, Toby.'

Kroger's head is shaking from side to side. 'I didn't touch her, I tell you. I just took the footage. Nobody raped her.'

Drury leans closer. 'You keep thinking that someone is going to save you. That this is all going to blow over. You're wrong. You had your chance and you blew it. Your mate Craig Gould is downstairs and he's going to sing like Amy Winehouse. He'll cut a deal. Name names.'

Drury gets to his feet. I haven't moved.

'I walk out that door and you spend the next twelve years inside.'

He doesn't take more than three paces.

'OK, OK, sit down,' says Kroger, snivelling. 'Nobody raped her, OK, but I'll tell you what happened.'

Drury takes a seat. 'Where was the film taken?'

'The changing rooms at Bingham Leisure Centre.'

'What about Piper Hadley?'

'She was outside. We tied her up.'

'Where is she now?'

Kroger frowns. Shrugs. He raises his eyebrows, not understanding the question. The penny drops.

'We didn't take them girls. We let 'em go.'

'Where?'

'At the swimming pool.' He makes it sound obvious. 'We didn't take them, I promise you.' He looks up at me again. 'It's the truth. Honest.'

'What did you do?'

'We roughed Tash up a little. Made her dance. Then we put her in the shower and cleaned her up, but that's all. She was fine.'

'Fine?'

'You know what I mean.'

Drury tosses a pad onto the table.

'I want the names. Every last one of them.'

When it was over,

I helped Tash put on her clothes and washed the blood from beneath her nose. She moved in slow motion, hurting in places I could never understand. There were red welts on her thighs and stomach, back and arms. Bruises coming.

They had warned us what would happen if we told anyone. There were photographs, they said, footage of Tash naked. They would upload it on the Internet and post the pictures on Facebook.

Then they told us to count to a thousand, so that's what I did. I counted to a thousand and then I counted to two thousand.

Tash didn't say anything. She could have been asleep.

Then I heard her voice, quiet and unsure. 'Piper?' she said. 'I want to leave now.'

I thought she meant go home, but she meant run away.

'I have five hundred pounds. How much can you get?'

I didn't say right away.

'Don't worry. I have enough.'

'We should tell the police.'

'No.'

'But you're hurt.'

'I don't feel anything.'

'You're bleeding.'

'It doesn't matter.'

She made it sound as though someone had turned off a switch in her body and she couldn't be hurt any more.

'What about Emily?'

'You go to her house. Tell her that we'll meet her tomorrow morning, first thing. She doesn't have to come, but I'm not changing my mind.'

My stomach twisted and coiled like a snake inside me. Tash looked at me as though I were made of glass and she could see right through me.

'I know you're scared,' she said. 'So am I.'

I couldn't think of anything to say that would change things. In her mind, Tash was already running. She wanted me to catch up with her. It's what I do, I told myself. I'm a runner.

39

An hour before first light on Christmas Eve, armed response teams gather at Abingdon Police Station. Seven addresses have been identified. Five more suspects are being sought. I'm barely awake when these men are dragged from warm beds, handcuffed in front of their families and bundled into police cars.

Theo Loach arrives at the station with his shoulders back and head up, shunning the offer of a coat to cover his head. His gunmetal hair is trimmed tight to his scalp and the only sign of disruption to his normal routine is the stubble on his chin.

Reuben Loach, Callum's older brother, has a cyclist's ropy build and trim black hair that clings to his skull like a helmet. He doesn't stop talking, insisting there's been a mistake.

Callum's uncle, Thomas Rastani, is a fifty-year-old insurance salesman with a wife and three children. Overweight and sweating in the cold, he hammers on his cell door, pleading to speak to his wife.

Scott Everett is another of Callum's friends. In his twenties, with a foppish fringe and eyes the colour of pea soup, he crouches beneath the blanket as though hoping it might make him invisible. Within minutes his father has arrived, politeness personified, but dropping the name of the barrister he's hiring.

The last suspect seems to have no obvious links to Aiden Foster or Callum Loach. Nelson Stokes, the former school caretaker, doesn't seem surprised by his arrest. He knows the drill – when to duck his head, when to cover it, when to keep quiet.

The men are brought in separately. Fingerprinted. Photographed. Read their rights.

By 9 a.m. the mood at the station is a festive one. There is a sense of expectation – a major case about to be cracked, the suspects in custody, the truth only hours away, or days. Phone records will link each suspect to the scene of the attack and to each other. They will deny everything initially, until one of them breaks ranks and tries to cut a deal. Then they'll turn on each other like guests on Jerry Springer.

I watch the early interviews, hoping for some sign that sets one of these men apart. Each of them is guilty of sexual assault and conspiracy and false imprisonment. They held her against her will. They cut off her clothes. They made her dance. They ignored her pleas. I don't know if they raped her or penetrated her, but one of these men is likely to have kidnapped the girls. Who among them is the collector?

According to Toby Kroger's statement, Theo Loach came up with the plan to punish Natasha. Aiden Foster had gone to prison for crippling Callum, but Natasha was equally culpable in Theo's eyes. She caused the fight. She provided the drugs. She walked free. His sense of outrage only grew when he saw her flaunting herself, flirting with boys, turning heads, walking on two legs. Someone should teach her a lesson. Show her that actions have consequences.

He recruited the others with the help of Kroger and Gould, organising a meeting at a pub in Abingdon.

'We were only supposed to scare her,' Kroger said. 'Theo talked about using acid on her face or tattooing something on her back, but we didn't want no part of that. So we agreed we were going to shave off her hair. Nelson said that's what they did to women in the war who fraternised with the enemy, you know, the Germans.'

Watching the interviews from behind the mirror, I learn what I can about the suspects. Theo Loach appears unrepentant. Reuben Loach is strangely silent, pushing his glasses up his nose and frowning at every question. Thomas Rastani is in denial, asking when he can go home. Scott Everett is defensive and difficult. Craig Gould cries twice during the interview and keeps apologising for his tears.

Shown footage of the assault, he says, 'I know it looks bad, but she was just dancing. Nothing else happened.'

Only Nelson Stokes appears unperturbed. He doesn't act hunted or feign contrition or construct a defence for himself. He's not delaying his answers or embellishing them with extra details. There are no outward signs of stress in his posture or his face. He's even playing games, jotting down numbers on scraps of paper, refusing to say if they're map references or coded messages.

Often the guilty look relaxed because they have less to worry about – they've already been caught. The innocent have more to fear because mistakes can be made. Witnesses can lie. Evidence can be lost. There are the dodgy juries, hanging judges and corrupt police.

No matter how hard I try, I still can't picture Stokes as the kidnapper. He's a pervert and a peeping tom, but on the continuum of sex crimes it is a major leap to have kidnapped and imprisoned the girls . . . to have mutilated Natasha. Not impossible. Not unprecedented. Unlikely.

Leaving the interviews, I wander upstairs to the incident room. DS Casey is updating the whiteboards with new infor-mation that links each suspect to the leisure centre.

'How many of them have alibis for the Saturday night of the blizzard?' I ask.

'The Loaches, Rastani and Everett.' He points to their photographs. 'Gould and Kroger are claiming they were with each other.'

'What about Stokes?'

'Says he can't remember. He's a cocky bastard.'

'What about the fingerprints at the farmhouse?'

'Forensics will be another few hours but we won't have DNA profiles until after Christmas.'

Drury appears upstairs with DS Middleton.

'Gould has given a statement,' he says. 'He's implicated the others.' There are cheers and high-fives among the assembled detectives. 'I want them charged. A special bail hearing has been convened. We're not opposing bail for Theo and Reuben Loach, Rastani, Gould or Everett but we'll be asking for provisions: no contact with each other or any witnesses. Kroger and Stokes have breached parole. We'll apply to have them remanded in custody.'

'What about Piper Hadley?' I ask.

'Gould and Kroger are both denying they have her. The others aren't talking. We'll keep asking the questions and tracing their movements.' Drury addresses the assembled detectives. 'The job isn't over, ladies and gentlemen. Let's get busy. The sooner we get them charged, the sooner we get home for Christmas.'

I hear him coming this time.

He's moving boxes and furniture.

'Knock, knock,' he says, tapping his knuckles on the trapdoor.

His face appears, smiling. 'Did you miss me? I've brought you a present.'

'Why?'

'It's Christmas Eve. I have lovely hot soup and fresh bread rolls and something sweet for afterwards.'

'Can we eat with Tash?' I ask.

His voice turns cold. 'Don't start.'

Climbing the ladder, I raise my arms. He lifts me easily, pinching the skin on my wrists beneath his thumbs. I rub the marks and walk ahead of him into the main room. The bamboo skewer is pressed into the small of my back, held against my spine by the elastic of my knickers. I'm scared it's going to slip out and fall through the leg of my jeans onto the floor.

'Shall we eat or wash?' he asks.

'I'm so hungry I'm feeling woozy,' I say. 'Can we eat first? Please.'

'Since you asked so politely, the answer is yes.'

He holds out the chair for me and sits opposite. He looks happier today, almost carefree, as though a weight has been lifted. We eat soup. I have difficulty swallowing because my throat is closing, but I'm also starving and the smell is making me feel weak. He eats with his head down, picking at his bread, tearing it into smaller and smaller chunks. He doesn't close his mouth, showing me glimpses of masticated food churning between his teeth and tongue.

I sneak glances around the room. His coat is on the back of his chair. Old bricks are stacked against the wall next to a bag of charcoal for the wood boiler.

He makes small talk. I ask about Christmas. Does he have a tree? A family? He says of course, but doesn't add any more.

After the soup he produces a bag of four cream buns. I can smell the sweetness of the cream and icing sugar. I want to take them back to the basement, but he wants to see me eat my share. They're sticky and sweet and the cream squeezes out onto the corners of my mouth. He reaches across the table and uses his thumb to wipe cream from the tip of my nose.

My hands are sticky. I get up from the table and he puts his leg out to prevent me leaving.

'Where do you think you're going?'

'I want to wash my hands.'

'I didn't give you permission.'

A pain darts up from my bladder and rushes to my throat. I sit back down again.

He's eating a cream bun. His mouth is full of sodden bread and jam and he doesn't bother swallowing before he speaks again.

'Do I look different today?' he asks.

'No.'

'You're staring at me. Why are you staring at me?'

'I'm not.'

He pushes himself away from the table and stands. I stand with him. He's six inches taller and leans over me.

'You were staring at me.'

'I'm sorry. I won't do it again.'

His anger is immediate, as though he's been saving it up, waiting for me to make a mistake. I'm frightened, but I'm also annoyed because I've done nothing wrong.

'It's a bad habit of mine,' I say.

'Maybe you should get out of the habit.'

'I will.'

I can feel the skewer against my back. I have to do this before I undress or he'll see it. I have to do it when he turns away.

His face softens. He leans across and kisses me near the mouth. He still has cream on his top lip. I have to stop myself from turning away.

He smiles and glances at the bath. 'Are you ready?'

'It's so cold,' I say. 'I don't want a bath. I'm clean.' I crawl onto the bed, wanting to reach the pillow. 'You can warm me up.'

He smiles, pleased with the change in me. My heart is beating itself against my ribs.

Sitting on the bed, he kicks off his shoes and socks, unbuttoning his shirt.

'I should brush my teeth,' I say, going to the sink and putting toothpaste on a brush. I look at my face in the small mirror on a stand. This is it, I think . . . now or never.

Taking off my clothes, I fold them neatly, slipping the skewer between the threadbare jumper and faded jeans before carrying them to the bed. He has set out baby doll pyjamas for me to wear. They make me look eight years old!

I pull on the panties and he folds back the bedclothes, already naked, erect.

I let him kiss me. I let him touch me. I let him lie on top of me. My right hand has found the skewer. I hold it against the mattress, willing myself, waiting for the moment.

I drive it hard into the side of his chest where I think his heart might be. I don't see myself doing it or feel myself doing it. The skewer breaks and I'm holding the makeshift handle. The sharp end is sticking out of his chest.

He grunts and turns on his side, his body shuddering and his legs kicking as though he's struggling to get up. I roll away and spring across the room. He's sitting up, holding the wound. The blood seems to animate him. He roars.

Picking up a brick, I swing it through a full arc, hitting him hard on the side of the head as he tries to stand. He falls backwards. The brick thuds to the floor. I should pick it up. I should hit him again. I don't know how to kill a person. Maybe he's already dead. He's not moving.

Spinning around, I grab my clothes, pulling on the jeans, jumper and dirty canvas shoes. I grab his coat, which is thick and heavy. Every part of me is screaming to run, but I have to find Tash. She must be *in one of the other rooms. I try the doors, calling her name, whispering rather than shouting. I can't find her. Maybe he lied to me. I can't leave her. I can't stay.*

Most of the rooms are full of old machinery and rusting drums. Some are locked. He must have a key. He keeps a keychain in his trousers. They're on the chair. I move towards the bed, but hear him groan, dragging snot through his nose. He turns his head. His eyes open.

I scream as he rolls and reaches for me, falling off the bed. He's lying on the floor, still holding his chest, trying to stand.

Running through rooms, I reach the outer door. It's locked. I turn and take the stairs, feeling the rickety metal frame rattle and shake beneath my weight, threatening to come loose from the wall. He's behind me, climbing the stairs slowly. I reach another door. Propped open. I move a drum and rubbish. Push the door closed. Slide a deadbolt into place.

I'm in a large room, empty except for a table and mismatched chairs. There's a window. I peer through the dirty glass and see a flat roof.

George's body hits the door and I scream at the sound. He talks to me through the door, speaking softly, saying that he isn't angry. He can forgive me. I have to say that I'm sorry. I have to open the door.

I don't answer. The door shakes as he crashes against it.

'I'll kill you, bitch, I'll cut you up! You're dead.'

I want to shout back, I've been dead for three years.

Balling his coat around my fist I punch at the window, but I'm not strong enough to break the glass. I pull a table closer and lie backwards across it, bracing my arms and kicking at the window with both feet. Once, twice, three times. The glass shatters and pieces fall outwards, tinkling against the roof below.

Using the coat, I clear the sharp edges and crawl outside, feeling the metal roof buckle and creak. I look for a way down. I can see the ground below, overgrown with weeds, littered with rubbish. I drop his coat. It doesn't make a sound when it lands.

Behind me the door breaks open. George appears at the window.

I start yelling from the rooftop.

'Help! Somebody help me!'

'Nobody can hear you,' he says.

I'm sitting on the edge. I look at the ground. It's too high.

'You'll break your legs,' he says. 'And then I'll have to shoot you like a horse.'

'I don't care.'

'Yes, you do.'

'Come any closer and I'll jump.'

'You'll never be able to see Tash.'

'I don't think she's here.'

'I'll take you to her now.'

'You're lying.'

He slides one leg out the window.

'Don't come any closer.'

'You're not going to jump.'

He keeps climbing out. Turning onto my stomach, I slide backwards over the edge, holding onto the rusting gutter, feeling the jagged edges bite into my fingers.

I hear him coming and let go. Falling. I expect to break my legs. I expect to die. The weeds and the overgrown bracken and George's coat help break my fall. I lie on my back, staring up at the roof. His face appears above me. I've surprised him. I'm alive.

Up again, I drag myself through the brambles, which catch on my clothes. There are buildings around me. Abandoned. Derelict. A water tower. A blackened chimney. A wire fence is draped in black-berry vines.

Running along the perimeter, I scan the wire. There's a gap beneath the lowest strand. I drop to my knees and scoop away dirt and leaves, making the hole bigger. Glancing over my shoulder, I can't see George, but I know he's coming. First I push through the coat and then I try to slither under the wire. My head and arms get through, but my jumper snags on something sharp, digging into my back. I claw at the earth and weeds, trying to pull myself forward. The jumper tears, flapping across my back. I'm sitting on the wet ground in the decaying leaf mould.

George comes round the corner of the building, still a vague shape with a bloodstained shirt. Closer now. Coming for me.

I scramble up and start running, fighting my way through branches that whip at my face and thorns that try to hold me back. I have forgotten what it's like to be outside, the malevolence of bush and briar. I'm a runner. If I find open ground, I can outpace him. But in the open he can see me. In the open I can't hide.

I can hear George cursing and swatting at the branches behind me, screaming threats. Pleading.

Stumbling into a clearing, I notice a winding path through larger trees. The ground slopes upwards and my canvas shoes are slipping and sliding on the mud and rocks.

Ahead of me the path divides. One track looks more worn, but I choose the other, which takes me deeper into the forest. I'm trying to second-guess him. The path narrows and rises, twisting along the side of a wooded gorge with steep rocky banks. I skirt the edge, dodging puddles and fallen branches.

The path turns suddenly. I change direction, but my right foot slips sideways and I can't rebalance quickly enough. Falling, I tumble down the embankment, rolling, picking up speed, banging my shoulder hard against a tree.

When gravity lets me go, I'm lying on my back, sucking ragged gulps of air into my lungs. My shoulder is on fire. Surely I've broken something.

Suddenly, I need to be quiet. I stop. Wait. He's above me on the path, less than thirty yards away. I can see him through the curtain of leaves and branches.

He pauses and listens, looking for me. Hunting me. I hold my breath. We're both listening to the sound of running water and the breeze in the trees. I have to breathe, taking tiny quiet gasps. The cold is leaking through my clothes, into my bones.

'Piper?'

He listens.

'I know you can hear me.'

Again he waits.

340

'If you come back now, I won't be angry and I'll let you see Tash.'

I have to cough, but I muffle it with my fist.

'And if you come back, I won't get Emily. I know where she lives. She's at work today . . . Piper? This is your last chance.'

He moves away, going further along the path. Every so often, I hear him calling for me.

Lying on my back, I stare at the clouds that are moving behind the branches. I'm lying on a rock, just out of the water. My jeans are torn and my knees are bleeding.

Above me there is a crevice carved by centuries of rain. The gap is just wide enough for me to crawl inside. I slither through the leaves and pull myself between the boulders, wedging myself there, with the coat behind me. Once I've wriggled inside, I drag the coat over my legs and curl into a ball, trying to get warm.

Exhaustion presses on my eyelids. I just want to rest for a few minutes; close my eyes. Sleep. Then I'll be able to run.

40

The caretaker at the Bingham Leisure Centre walks with a limp and has a hanging left arm, paralysed by a stroke. His name is Creighton and despite the customary rehab, his speech is still thick and wet with tongue and spit.

'We're closed over the winter,' he explains. 'Pools are too expensive to heat.'

He holds a set of keys in his teeth as he unhooks a chain with his good hand and slides a deadbolt from the ring. The gate moves grudgingly on stiff runners.

Collecting another set of keys from the admin office, he flicks a series of switches. It takes a few seconds for the neon tubes to heat and illuminate, casting a blue glow over water and air. The Olympic-size pool stretches out lengthwise beneath its domed roof. There are low stands on the far side and starting blocks angled towards the surface of the water.

'The police were here this morning,' he says. 'Didn't find anything. Don't know what they expected.' He hitches up his trousers with one hand. 'What do you want to see?'

'The changing rooms.'

'Figured as much.'

He puts the set of keys on the counter and thumbs through them.

'Come on then.'

I follow him along the side of the pool where the lights bounce off the water and throw rippling patterns on the walls.

'Who has access when the centre is closed?'

'There are four keyholders.'

'Ever had any security issues?'

'Kids sometimes break in looking for cash in the register or raiding the shop. The coppers said something about a sexual assault. Never had something like that. They asked about CCTV cameras. Can't have cameras in changing rooms. Imagine the problems. Privacy issues.'

The male and female changing rooms are in opposite corners. Opening a control panel, he flicks more switches and unlocks the doors. Rubber non-slip mats form a rippled path between the pool and the showers. Rows of lockers are arranged into alcoves with wooden benches in between.

I recognise the benches. This is where they sat as Natasha danced. Seven men set out to punish her. They talked of cutting her hair or scarring her face. Branding her. This is the power of people combining, when individual responsibility is diminished and the mob holds sway. It happened on the night that Augie Shaw died. It happened during the summer riots in London.

Regardless of the hows and whys, the psychology remains the same. The crowd provides anonymity, it abrogates responsibility, it diminishes any sense of 'self'. People don't lose their identity – they gain a new one. They unite against a common enemy, perceived or otherwise. They become a tribe.

Seven men imprisoned and assaulted a teenage girl. I don't know if they raped her. Collectively they justified something that individually they would never contemplate or carry out. They whipped her, making her dance, treating her like a performing animal instead of a human being.

343

Yet under different circumstances, if I had met some of these men on their own, I might have seen decent, hard-working, law-abiding human beings; men who love their kids, are loyal to their wives and are kind to animals. I'm not trying to excuse their behaviour; I'm trying to explain it.

The assault footage was time-coded. The camera stopped at 11.17 p.m. Piper Hadley showed up at Emily's house just before midnight. She could have gone to the police, but she didn't. Maybe she was scared. The last time Natasha was a witness at a trial, she was treated like the accused and Piper was sent away to a school for troubled teenagers.

The girls didn't spend the night at Natasha's house and Mrs McBain didn't wake them in the morning. So where did they go? When were they taken? Most likely the kidnapper was one of the men who imprisoned and assaulted them earlier in the night. He came back afterwards, or intercepted the girls. Chose the right moment.

Mr Creighton is growing impatient. I follow him along the pool deck and out through a side door, where dead leaves have piled up against the fences, marshalled by the wind. The air is cold and bright, smelling of woodsmoke and wet clay.

My mobile vibrates against my heart. There is a text message from Dr Leece at the hospital: he wants to see me.

The vertical blinds are drawn in the pathologist's office. I knock. A voice tells me to enter. John Leece is sitting in semi-darkness, reclined on a leather office chair with a wet flannel over his eyes. A lone desk lamp throws a circle of light over a series of post-mortem photographs arranged on his desk.

'A migraine,' he explains, without removing the flannel. 'I've been plagued by them since childhood.'

He motions me to sit down.

'There are times when I'd gladly put a bullet in my head to be rid of the pain.'

'Quicker than aspirin,' I say.

'Rather more permanent.'

He folds the flannel and dips his fingers in a glass of water before wiping them across his eyelids. I'm studying the photographs on his desk. One of them shows Natasha's body beneath the ice, her face in soft focus. A shaft of sunlight has pierced the clouds and illuminated the snow, creating a halo around her head. She looks almost peaceful, as though she's been laid to rest in a mausoleum of ice.

'You wanted to see me.'

'Have you heard of tritium?'

'No.'

'It's a hydrogen atom that has two neutrons in the nucleus and a single proton. Although it can be a gas, it most commonly reacts with H_2O to form tritiated water. Colourless. Odourless. Although not particularly dangerous, it's considered to be a low-level radioactive hazard with a half-life of 12.3 years. The molecule is so small it enters the body very easily – inhalation, ingestion, even through the skin.'

'Why are you telling me this?'

'Traces of tritium showed up in Natasha's urine. At some point she ingested the molecules, probably in contaminated water. Maybe she bathed in the water or was given it to drink.'

'Radioactive water?'

'Normally it would be excreted through her urine within about thirty days of ingestion, so she must have been contaminated in the past month.'

'Is it dangerous?'

'Tritium is created naturally in the upper atmosphere when cosmic rays strike air molecules, but it's also produced during nuclear weapons explosions or as a by-product of nuclear reactors. It's a pollutant that in large enough doses can cause cancers, congenital malformations and genetic mutations.'

'Where was she contaminated? Radley Lakes?'

'It's a wildlife sanctuary. They test the water regularly. Contamination at these levels would have showed up.' He gets to his feet and crosses the office to his desk. 'I talked to someone from the Nuclear Decommissioning Authority. He didn't believe me at first. He said tritium exposure is almost unknown but that occasionally there had been accidental releases into the cooling water of nuclear power plants or into the effluent stream as waste.'

'So what you're saying is that Natasha was exposed to some form of nuclear waste or spillage?'

'Yes.'

'From a nuclear power plant?'

'That's the most likely source.'

'Didcot Power Station?'

'Didcot is coal and oil,' says Leece.

'Where then?'

'I was thinking about Harwell. It's only sixteen miles south of here.'

'I thought it was decommissioned years ago,' I say.

'The last three reactors were closed in 1990 and the land was remediated, but there are still storage sites with radioactive material. It's going to take another ten years to clean them up.'

Dr Leece opens his laptop and calls up the results of an Internet search. Harwell was Britain's first nuclear reactor, set up in the 1940s when the government handed over an RAF base to the Atomic Energy Research Establishment.

'Treated waste water from the old nuclear plant was piped to the Thames at a place called Sutton Courtenay, which is only a couple of miles south of Radley Lakes.'

He calls up Google Earth. A picture of the planet appears on screen, as though taken from outer space. The camera plunges towards the surface, falling onto Oxfordshire. Slowing. Stopping. Focusing.

'There's also this place,' says Dr Leece. 'The Culham Science Centre is a research laboratory experimenting with nuclear fusion as part of the Joint European Torus project.'

'Where is it?'

'About a mile south of Radley Lakes.'

'So the tritium could have come from there?'

'I'm just suggesting it's a possibility.'

I look at the screen. The main railway line from Oxford to Didcot runs past the research centre. Natasha McBain could have followed the tracks in the blizzard, trying to get home.

'Does DCI Drury know this?'

'I left him a message.'

'This is where they should be searching.'

'They won't look now – not until after Christmas.'

I wake shivering.

I don't know how long I've slept, but I can't feel my feet or my toes. The blood has dried on my knees, but the scabs split when I bend and the wounds begin weeping again.

George said it was Christmas Eve. I dreamt that I could see my family around the table: Dad, Mum, Phoebe, Ben, Granddad and the little sister I haven't met.

I slide on my stomach to the edge of the overhanging rock. The ground is wet and it seems colder now, cold enough to snow.

Climbing out of the crevice, I peer over the top of the rocks, studying the path. I can't see George. Can't hear him. The trees are like charcoal drawings above me.

I pick up the coat and brush off the leaves, putting my arms through the sleeves. It's too long for me. I fold up the sleeves and put my hands deep in the pockets. It smells of George.

My fingers touch his mobile phone. I'm so surprised that I almost drop it. Two hands. I turn it over. Look for the power button. The screen lights up and welcomes me with music. There are no bars of signal. If I get higher, I might pick up a phone mast.

Scrambling up the embankment, I keep tripping over the hem of the coat. I have to hike it up and hold it under my arms, which makes it hard to climb because I can't hold onto the trees.

When I reach the path, I crouch behind a rock, peering both ways. I can't see him. I don't want to go back the way I've come, so I keep following the path, away from the factory, looking for a road or a house or a car.

It's raining and misty, but I can make out a trail that snakes between the trees. I'm climbing. That's good. Maybe I'll get a signal from higher ground.

Every few minutes, I stop and look at the phone, checking the signal. One bar blinks for a moment and then disappears. I wait. It flashes again. I scramble onto a rock and hold the phone above my head. A second bar of signal appears alongside the first. Wider. Stronger.

I dial 999. An operator answers.

'Hello, what service do you require, police, fire or ambulance?'

'Police. I need help.'

'Can I have your name please?'

'I'm Piper. He's chasing me, please hurry.'

'Hold the line.'

A different voice answers this time. A woman.

'You're through to the police. Can I have your name please?'

'I need you to come and get me. He's going to kill me.'

'Please, tell me your name?'

'Piper Hadley.'

'Has there been an accident, Piper?'

'No. He's coming, please help.'

'Who is coming?'

'I don't know his name. This is his phone.'

'Where are you, Piper?'

'In a forest.'

'Whereabouts?'

'I don't know.'

'So you've just wandered into nowhere?'

'I was kidnapped. I've managed to get away. You have to come quickly. He's got Tash. I know he'll punish her.'

'Who is Tash?'

'She's my friend. We were kidnapped together.'

'What's your friend's name?'

'Natasha McBain.'

'You're breaking up, Piper. Can you please repeat the name?'

'I said Natasha McBain.'

'Is this a hoax call?'

'What?'

'Do you know the penalty for making false emergency calls?'

'It's not a hoax! It's not!'

'There's no need to yell, Piper. If you become abusive, I will terminate the call.'

'I'm not being abusive. I'm telling you the truth.'

'I'm going to need a better location. I need a street or a cross-street.'

'There are no streets.'

'I didn't catch the name of the street.'

'There are none. I'm in a forest.'

'Where is the forest?'

'I don't know.'

'The nearest road?'

'I don't know.'

I feel myself beginning to cry. She doesn't believe me. They're not going to come. She tells me to hold. She's getting her supervisor. Another woman comes on the line.

'OK, love, my name is Samantha, what's yours?'

'Piper Hadley.'

'Where do you live, Piper?'

'I come from Bingham. It's near Abingdon. Priory Corner. It's called The Old Vicarage.'

'Listen, Piper, don't get upset. Stay calm. We're trying to trace the call. Do you know the name of the nearest town?'

'No.'

'What about the county?'

'No.'

'OK, don't worry. We'll find you.'

'Hurry.'

'I will.'

'It's getting dark and I'm cold.'

'Can you go somewhere warm?'

'I don't know where I am.'

'Can you see any lights?'

'No.'

'Can you call out?'

'I can only whisper. I don't want him to hear me.'

'Who will hear you?'

'The man who took me.'

'Who's that?'

'I don't know his real name. Please help me.'

'Don't cry, Piper.'

'I can't help it.'

'You're doing really well, Piper. I can see that you're in Oxfordshire. I'm going to call the nearest police station. I just need you to stay on the line.'

41

There's an envelope being held for me at the hotel. I ask the receptionist to prepare my bill and I head towards the lift. That's when I notice Ruiz sitting in the Morse Bar, reading a paper and nursing a pint glass of water.

'Where were you last night?' I ask.

'I caught up with Tom Fryer and some of his old rugby mates.'

'How big is the hangover?'

He points to the water. 'I've had two bacon rolls, three cups of coffee and a litre of Diet Coke and I haven't peed once.'

'Congratulations.'

Ruiz has already checked out of his room. He follows me upstairs and sits in the corner as I pack. I'm shoving dirty clothes into a holdall and collecting my toiletries. He notices the envelope and holds it up to the light.

'You should open it,' he says. 'It's from Victoria Naparstek.'

'How do you know?'

'I'm psychic.'

'You saw her deliver it.'

'That too.'

Opening the envelope, I slip the card free and read the short message: *I'd like to see you again. Give me a call some time . . . if you want to.*

She's given me her mobile phone number. I put the card in my pocket and crumple the envelope into a ball. Continuing to pack, I tell Ruiz about the arrests and interrogations, as well as Dr Leece's revelations about the tritium in Natasha's urine.

'So you figure she might have been kept somewhere near this research centre.'

'It's feasible.'

'And one of the guys who assaulted her is probably the kidnapper?'

'Most likely.'

'You don't sound convinced.'

'I'm not.'

'You don't think they match the psychological profile. Maybe you got it wrong.'

'Maybe.'

I look at my watch. It's just gone three o'clock. Four of the men will have posted bail by now. They'll be home for Christmas. Drury won't have surveillance teams working over the holidays. If one of these men is the kidnapper, he'll have time to dispose of Piper and destroy the evidence.

Ruiz fills a glass of water from the bathroom and sips it thoughtfully, contemplating the same possibility.

'Capable Jones got back to me,' he says. 'You still interested in Phillip Martinez?'

'It can wait.'

Downstairs, I hand my credit card to the receptionist, who hopes I had a pleasant stay. The printer warms up and produces my itemised bill. I glance at the total and hope the chief constable is a man of his word.

Ruiz spreads his arms. 'So I guess this is it, amigo.'

We hug. It's like being squeezed by a bear.

Over Ruiz's shoulder I see Dale Hadley stumble from the

revolving door as though spat out by a dispensing machine. Dressed in baggy trousers and a shapeless shirt, he looks disorientated and hollowed out.

His eyes meet mine. 'We have to talk.'

'I'm about to leave.'

Grabbing my arm, he pulls me away, looking for somewhere quiet. Checking doors. He finds an empty lounge.

'I know,' he says, squeezing his hands into fists.

'Pardon?'

'I know what she's been doing.'

'Piper?'

'No! Sarah. I know she's been sleeping with Victor McBain. She confessed. She said you knew. How?'

'I guessed.'

He can't look at my face, cannot speak. He's not a big man, but he looks diminished. Wounded. It's like walking past a cage at a zoo and seeing a decrepit lion or tiger that has been imprisoned for too long.

'My father warned me about Sarah. He said that when you marry a beautiful woman, you have to live with the possibility that other men will try to take her away. Do not covet thy neighbour's wife. Don't fuck her.'

He's taken a seat on a Chesterfield sofa.

'I gave her everything. I bought her the big house, a nice car. Jewellery. Dresses. I've never been unfaithful. Never even thought about it.'

'You should go home, Mr Hadley.'

He doesn't seem to be listening. 'Things used to be all right before Piper went missing, but after that everything changed. Losing Piper crippled Sarah emotionally. She changed. We hardly touch each other. It's been months . . .'

I don't need to know this. I don't *want* to know this.

'I gave her time. Space. I supported her.'

'You did the right thing.'

'Really? Do you think so?'

354

'Yes.'

'Why did she sleep with Vic McBain? He's uneducated, uncouth, foul-mouthed . . .'

Because he's not you, I want to say, but I don't. When Sarah Hadley looks at Vic McBain, she doesn't have to soak up anyone else's pain. She can deal with her own grief, without having to share someone else's. She can look into someone else's eyes and feel something other than pain and loss.

I don't say any of these things because his mobile is ringing. He doesn't recognise the number. He's about to cut off the call, but changes his mind.

'Hello?'

. . .

'Who is this?'

. . .

'I'm sorry, I can't hear . . . can you say that again?'

. . .

'Piper? Oh my God! Piper!'

. . .

'We've been so worried. We've looked everywhere. We didn't stop looking. I can't believe it, sweetheart. Where are you?'

. . .

'Wait. I'm going to put you on speakerphone.'

'Daddy?'

'I'm here.'

'You have to come and get me.'

'I will. Tell me where you are?'

'I don't know. But he's after me.'

'Who?'

'The man who owns this phone. I don't know his name, but he's looking for me. I called the police, but they wanted me to give them a street or a house number and I told them I don't know where I am. He has Tash, Daddy. He caught her when she tried to run away. You have to help us.'

'You're breaking up, Piper. Try to stand still.'

355

'Can you hear me now?'

'Yes.'

'Are you crying, Daddy?'

'I'm just really happy.'

'So am I. It's so good to hear your voice'

'Yours too.'

'I didn't run away, Daddy. We talked about doing it, but we didn't get a chance. A man took us. Can you tell Mum? I don't want her thinking that I don't love her. And tell Phoebe and Ben and my little sister. What's her name?'

'Jessica.'

'That's pretty.'

'What did you tell the police?'

'Just what I told you. Tash escaped but he caught her again. I couldn't find her and I'm scared he's going to do something to her if I don't go back.'

'Don't worry about Tash. Tell me where you are.'

'I don't know.'

'We're going to find you, baby. They'll trace the call.'

'He's still looking for me. I have to hide.'

'Can you wait a second, sweetheart?'

'Don't go away.'

'I won't.'

I can hear him having a conversation. Someone is talking about calling the police.

'Are you there?'

'I'm here, Daddy.'

'The police are trying to find you. Stay on the line. Don't move, Piper.'

'What if he comes? I'm scared.'

'I know you are. I'm with a man called Joe. He's going to talk to you.'

'Hello, Piper.'

'Hi.'

He has a nice voice, soft but strong, not wheedling like George.

'Where are you right now?' he asks. 'Describe it for me.'

'I'm in a forest, standing on a ridge. I couldn't get any signal so I climbed higher. I don't have much battery left.'

'Where did you get the phone?'

'I took it from George.'

'Is that the man who's been holding you?'

'Yeah.'

'His name is George?'

'I don't know. Tash called him George. She said he looked like George Clooney, but he doesn't really, not unless George Clooney has put on weight and got ugly. Has he got ugly?'

'My wife doesn't think so.'

'That's good.'

'What can you see, Piper?'

'Trees.'

'Anything else — a landmark, a river, or a road or a railway line?'

'No.'

'You said you escaped.'

'Yes.'

'Where did you escape from?'

'It was some sort of factory but it's empty and everything is broken and overgrown. Are you there, Daddy?'

'I'm here.'

'Please come and get me.'

'I will.'

'It's getting dark and I can't stop shivering.'

A bird lifts from the trees behind me. Jerking my head around, I search the shadows.

'Piper?'

'I thought I heard something.'

'Why are you whispering?'

'I can't talk very loud in case he hears me.'

Joe speaks. 'When did you last see George?'

'I don't know what time it was. He said he was going to get Emily.'

'What?'

'He had a photograph of Emily in his wallet. He said he was going to get me a friend. I told him I didn't want a friend. You have to stop him. You have to warn her.'

'We will. What does George look like?'

'He's old and ugly.'

'What colour is his hair?'

'Brown.'

'How old is he?'

'I don't know — thirty or forty.'

'Is he tall?'

'Taller than Daddy, but he has small hands. I'm wearing his coat. It hangs down to my ankles. Are you still there, Daddy?'

'I'm here. The police are tracking the signal. I want you to stay put.'

'It's getting dark.'

'I know.'

'What about Emily?'

Joe answers. 'We'll make sure she's safe.'

'It's starting to rain.'

'Can you find somewhere out of the rain?'

'I don't know. I just want to curl up and go to sleep.'

'No,' says Joe. 'You mustn't fall asleep. You should keep moving.'

'Daddy told me to stay still.'

'You mustn't fall asleep. Try to stay warm.'

'OK. I can't feel my fingers. I'm just going to swap hands . . .'

. . .

'Hello?'

. . .

'*Daddy?*'

. . .

'*Joe.*'

. . .

'*Are you there?*'

42

Dale Hadley is cradling his phone in both hands as though he's dropped a priceless vase and is holding the broken pieces.

'The line went dead.'

'She'll call back.'

'There's no number on the screen.'

'She'll call.'

'What if the battery has run out?'

'They'll still be able to track the previous signal.'

'She's cold. I could hear her teeth chattering.'

'They'll find her.'

'She was slurring her words.' He groans helplessly. 'Oh God, oh God, we can't lose her now.'

I hold his shoulders, tell him to breathe. Relax. Stay calm. Piper is going to need him. She's going to hang on, but only if he does the same.

Ruiz has DCI Drury on the line. I take the phone and can hear Drury yelling instructions across the incident room. He's with me now.

'Piper Hadley called 999 twenty minutes ago but the signal

dropped out. She's on a mobile. We've been tracing a second call but lost it two minutes ago.'

'She was talking to her father. The call dropped out.'

'We have the number but the mobile isn't transmitting any more. The initial call came into the control centre at Milton Keynes and was transferred to Abingdon. The number is listed to a pay-as-you-go subscriber. The handset doesn't have a GPS locator, but the control room has tracking technology. The call was picked up by three towers, which means we can triangulate the signal.'

'What about the nearest base station?'

'It's a thirty-two-metre tower in a field about half a mile north of Culham Railway Station.'

'Dr Leece mentioned Culham.'

'Why?'

'They found traces of tritium in Natasha's urine. It's a low-level radioactive pollutant – a by-product of nuclear reactors. She must have consumed tritiated water.'

'There are no nuclear reactors in Oxfordshire.'

'There's a nuclear fusion research laboratory just outside of Culham.'

Drury yells more instructions across the incident room, fortified and energised. He's on the scent.

'I'm cancelling Christmas leave. Recalling officers. I can put forty bodies on the ground. Civilian search and rescue teams will give us twice that number. We're focusing on the closest phone tower until we get a more precise location. I'll send a team to the research centre. There are police choppers at Luton and Benson, but the weather is shit and it's going to be dark in an hour.'

Dale Hadley is listening to the conversation. I don't want to voice my main concern. Piper won't survive another night outdoors. Either we find her or she has to find somewhere warm and protected.

The DCI hangs up. He wants us back at the station.

Dale Hadley is still nursing his phone. 'Maybe George found her,' he says. 'Why else would the phone be turned off?'

'There could be other explanations.'

'Like what?'

'The batteries might be flat. She might be out of range.'

I take him back over Piper's call, gleaning every detail. She called the man George but said it was just a nickname. He was tall with brown hair, aged thirty to forty with small hands. He had a photograph of Emily Martinez in his wallet.

I turn to Ruiz. 'Let me ask you something: what sort of man keeps a photograph of a teenage girl in his wallet?'

'A boyfriend.'

'Someone older.'

'A father.'

'Come on.'

Ruiz is behind the wheel, braking late, throwing the Range Rover around corners. Wiper blades slap against the rim of the windscreen.

Dale Hadley sits in the back, staring at his mobile phone, willing it to ring. He's trying to remember every word that Piper said to him, replaying their conversation as though it might give him a clue. A short while ago he was consumed by thoughts of his wife's betrayal. Forgotten now.

'Someone will tell Sarah, won't they?' he asks. 'The police will call her.'

'I'm sure they will.'

'You told Piper to keep moving. Should we have told her to stay put?'

'She has to keep warm.'

'But how will they—'

'The police can track the signal even if she's moving.'

He nods, looking at his phone again.

'Can I ask you a question?' I ask. 'Did Piper ever meet Phillip Martinez?'

'Emily's father – I don't know. Emily used to live with her mother. Her father was in the States. He moved back after Amanda had a breakdown.'

Still driving, Ruiz interrupts, rattling off the background details that Capable Jones uncovered. Phillip Martinez was born in Manchester in 1972 and went to a selective grammar school, before studying medicine at King's College in London and doing a postgraduate research degree in Boston.

'He didn't practise,' says Ruiz. 'Instead, he focused on medical research, working for pharmaceutical companies and hospitals in Chicago and Hawaii before he took up a position in Oxford. Capable talked to one of his former lecturers, who said Martinez didn't lack confidence. He was convinced he was going to win a Nobel Prize. It was just a matter of time.

'That was until he blotted his copybook. Five years ago, working in Honolulu, he faced allegations that he falsified data on biomarkers and treatments for cancer in two journal articles. He denied it and later blamed a research graduate who was working with him. He claimed she doctored the figures. She lost her job. Left a suicide note. Disappeared into the sea.'

'What about Martinez?'

'The Office of Research Integrity conducted an inquiry, but the findings were inconclusive. He had to pay back two hundred thousand dollars in research grants. That's when he moved back to England.'

'What about Mrs Martinez?'

'Amanda Lowe grew up in London. She was a freewheeling hippie type; a rampant socialist at university, according to her friends, but she settled down when she married. It was an odd sort of match. The good doctor is a raging conservative, control-ling, pedantic, apparently quite brilliant. The marriage lasted nine years until it broke down around the time of the research scandal. Initially Martinez didn't fight for custody, but he came back again when his wife had a breakdown. He accused Amanda of substance abuse and alcoholism; subpoenaed her medical records. Her two stints in a psych hospital swayed the court. Emily went to her father.'

The uneasy sense of disquiet within me has bloomed like a noxious weed. Martinez studied medicine. He would have done a surgical rotation. According to Dr Leece, whoever mutilated Natasha had some knowledge of surgery or a limited degree of medical training.

Martinez is a research scientist. He's accustomed to controlling his experiments, knowing the variables, removing them. Scientific research is about questions and observations, striving for facts unencumbered by bias or distortion. It's about objectivity, reproducibility, exactness and demonstrability.

His model trains are another example of his meticulousness. He fashioned a miniature world in precise detail where he can control everything, the lights, the switches, the trains, the timetables . . . Most psychopaths build rich fantasy worlds in their heads – he created one in real life.

The Range Rover floats through the outskirts of Oxford, the streets surprisingly empty. Most people have left for the holidays. The stragglers are getting off buses and carrying home provisions.

Ruiz pulls up in front of the house. The driveway is empty. Nobody answers the doorbell. I check the garage. It's in darkness.

'Nobody's home,' yells Ruiz, having tried the back door.

I look at my watch. It's four o'clock on Christmas Eve.

Emily gave me her mobile number. I find her contact details and press the call button. She's not answering. Her voicemail triggers.

'Hi, it's me. I'm obviously doing something very cool and exciting, which is why I can't answer your call. Leave me a message and I may or may not get back to you. After the tone . . . Ciao.'

I turn to Ruiz.

'Any ideas?'

'She could be working?'

Directory assistance patches me through to the pharmacy. A woman answers. Busy. Flustered.

'Is Emily Martinez working today?' I ask.

The woman sighs. Disgusted. 'She didn't show up for work; left us short-handed.'

'Did she call?'

'No. Are you a friend of hers?'

'More of an acquaintance.'

'Well, if you see her, tell her she's fired.'

Idiot! Stupid, stupid girl!

I dropped the phone. My hands were so cold that I couldn't close my fingers. And instead of catching it, I stuck out my foot and kicked it into a puddle. The screen is cracked. Nothing lights up.

I've broken it. Shit! Shit! Shit!

I hold the button down. Nothing. I slap the handset against the palm of my hand. It's dead.

How are they going to find me now?

I look around, trying to get my bearings. The fog has lifted and below me, through the trees, half a mile from here, there is a ploughed field streaked with snow. An electricity pylon rises from the mud and ice, strung with power cables. Power cables lead to places where people live. They thread towns together.

I head down from the ridge, climbing over rocks and weaving between trees. The going is slow because I don't want to fall. There is wood everywhere, dead limbs and branches scattered over the ground.

A misty rain has started falling. Droplets cling to the shoulders of the overcoat like glass beads sewn onto the wool. My feet have stopped being numb. Now they're burning and itchy.

The field had seemed nearer. I can't see it any more. All the trees look the same. I panic for a moment, thinking I've lost my bearings and have been walking in circles. But I'm still heading down the slope.

The man called Joe said the police were coming. He sounded nice. He told me to keep moving, to stay warm.

The trees grow thinner. The field is in front of me. I can see the electricity pylon and a line of distant trees that could be a road. Hope flares in my chest. A road will lead to a house or a farm.

There's a fallen tree. I clamber onto the log and use a branch to balance as I climb the fence. My overcoat is too long. I take it off and throw it over, jumping after it.

Instead of being muddy, the ground is hard. Frozen. The rain is heavier now, hitting my cheeks like grains of sand kicked up by the wind. The sky has grown darker and the temperature is dropping.

Crossing the field, leaping between ploughed ruts, I reach the pylon and I stand for a while, wrapped in the overcoat, trying to get my bearings. I look up at the metal spars and beams, the hammered rivets. The electricity cables sweep over my head, descending and then rising to another pylon and then another.

I don't like being in the open. George could be watching me from the ridge. Veering away from the pylon, I head towards the line of trees and climb another fence to a narrow farm track, dotted with puddles. I can see tyre treads in the mud.

Peering into the gloom, I look beyond the curve in the road and can make out the angled roofline of a house or a barn just visible against the sky. I want to run, but the air has become like water and I feel like a greased swimmer, crossing the Channel.

Everything hurts. Walking. Breathing. Swallowing. I follow the road past the bend and come to an old mailbox and then a house in the middle of an overgrown orchard.

I try the gate. The latch is stiff. Rusted in place. Working it back and forth, I scrape my knuckles, but manage to slide it open. The hinges groan in protest. Weeds grow along the path. The nettles sting my legs where my jeans are torn.

I look up at the windows for a sign of life. The house frowns back at me. Rusting bits of machinery are strewn on the porch — the door of a refrigerator, a mangle, something charred with wires sticking out the top.

The front door is boarded up with cheap plywood. I feel like crying. I look back towards the road and wonder if I should keep walking or try to get inside and stay warm. There could be blankets. Maybe I could light a fire.

Hooking my fingers around the plywood, I work it back and forth, pulling nails from the rotten wood. Cursing my useless hands. When the gap is big enough, I crawl through on my hands and knees, sitting for a moment until my eyes adjust to the darkness.

The house is old and smells of mildew and damp. The rooms are empty except for broken ceiling panels and odd bits of discarded furniture. I can't find any blankets and I don't have any matches to start a fire.

A red Formica table has been left behind in the kitchen. At the sink I turn on the tap. The handle spins aimlessly. Dry. I'm thirsty.

Through the dirt-streaked window I notice a barn. It has a pitched roof but no walls. Round bales of straw or hay are stacked up to the roof. There must be a farmhouse nearby.

I unbolt the kitchen door and go outside. There's a water tank with a tap on the side. I turn it on and let the water run for a few seconds. The water is sweet. I can smell it. I scoop it up by the handful, lifting it to my mouth. Nothing has ever tasted so good.

43

Ruiz is standing in the front garden, peering through a window. He cups his hands against the glass, letting his eyes adjust.

'Can you see anything?'

'Something is broken on the kitchen floor,' he says.

'What is it?'

'A vase or maybe a plate.'

'Accidental?'

'Maybe.'

Dale Hadley is waiting in the car. Ruiz walks back to the main door. 'Do you know the difference between reasonable suspicion and probable cause?'

'Not really.'

'Reasonable suspicion is where a reasonable person *suspects* that a crime has been committed or is in the process of being committed. Probable cause is when a reasonable person *believes* that a crime is being committed or about to be committed. You see the difference?'

'Sort of.'

'Good. Explain it to me later.'

Pivoting on one foot, he hammers the lock with the heel

of his boot. Wood splinters. The door swings open, banging on its hinges. He moves through the open-plan living room, yelling Emily's name. Broken crockery litters the kitchen floor. Thrown, not dropped.

Ruiz searches downstairs and I take upstairs. Emily's room is on the right side of the landing. Her bed is unmade and clothes are spilling from drawers. It contrasts starkly with the rest of the house, which is ordered and neat.

The untidiness is probably teenage-induced – I have one of them at home – although Emily didn't strike me as being as sullen and disorganised as Charlie. Pages have been torn from one of her schoolbooks. A train timetable lies in the wastepaper bin.

Opening the topmost drawer, I see a picture frame resting upside down beneath a folder. It's a woman's portrait. Pretty and smiling, she has long hair and familiar eyes: Emily's mother.

Ruiz yells from downstairs. I follow the sound of his voice to the garage. He's discovered the model railway and is grinning like a schoolboy.

'How cool is this?'

'Don't you mean nerdish?'

'Come on, didn't you ever want to be a train driver?'

'No.'

'Let me guess – you grew up wanting to be a psychologist?'

'What's wrong with that?'

'You were one sad, sad child.'

My mobile shudders to life. I flip it open.

'We've triangulated the signal,' says Drury. 'Piper's call came from a heavily wooded area half a mile north of the conference centre, east of the Thames. The margin for error is about two hundred yards because the trees could be skewing the signal. I'm heading there now.' He yells at someone to hold the lift. 'Where are you?'

'At the Martinez house.' I glance at Ruiz. 'Emily Martinez didn't turn up for work today and there are broken dishes in the kitchen. You might want to send a forensic team.'

'Where is Phillip Martinez?'

'He's not here.'

There is a pause. Drury has stopped walking. 'What should I know, Professor?'

'Piper said that George had a photograph of Emily in his wallet.'

'And you think Phillip Martinez?'

'I think we're talking about the same person.'

'Why didn't Piper say that?'

'I doubt that she's ever met Phillip Martinez or knows what he looks like. Martinez didn't move to Abingdon until after the divorce. He fought for custody after his wife's breakdown.'

'Why would he kidnap Piper and Natasha?'

'He spent two years fighting for custody of Emily. He wasn't going to let someone take her away. He treats her like a possession. Like he *owns* her.'

'But you said—'

'He matches the profile. He's a control freak. He has medical training. He was also at the house when Piper turned up on the last night of the festival. He could have overheard her talking to Emily. That's how he knew they were planning to run away.'

'You said the kidnapping was most likely organised in advance.'

'I said he targeted the girls for a reason. It wasn't random.'

'What about the letters that were sent to Emily and Aiden Foster?'

'Martinez could have organised it. He expected the letters to be given to the police – to throw you off the trail.'

'But he brought Emily's letter to the station.'

'It was a fishing exercise. He wanted to find out how much you knew.'

I can hear Drury breathing down the phone. He cups the receiver and yells down the corridor. *'Put out a missing person's bulletin on Emily Martinez.'*

It's dark.

I can keep to the road by feeling the hardness of the dirt beneath my shoes, but I can't avoid the puddles. The rain has eased, but in the distance I can see shimmerings of lightning above the trees, followed by a dull rumbling.

The phone is still in my pocket. I can feel it with my fingers as I walk. I take it out, turn it over and feel for the catch to the battery compartment. The rear panel slides off and I use my thumbnail to lever the battery from its slot, before putting it back in again and replacing the panel.

I turn the phone on again. The screen lights up.

I call the last number.

'Daddy?'

'Piper! Thank God! We were worried.'

'I dropped the phone. My hands were so cold.'

'Are you OK? Where are you?'

'Are the police coming?'

'Yes. Where are you?'

'On a dirt road.'

'Can you see any lights?'

'No. Tell them to hurry.'

'I will.'

'Have they found Tash?'

Daddy doesn't answer. Joe takes the phone.

'What's wrong?' *I ask.*

'Your dad needs a minute. He's a little overwhelmed. I need to ask you some questions.'

'OK.'

'Have you walked very far since we last spoke?'

372

'It feels like a long way because my feet hurt, but I don't think it is.'

'Where are you now?'

'I'm on a dirt road. I passed an old house and a barn, but nobody lives there.'

'OK, just hold on, I'm going to relay that information to the police.' I can hear him talking to someone.

'OK, Piper, what else can you see from the road?'

'Nothing now, it's too dark. Before there was a pylon in a field.'

'Have you seen the river?'

'No.'

'What about a railway line?'

'I used to hear trains when I was in the basement.'

'That's good information, Piper. One more thing – have you ever met Emily's father?'

'No.'

'Do you know what he looks like?'

'No. Why?'

'The man you call George – had you ever seen him before?'

'I don't think so. He knew stuff about us. He knew we'd given evidence in Aiden Foster's trial. He knew that Daddy worked in the City and that Tash's dad had been to prison.'

'Is that all?'

'Uh-huh. I'm getting tired, Joe. My feet hurt. Do you think I could sit down for a while?'

Piper's body is closing down. Her words are getting slower and thicker. I turn to Ruiz. 'Where are they?'

He relays the question to Drury, who's on the phone. 'How close?'

Ruiz gives me the thumbs up. 'They know the road. Cars are on their way.'

'Did you hear that, Piper? They're close. Just a few more minutes.'

'Mmmmm,' she says.

'Keep talking, Piper . . . are you still there?'

'Uh-huh.'

'I have a daughter about your age.'

'What's her name?'

'Charlie.'

'Where does she go to school?'

'Shepparton Park School – it's on the outskirts of Bath.'

'Does she like it?'

'I think so.'

'I've missed so much school. I don't suppose I'll ever catch up.'

'Sure you will. Bright girl like you.'

Her teeth are chattering. 'I'm getting very tired, Joe. I'm going to close my eyes for a little while.'

'Stay awake, sweetheart. They won't be long. It's Christmas tomorrow.'

'That's what George told me. Did they have the Christmas procession with all the lanterns at Oxford Castle?'

I look at Dale Hadley, who nods.

Piper yells excitedly. 'Hey, I've just seen something. Lights. I can see lights flashing. It's a car!'

'Stay on the phone, Piper.'

'I'M HERE! I'M HERE!' she yells. 'They've seen me. They're slowing down. Tell Daddy I'll see him soon.'

'Don't hang up . . . Piper?'

I'm listening to dead air.

Dale Hadley is in tears. He hugs Ruiz and he hugs me and then he hugs Ruiz again. He's like a man who's been given a second chance, who wants to stop people in the street and say how wonderful it is to be alive.

'They'll take her to the hospital first,' I tell him. 'They'll want to make sure she's all right.'

'Can we go there?'

'Of course, but first we stop at the police station.'

44

Julianne calls. She's at home with the girls. I can hear them laughing in the background, Charlie tickling Emma, Christmas carols on the stereo.

'Where are you?' she says. 'We're waiting.'

'I'm truly sorry – but I won't make it tonight.'

I don't have to see her face to gauge her reaction. It doesn't take words or sighs or a sullen silence. I know I've disappointed her. It's what she expected.

Rain zigzags off the windscreen, trembling at the edges of the glass. 'Piper Hadley is alive,' I say. 'The police have found her. She's on her way to hospital.'

'So you're the white knight again?'

'It's not like that.'

In the silence that follows, Julianne chastises herself for being unreasonable. 'I'm sorry. That was a terrible thing for me to say. Forgive me.'

'Of course.'

There is another long pause. I can picture her standing in the living room, biting on the corner of her lip. She's stronger than I am, surer of her place in the world, less burdened without me. I guess that makes her happier.

'I'll save you some dinner just in case you make it down. And I'll leave the key in the usual place.'

'Thank you.'

'I'm really happy about Piper Hadley. What a wonderful Christmas present for her family.'

'Yes, it is.'

The Range Rover pulls into a parking spot. Abingdon Police Station is lit up like a spaceship with an angled turret that looks like a flying saucer has crashed into the roof and become stuck there.

From the moment I step through the door, I sense something is wrong. The incident room is deserted. Drury isn't in his office. A dozen people are crowded around the doorway of the control room. Pushing between shoulders, I make my way to the front. Dale Hadley follows me.

DCI Drury's voice comes over the two-way. Angry. Frustrated.

'*OK, I want to go through this again. Mobile units, I want call signs, exact locations and personnel. Who picked up Piper Hadley? Which cars were on the road?*'

One by one, the cars respond. DS Casey is using coloured circles to represent each vehicle on a map of the area.

Drury's voice again.

'*So what you're telling me is that not one of you has Piper Hadley?*'

There is silence.

'*I want roadblocks. Seal off the area. I want vehicles stopped and searched. Farmhouses, barns, outhouses, garden sheds − I want them all searched.*'

Dale Hadley looks from face to face. 'We heard her. She saw headlights.'

'It wasn't one of our vehicles,' says DS Casey.

'Piper saw flashing lights?'

376

'She saw lights *flashing* through the trees,' I say, 'which is not the same thing.'

Dale Hadley pauses, his mouth opens. No sound emerges. He's locked in a terrible wordless commune with himself. His legs buckle. Someone helps him to a seat.

'Where's Drury now?' I ask Casey.

'On his way back.' He turns to Mr Hadley. 'I want to reassure you, sir, that we're doing everything we can to find your daughter. We know her last location. We have sealed off the area. We're also tracing the phone she was using. Previous calls. The positions. We'll unlock the history. Find out where she was held.'

Hollow words. Dale Hadley has heard them before, the reassurances and guarantees. Less than two hours ago, he rediscovered his daughter. Twenty minutes ago, he thought she was safe. Now she's been snatched away again and he won't accept excuses or promises.

'I will get a family liaison officer to take Mr Hadley home,' says Casey.

'No, I want to stay.'

'We'll keep you informed, sir.'

'What if she calls me again? I should be here.'

DS Casey gives in grudgingly.

'You'll have to allow us to do our jobs, Mr Hadley. It's important we move quickly.'

'Ruiz can look after him,' I say. 'He knows how it works.'

DCI Drury arrives alone. The rest of his team have stayed at the scene, manning roadblocks and searching the surrounding fields. Several officers bring him up to speed. Drury is staring blankly at the floor. Something has gone horribly wrong. He can't explain how or why. He wants today over again or at least a second chance. He goes into his office, motioning me to follow.

Opening a bottom drawer, he produces a bottle of whisky,

cracking the seal and pouring himself a slug in a coffee mug. He swallows it and squeezes his eyes shut as the liquor scalds his tongue and the warmth explodes in his empty stomach.

He raises the bottle.

'No thanks.'

He pours another shot and screws on the lid, replacing the bottle in the drawer.

'How?' he mutters. 'It was a private road. There can't be more than twenty cars a day. A member of the public would have called us by now. So who picked her up?'

'He must have been following her.'

Drury rests his elbows on his desk, pressing his thumbpads into his eyes.

'The mobile phone that Piper used was purchased from a Vodafone shop in south London eighteen months ago. It was registered to a Trevor Bryant, an alias used by a local drug dealer called Eddie Marsh. We raided some of Eddie's properties a few months back.'

'Where is Eddie Marsh now?'

'He jumped bail. In Marbella according to his ex-girlfriend.'

'Does Marsh have any history of sexual offences?'

'No.'

'What about links with the men you've charged with assault?'

'We're looking.' Drury changes tack. 'Emily Martinez isn't answering her phone and her father didn't show up at work today. What can you tell me about him?'

'He matches the psychological profile.'

'I can't base an arrest on a profile.'

'He has the intellect, the experience, the knowledge and the motive.'

'Still not hard evidence.'

'You'll find it. You'll match his DNA to the farmhouse or you'll find his fingerprints.'

The DCI looks rueful. 'It's easy to have faith when you don't have to wear the failure.'

There's a knock on the door. DS Casey appears. 'Phone call, boss.'

Drury picks up.

'Where? . . . Who owns the property? . . . You're sure? Check again.' Strange bright fragments of possibility are firing in his mind. 'Is there a caretaker? . . . Yeah . . . OK, contact him . . . I'm on my way.'

He looks up at me.

'We've found where he kept the girls.'

45

On the journey south to Culham we pass through two police checkpoints patrolled by officers in reflective vests, waving motorists to the side of the road. Car boots are searched. Trucks. Trailers. Caravans.

Drury flashes his badge. A glowing wand waves us through. Less than half a mile further on we turn off onto an unmarked road that is guarded by a single-bar gate counterweighted with a metal block, padlocked in place. A wooden notice reads: PRIVATE ROAD – NO ACCESS.

Continuing along a muddy track, weaving between potholes, the road almost disappears in places, surrendering to the undergrowth. Other vehicles have forged a path. We come to a line of parked police cars and a white van. The doors open and two police dogs bound out, sniffing at tyres and trees.

Ahead of us, an abandoned factory or warehouse is partially illuminated by headlights. Most of the buildings are single-storey although exhaust stacks and flues suggest larger structures might lie below ground. The surrounding chain-link fence has collapsed in places under the weight of dead vines and trees felled by past storms.

The main gate cants drunkenly on wooden posts that have rotted to crumbling stumps. Immediately beyond, the road disappears beneath a mass of tangled brambles and spindly vines, grown to shoulder-height in places. A path has been hacked through the foliage.

Torches swing from building to building, lighting up small sections. Graffiti stains some of the more prominent walls, but the evidence is aged and faded. Windows are boarded up or broken. Doors are sealed or gape blackly open.

'It was abandoned in the eighties,' says Drury. 'Before that it was an emergency relocation site for the government – some sort of shelter in case the Ruskies launched a missile strike on the Harwell reactors. There were half a dozen complexes like this one.'

The DCI shines a torch on a wall of rock that rises almost vertically above the compound.

'The whole site was once a quarry. They mined the rock for track ballast when they built the Great Western Railway. The main line is less than a hundred yards to the west of here.'

'Who looks after it now?' I ask.

'It's administered by the Atomic Energy Authority, which means it's under the jurisdiction of the CNC.'

'The CNC?'

'The Civil Nuclear Constabulary: it's a security force that protects nuclear installations. They don't know if they're soldiers or make-believe coppers.' Drury motions ahead to a small group of detectives. Among them is a uniformed man, not a police officer, who is trying to look like one of the lads.

'This is Sergeant Moretti,' says Drury. 'He has the keys.'

I glance at the surfeit of broken doors, but don't comment.

Moretti stands to attention, sucking in his stomach. Pale as a plucked chicken, he has the word POLICE stitched into the breast pocket of his waterproof jacket.

'How often is this site patrolled?' asks the DCI.

'It's not on any regular routes.'

'What does that mean?'

'The place hasn't been used for thirty years.'

Drury blows air from his nose. 'Really?'

White surgical gloves are distributed and the DCI follows Moretti through the first door. Lights are triggered. Most of the bulbs are broken, but enough shine unsteadily to reveal a large room littered with torn fittings and collapsed heating ducts.

'Why is the power still connected?' asks Drury.

'Can't tell you, sir,' answers Moretti. 'Above my pay grade.'

A metal trough along one wall has a sign above it that reads: USE GLOVES AND EYE PROTECTION. Nearby, a control panel has a row of red and green buttons. The wiring has been ripped out.

A rusting staircase turns back on itself and rises to the upper floor, fifteen feet above. Beneath the stairs an old boiler has been wedged sideways, partially concealing a door. Moretti goes first, pulling aside two drums that slosh with unknown liquids.

The second room is smaller, with a table, two chairs, a double bed, a bath and a wood-fired boiler or stove. Someone has doused every hard surface with bleach or some other chemical cleaner. The caustic stench hooks at the back of my throat and tries to scald my lungs.

It's the same smell I remember from the farmhouse where the Heymans died.

'What's upstairs?' asks Drury.

'More of the same,' says Moretti.

'Show me.'

The rattling metal staircase pulls more plaster from the walls. I stay behind with DS Casey, walking the room again. The old-fashioned bathtub was lifted into place using a block and tackle. The ropes have left marks on the overhead pipes. A razor rests on the rim of the tub. The nearest shelf holds bottles of toiletries.

The iron-sprung bed has been stripped of bedding and a

quarter-inch thick chain is looped around one metal leg. At the opposite end of the chain is a leather cuff, sweat-stained and secured by a padlock. It can be adjusted to fit around a person's wrist or neck.

Beside the bed there is a wooden trunk with a curved lid. Using a fountain pen, I lever it open. The trunk looks empty at first glance, but then I spy a thin piece of black fabric hooked on the corner of a loose hinge; a g-string with a lace edging.

DS Casey opens a plastic evidence bag and I drop the lingerie inside.

The bedding was thrown into the corner and set on fire. Crouching beside the charred mess, I use the pen to lift a tacky section of the fabric. The remnants include a scorched corner of a pizza box and a foil takeaway container. Something else catches my eye – a small moulded plastic figure, less than an inch high. A stationmaster dressed in a blue waistcoat holding a flag.

'I need another evidence bag,' I say.

'What is that?'

'A collector's piece.'

Straightening up, I gaze around again, bothered by something that I can't quite quantify. I look across the room. Anyone coming into the main building could easily have found the door beneath the stairs. And this second chamber isn't particularly secure or soundproof. The bed has only one manacle yet there were two captives. He couldn't watch both girls constantly. How did he control them?

Natasha had pre-mortem scratches on her hips. Dr Leece speculated that she might have squeezed through a narrow opening like a window. This place has none.

'Did you notice the pipes on the walls outside?' I ask.

Casey shakes his head.

Crossing the room, I push aside several boxes and find an empty metal storage cabinet. There are scratches in the concrete where the cabinet has been dragged across the floor.

'Here, help me lift this.'

Casey takes one side and we pull the cabinet away from the wall, exposing a trapdoor with a rope handle. On my knees, I pull it open, levering it backwards on stiff hinges. The room below is a dark pit.

'Lend me your torch.'

Crouching over the hole, I direct the beam. Dust motes reflect in the light as the dungeon is revealed piece by piece, like a jigsaw created in hell. Two bunks. A table. Chairs. Shelves. A sink. Magazines. A saucepan. A bedpan. Thin grey blankets. Scattered clothes.

The ladder only reaches halfway to the ceiling. The lone window is high on the wall above the sink. Sealed. It doesn't seem big enough for a person to squeeze through.

The torch beam continues moving. I notice a poster of Brighton Pier and a collage, made of cut-up pictures torn from magazines. Cans of food are stacked on the shelves. A jar of teabags is resting near the gas ring burner.

When I'm sure the basement is empty, I pull away, desperate to be outside, to be away from here.

The rain has started up again and I don't have an umbrella. I walk away from the buildings, climb the embankment and look down from the top of the quarry. Standing there, with my head bowed, arms hanging, I let the rain run over my scalp and into my eyebrows and down my face. I have never adored nature. I can appreciate its beauty, but I'm indifferent to its vagaries. Nature can do some appalling things, but it always endures and remains unmoved by human suffering.

Below me, men and women in blue overalls are moving into the compound, following a path cut through the brambles. They're looking for blood, ballistics, fingerprints and body fluids – the remnants of death, the signs of life.

Piper was here. She ran from him, but he tracked her down. What will he do now? Unless this man has developed a special bond with Piper, unless she's become indispensable to his fantasies, she will be expendable, another loose end to be tied up.

Gazing into the sky, I search forlornly for a star through the thick cloud cover. Two thousand years ago, according to the Bible, three wise men followed a star and found a saviour lying in a manger. I don't believe in miracles, but Piper Hadley needs one tonight.

The headlights were blinding me at first.

It was only when the driver's door opened and he moved forward into the light that I knew he had found me. I lost control. The wetness ran down my legs and filled my shoes.

I couldn't run. I couldn't cry out. I had nothing left. He took my hand and led me to the car. He put tape around my hands and feet and made me swallow two small white pills.

Gentle as a lamb, I let him lift me into the boot. He put tape on my mouth and pulled a sack over my head. I coughed into the dust, struggling to breathe. Then I closed my eyes and went to sleep.

I have a vague recollection of the car stopping and George talking to someone, but then the car was moving again and I slept, not expecting to wake up.

And now I'm here, lying in a lovely bed, wearing clean pyjamas. It's the same attic room that Tash and I first came to after he took us. The furniture hasn't changed, but he doesn't have the black and white TV any more. Maybe he threw it away.

I don't remember how he got me up the stairs. And I haven't moved since I woke up. Exhaustion keeps me pressed to these white sheets like an insect pinned to a piece of cardboard. I once visited the Natural History Museum in London on a school excursion. We were taken to the Entomology Department where there were 140,000 wooden drawers with 28 million specimens. I didn't know there were that many different insects in the world. I don't like bugs, but I don't squash them any more.

I'm so tired. I just want to sleep. George can do what he likes. I don't care any more.

Some time later, I wake with the memory of having screamed, but the sound has dissipated and the room is full of dark shadows.

'Is anyone there?' I ask.

There's no answer.

'Talk to me, please.'

'What would you like me to say?' asks George.

He is sitting on a chair between the wardrobe and the window, leaning back against the wall. I can't see his face.

'What was your nightmare about?'

'I didn't have a nightmare.'

'Yes, you did.'

'I don't remember.'

'Dreams are funny like that,' he says. 'I don't remember mine.'

'Am I a long way from home?'

'What do you mean?'

'I mean in miles. Is it a long way?'

'No.'

'Could I make it if I walked all day?'

'Perhaps.'

'Are you just saying that to make me happy?'

'Yes.'

46

It is past midnight on Christmas morning and the only creatures
stirring are being nourished by machine coffee and the chocolate bars with raisins that nobody likes. Every available officer
has been recalled. Leave cancelled. Festivities put on hold.

The roadblocks have been maintained throughout the night
and plans are being prepared for a major ground search at first
light using volunteers, dogs, helicopters and heat-sensing radar.

On a whiteboard in the incident room, somebody has written,
'Piper Hadley is coming home.' Yesterday's message. Premature.
Out of date. Nobody has the energy to scrub it off.

Drury moves down the corridor as though walking in his
sleep. At the coffee machine he presses a button and listens to
the machine give an emphysemic cough and hack, spitting out
coffee that looks like tar.

He takes a sealed evidence bag from his pocket and studies
the tiny manikin of the stationmaster.

'Are you sure it belongs to Martinez?'

'Yes.'

He runs his thumb over the model piece.

'It's not much of a smoking gun.'

'If you wait for fingerprints or DNA, it could take days. Piper doesn't have that long.'

The DCI's face twists. 'We've issued an arrest warrant for Martinez and circulated details of his vehicle.'

'What about going public?'

'He could have Emily and Piper. It's too big a risk.'

Drury sips the coffee and almost spits it out. He pours the dregs into the sink, crushing the plastic cup in his fist.

'Are you sleeping with Victoria Naparstek?' he asks.

'What?'

'You heard the question.'

'I don't think that's any—'

'I'll take that as a yes.' He rocks back on his heels, flexing his fingers against his thighs. 'I think you should leave her alone.'

'Why?'

'I'm concerned for her.'

'You care for her?'

'Yes.'

'Does your wife know?'

He smiles tightly. No teeth. 'My wife and I have an under-standing. I know it sounds like a cliché.'

'You have an open marriage?'

'If you want to call it that.'

'Does your wife see other men?'

'She could.'

As soon as he utters the statement, he's aware of how self-absorbed and insincere it sounds. Elevating his chin, he presses his lips into thin lines.

'Are you married?' he asks.

'My wife and I are separated.'

'I notice that you still wear a wedding ring. I guess that makes us both hypocrites, but only one of us is a showboat.'

He leaves me then, striding down the corridor like a soldier marching into battle. How can a man with so much ego and self-hatred survive in a job with so few highs and so many lows? I fear for his sanity. I feel for his wife.

Ruiz wakes me just after 4 a.m. I've fallen asleep on a desk, head resting on my forearms, dribble on the blotter beneath my chin. I sit up, dry-mouthed, thirsty.

'You don't twitch when you sleep,' he says. 'It's like your Parkinson's takes the night off.'

My arms and head are moving now, jerking and spasming. It's a strange dance, self-conscious and nerdish. I take two pills from a childproof bottle and Ruiz gets me a cup of water from the cooler.

'Merry Christmas,' he says.

'Ditto, big man.'

I'm waiting for the medication to take hold. Then I'll be 'on' – as they say in Parkinson's parlance – as opposed to 'off'.

'Where have you been?'

'I took Dale Hadley home. Nice house. Good-looking children. They're like a Disney family.'

'With a missing daughter.'

'Swings and roundabouts.'

Ruiz has news. Phillip Martinez was picked up two hours ago by a highway patrol car on the M40 near Stokenchurch. He was alone in the car.

'Where is he now?'

'Downstairs. Drury is about to interview him. I thought you'd want to watch.'

I wash my face with cold water. Ruiz waits. Then we take the lift downstairs. Phillip Martinez is sitting alone in the interview suite. He glances at the ceiling like a man who is trapped at the bottom of a deep dark well, who can see a circle of blue sky above him.

Dishevelled and tired, he raises his hairless hand, scratching the stubble on his jaw. One side of his face is bruised and swollen, slowly changing colour.

DCI Drury and DS Casey enter the room. Martinez leaps to his feet.

'It's about bloody time.'

'Sit down, please,' says Drury.

'Have you found Emily? Did you talk to her mother?'

'Sit down.'

'That bitch is behind this. She's been planning it all long.'

Drury points again to the chair. The two men stare at each other and Martinez blinks first, taking a seat. He crosses his legs and his upper foot jiggles up and down.

'For the record,' says the DCI, 'we are recording this conversation. Can you confirm, Mr Martinez, that you have been read your rights?'

'Yes.'

'You have also been given the opportunity to have a lawyer present, but you have declined.'

'Yes.'

'Where were you between 2 p.m. and 3 p.m. yesterday afternoon?'

'I was looking for my daughter. She ran away.'

'Why?'

'We had an argument.'

'How did you get the bruises and scratches on your face?'

Martinez touches his cheek. 'She was upset. She threw a few things.'

'What was this argument about?'

Martinez sighs. 'Emily wanted to spend Christmas with her mother. I told her that she could go to London on Boxing Day but not before. She wouldn't listen.'

'She hit you?'

'Yes.'

'Did you hit her?'

'No. I mean . . . I tried to stop her hurting herself. She was out of control. Hysterical.'

'Did you hit her?'

391

'Is that what she said? She's exaggerating. She's a typical teenager. Headstrong. Ungrateful. Melodramatic.'

'When did you last see her?'

'Eight–fifteen yesterday morning.'

'Why didn't you report her missing?'

'I didn't know she'd run away until later. I thought she'd gone to work. When she didn't come home at midday I started to worry.'

'What did you do then?'

'I went looking for her. I called her friends. I found a train timetable in her room. That's when I realised that she'd gone to London. Her mother lives at a hostel in Ealing. I drove there but Amanda wouldn't see me and the staff threatened to call the police.'

'You didn't see Emily?'

'They were hiding her.'

Drury pauses. With deliberate slowness, he places a sealed evidence bag in front of Martinez.

'Is this your wallet?'

'Yes.'

'There is a photograph in the inside sleeve of a young woman.'

'Emily. So what?'

Drury places a second plastic bag on the table.

'Do you recognise this?'

'That's one of my pieces: the stationmaster. I have a model railway. Where did you get it?'

'You're sure it belongs to you?'

'Positive. I commissioned it from Aiden Campbell, a famous model maker. I supplied him with a photograph. How did you get it?'

'It was found at an abandoned factory where we believe Piper Hadley and Natasha McBain were imprisoned for three years.'

Martinez blinks at Drury incredulously, his eyebrows raised, his palms open. He's unsure if he's missing something.

'You must be joking.'

Drury doesn't respond.

Martinez wags his finger in the air. 'Oh, no, you're not suggesting—'

'I'm asking for an explanation.'

Martinez frowns, his features bunching together in the centre of his face. 'This is ridiculous. Somebody is winding you up.'

Martinez turns to the mirror, as though aware that someone is watching him. Or maybe he's looking at his own reflection, needing confirmation that this is really happening to him.

Watching from behind the one-way mirror, I look for signs of stress and deception. There nothing disjointed or improvised or put together in haste.

'He's good,' says Ruiz.

'Yes, he is.'

'Is he telling the truth?'

'About Emily . . . possibly.' I saw the train timetable in her room.

'I should check on the ex-wife. I could drive to London.'

'It's worth a shot.'

I hug the big man and wish him Merry Christmas again.

'What are you going to do?' he asks.

'I'll hang around a bit longer.'

'What about Julianne and the girls?'

'I'll call them.'

Ruiz leaves and I turn back to the interview. Drury has placed a photograph on the table in front of Phillip Martinez.

'Recognise this place?'

'No.'

'Take a closer look.'

'What is it?'

'It's where you kept Piper and Natasha. You tried to clean up, but didn't do a very good job. One skin cell is all it takes to get a DNA profile. We're dismantling the pipes and vacuuming the floors. The same thing is happening downstairs. We're taking your car apart. We're going to find the evidence. We're going to link you to this.'

'This is completely ridiculous. I have no idea what you're talking about.'

'I'm giving you a chance to redeem yourself. Tell us where Piper is. Tell us what you did to Emily.'

Martinez tries to stand. DS Casey matches his movements. He's bigger. Stronger. More intimidating.

'I won custody of my daughter. She belongs to me. Why aren't you looking for her?'

'Answer my question, Mr Martinez.'

'I don't have to listen to you.'

'But you do have to sit down.'

The scientist retakes his seat. Shocked. Angry.

This man is either telling the truth or he's an expert liar, practised to the point of being pathologically good. Drury has done everything right – pushing for details, looking for the minutiae that so often trip up a suspect because lying is harder to sustain than the truth. But Phillip Martinez is even more remarkable. His answers sound so credible. He doesn't embellish or avoid eye contact. There are no gaps or clumsy repetitions. He is genuinely concerned about Emily – asking about her constantly, accusing his ex-wife of orchestrating her disappearance.

On the night of the Bingham festival he had a phone call from a doctor saying that his ex-wife had been admitted to Littlemore Hospital in Oxford suffering from auditory hallucinations. He called Emily and met her at the house and that's where he spent the night. He didn't see Piper arrive. He didn't know Emily was planning to run away.

It's the same story when he's questioned about the blizzard. He and Emily ate dinner and watched TV until the power went out. Then they played a game of Scrabble by candlelight before going to bed.

It's a bravura performance of a wronged man. Misunderstood. Angry. Frustrated. Prickly.

Drury takes a break after two hours. Regulations must be followed. I meet him in the corridor.

'Have you been listening?' he asks, taking deep swallows from a bottle of water.

'Yes.'

'It's like he knows the questions are coming.'

'He's had three years to prepare.'

Drury's chest expands as though plates of muscle are moving beneath his shirt. 'How do I break him down?'

'Maybe you can't. The very best liars are those people who are good at lying to themselves.'

'He's delusional?'

'Not at all. Deception and self-deception require the same skills. Haven't you ever wondered why people cheat at solitaire or peek at the answers to a crossword puzzle? It's not a competition and there's no prize, yet they still do it.'

'They want to feel good about themselves.'

'By cheating?'

Drury shrugs. 'So why do they do it?'

'It's an evolutionary process. Forty years ago a biologist called Robert Trivers argued that our flair for self-deception dated back to prehistoric times when we first formed into tribes. Communities have always punished cheats and liars but as highly intelligent primates we became aware of the risks of being ostracised and fed to the hyenas if we were caught. It didn't stop us lying. We just got better at it. We learned to get away with more.'

'So you're saying we evolved into liars?'

'I'm saying it's a theory. It's why Mark Twain wrote: "When a person cannot deceive himself, how is he going to deceive other people?"'

Drury looks at his watch.

'My kids are going wake up in a few hours. Their presents are under the tree. I'd like to be there.'

'Let me talk to Martinez.'

'Can't do that – against the rules.'

'Sign me in as a visitor. No cameras. No recording.'

'It won't be admissible in any court.'

'Finding Piper is more important.'

The DCI pulls his head from side to side, sucking saliva through his teeth.'Martinez would have to agree.'

'Ask him.'

'Why would he say yes?'

'He's a showman. He wants an audience.'

47

Phillip Martinez looks up as the door opens, eyes on mine, caught between hope and trepidation.

'Have they found my Emily?'

'Not yet.'

He closes his eyes, shows his long lashes, a picture of misery; a man marooned on a desert island, waiting for rescue. As the air shifts, I catch a whiff of his sweat dried in his clothes.

'Do you remember me?' I ask, sitting opposite him.

'Of course.' He watches me cautiously. 'Should I call you Professor or Doctor?'

'I'm not a doctor.'

'You trained for a while. Three years of medicine.'

'How did you know that?'

Martinez allows himself to smile. 'You have talked to my daughter three times. In your wildest dreams did you imagine that I wouldn't check up on you?'

'That's very diligent.'

'I am always diligent, Professor. I am the senior scientist at one of the biggest research institutes in Europe. I have a staff of twenty and a budget of thirteen million pounds. Don't mistake me for a stupid man.'

'I would never do that.'

He leans back, satisfied with his first salvo.

'We got off to a bad start,' I say. 'I won't lie to you if you don't lie to me.'

'I haven't yet,' he says.

'You lied about why you came back from America. You were accused of falsifying data on treatments for cancer and were publicly rebuked by your peer reviewers.'

Martinez barely moves a muscle. His glossy avid eyes remind me of a ventriloquist's dummy.

I keep pushing. 'Two journal articles were published under your name. You took research funds under false pretences. You had to pay the money back.'

His jaw flexes and his eyes glaze over.

'In your wildest dreams, Mr Martinez, did you imagine that I wouldn't check up on you?'

There it is – his breaking point. He rocks forward in his chair, his lips peeled back, canine teeth bared.

'How dare you,' he spits. 'How dare you insult me and question my ethics. Look at you! You're diseased! You're only functioning because of the drugs that people like me have discovered and tested. Your condition is getting worse – eating away at your nerves, robbing you of balance, movement, speech and eventually your mind. One day, not so many years from now, you'll be a jerking, shitting, quivering sack of bones, unable to walk or talk or feed yourself. Instead of insulting my reputation, you should be praying I find a cure. You should be begging for my help, you pompous, self-righteous schmuck. You *need* people like me.'

Watching spit fly from his mouth, I recognise a classic narcissist, a perfectionist governed by his own ego and sense of worth, someone who cannot accept anyone who questions the carefully crafted, flawless image he has manufactured of himself. He will destroy the messenger, rather than hear the message.

He leans back, fire still burning inside him. He wants me to apologise. Expects it.

I give him that much. 'I'm sorry, Mr Martinez. I didn't mean to question your professional integrity.'

He waves his hand dismissively.

'Can I ask you some questions?'

He nods.

'Does the name George mean anything to you?'

'Why?'

'It's a simple enough question.'

'It's a nickname. When we first married my wife called me Gorgeous George. She thought I looked like some wrestler who was big in the fifties. We both had curly hair.'

'How did you get the bruise on your face?'

He touches the side of his head. 'I told the police. Emily threw a plate at me because I wouldn't give in to her blackmail.'

'Why would she blackmail you?'

'She wanted to spend Christmas with her mother. I told her no. She threatened to accuse me of molesting her unless I gave in.'

'She doesn't like living with you.'

'We disagree on certain things.'

'Such as?'

'I don't believe in coddling children, Professor. I will not become a slave like other parents. I am not a servant, chauffeur and secretary to my daughter. Other parents pamper and create monsters. Driving them everywhere, fulfilling their every wish – birthday parties, ballet, football practice, piano, violin, tennis; Ritalin if they're hyperactive, Prozac if they're depressed, antibiotics if they sniffle. Not me. I am a parent, not a best friend or confidant . . . and certainly not a slave.'

'Congratulations. You're father of the year.'

He doesn't react.

'Where were you yesterday afternoon?'

'I drove to London.'

'What time did you arrive?'

'I don't know. It was quite late, nine, maybe ten o'clock. You can ask the landlady at the hostel. She wouldn't let me see my wife.'

The drive to London takes less than two hours. He had ample time to snatch Piper, clean up the basement and hide her somewhere before driving to the capital.

'How do you explain your stationmaster turning up at the scene?'

He hesitates. 'Isn't it obvious? Somebody planted it there. They're trying to frame me.'

'Who would do that?'

He shrugs. 'It's happened before. That business with the falsified test results – somebody sabotaged my experiments. I was set up.'

'Why?'

'To discredit me, of course.' He makes it sound so obvious. 'Medical research is full of venal people: rivals jealous of my success, trying to steal my funding, scared they might be beaten to a breakthrough that could be worth billions of dollars.'

'You don't really believe a rival would try to frame you for kidnapping and murder.'

He shrugs dismissively. 'This is a waste of time. I had nothing to do with the Bingham Girls. Never met them. I wasn't living in Abingdon when they went missing.'

'Don't you think it's odd, you finding a letter from Piper among Emily's things?'

'I was searching her room.'

'Why?'

'I was looking for drugs.'

'You think she's using?'

'Like I said – I'm diligent.'

'You search your daughter's room; do you read her emails?'

'Yes, as it happens.' He laughs at my surprise. 'You don't agree with my methods?'

'No.'

'When your daughter is sucking on a crack pipe in some filthy council estate, you can come and ask for my advice on parenting.'

'Where is Piper Hadley?'

'I have no idea.'

'Where is Emily?'

'She's with her mother.'

He holds my gaze defiantly. 'I didn't take those girls. You people can plant whatever evidence you like, but it won't make me guilty.'

The key turns in the lock.

The door opens. George is wearing a dressing gown and carrying a tray with a sandwich and a mug of tea. He puts the tray on a table beside my head. I stare at the steam, watching it twist and curl into nothingness.

My left wrist is handcuffed to the metal bedhead. I use the other to pull the bedclothes around me, but I can't reach the sheet. I must have kicked it off when I was sleeping.

'You should drink something.'

There is a long silence. My chest tightens and I can't breathe. George sits next to me and puts his hand near my leg, telling me to stay calm. His hand slides closer until his fingers brush against my thigh.

'You shouldn't have run away. I want you to say you're sorry.'

I don't answer him.

His hand touches my skin where my pyjama top and the trousers meet.

'Did you hear me, Piper?'

'Yes.'

'Say you're sorry.'

I shake my head.

He strikes on my blind side, the punch sinking deep into my stomach, where he twists his fist under my ribs until I imagine that every organ has been ruptured and the blood and bile are spilling into my chest. I cannot breathe. He waits.

'Say you're sorry.'

I blink again. The next blow lifts my body off the bed, holding me against the wall, convulsing.

'Say you're sorry.'

'I'm sorry, I'm sorry,' I sob, trying to breathe.

I'm sorry you're a sad sadistic prick. I'm sorry I didn't stab you through the eye. I'm sorry I didn't crush your skull with the brick. I'm sorry I can't scratch your eyes out. I want to scream these things, but none of the words come out. Instead, I crumple to the bed and curl into a ball.

'That's better,' he says. 'Now we can be friends again.' He cradles me, rocking me back and forth, stroking my hair. 'Would you like to meet Emily?'

I try to pull away, but he grips me harder.

'You didn't . . . you promised me.'

'Why should I keep my promises to you?'

'I said I was sorry.'

'Yes, you did.'

'Where is she?'

He smiles. 'We'll save that surprise for another day.'

Pushing himself away from the bed, he goes to the window. 'Shall I tell you what it looks like outside?'

'What do you mean?'

'It's Christmas — do you want to know what sort of day it is?'

'OK.'

'It's overcast, but we might get some sun later.'

'Describe something else.'

'What?'

'Anything.'

'I can see a church steeple and a park. Some kid is riding a new bicycle.'

'It must have been a present.'

'Yes.'

'What's your favourite movie?'

'I don't watch many movies.'

'What about TV?'

'I like Strictly Come Dancing, but it's not on over Christmas.'

'Do you watch EastEnders?'

'No.'

He looks genuinely sorry. Reaching into his pocket, he produces two white pills.

'I have to go out for a while. I'll be back later. These will help you sleep. You shouldn't have them on an empty stomach.'

'I don't think I can eat anything.'

'When you're stronger we'll start all over again. It will be just like old times.'

48

DS Blake sprints down the corridor, taking the corner so quickly he almost loses control and has to leap an office plant. One of the uppermost leaves rocks to the floor like a dropped sheet of paper.

'We found it, boss,' he says, hammering on Drury's door. The DCI has been sleeping. Blake continues. 'Martinez has another house. It's in Oxford. He rented it when he moved back from the States. He lived there until he won custody of Emily, but he never relinquished the lease.'

Drury appears, sleep-stung.

Blake is still talking. 'The owner of the house died in 2009, but Martinez did a deal with the son to keep the lease going.'

'Why does a man need two houses?' asks Drury.

'Exactly my thoughts, boss.' Blake looks pleased with himself. 'The son said something else. His old man had an early-model Land Rover. It was kept in the garage of the rented house.'

'Where is it now?'

'He doesn't know.'

'So Martinez could have had access? That explains why his Lexus is so bloody clean.'

The DCI is fully awake and moving. 'Briefing in fifteen. I want a dozen officers with me. Get me aerial maps of the street and the house. See if the council has a floor plan.'

'It's Christmas, boss.'

Drury curses. 'OK, but get me a child protection officer. I want one with us.'

The mood in the incident room has been completely transformed. Exhausted bodies are energised. Tiredness has been forgotten.

Watching and listening, I realise how much I stand apart from these officers. I am an outsider, a civilian. On top of this I'm a psychologist, a profession they mistrust. They imagine that I'm constantly reading their body language, probing for weaknesses or hidden meanings, like a man with x-ray eyes who can peer into the depths of their souls. Such fears are irrational and baseless, but it doesn't change the reality. Some people cannot relax around a police officer or a priest or an abortionist; the same is true of a psychologist.

Drury's mobile rings again. He answers it. Hurried. Irritated. It's the chief constable.

'Yes, sir, I'm on top of this. We have a good lead on where Piper Hadley might be . . . North Oxford . . . That's right, sir . . . We can link him to the abandoned factory and to both girls . . . I understand your concerns, sir, but things are under control . . . In the next hour . . . As soon as I know.'

Casey emerges from the lift. His tweed jacket has beads of rain on the shoulders and his wet hair looks even more like a helmet than usual. He has spent all morning in the search area, marshalling volunteers. Most of them now want to go home for Christmas dinner.

'What do you want to do, boss?' he asks, flexing the cold from his fingers.

'See how many you can keep in the field,' says Drury. 'Call it off when it gets dark.'

The briefing is over. The team assembles downstairs. Vehicles standing ready, engines running. Drury takes the lead car, dressed in a bulletproof vest, a man completely in charge. He hasn't asked for my help. Hasn't spoken to me. This is his show.

My mobile is ringing. It's Ruiz.

'What's the difference between a snowman and a snow woman?'

'Snowballs,' I say.

'You've heard it.'

'Noah had heard it.'

Ruiz sighs and tries to think of another joke.

'Any news?' I ask.

'I should set up my own detective agency.'

'You hated being a detective.'

'Yes, but I was pretty good at it. I found Emily Martinez. She's with her mother.'

'You talked to her.'

'Yep. She arrived at the hostel yesterday around lunchtime. It took a while to convince Amanda Martinez to trust me. She thought I was working for her husband.'

'What did Emily say about the fight?'

'It was just as Martinez described it.'

'So he was telling the truth.'

'About that much anyway,' says Ruiz.

He continues talking as I watch a bus pull into the parking area carrying volunteers returning from the search. They disembark wearing mud-stained boots and creased white overalls. As they walk towards their cars, they remind me of emaciated snowmen.

As the image occurs to me, I get a tingling sensation in my fingertips.

'I got to go,' I tell Ruiz.

'What's up?'

'Maybe nothing.'

Climbing the stairs, two at a time, I reach the incident room. DS Casey is on the radio organising refreshments for the search teams that are still at the scene. I wait for him to finish.

'The CCTV footage from the Bingham festival – where will I find it?'

'It should be on the database,' he says.

'Can you call it up?'

He logs me into the nearest terminal, linking me into the Police National Computer, a vast database containing the details of every known offender and 'person of interest' in the UK: their names, nicknames, aliases, scars, tattoos, accents, shoe size, height, age, hair colour, eye colour, offence history, associates and modus operandi. It also hosts the case files of active investigations, allowing detectives to cross-reference details and search for links.

The Bingham festival footage is catalogued in a dozen different ways. It was shot from a CCTV camera opposite the bus stop at the entrance to the village green. Twenty-eight seconds of recording show Piper and Natasha leaving the funfair, walking along a sideshow alley and turning out of the gate.

I open another file, this one containing a series of images taken by a photographer for the *Oxford Mail*. He shot mostly kids eating candyfloss and riding on the carousel, but one sequence near the dodgem cars shows Piper and Natasha standing in the background.

I zoom in on the girls, moving through the images frame by frame. Behind them, parked on the road, I can see a patrol car with a police officer standing alongside, leaning on the open door. The image is too blurred and distant to recognise a face, but the stance is familiar.

Another photograph comes to mind – the one of Natasha McBain outside Oxford Crown Court, being escorted through a hate-filled crowd by a court security officer. His face is hidden behind a raised forearm as he pushes people aside.

Thoughts are now splattering into my consciousness like fat drops of rain on a dry road. First one then another . . . snowmen, stationmasters, missing girls . . . The truth isn't a blinding light or a cold bucket of water in the face. It leaks into my consciousness one drop at a time.

Pushing back from the desk, I cross the incident room and take a corridor as far as the changing rooms. Each officer has a steel storage locker for his or her uniform and kit. I walk down the rows of lockers, looking at the numbers and initials.

The locker is secured with a combination padlock. I look for something heavy. The fire extinguisher is buckled against the wall. I pull it free, raise it above my shoulders and smash it against the padlock. The door buckles, the lock breaks. I'm looking at body armour, police boots and a reflective vest. Hanging at the back of the locker is a pair of white overalls with OxSAR sewn into the breast pocket. The trouser cuffs are stained with soot and I smell bleach on the fabric.

DS Casey is at the radio, listening to the police operation in North Oxford. The cars are getting closer, sealing off the street.

'I need to ask you something. When the chief constable cancelled all holiday leave and officers were recalled, did that include everyone?'

'Yeah.'

'Where was Grievous yesterday?'

'I saw him at one of the roadblocks.'

'Where?'

'On the Silo Road.'

'What about today?'

'I haven't seen him. What's this about?'

I don't answer for a moment. And then: 'What's his full name?'

'Pardon?'

'His name . . . his proper one.'

'Brindle Hughes.'

'What about his first name?'

'Gerald.'

'Does anybody ever call him George?'

'Everbody calls him Grievous.'

Sitting at the computer terminal, I type a new search looking for a witness statement. The screen refreshes. I scan the list. The statement is signed and dated by Probationary Constable Gerald Brindle Hughes. He describes being on patrol on the Saturday night that the Bingham girls disappeared. He saw two girls matching the descriptions of Piper Hadley and Natasha McBain leaving the funfair at approximately ten o'clock.

'Where does Grievous live?'

Casey looks up from the radio. 'Why?'

'We have to find him.'

Casey looks at me apprehensively. His hairline creeps closer to his eyes.

'What's he done?'

'I'm not sure, but I need you to trust me. If I'm right, it could make your career. If I'm wrong . . .'

I don't finish the sentence. Casey has grown nervous. 'Maybe I should call the boss.'

'Don't use the radio. He'll be listening.'

'Who?'

'Grievous. That's how he found Piper.'

'What are you talking about?'

'He's been monitoring the police radio messages. That's how he knew where to find Piper. He heard her location being given over the radio. He got there before anyone else.'

'But how?'

'He knew where she escaped from.'

The penny drops. Casey looks at me in disbelief. 'Are we talking about the same person? Trainee Detective Constable Brindle Hughes?'

'I hope I'm wrong. Please, we have to hurry.'

49

DS Casey shoulders open the external fire door and points his keys at an unmarked police car. Lights flash and doors unlock.

'The boss's phone is turned off,' he says, holding a mobile to his ear. 'He won't turn it on until after the operation. It's procedure. Urgent comms only.'

Casey stares at the screen, pondering whether to leave a message. He wants to cover himself.

'I'll explain it to DCI Drury,' I say, sliding into the passenger seat.

Moments later we pull out of the parking area and accelerate along Marcham Road. The streets are deserted. People are indoors, celebrating Christmas, eating turkey and the trimmings, plum pudding with custard, dozing off in front of the TV before the Queen makes her speech.

'I still can't believe we're doing this,' says Casey. 'Grievous is one of the lads.'

'How well do you know him?'

'He's a mate.'

'So you've been to his place?'

'No.'

'Have you met his fiancée?'

'Not yet.'

'She's never come to the pub for a drink or dropped Grievous at the station?'

'No.' Casey falters. 'He hasn't been with us long. Six months maybe.'

'Where was he before that?'

'In uniform . . . working downstairs.'

The DS swings hard into Drayton Road, past Ock Meadow, heading south, accelerating between intersections.

Facts are shifting in my head, detaching and re-forming into new pictures like the fragments of a montage, creating different realities. The past reshaped, history rewritten, explanations turned upside down.

Thinking out loud, I explain how Grievous was working the night that Piper and Natasha disappeared. The girls must have walked right past him as they headed for the leisure centre. He was also working as a court security officer when they gave evidence against Aiden Foster at Oxford Crown Court.

'That could be just a coincidence,' says Casey.

'Remember the farmhouse on the night of the blizzard? Augie Shaw said he saw Natasha on the road. Barefoot. Terrified. There was someone chasing her.'

'The snowman,' says Casey.

'I think it was someone dressed in white overalls, a search and rescue volunteer. Grievous works for OxSAR.'

'A lot of guys work as volunteers.'

'His overalls smell of bleach.'

'Is that the best you have? Phillip Martinez has a motive and no alibi. The guy is a control freak, you said so yourself. He's got medical training. He could have done that stuff . . . you know . . . to Natasha.'

Casey won't use the words.

'Grievous did two years of nursing before he became a court security officer.'

'How do you know?'

'He told me.'

'What about the figurine you found at the abandoned factory?'

'Grievous was with me when I went to see Phillip Martinez. He saw the model railway. He could have picked up the station-master and planted it to implicate Martinez.'

'You're making him sound like a master criminal. He's a trainee detective constable, for Christ's sake.'

'Humour me then. We'll knock on the door, say hello, wish him a Merry Christmas.'

'Then what?'

'We'll leave. One drink. That's all.'

The DS isn't convinced. I'm asking him to distrust a colleague, to break a special bond. Police officers look after each other and cover each other's backs. They socialise together and take holidays and marry into each other's families. They're comrades in arms, outsiders, hated until needed, undertakers to the living.

The raid in North Oxford has unfolded over the two-way radio. Police are going from floor to floor, searching the basement for hidden tunnels and secret rooms.

We're getting close. Casey pulls over a hundred yards from the address. This is a newer part of Abingdon with two-storey semi-detached houses, some with loft conversions and garages. The painted brick façades stand out brightly against the winter trees. Some have Christmas lights strung under the eaves or around the windows.

'So we're just going to say hello?' says Casey.

'Absolutely.'

'And then we'll leave?'

'Of course.'

'And you won't embarrass me by mentioning any of your theories to Grievous?'

'No.'

We walk through the gate and along the path. Casey rings the doorbell. Nobody answers.

'He's not home.'

'Try again.'

'I should never have let you talk me into this.'

The door opens. Grievous looks perplexed and then smiles broadly. 'Is everything all right, lads?'

'Yeah, course,' says Casey. 'We were passing and thought we'd drop in.'

'Merry Christmas,' I say.

'And to you.'

He hasn't fully opened the door.

'Do you have company?' I ask.

'No.'

'Where's your fiancée?'

'She's spending Christmas with her folks in Cornwall.'

'Shame, I was hoping to meet her,' says Casey. 'You didn't come to work today.'

'I didn't finish until late. Slept in. The boss said it was OK to take the day off. My mum's not well. Could be her last Christmas.'

'Sorry to hear that.'

'I was just going over there now. She lives around the corner.'

'Surely there's time for a quick drink,' says Casey, giving him a warm grin. He pushes past Grievous and stands in the hallway, glancing into a darkened front room.

'Nice place, lived here long?'

'A few years.'

We're led down the hallway to a drab *circa*-1970 kitchen with wood veneer cabinets, a porcelain sink and a worn linoleum floor. Coats are shrugged off and hung over chairs. Casey takes a seat, spreads his knees, a big man's pose.

'We should be celebrating,' he says.

'Why?' Grievous asks.

'We arrested Phillip Martinez for kidnapping the Bingham Girls. You missed a big day. Martinez had a second house. They're searching it now, looking for Piper Hadley. We were just on our way there.'

'North Oxford is the other direction,' says Grievous.

'How did you know it was in North Oxford?' asks Casey.

'You mentioned it.'

'No, I didn't.'

There is a moment, a heartbeat of silence, when the two men stare at each other. One is searching for clarity, the other for a way out. There is a tiny twitch in Grievous' eyes. The 'tell'.

'I've been caught out,' he says, looking embarrassed. 'I have a scanner upstairs. I've been listening to the police radio. Even when I'm not working, I can't leave the job alone.'

Casey laughs with him. 'You need to get married, pal.'

'Yeah, you're right,' says Grievous, glancing at me. I see nothing in his eyes. 'So why are you really here?'

'I'm heading back to London,' I say. 'I wanted to thank you for driving me around. I didn't get a chance to say goodbye.'

'Oh,' says Grievous, relaxing. 'Well, it was a pleasure meeting you, Professor.'

'You never did learn to call me Joe,' I say, shaking his hand, holding it a second longer than expected, studying his face. I release him. 'Can I use your toilet, Grievous?'

'Sure, it's up the stairs, first door on the right.'

I try to make eye contact with Casey but he's talking to Grievous about kitchen renovations. As I climb to the first floor, I glance quickly over the banister before opening the bathroom door.

I run the tap and open the cabinet. Shaving foam. Dental floss. Toothpaste. Hair gel. No women's products. Opening the door, I cross the landing to the nearest bedroom. I can hear Casey and Grievous popping cans of lager.

The room has been set up as a gymnasium with a bench and free weights that are stacked on a rack or threaded on a horizontal bar. The only other significant furniture is an old-fashioned roller desk with small wooden drawers. A laptop computer is closed on the slide-away table and the upper shelf has a police scanner blinking out green digital numbers.

415

I move diagonally across the landing and come to the main bedroom. It has a queen-size bed, unmade, cheap cotton sheets tossed aside. A flat-screen TV is propped on a stand in front of the bay window. DVDs are stacked on either side. Pirated movies. The large mahogany wardrobe has three doors, the centre one with a full-length mirror. Two pairs of trainers are lined up beneath the bed. Clothes are folded on a chair. A comb is stuck on a hairbrush.

There are two more rooms. One is made up as a guest room with an old-fashioned bedspread and a dressing table with an oval mirror that pivots up and down. The other room is used for storage.

I go back to the bathroom and flush the toilet.

The only place left is the loft conversion, up a narrow set of stairs. I climb slowly, trying not to make a sound. I glance over the banister. I can't hear voices any more.

The door is locked. My fingers turn the key. The door opens inwards and my pupils take a moment to adjust to the partial light. The roof slopes down on either side of the room. Against the far wall, beneath a covered skylight, I can see a bed and a bundle of bedclothes.

The room looks empty. I'm about to leave, when I hear a sound.

Crossing the room, I find a girl asleep beneath bedding, whimpering in her dreams, rocking her head from side to side. A nightmare has taken hold and her body jerks in protest. My fingers touch her arm. Her eyes open, but nothing registers.

'Piper?'

She doesn't answer.

'Can you hear me, Piper?'

Her pupils are dilated. She's drugged.

'I'm Joe. We talked yesterday.'

Her eyes are closing. She tries to roll over, but her left wrist is attached to the bedhead by a set of silver handcuffs.

Police issue. There's no way to free her without a key or a hacksaw.

I open my mobile and send a text message to DS Casey.

Piper is upstairs. Be careful.

I call Drury's number. He's still not answering. What next? 999. I ask for an ambulance and the police. The operator wants me to stay on the line, but I give my name and hang up.

I stroke hair away from Piper's eyes. They open.

'You said you were coming to get me yesterday.'

'I know. I'm sorry.'

'Don't let him hurt me.'

'I won't.'

Her eyes close. She's breathing deeply. Asleep again. I make my way downstairs, peering over the banister, listening for voices. Instead, I hear silence. I descend again, creeping towards the kitchen.

The room comes into view slowly. I see cans of beer on the table. Two glasses.

DS Casey is sitting in the same chair. His head has rocked forwards and his hand is clutching his throat, trying to stop the blood that is bubbling through his fingers. He groans and his chin lifts, his eyes meeting mine, death within them. Coming soon.

I hold my hand over his throat, my fingers covering his hand, increasing the pressure, but his carotid artery has been severed. He's bleeding out. Losing consciousness. I want to tell him I'm sorry. I should have stayed with him. Together . . . maybe . . .

On the table in front of him a mobile phone, my message on the screen. The last thing he read. A humming refrigerator rattles into stillness. At the same moment, his head rocks forward and his body shudders once before his heart stops, the pump dry. In the sudden quietness, I feel a small ceaseless tremor vibrating inside me, expanding, filling my chest and throat. I look along the hallway. Grievous could be waiting in any one of the rooms.

I could run. I could get outside and wait for the police. But that means leaving Piper.

There is something else on the kitchen table: a small silver key lying next to Casey's mobile. The key belongs to the set of handcuffs.

I look along the hallway again.

'Can you hear me, Grievous?'

The silence seems to be mocking me.

'We should talk,' I say. 'I'm good at listening.'

Still nothing.

Maybe he's gone. Fled the scene. He's left me the key. Surely he can't expect to get away. I wipe my hands on my thighs, pick up the key and move back towards the stairs, stopping at each door to glance inside.

There is a creaking sound above me.

'Grievous?'

Nothing.

From across the street, I hear a burst of laughter and the sound of Christmas crackers being pulled. Cheers. Applause.

I climb to the first landing, moving from room to room. Tiptoeing. Trying not to make a sound. Even before I finish the search, I know where I'll find him. Mounting the final staircase, I nudge the door with my foot.

Grievous is sitting on the bed with his back to the wall. His arms and legs are wrapped around Piper, hugging her against his chest. She's a human shield, asleep with her head on his shoulder.

'I thought you'd run away,' he says.

'Ditto,' I reply.

His hair is plastered down one side of his face and his eyes are like dark holes full of shadow and menace. He motions towards the end of the bed. There is a pistol lying on the bedspread, closer to me than to him. Polymer-framed, black as pitch. The ammunition clip has been placed alongside the weapon.

418

'That's for you,' he says.

I stare at the gun, trying to make sense of the offer.

'Pick it up. It won't bite.'

Piper is like a rag doll in his arms, her head slumped to one side, her eyes closed, her breathing shallow.

'What did you give her?'

He motions to the empty pill bottle on the table to his left. 'Diazepam. She won't feel a thing.'

'What isn't she supposed to feel?'

'Dying, of course.'

'You don't have to kill her.'

'It's a bit late now. She swallowed the lot. We're going to die together.'

He raises his left wrist and shows me how they are hand-cuffed together. His other hand, hidden until now, has a knife pressed flat against her body, the point roughly over her heart.

'There must have been thirty pills in that bottle. I don't think she'll survive even if they pump out her stomach. No time to waste, really. If you shoot me, you might save her.'

'I'm not going to shoot you.'

He looks at me sadly and kisses her forehead. 'Then we'll both watch her die.' He twirls her hair with his fingertips. 'It's such a pity. She's been a dear, dear thing.'

'Why are you doing this?'

'You're the psychologist, you tell me.'

Stepping closer, I crouch and take the pistol and ammunition clip.

'It slides in and clicks into place,' he says. 'Now release the safety.'

I have never fired a gun. I hate them. I know some people who argue they're just a tool, like a shifting spanner or a ballpoint hammer, but let's be honest and accept that guns are designed to be lethal weapons. There are a lot of things I haven't done. I haven't had a body piercing or jumped out of a plane or tried to tip a cow. All of these things seem preferable at the moment to holding a pistol in both hands, trying not to shake.

'Careful, you might shoot someone,' he says, smiling.

'Let Piper go?'

'Shoot me and you can have her.'

I point the gun at his head.

'That's the way.'

'I'm not going to shoot you. Nobody has to die.'

He smiles. He smells almost perfumed, as though he's showered and shaved and doused himself in cologne.

'You weren't in the service, were you?' he asks.

'Neither were you.'

'I got close.'

'That's like saying you nearly had sex, Grievous. You either did or you didn't – anything else is wanking.'

Anger lights up his eyes. I haven't seen his temper before. He's learned to hide it well.

'Should I call you Gerald or George?'

'Call me what you like.'

'Piper and Natasha called you George. It suits you.' I take a step closer. 'I'm going to undo the handcuffs.'

He shows me the knife again. 'I can flick my wrist and reach her heart before you take another step. How good a doctor are you? Can you patch a broken heart?'

I step back and find a straight-backed chair. I straddle it, resting my outstretched forearms on the top spar. I can hold the gun steadier now.

'This crime of mine,' says Grievous. 'Kidnapping the girls, raping them – in the grand scheme of things it doesn't mean very much. A thousand years from now nobody is going to care about the Bingham Girls or what I did to them. Not in a hundred years. Let's face it, Professor, men have been penetrating women since our species began. It's how we survive. So what if we don't say please beforehand and thank you afterwards. It doesn't alter the act. We penetrate. We procreate.'

'That's an interesting philosophy, George. Your mother would be very proud.'

'Leave my mother out of it.'

'Is that who you're trying to punish?'

'Oh, dear me, how disappointing,' he sighs. 'Is that the best you can do – Freudian hostility, a mummy fixation? Please. I expected more.'

'You don't have a fiancée, Grievous. She's another fiction. That's your problem, isn't it? You can't find anyone to love. It's always been that way, ever since puberty when all those hormones were playing havoc with your thinking. You wanted a girlfriend, but you had a problem. You were deaf in one ear and couldn't quite tune into what people were saying. Nobody knew about the brain tumour slowly growing, benign.

'You refused to wear a hearing aid or to sit up front in class. You didn't want anyone to know, particularly the girls. You wanted to be one of the cool group sitting up the back, passing notes to each other.

'Do you know, Grievous, there is a correlation between deafness and paranoid thinking? If you can't hear particularly well, it's easy to think people might be talking about you, laughing and joking at your expense, putting you down. Isn't that true?'

He doesn't answer me, but seems to be pressing the knife tighter against Piper's chest.

'Even the teachers thought you were slow and stupid, even your family. And every time someone laughed or behaved a little differently, you were sure they were making fun of you, whispering behind your back, sharing a private joke.

'You wanted a girlfriend, you were desperate for one, but girls rejected your pathetic attempts to woo them. I'm not criticising you or being patronising. It wasn't your fault. You adored those girls. You would have treated them like goddesses. Showered them with love. Written them poetry. Sung them love songs. But they didn't choose you, did they? They chose the arm-candy, the boys who made them look good and gave them status, the ones they swooned over.

'You fantasised about those unattainable girls. You pictured them as you worked out in weight rooms, shedding those pounds. You starved yourself. And then one day they discovered the tumour in your head and the surgeons cut it out and suddenly you could hear. You were whole. Nothing would stop you now.'

I pause, watching him, sensing how close I am to the truth. He has a lock of Piper's hair in his mouth.

'So what happened?' I ask.

He doesn't answer.

'Let me guess. You asked one of the unattainable girls to go out with you and she said yes. She was nice. Friendly. Pretty. She didn't tease you. She didn't call you names. She didn't make fun of your hearing problems. You were over the moon. You walked on air. You had never been happier in your entire life.

'It's not that you wanted to have sex with this girl – not straight away – you wanted to talk, to romance her, to show her what you had to offer. But then you froze. You got tongue-tied. Being able to hear didn't make any difference because you'd grown up being nervous and slow. You didn't know how to relax and just be yourself. Instead of being a new man, you were the same old Gerald – the slow Gerald, the paranoid Gerald.

'Did she laugh at your first crude attempt to kiss her? Or was the whole date a joke? Maybe her pretty friends put her up to it. Is that why you chose Natasha? She reminded you of those girls who laughed at you. She was provocative, flirtatious, vain, out of your league . . .'

His eyes flash open, full of hatred. Violence. 'You think I cared about that slut?'

'I think that answers my question.'

'She got what she deserved.'

'That's why you mutilated Natasha. It was hatred, not love.

Your desire had become twisted. Corrupted. Violent. It demanded you step aside. It negated the rights of others. It cleansed. It poisoned. It dictated your beliefs. You must have dragged that hatred around with you for years. It was gnawing away inside you while you watched other lads get the pretty girls, walking them home, getting invited inside, despoiling those sweet young bodies and then boasting about it afterwards.'

'Keep talking, Professor, it's *her* time you're wasting.'

I glance at Piper. Her breathing has grown ragged. The sedatives are being absorbed into her bloodstream.

'Why is it so important that I kill you?' I ask.

'It's over for me. There's nowhere else to go.'

'Give me Piper and I'll leave you the gun.'

He shakes his head. 'I want you to pull the trigger.'

'Why?'

He smiles. 'It's like I told you that first day I drove you to Bingham – killers and kidnappers know when they cross a line. They can't expect sympathy or understanding. Gideon Tyler took your wife and child. He did terrible things to them, but you said you wouldn't have pulled the trigger to stop him.'

'I lied.'

'Show me. Shoot me now. Prove you can do it, Professor. Learn how it feels.'

'I don't want to know how it feels.'

He runs his finger along Piper's cheek. 'Maybe if she were your daughter, you'd think differently. Perhaps Piper doesn't mean enough to you.'

'That's not true.'

He smiles. 'You think you can read people, Professor. You pick apart their motives and peer inside their heads, but I wonder if you ever look at yourself. I think you're a coward. I'm going to make you brave.'

'I live with a disease that makes me brave.'

'It gives you an excuse.' He spits the words. 'You couldn't stop the man who kidnapped your wife and daughter and now you're baulking at this. You're making excuses. Stop me. She's dying. Just do it!'

He lifts Piper's eyelids. Her pupils have rolled back into her head and white foam is leaking from one corner of her mouth. Every minute gives the pills longer to dissolve in her stomach and enter her bloodstream. Five minutes after ingestion she has a 90 per cent chance of survival. By sixty minutes it falls to less than 15 per cent.

The pistol has grown hot in my hands. I stare along the barrel with a mixture of loathing and awe.

'Let her go.'

'Shoot me. It's not difficult. You walk over here. Point the gun at my head and pull the trigger. Don't go trying to miss. I don't want to be left a vegetable. And don't try shooting me in the leg or shoulder. This knife is very sharp. It won't take much to slice into her chest.'

The pistol is growing heavier. I look at Piper and imagine her heartbeat slowing and her organs failing. In the next breath I can picture Charlie lying on a filthy mattress, chained to a radiator with masking tape wrapped around her head, breathing through a hose. I would have pulled a trigger a dozen times over to save her and Julianne. I would have emptied the magazine and reloaded. I would have done anything . . . given anything . . . if only . . .

'If I hear sirens, I will kill her, Professor. You're running out of time.' He is rocking Piper in his arms. 'Pull the trigger. People take lives all the time. You might even enjoy it. It could be cathartic. I mean, you're separated, your wife left you, you're riddled with disease, so much for "in sickness and in health".'

'That's not why she left me.'

'You must really hate her.'

'No.'

'Liar!'

I scream at him then. Aiming the gun at this head. Stepping closer.

'PUT DOWN THE KNIFE!'

'No.'

'LET HER GO!'

'Shoot me.'

'NO!'

'Tick tock, tick tock.'

'LET HER GO!'

'Pull the trigger.'

'SHE'S DYING!'

Grievous begins screaming back at me. 'SAVE HER! JUST DO IT! PULL THE TRIGGER! DO IT. SHOOT ME! PULL THE FUCKING TRIG—'

The gun recoils and a noise seems to detonate directly inside my head. Echoing. Drawn out. Groaning like a turntable on the wrong speed. I stare at the gun and smell the cordite.

My finger is still on the trigger. I'm locked in place as though turned to stone, while the Earth has turned ten thousand revolutions. Nothing stirs or shifts until Piper slides sideways, her hair plastered to the back of her head, slick with blood.

For a moment I think I must have shot her. Somehow the bullet must have ricocheted off the wall. I put my hand over the back of her head and discover the blood isn't hers.

Grievous is staring at me with his lips peeled back and mouth open, his last sentence cut short. The entry wound in his forehead is smaller than a five pence piece, while the exit wound has sprayed blood and brain matter across the painted wall.

Fumbling with the key, I remove the handcuffs and reach under Piper, lifting her easily and carrying her to the door and down two flights of stairs.

Adrenalin is still surging through me like the bass beat at a rock concert. Setting her down in the hallway near the front door, I put my ear to her mouth and nose and my hand on her lower chest. She's breathing, but her eyes are fixed. Dilated. I turn her on her side, putting her in the recovery position.

Where are the paramedics? I call 999 again, yelling at the

operator, telling them to hurry. The sedative has been in Piper's system for nearly thirty minutes.

I have to act now. Gastric lavage. Pump her stomach. I remember my medical training – three years of studying to be a doctor, doing my filial duty because God's-personal-physician-in-waiting wanted me to carry on the family tradition.

I rip open kitchen cupboards and grab a container of salt and run the hot tap until the water is warm. Mixing the water and salt in a clean plastic container, I create a saline solution. Next I need a tube: something about the width of my pinkie and three feet long.

Beneath the sink is a water filter with a flexible blue plastic pipe. I tear it away from the fittings and cut off the ends, hoping it's long enough. Crouching next to Piper, I turn her head to one side and lubricate the end of the tube with soap, before inserting it through her nose, pushing it gently until it reaches the pharynx. I feel the slight resistance and turn the tube 180 degrees. It continues sliding towards her stomach.

I put my head on her chest and blow a puff of air through the tube, listening for the telltale bubbles from the fluid in her stomach. Holding the plastic container of saline solution above her head, I punch a hole through the base and insert the tube, letting about 300 ml of the warm fluid flow into her stomach.

Then I suction, letting the mixture of saline and her stomach contents flow out onto the floor. Repeating the process, I keep going until the liquid runs clearer. My mobile has been ringing. I've been too busy to answer it.

Drury's name appears on screen.

'What's happened in there? Neighbours reported a gunshot.'

'Where are the paramedics?'

'Outside. They're waiting for the all clear.'

'It's clear. Tell them to hurry.'

'Where's Grievous?'

'Dead.'

'Casey?'

'I'm sorry.'

Moments later the door jerks open and the DCI's eyes meet mine. He's wearing a bulletproof vest and helmet, like a modern-day warrior. In the dim light the scar on his cheek looks like a birthmark.

A dozen police officers surge into the house. Behind them I see two ambulances, their lights beating with colour, sirens muted. Four paramedics follow. Two of them crouch beside Piper. The younger one has a farm girl face.

'What did she take?'

'Diazepam.'

'How much?'

'Unknown.'

'How long has she been unconscious?'

'Thirty minutes, maybe longer.' I point to the tube. 'I've done a nasotracheal intubation and a gastric lavage. She needs activated charcoal to absorb the rest.'

'We can take it from here, sir.'

Drury appears at the top of the stairs. Ashen-faced. Tortured by what he's witnessed. Two colleagues are dead. A kidnapped girl is alive. It doesn't feel like a victory.

On the night we were taken,

I left Tash at the church while I went to Emily's house and told her that we were running away. In the winter Reverend Trevor leaves the small door open at the side of St Mark's of a Saturday night so that parishioners who arrive early on Sunday morning don't have to wait in the cold for the curate to unlock the door. I left Tash lying on a pew, curled up like a kitten.

It was well after midnight when I got back. The funfair had closed down and the rides were being dismantled or folded up like Transformer toys. Scaffolding pipes were loaded onto trucks and canvas tents rolled into tubes.

Tash wasn't where I left her. I thought she must have found some-where warmer in the choir stalls or under the baptismal font. It was scary walking through the darkened church, but I couldn't risk turning on the lights, so I lit one of the prayer candles and tried not to spill hot wax on my hands.

I walked towards the main doors and that's when I saw George. He was sitting straight-backed in a pew. Tash was asleep with her head on his thigh.

George held a finger to his lips, not wanting to wake her.

'Hello, Piper,' he whispered.

'How do you know who I am?'

'You're the runner,' he said, stroking Tash's hair. 'She's sleeping. She told me what happened. I've been waiting for you.'

'Why?'

'We have to go to the police station. We have to tell them what happened.'

'Tash didn't want to tell anyone.'

'I made her change her mind.'

'Who are you?' I asked.

'I've come to help.'

He was wearing black combat trousers and dark boots laced to his shins. A dark shirt was visible beneath his waterproof jacket. I thought he looked like someone official — like a soldier or a police officer — except for his jacket, which was old and stained.

Sliding Tash's head from his lap, he sat her up, leaning her head against his shoulder.

'My car is outside,' he said. 'Here, help me lift her.'

I reached down and took Tash's arm, but that's when his hand slipped over my mouth and nose, stopping me in mid-breath, squeezing. His other arm wrapped around my chest, pinning my arms and lifting my feet from the ground. I couldn't breathe. I couldn't run.

'Shhhhhh,' he whispered. 'Sleep now, Princess. You'll be home soon.'

50

They let me ride in the ambulance with Piper. Although she is unconscious, her vital signs are stronger. They can put her on dialysis and clean her blood. She'll recover. She'll see in the New Year and meet her new baby sister.

Seated on a side bench, my knees touching the stretcher, I sway through every corner of the journey to hospital. I can see a face reflected in the chrome, but it doesn't look like me. My body is shaking. I don't know if it's the Parkinson's or the cold or something more elemental. I killed a man. I took a life.

Piper's eyes flutter open, wide with shock at first. She recognises me. Relaxes.

'Hello,' I say, holding her hand.

She can't answer because of the oxygen mask.

'You're safe. We're going to the hospital.'

Her fingers squeeze mine.

Her other hand reaches for her mask. The paramedic wants her to keep it on. Piper insists. She mouths the word. I lean closer and hear her whisper.

'Tash?'

'I'm sorry,' I say. 'Tash didn't make it home. She died in the blizzard, but she helped us find you.'

Piper squeezes her eyes shut and a tiny marble-like tear rolls down her cheek and stops at the edge of the mask.

This was always going to be the hardest news and it will hurt her more than anyone imagines – a survivor's guilt and a sense that the world has moved on without her. There is nobody left who understands what she's been through.

51

It's after midnight when I arrive at the cottage. The key is under the third brick beneath the foxglove plant. Letting myself in, I use the glow of the Christmas lights to navigate along the hallway, trying not to make a sound.

In the sitting room, I slump onto the couch and close my eyes. Too exhausted to get up the stairs, too wired to sleep.

'Hello.'

Julianne is standing at the doorway. She's wearing flannelette pyjamas, which she buys a size too large because she says they're more comfortable. The trousers hang low on her hips and the shirt is unbuttoned to reveal the shadow between her breasts.

'I heard the news,' she says. 'Is she going to be OK?'

'Yes.'

'They said a man was shot.'

I nod.

My hands are shaking. I look into her eyes and something small and delicate shreds inside me. I feel the tears coming. I try to hold them back, but she sits beside me and presses her face to mine.

I sob.

She soothes.

'I killed a man.'

'You saved a girl.'

Her arms are around me now, hugging me like a child.

'When I was holding that gun, all I could think about was Charlie. I could picture when Gideon Tyler kidnapped her; how helpless I felt, how completely and utterly useless. I remember you standing in this room, unable to look at me. I couldn't think of anything to say to you. I couldn't make it better. I couldn't share your pain because I knew that if I took your sorrow and anger and added it to mine it would fucking bury me . . . I'd never survive.'

'Don't torture yourself, Joe.'

'That was the beginning of the end for us. I knew it. You knew it.'

'Charlie is fine. I'm fine. You have to stop punishing yourself.' She strokes my hair. 'I think you should talk to someone.'

'Who?'

'A professional.'

'You think I should see a therapist.'

'Yes.'

'Are you seeing one?'

She nods. 'It's helping.'

'Who?'

'I'm not saying. You'll tell me there's someone better.'

I try to laugh because I know she's right. We sit like this for a long while, listening to the silence, enjoying each other's warmth.

'How was Christmas?' I ask.

'Postponed.' She points to the Christmas tree, where brightly wrapped gifts lie unopened beneath the lower branches. 'We decided that we didn't want Christmas without you so we put it off until tomorrow . . . or I should say today.'

'What about Santa Claus?'

'Oh, he came.'

'And Emma didn't want to open her presents?'

'Oh, she did. It almost killed her, but she wanted you here.' She lightly kisses my lips. 'We all did.'

Julianne slides her body away from mine and stands, pulling me upwards. 'To bed with you.'

'Let me sleep here.'

'No.'

She leads me upstairs, pausing at the open door to Emma's room where we watch our youngest sleeping, surrounded by stuffed animals and her gloriously imaginative paintings.

Then we pass Charlie's room, which has a sign on the door banning entry to little sisters and anyone below a certain height. A height chart is helpfully provided.

Julianne doesn't stop outside the guest room. Pulling me onwards, she takes me into the bedroom we once shared and helps me undress. When I try to speak, she puts her finger over my lips and draws me to the bed and wraps my arms around her body, across her breasts.

I smell her hair. I feel her heart. I listen to her sleeping. I want for nothing.

My name is Piper Hadley and

I went missing three years ago on the last Saturday of the summer holidays.

    Today I came home.